The
BLESSED

The
BLESSED

TONYA HURLEY

Hodder
Children's
Books

A division of Hachette Children's Books

For my mother, sister, and daughter

Lucy's Lament

I am alone. Cornered. Next to nothing and the dogs are at my door.
The assembly of the wicked surrounds me. I am mocked and
shunned. Abandoned. Lies and pain, my sole companions.

*Do not leave me now. I'm shaking and desperate for the comfort
of your arms.*

Tongues of flames licking my conscience.

*The tormentors laugh and grab. I am torn and shredded. Insides
out. Without mercy.*

Is there no one who can save me?

'Save yourself,' you said.

*Corpse flowers bloom beautifully beneath my feet. They fill the
air with the scent of rotting flesh.*

*Tears of blood trickle from my eyes and pool upon the ground, a
lake of purple and crimson my only mirror now. I am emptied of
all but my ghost.*

My sorrow is continually before me.

You think there are other ways, but there aren't.

I've made my choice. And it has made me. The path before me is clear.

I am not innocent. I am not ashamed.

I am ready for testing. I demand your worst.

'Do not be afraid,' you said.

Here I am.

Stripped down bare. Dressed in blind faith. Filled with fight and fire.

Vide et creder.

Visiting Hour

'Agnes!' Martha wailed, clutching the pale arm of her only daughter. 'Is he really worth it? Worth this?'

Agnes's blank eyes were fixed on her mother as she went in and out of consciousness. Her body was unloaded from the back of the ambulance like a raw meat delivery to the local butcher. She was unable to muster the energy to raise her head or her voice in response. Blood soaked through to the pleather pad beneath her, collecting and then streaming toward her dark teal ballet flats before finally trickling down the stainless steel leg of the stretcher.

'Agnes, answer me!' Martha demanded, anger more than empathy colouring her tone as an Emergency Medical

Technician applied pressure to her daughter's wounds.

Her shrill cry cut through the grating static of police radios and EMT dispatch scanners. The emergency doors flew open. The hard rubber stretcher wheels clacked metronomically as they rolled over the aged linoleum floor of Perpetual Help Hospital in Brooklyn, keeping time with the blips coming from the heart monitor attached to the patient on board. The distraught woman was running, but still could not catch up to her daughter. She could only watch while the plasma – or liquid stubbornness and idealism, as she saw it – drained from her only child.

'Sixteen-year-old female. B.P. one hundred over fifty-eight and dropping. Ten fifty-six A.'

The police code for a suicide attempt was all too familiar to the ER team.

'She's hypovolemic,' the nurse observed, grasping the young patient's cold and clammy forearm. 'Bleeding out.'

The nurse reached for a pair of shears and carefully but quickly cut through the side seam of Agnes's T-shirt and removed it, revealing a bloodstained cami beneath.

'Look what he did to you! Look at you!' Martha scolded as she stroked Agnes's long, wavy auburn hair. She studied the girl's glamorous, old-Hollywood looks in wonder, her perfect skin and the brassy hair that fell in finger waves around her face, even more perplexed that she could do something so drastic over a guy. *That* guy.

'And where is he now? Not here! I told you over and over again. And, now, this, THIS, is what it got you!'

'We're going to need you to calm down, ma'am,' the EMT advised, holding Agnes's mother back at arm's length as the stretcher made a sharp turn toward the curtained triage area. 'Now is not the time.'

'Is she going to be OK?' Martha pleaded. 'If something happens to her, I don't know what I'll do.'

'Something has already happened to her,' the nurse said.

'I'm just so . . . disappointed,' Martha confided, drying her eyes. 'I didn't raise her to behave so thoughtlessly.'

The nurse just raised her eyebrows at the unexpected lack of compassion.

Agnes heard clearly enough but said nothing, unsurprised that her mother needed comforting, validation that she was indeed a good parent, even under these circumstances.

'You're not allowed back in the trauma rooms,' the nurse said to Martha, thinking it might be a good idea for her to cool off. 'There's nothing you can do right now, so why don't you go home and get some fresh clothes for her?'

Martha, a rail-thin woman with short black hair, nodded, eyes glazed over, as she watched her daughter disappear down the harshly bright hallway. The nurse stayed behind and handed Martha Agnes's drenched teal T-shirt. Some of it was still wet with bright red ooze, and part was already dried black and cracking as Martha folded it and crunched it in her arms.

There were no tears shed.

'She's not going to die, is she?' Martha asked.

'Not today,' the nurse responded.

Agnes couldn't speak. She was dazed, still more in shock than in pain. White cotton bandages were fastened around her wrists, tight enough to both staunch the bleeding and absorb it. Staring up at the rectangular fluorescent ceiling lights that passed one after another, Agnes felt as if she were speeding down a runway, about to take off – for where exactly was anybody's guess.

Once she arrived in the trauma area, the scene grew even more frantic, as the ER doctors and nurses fussed over her, lifting her on to a bed, attaching the various monitors, inserting an IV, checking her vitals. She had the sensation of walking into a surprise birthday party – everything seemed to be going on for her, but without her.

Dr Moss grabbed her right wrist, unwrapped the bandages, and turned it firmly into the light above his head to peer at the bloody crevice. He did the same with her left wrist, and recited his observations to the nurse at his side for the record. Agnes, now slightly more responsive, managed to look away.

'Five-centimetre vertical wounds on each wrist,' he dictated. 'Laceration of skin, vein, subcutaneous vessels, and ligament tissue. More than a cry for help going on here,' he said, noting the severity and location of the gashes and looking her directly

in the eyes. 'Opening your veins in the bath – old-school.'

A transfusion was started and she began to come to, slowly. She watched wearily, transfixed, as some stranger's blood dripped into her body, and she wondered if she'd be changed by it. This certainly wasn't a heart transplant, but the blood inside her heart would not be entirely her own.

Agnes started to moan and then became somewhat combative.

'Not a cry for help,' she said, indicating she knew full well what she was doing. 'Let me go.'

'You're lucky your mom was around,' he advised.

Agnes mustered a slight eye-roll.

After a short while, she heard the snap of the doctor removing his latex glove.

'Stitch her up,' he ordered. 'And send her up to Psych for an eval after she's fully transfused and . . . stable.'

'To Dr Frey?' the nurse asked.

'He's still up there? At this hour?'

'It's Halloween, isn't it?' she groused. 'Just him and a skeleton crew.'

'That's dedication,' Moss observed.

'Maybe, but I think he likes it up there.'

'He's got some of the worst of the worst in that ward. I'm not sure he has a choice.'

Agnes overheard and couldn't get the image out of her head of a Mad Monster Party going on up there. And if they were

waiting for her to 'stabilise', they would be waiting a hell of a lot longer than even the poor uninsured souls in the waiting room seeking treatment.

'Another body outlasting the mind,' Dr Moss said under his breath as he stepped behind the next curtain to assist with a CPR case, already well underway. Agnes was feeling more herself and she selfishly welcomed the tumult, if only to distract her from her own problems for a minute. She offered her wrist to the physician's assistant and tuned into the commotion next to her, like the unwelcome music blaring from a car stereo outside her apartment window on a hot summer night.

'Seventeen-year-old female,' the EMT shouted, as she continued compressions. 'Suspected drowning.'

The bony, blue-lipped girl in front of the intern was lifeless and turning whiter shades of pale with each passing second. He tried to examine her nails, but they were already painted blue.

'In the river?' the intern asked.

'On the street,' the EMT offered, drawing raised eyebrows from everyone in the room. 'Facedown in a pothole.'

'She's in full arrest. Defib.'

After several rounds of computer-assisted shocks were applied to her chest and rib cage, the tattooed teen bounced, spasmed, and came to.

'Bag her!' a nurse ordered.

Before they could get the intubation tube down her throat, she started coughing and spewing dirty water on the surgical gowns of her caretakers until some spittle ran down her chin. She might even have vomited if she had eaten anything that day. Tinted by her smeared red lipstick, the gravelly discharge left her looking bloody and muddy. Some murky runoff dripped down her underfed abdomen and collected in her belly button, flooding the innie and causing her steel ball barbell piercing to look more like a diving board, one end bobbing slightly up and down.

An IV was started; labs were drawn and sent off for testing.

'What's your name?' the nurse asked, checking her faculties.

'CeCe,' the girl said wearily. 'Cecilia.'

'Do you know where you are?' the nurse pressed.

CeCe looked around her. She saw nurses and doctors scurrying around and heard relentless moans coming from some homeless people on stretchers parked in the hallway.

'Hell,' she answered.

Cecilia looked up at the crucifix posted above the doorway and rethought her response. 'The hospital.' She looked at the mud on her secondhand faded Vivienne Westwood bodice, double bird claw ring – gunmetal gold pheasant talons gripping her middle and ring finger – leather leggings, and black ankle boots. 'What am I doing here?'

'Technically, you drowned,' the nurse said. 'You were found facedown in about an inch of water.'

'Oh, my God,' Cecilia cried, shortly before busting out into hysterics.

The nurse held her hand and tried to calm her before discovering that Cecilia wasn't crying, but instead, laughing uncontrollably. So much so that she couldn't catch her precious breath, further depleting her of oxygen.

'There's nothing funny going on here.' Dr Moss eyed the dirty residue and acrylic tubes emanating from her. 'You almost died.'

Of course he was right, but she wasn't laughing at the staff, just at the pathetic train wreck she'd become. Inhaling a puddle full of street gravy. How low can you get? Literally. Her friend Jim, who killed himself by jumping off the Brooklyn Bridge and sucking down thick, murky East River 'Chop Suey' water sure would have got a kick out of this. The thought sobered her up enough to replay the evening, to visualize the guy she was making out with on the F train back to Brooklyn from the Bowery and whose name she couldn't remember, and the gig she wasn't paid for.

'Emergency contact?' the nurse asked.

Cecilia shook her head *no*. 'Where's my guitar?' She felt around the stretcher like an amputee for a lost limb.

She was naturally beautiful, gifted with deep green almond eyes and sharp features from early childhood. Her dark hair was shoulder-length, carefully unkempt in an edgy style. Tall and lean, with long bones and muscles. She would've had an

easier time becoming a model, she was often told, and not just the kind recruited at shopping mall kiosks by pretty part time employees with tans and cropped shirts – but the real deal. And fashion was important to her. But she just couldn't stand the idea of becoming a billboard for someone else's creativity. It was stressful enough hawking her own. If she was going to be a messenger for anyone, it might as well be herself. Besides, music and her look was what got her out of bed in the early afternoon. It was what she lived for.

'The admission desk will have a record of whatever you were brought in with,' Dr Moss said. 'I'll check on your guitar when things settle down around here.'

'Do they ever?' she asked. The little smile she got out of him fuelled her.

'Thanks,' Cecilia said sincerely, as the doctor left her to contemplate her situation. 'You're a goddamn angel.'

'No, I'm a doctor. I can only fix damaged bodies.'

'Doctor! Stat!' the charge nurse ordered, interrupting his attempt at a made-for-TV moralism. Without warning, madness burst through the ER entrance, signalling to Cecilia that it might be a while before she got the GPS on her instrument.

'Holy breast-fed Jesus,' CeCe said, trying to decipher what the bright flashes of light against the wall above her cloth divider could be. It was like nothing they'd ever seen, or heard, before. It was almost as if a lightning storm had made its way into triage. The yelling that accompanied the flashes sounded

like a pack of famished beasts picking over bones. It was the blaze of camera flashes and the cursing of paparazzi, all jockeying for position. All trying to get a shot. THE shot.

'Lucy, over here!' one yelled.

'Lucy, one shot of you and your IV bag!' another demanded.

'I can't see,' Lucy mumbled as she put her vintage blond mink jacket over her head to shield her eyes and shroud her face, before promptly passing out.

'Back the hell up,' a security guard at the visitor desk shouted repeatedly.

Neither Agnes nor Cecilia could make out much except what they could see beneath the hanging curtain and hearing the term 'OD' thrown around. Articles of clothing began hitting the floor, first one spiked stiletto and then another, black leggings, a strapless push-up bra, Swarovski headband, vintage Chanel purse, and finally a silk dress that seemed to gently float down like a little black parachute.

'Looks like another recessionista's charge account came due,' Cecilia said under her breath.

'What is this, teen night?' Dr Moss asked rhetorically as he prepped the oral charcoal.

'No, just Saturday night in Brooklyn,' the nurse responded. 'Mondays are heart attacks—'

'Lucy!' another nurse shouted. 'Lucy, can you hear me?' The nurse didn't need to check the clipboard for her name. Anyone who read the blogs or local gossip pages knew who she was and

why she was accosted by the screaming paps.

Agnes overheard the chatter between the doctor and the hospital public relations officer who were standing outside her curtain.

'Keep those vultures out of here,' he ordered, looking over at the salivating row of photographers perched restlessly in the waiting room. 'No comment and no confirmations from anyone, got it?'

Dr Moss walked in to examine Lucy. The oral-activated charcoal treatment had already been started. She was gagging on the tube, which he took as a good sign. She awoke abruptly, as if the starter rope was being pulled on a lawnmower. Fully aware and completely awake.

'Get me out of here,' Lucy screamed, wrenching the tube from her throat. She was fidgety, crazed, almost manic.

'Relax, honey,' a large-and-in-charge nurse said, pushing gently down on her shoulders. 'You're safe from all those reporters out there.'

'Safe?' Lucy scoffed, fussing blindly with her makeup, her voice raspy. 'Are you kidding me? This shot is gonna put someone's kid through college.'

The nurse was clearly taken aback not only by her comment, but also by the fact that the girl lying on the stretcher was in full media mode.

'What are you talking about?'

'An emergency room photo? Do you know what kind of

placement those get?' Lucy gave the irascible health aide the once-over and realized that she probably didn't. 'Like you'd understand,' Lucy pulled the overhead examination lamp closer and checked out her reflection in the chrome tray positioned over her stretcher.

'Well, then, maybe you can get that officer outside to understand a little better what someone your age was doing passed out in the bathroom of a club?'

Lucy refused to acknowledge the seriousness of her condition, medically or legally, and reached down for the pieces of her scattered outfit. A searing pain stopped her short, and she doubled over, clenching her stomach in agony.

The nurse placed sticky-back electrodes on Lucy's chest and wired her to the cardiac monitor at her bedside. The switch was flipped and instead of the expected *beep . . . beep* of Lucy's heart rate, the sound was one long extended tone, indicating a flat line.

Then . . . nothing.

Lucy's eyebrows perked up nervously as the nurse fiddled with the machinery.

'Everyone says I'm heartless,' Lucy jibed.

'Stop moving around,' the nurse ordered. 'You're messing with the monitor.'

'Ugh, I think I'm getting my period.' Lucy dropped her head down on the tiny pillow beneath her head. 'Get me some Vicodin.'

Dr Moss shook his head and left the curtained cubicle. He noticed the photographers and bloggers uploading and posting from their mobiles, calling sources, vigorously updating editors on the second-rate 'it' girl's breaking news. Suddenly, as if the fire alarm had gone off, the crowd dispersed, off to chase the next ambulance.

The nurse poked her head into Lucy's bay to let her know things had settled down.

'Shit!' Lucy spat, her chance for a little cheap ink thwarted by someone else's personal tragedy.

Hours passed, lights dimmed, staff, shifts, and dressings changed, and fifteen-minute-interval checks on Agnes's restraints took place – also mandatory procedure – but the sounds of the sick, the injured, and the dying persisted long past visiting hours, into the night. It was sobering and depressing. Patients came and went, some discharged, some admitted, others like Agnes, Cecilia, and Lucy left in limbo, waiting for a bed or further observation, forced to endure the suffering of others as well as their own.

Agnes's mobile went off and she knew immediately by the *Dynasty* TV-theme ringtone that it was her mother. She hit the mute button and tossed the phone, limp-wristed, on to the monitor stand next to her stretcher, ignoring the caller just as she had the digital cascade of text messages that now clogged her mailbox. She sighed and drifted off to sleep, like Lucy,

whose lost photo op, and a first round of questioning by the NYPD, proved totally exhausting.

It was practically silent. Still.

An ER tech ripped open the curtain all at once, as if he were ripping off a plaster, and wheeled in a computer on a mobile stand. 'I need to ask you a few questions, Cecilia . . . Trent.'

Cecilia didn't budge.

'Address?'

'Pass.'

'Ah, OK.' He skimmed the screen for an easier question. 'Religion?'

'Currently, I'm practicing the ancient art of' – she paused as he typed – 'I don't give a crap-ism.'

He continued typing until the end and then pressed the delete button. 'I can't type that.'

'Sure you can.'

'No, I can't.'

'And they say this is a free country,' Cecilia said. 'OK, I'm a practising nihilist.'

'Why don't I come back later.' He pushed his computer cart out of the room as he closed the curtain.

'Don't be like that,' she called after him apologetically. 'I'm just bored.'

'Get some rest.'

She should have been able to, with all that sedation flowing

through her, but she couldn't. She kept replaying the evening over and over in her head, the little she could remember of it. After a while, the ER went almost totally quiet except for the sound of hurried footsteps. They sounded heavy, not like the surgeons' paper booties or the nurses' rubber soles that had been scurrying through the ward until then. Cecilia, an experienced night owl by nature and profession, felt uneasy for the first time in a very long time.

Cecilia looked up and noticed the shadow of a male figure on her curtain, passing by her bay. 'Coming back for more? They always do.'

She glanced down and saw the coolest pair of black biker boots she'd ever seen. Even in silhouette she could tell, whoever he was, he was hot. Definitely not the douche bag ER tech. She'd got really good at determining a guy's 'attributes' in the dark.

He stood still, as if he were intensely plotting, his back to her curtain divider, giving her time to wonder about him. Visiting hours were over, and from the almost chiaroscuro outline of his hair, jeans, and jacket, she wondered if this was the guy she'd hooked up with earlier. She could barely remember what he looked like, but maybe he'd snuck past the desk, to see her. See if she was OK. Even if it was out of guilt.

'Are you decent?' he asked. 'Can I come in?'

'No and yes. Two things about me – I never get on a plane with a country star and I tend to never say "no" to a guy.'

She felt a tingle in her stomach as he slid aside the curtain. He looked anxious, almost like a chain smoker who had given up cigarettes earlier that day. Tense. He ducked quickly into the space. He was tall and lean, olive-skinned, with thick, styled hair, long, slightly muscled arms, and a barrel chest that was barely enclosed by his jacket and a T-shirt of The Kills.

A vision.

'I didn't think anyone was awake,' he said in a baritone whisper.

'Here to give me last rites?'

'You have a death wish?'

'After last night, possibly.'

'Do you always invite strangers into your room?'

'I prefer the company of people I don't know very well.'

'Sounds lonely.'

There was an awkward silence and Cecilia had to look away from him. The understanding and compassion in his voice was overwhelming. Her eyes welled unexpectedly with tears. 'I'm not crying. I must still be high or something.'

'I understand.' He stepped forward. Closer to her. Shrinking the space between them. He smelled like incense. Cecilia began to question the wisdom of confiding in this guy. Hot guys cruising clubs was one thing, but hot guys creeping hospitals was quite another. She tensed up. 'Do I know you?'

'Wouldn't you know if you knew me?'

The truth was she hung out with a lot of guys, and it was difficult to keep them straight. So running into one turned into a game of Twenty Questions with her. Something she was good at. 'Were you at my gig tonight? Did you bring me here?'

'No . . .' he said slowly. 'Cecilia.'

'You know my name? You better be psychic or I'm screaming,' she said, backing away suddenly.

He pointed to the foot of her bed. 'Your name is on your clipboard.'

'What do you want from me?' Cecilia asked, holding her punctured arms up as far as the vinyl tubes would stretch, like a medicated marionette. 'I can take care of myself. Despite what it looks like.'

'I can see that.' He nodded and tapped her hand gently.

'Who are you?' she asked immediately pulling away.

'Sebastian,' he said, reaching for her again.

She relaxed into his touch.

He took notice of the hard-shell guitar case leaning upright against the wall beside her bed. It was stickered, stained, chipped, and battered. It had seen better days, but he had the sense it was protecting something precious. 'You're a musician?'

'That's what I told my parents when I ran away.'

'Everyone's either running from something or toward something.'

'Well, then,' she said, feeling some camaraderie. 'Which way are you headed?'

'Both, I guess.'

'At least one thing we have in common.'

'At least.'

'Seriously, I just always felt like there was something deep inside of me I needed to say,' CeCe tried to explain. 'Something . . .'

'Trying to get out?' he asked.

She looked up at him in surprise. He understood.

'Yeah.'

'Another thing we have in common,' he said.

He moved in even closer. Into the light. Close enough for her to feel the warmth of his body and his breath. To see him. To smell him.

'So, Sebastian . . .' Even his name appealed to her. It fit him. She knew his type. Devastatingly good-looking guy, nice moves, but probably cheating on his night nurse girlfriend right under her nose. 'What are you doing here?'

'Visiting.'

'A girlfriend?'

'No.'

'Well, you don't look like a blood farmer, organ broker, or bone thief . . .' she said. 'Are you one of those dudes who cruises the hospital for sick chicks?'

The loud clang of a tray dropping and some hallway chatter

startled them. He'd looked edgy since he'd walked in, but she could sense he was ready to leave. Right then. 'You looking for someone or is someone looking for you?'

'I found what I was looking for,' he said, reaching down into his jeans pocket.

'Whoa, what the hell are you doing?' Cecilia reached for the nurse call button. He beat her to it, snatching it away. She immediately extended her hand to grab it, then winced in pain, pulling back as the IV lines stretched to their limit and tugged at her veins. 'Point blank, I *will* hurt you.'

He pulled out a gorgeous bracelet made from what looked to be the oldest, most extraordinary rough ivory beads, and dangling from it, an antique gold charm of a thin, bowed sword.

'Holy shit.' Cecilia marvelled at it and was both touched and spooked that a total stranger would give her such a stunning, obviously ridiculously expensive, personal, and unique gift. 'Were you the one who brought me here?' she asked. 'Were you the one who saved me?'

Sebastian placed the bracelet in her hand and clasped his around it, gently but firmly, and backed away toward the curtain. 'Later.'

Something in his voice sounded to her like he meant it literally. She believed him. This was the most honest conversation she'd had with a guy maybe ever. And he was a total stranger. But an old soul. Like her.

'Listen. I have a few gigs this week. Cecilia Trent. Google me. Maybe you'll find me and come down and check me out minus the IVs.'

'Maybe you'll find me first,' he said.

'Wait,' Cecilia whispered hoarsely after him, holding up her wrist adorned with the bracelet. 'What is this?'

'Something to hold on to.'

2

Pilgrimage of Shame

S unday morning.

The day of rest. Regret. And cotton mouth.

Lucy was lying on her side when she came to. She listened for a while before opening her eyes, holding on to that serene moment before what she had done the previous night revealed itself to her sober and fully conscious mind. The sliver of time before excuses of a sick grandmother or friend in turmoil emerged, all while performing an underwear scavenger hunt.

Her first reflex was to feel beneath the pillow for her Hermès flask, half grey and half salmon-hued with black leather straps and a sterling silver lid; it resembled an oversized necklace rather than something camouflaging alcohol. The promoters at Sacrifice, an upscale Manhattan nightclub, gave it to her after they hosted an exclusive Hermès party for fashion week . . . along with free top-shelf refills for life, which always kept her coming back, because drink tickets were so last millennium. This morning, however, there was no comfort to be found, under her pillow or anywhere else; she didn't feel a flask.

The pillowcase had slid partially off and her mouth was in direct contact with the plastic blue cushion. It took an instant before she realized this and panicked, logging a mental inventory of who could have potentially died on it and then lay there for hours, leaking body fluids over it and inside it. Hospital pillows, like airline pillows, were reusable and no one had actually ever seen them changed, she was sure. The plastic cover didn't fool her one bit – all of its infectious contents were now swirling around her mouth playing a game of tag with her immune system. Whatever it was, it was in her.

Lucy opened her ghostly pale blue eyes – blood vessels creeping through the whites of them like a spiderweb – and knew she was in a hospital. She tried to go back to sleep, back to numb, but the whiz and buzz of medical equipment booting up along with the hallway chatter made it impossible as did the commingling vapors of ammonia, feces, drying blood, and puke that seemed to permeate the entire ER.

'I need to get out of here,' Lucy said, peeling her face off of the plastic pillow.

The nurse simply ignored her and began taking Lucy's vitals before she retreated to paperwork. Lucy's eyes were fixed on her Parisian weekender, the one that she got from her dad when they visited a flea market in France. It was made from an antique rug – hand-woven blooms of rich reds, bright magentas, royal blues, and peridots.

He took her to Paris when she was ten, right before her mother left them, saying that he wanted her first trip to Paris to be with a man who would always love her. Lucy's mother left when she was young. She decided that she didn't want to be tied down with a husband and a kid. She up and moved to LA. Later, Lucy realized that those, too, were her initials. Los Angeles, the city of angels, among other things. Whether the abrupt move was some previously unfulfilled ambition or just a fight-or-flight response to a traditional lifestyle, she never really knew. For Lucy, it was both formative and informative, colouring her views of life and love with a decidedly unsentimental palette.

Whatever the reason, her dad was all that she had, and now she barely even talked to him. Unless there was a problem with her rent cheque. She held on to that bag and to what he said as it shifted from a sweet memory to a bitter lie. All that was left – baggage. When she did talk to him, she was always accused of being just like her mother, which to her father unforgivable.

Lucy grabbed her clothing from the night before out of the

bag. It was bad enough, she thought, that she'd wound up in the hospital, but without anything else to wear, a 'walk of shame' was guaranteed. She wondered who might pay for such a shot and how much, and instantly reached for her mobile phone, and as she did, something dropped to the floor.

She looked down and saw a bracelet made up of the most exquisite off-white beads with a most peculiar, double-eyed gold charm.

Some Fifth Avenue version of the Kabbalah bracelet, Lucy thought, leaning over to pick it up. *Probably some Holy Roller looking for a handout.*

Before it even made it up to her eyes, she decided to incorporate it into her look. Barney's New York was doing a whole SACRED line for next fall, and this little number would give her a jump on the season. *Definitely fake, but I can make it work.*

As she brought the piece closer to her face and studied it, she realized that it was anything but fake. The reflection from the fluorescent light above caused her to squint like a jeweller. She could usually tell cheap from a mile away, and this was the real thing. It was unbelievable. Looked as if it were antique. Heavy. Hand-carved. She fantasized for a moment that it had been passed down through the ages like estate jewellery or hidden like buried treasure only to be found centuries later.

Unearthed.

I'll bet this cost a freakin' fortune. Not like those gum-machine

knockoffs for sale on the flying carpets along the sidewalks of Atlantic Avenue, she thought. She turned over on to her back and held it up in front of her face, fingering the golden charm. It was unlike anything she'd ever seen, not even at celebrity auctions, and it was certainly one of a kind. Strange and familiar to her all at the same time. Almost too much to look at. But she felt, in a way she could not describe even to herself, that it should belong to her. And now it did.

'Was my father here?' Lucy asked the nurse, hope in her voice as if she were a little girl at Christmas again, fondling the rare find. 'Did *he* leave this for me?'

'No,' the nurse said, tamping down Lucy's childlike eagerness.

'Yeah, he would never step foot in a Brooklyn hospital. He rarely leaves Manhattan.'

The nurse just rolled her eyes.

'What time is checkout?' Lucy asked, still transfixed by the bauble.

The nurse shrugged dismissively and returned to her business.

'Bitch,' Lucy mumbled as the short and stubby nurse waddled away.

Watching the nurse leave, she noticed a familiar face across the hall – not a friend or even much of an acquaintance, but a former classmate and a die-hard competitor for precious gossip-column space. The girl never had a bad thing printed about

her, until recently when rumours of a pregnancy by an ex-boyfriend, now in college, began to circulate. Lucy knew all about it because she had started the rumour. And right next to her was the girl's boyfriend.

There was no curtain on their bay. They were totally exposed.

'Hey, Sadie,' Lucy called out, getting the girl's attention.

Sadie was clenched over in pain, moaning, holding her stomach. She was too weak to respond or to defend herself.

'Wow. Can't believe how fantastic your postpregnancy bod looks,' Lucy said. 'Hard to believe you were pregnant like . . . an hour ago.'

The girl tucked her head inside her hoodie, knowing what was about to happen, much like a mobster who'd been taken away in the backseat of a rival crime family's car. But, the guy didn't even try to hide his face. In fact, quite the opposite.

Ratting out Sadie would surely impress Jesse and get her E.R. story better placement. In fact, it might even warrant a vlog post. All she could think was *jackpot*. In her circle, teen pregnancy was one thing, good for a few days of embarrassing coverage before it got turned into some noble endeavour, but termination – that was quite another. That could mean exile. And for Lucy, one less rival. She couldn't count the number of times they had tried to humiliate her.

Eye for an eye.

Lucy took a picture with her mobile and looked it over. It was a perfect snap, capturing all Sadie's tears and torment. But the distraught look on Sadie's face, her vulnerability, reached Lucy in a way she hadn't expected. Even more moving to Lucy was Sadie's boyfriend, Tim, hand in hand with her, right by her side. There was no one there for Lucy. Not even the man who should have cared the most, her dad.

She locked eyes with the couple, felt them pleading silently with her for media mercy, felt their pain, which was completely unlike her, and pressed send.

'You're discharged,' the nurse said curtly to Lucy on her way down the corridor. 'Your things are in that bag and the paperwork is at the front desk.'

'That's it?' Lucy asked, somewhat disappointed.

'Ha! What did you expect?'

Lucy frowned only slightly, but still just enough to give the night nurse a smirk of satisfaction.

'What do you think?' Lucy inquired, brandishing her bejewelled wrist regally.

'I think it suits you,' the nurse said. 'Try not to pawn it too quickly.'

Lucy bared her teeth and raised her perfectly manicured hands into claws like an angry cat and hissed away the nurse's bad energy.

She grabbed her weekender bag and headed out through the revolving doors. It was dawn, the time when people were

getting up for work and, in her case, returning from going out. Her rush hour.

She walked to a food stand and ordered some scrambled egg whites and bacon on a bagel and a hot cup of coffee. Still thinking about what she'd just done to Sadie. How low she'd sunk. She watched the vendor crack the eggs and separate the yolk, the core, the most substantial part, and discard it.

'Scoop it,' she ordered, insisting he shell out the bagel, as she watched an obviously downtrodden couple order their toddler a Dr Pepper.

Right on cue, she felt a spindly hand grab her arm. She didn't need to look to know whose it was. Jesse's black-sleeved jacket was a dead giveaway.

'Get your hands off me, prick,' she barked, jerking free without even turning around to face him. Jesse was tall, slightly hunched over from all that time spent on the computer, and thin. He tried, to a fault, to be on trend, and looked as if he were uncomfortably dressed by a girlfriend – which he did not have.

'Awwww,' he whined. 'Wake up on the wrong side of the stretcher?'

Lucy was suddenly struck by the reflection of the sun bouncing from the double-eyed charm. She could have sworn it was staring back at her.

'I'm done, Jesse. This time I mean it.'

'Done with what? You're living the dream.'

'Whose dream?'

'Yours, remember?'

'All I know is I could have rotted away in there and nobody would give a rat's ass.'

'I'm here.'

'Like I said.'

'Don't be ridiculous, Lucy. You're all over the place.'

He wiggled his phone in his hand, screen side up.

'I don't mean morbidly curious about me, Jesse,' she said. 'I mean concerned.'

'You just need some sleep.'

'You have no idea what I need.'

Jesse studied the dishevelled girl in front of him. He was good at reading her, usually, but something was different this morning. She was more melancholy than he'd ever seen.

'You couldn't stop in the bathroom to fix your face?'

Lucy lifted her hand to her cheek, and as she did, he saw the bracelet.

'Nice,' he said, reaching for the dangling charm. 'Where'd you get it?'

'Don't touch it!'

'Damn. Well, at least somebody cares, right?'

'You're evil.'

'Takes one to know one.'

'I've gotta go.'

'Don't forget. We have a deal.'

Lucy couldn't help but notice that the shadow she cast completely engulfed him. 'I don't owe you anything.'

'Loved the snap of Sad Sadie. Already ran it.'

'Then we're more than even.'

'Did you catch something in that ER?' he ribbed, trying to keep up.

'Yeah, a conscience.' Lucy rummaged through her purse for a cigarette and taxi fare. 'Stay away from me, it might be contagious.'

Jesse saw that she came up empty-handed. 'Money for a cab?' He pulled a crisp bill from his jacket pocket and dangled a twenty from between his long, thin fingers.

'Don't tempt me like you do everyone else.'

'Too late for that, isn't it?'

'It's never too late.' Lucy spun around on her four-inch spikes, dropped her oversize rehab shades over her eyes, putting a proverbial period on the conversation, and walked away, brushing him off as only she could. She didn't have a penny and he knew it. Every cent she had, or had borrowed, she was wearing. If she were lucky, Lucy thought, the Metrocard she was carrying might have one fare left.

'Check your email when you get home,' Jesse called after her, unconcerned.

She stopped for just a second, pulled down her dress, which she could feel riding up her thighs, and continued down the block. Checking to make sure that no one was watching, she

then jaywalked over to a bus stop just across the avenue, praying no one would see her in her outfit from last night. Or worse, at a bus stop. All the walk of shame boxes were checked.

Hair – matted.

Lipstick – smeared.

Eyes – black from running mascara.

Clothes – stained and wrinkled.

Head – hung in shame.

Dignity – lost.

3

Watch Me Burn

The psychiatric floor of Perpetual Help also happened to be the highest floor. 'The Penthouse', as the ward staffers like to euphemize it. At that moment, all Agnes could think was that it was a pretty good place to jump from, which might have been what the administrators had in mind when they moved the unit up there. The simplest cost-cutting measure of all.

Agnes was wheeled into the waiting room flat on her back, but forced herself upright and into a sitting position after she was 'parked', slowly rotating her torso toward the edge of her stretcher until her legs fell over the side. She was dizzy and grabbed the edge of the stretcher and squeezed down, which, it turned out, hurt like hell. She hadn't realized how much the wrist and forearm muscles were used in steadying yourself like that. If she had, she might have sliced somewhere else. Agnes lifted her head to check out her surroundings.

It was grim, barred up, quiet, dimly lit, with walls painted in neutral colours and furniture discretely bolted down, not a sharp edge to be found. Dull and drab, with one exception: an ornate stained-glass window. Agnes bathed in the splintered morning light that blazed through it. It was the only colour to be found anywhere on the floor and the kaleidoscopic jewel-toned glow was soothing, maybe even a little mesmerizing. On the not-so-bright side, the place smelled like meat loaf, instant mashed potatoes, soggy canned green beans, and disinfectant. Nauseating. *Lunchtime for the lunatics*, she thought.

The wait seemed endless, but it did give her time to reflect. She was by herself without anyone in her ear. Suddenly, the door opened and a young nurse escorted a little boy into the room and locked him in behind her without saying a word. He was very young, not older than ten. Far too young to be there, surely, and definitely didn't fit the funny-farm profile she was expecting from the campfire stories her ER nurse was telling downstairs.

Agnes smiled at him, but he wasn't interested in gestures or even eye contact for that matter.

They were alone.

'What's your name?' Agnes asked.

The boy sat quietly for an uncomfortably long time. In his

own little world and not interested at all in small talk with some stranger.

'It's OK if you don't want to—'

'Jude!' he shouted, as if the word had been building pressure inside of him and had now been launched like a rocket. 'My. Name. Is. Jude.'

With that laboured introduction out of the way, Jude darted toward an old and weathered statue of Jesus, with its left hand pointed gently at its exposed heart. Time and indifference had taken its toll on it. Flecks of white where paint and plaster had chipped or broken off dotted the figure. Agnes guessed that it must have been moved up to the psych ward and out of the way, just like everything and everyone else up there. It reminded her of the statues that adorned her school lobby, Immaculate Heart Academy, but in worse condition, lending it, ironically, a kind of unforced sympathy, which was more than likely originally intended.

Out of nowhere. Without warning. The boy jumped up on the statue's pedestal and grabbed it with both arms, grunting and struggling with it as if it were fighting him back.

Maybe this kid isn't too young to be a mental patient after all, she thought.

'Say "Uncle", Jesus!' he said, trying to catch his breath.

Agnes tried not to look.

The boy was getting increasingly agitated and maniacal . . . hanging from the neck of an almost life-size statue, driving

his knuckles repeatedly into the Saviour's Plaster of Paris head.

'Say it!' the boy demanded as if the statue were resisting him.

Agnes was astonished at what kind of kid would bully a statue, let alone one of . . . Jesus. She stared intently at the painted face as several drops of blood suddenly appeared, trickling down the forehead and off the brow.

Her eyes incredulously followed the streams down as they fell to the floor, bright red spots peppering the white, waxed marble. Proving that one – a certain one perhaps – can indeed get blood from a stone.

Startled for a second, she thought she might be seeing things, something miraculous even, until she noticed Jude's knuckles, which were rubbed raw and bleeding. Undaunted, the boy examined his hand, shook it off, and returned quickly to his rubbing, stopping only to feel around behind the statue's head. As he pulled his hand away, and hopped off the pedestal and back toward her, Agnes noticed he was clutching something.

'He left this for you,' Jude said, handing Agnes the most spectacular white bracelet that she'd ever laid eyes on. 'He wanted me to make sure you got it.'

Agnes was stunned. Without words. Her heart felt as if it were going to beat right out of her chest and she was sure, if someone looked close enough, they could see it through her smock. The chunky beads – maybe pearls, she gathered – were strung beside an unpolished gold charm embossed with a

heart set aflame. She felt her incisions tingle and twitch as she gently fingered it.

'Tell him that I gave it to you,' the boy said proudly, without the slightest hesitation or stammer. 'OK?'

'Agnes Fremont,' the nurse called out.

Jude heard the nurse and dutifully returned to his seat and his silence.

'*Who? Tell who?*' Agnes queried the boy with sudden urgency, eyeing the statue suspiciously.

The boy did not answer her.

Agnes, meanwhile, was in a kind of shock. Whatever his problems, the trinket was extraordinary. Agnes hid the beads under her hospital gown and tucked the gold charm under her bandage to keep it safe and out of view. The flaming heart emblem that hung from it pressed uncomfortably into her wound. It hurt, but the pain it caused felt somewhat reassuring to her. She really was still alive.

'Agnes Fremont,' the nurse called out again, this time with more impatience. 'Are you coming?'

Agnes jumped off of her stretcher and waited anxiously by the door like a pet that hadn't been out all day. She looked back at the boy who was now sitting like an angel in his seat, and followed the nurse down the corridor.

As she was taken through, she stole peeks in the rooms. Having never been in a psych ward before, curiosity got the best of her, and she couldn't help but rubberneck. Besides,

all the girls in the tiny dormitory-style rooms were doing the same to her.

Face after face, all hopeless-looking and lost. Some just staring into nothingness and others just . . . waiting. She felt she had nothing in common with them, except she did.

The nurse gestured for her to enter an office until the doctor could see her. It wasn't like the movie psychiatrist's office she'd been expecting, with the heavy drapes, thick carpet, comfy couch, and box of tissues. A smouldering pipe burning cherry tobacco and wall-to-wall bookcases featuring Freud and Janov were nowhere to be found either. The room was tiny, sterile, painted beige, and harshly lit – a perfect match to the corridor, except for the noticeable lack of religious iconography that peppered the rest of the hospital. No statues, paintings, no Eyes-Follow-You-Jesus 3-D portraits. Against the wall stood a stainless steel apothecary cabinet filled with old charts and replicas of brains – whole and cross-sectioned. She took a seat in the chair, a padded pea-green job with metal armrests, an institutional desk, and standard issue high-back office chair. There was a nameplate on the desk but all she could read from this angle was CHIEF OF PSYCHIATRY. She was seeing the boss.

Agnes soon found herself mindlessly picking at the pus-coloured foam lurking just beneath the old, cracked leather seat covering, patience not being one of her virtues. If she wasn't picking at that, it would have been her wounds, but they were tightly bandaged enough that she couldn't do much more

damage. The austerity of the surroundings made her more and more nervous and she found herself thinking about the boy in the waiting room. He was so young to be so whacked-out. Until now, she imagined her youth, her obviously defiant nature might help to put her recent behaviour into perspective, to excuse it as a momentary lapse of judgment, and that she'd be let go with some kind of warning. Clearly, *she* wasn't mentally ill.

The door sprang open and a well-groomed middle-aged man in an old-fashioned white lab coat charged in. Agnes flicked away the last bits of foam from under her fingernails and sat at attention, hands clasped daintily over her abdomen. She noticed that her charm was peeking out from her bandage and quickly pulled her hair around and over her wrist to cover it.

'Hello . . .'

He paused. Scanning her chart to find her name.

'Agnes . . . I'm Dr Frey. Chief of Psychiatry.'

'So I see,' she said, unimpressed, tossing her gaze toward his desk plate.

One thing she hated about herself was her impulsivity. She tended to make quick judgments, and already she didn't like him. There was something about the rote politeness and elitist formality in his manner that put her off, but then she wasn't exactly planning to open up either. Or maybe it was simply that he hadn't bothered to find out her name before the appointment. Whatever. The doctor wasn't much for small

talk, it appeared. Neither was she. Agnes decided to cooperate for as long as it was in her interest. She wanted out.

'I'm sure you've heard this before but—' Agnes sputtered.

'But you're not crazy,' he interrupted, matter-of-factly finishing her sentence without even looking up at her.

'I don't belong here,' she almost pleaded, leaning in toward him with her hands outstretched, inadvertently revealing the bloodstains from her self-inflicted wounds.

'Are those tattoos, Miss Fremont?' He looked over the top of his glasses. 'No? Then you probably do belong here right now.'

Agnes pulled her arms back and dropped her chin, unable to look him in the eye, but she could still hear him and he kept on talking.

'It says in your file that you are a good student, very social, never been in trouble to mention, no history of depression.' He flipped back and forth between the stapled pages in a manila folder. 'So what changed?'

Agnes did not respond, shifting uncomfortably in her chair from both the pain of the question and the charm.

'Do you want to tell me about him?'

'Why does it always have to be about a guy?' Agnes blurted, trying to dam the tears that said otherwise.

'Because it usually is,' said Frey.

Agnes paused. She recalled in an instant almost every relationship she'd ever had, as far back as her first crush. There was definitely a pattern. They didn't last. Even her friends were

starting to joke that she couldn't hold on to a guy. As far as she was concerned, her heart was just too big for those boys to handle. If she could just find one who could, everything would be OK.

'My mom thinks I fall in love too easily.'

'Do you?'

'I just follow my heart. I always have.'

'That is a virtuous quality. But it almost led you to a dead end, Agnes.'

Agnes shrugged indifferently. 'When relationships end, it's like a death. There are always scars.'

'It is easy to be disappointed when you feel so deeply, isn't it?'

Agnes wasn't usually so cynical, but the doctor had hit a nerve.

'Yes.'

'What's his name?'

'Sayer.'

'Tell me about Sayer.'

Agnes was a little weirded-out talking openly with a nurse standing behind her – placed there mostly for the doctor's protection, legally and otherwise.

A witness.

'Well, according to my mom . . .' she began.

He waved her off and leaned forward, his chair creaking. 'What about according to you?' He paused. 'According to Agnes?'

'She wants to run my life because she hates hers,' Agnes exploded.

'I get that you and your mother disagree about things, but I asked you about the guy.' He was intent. Intense. What started off as an evaluation was snowballing into an interrogation.

It wasn't until that moment that Agnes realized that she hadn't given her temp boyfriend a thought since she'd been admitted, her interest in him draining out of her veins along with her blood the night before. 'Oh, Sayer wasn't really that important. Just the most recent.'

'Not important?' Frey squinted her wraps into focus. 'I can't help you if you aren't honest with me.'

'I liked him. OK, I liked him a lot. But my mom thought he was poison, just like every other guy I date. It put so much pressure on the . . . relationship. He couldn't stand it any more. Neither could I. Obviously.'

'What about him was wrong?'

'Everything, apparently. It's not even worth talking about.'

'But it's worth killing yourself over?' Dr Frey probed. 'Are you angry that it didn't work out or that she might have been right?'

She was starting to feel like her mom and the doctor shared a brain. He was reading her, pushing her places she didn't want to go, and she didn't like it. 'Maybe both. But I believe in love.'

'Did you feel pressure to have sex?'

'I didn't say sex. I said love. True love.'

'Do you think that may be a bit too idealistic at your age?'

'How old was Juliet?' she shot back.

He paused, noting her quick-wittedness, especially under the circumstances. It wasn't a medical diagnosis, but it occurred to him that she could probably be a handful.

'But that's just fiction, Agnes. Fantasy. And look how it turned out.'

'Without dreams there are only nightmares, Doctor.'

Agnes felt she'd schooled the expert.

'There are other ways to solve problems, to cope with them. Therapy, for example,' Dr Frey explained. 'Suicide is not a solution.'

She took it in, wondering seriously how much of this attempt was a suicide bid or simply a way to get revenge – to hurt Sayer for cheating, to hurt her mom for not being supportive – by hurting herself.

'I'm not sure there would even be a need for therapy,' Agnes said, 'if everyone had someone to love who loved them back equally. Unconditionally.'

Dr Frey smiled at her naïveté, or at least that's how she saw it. Clearly, for him, love was not the only answer.

'What do you think happens after we die, Doctor?' she asked, her attention shifting to the brain models neatly displayed in the apothecary cabinet.

'I think you are in a better position to answer that question than I am, Agnes,' Frey said, feeling agitated as if Agnes were

trying to get to him. 'You came pretty close yesterday.'

'I mean, you certainly talk to patients all the time who've tried to kill themselves or had some kind of out-of-body experience.'

'I'm afraid the afterlife is above my pay grade,' Frey explained coolly. 'I'm a scientist. I don't spend a lot of time speculating about things I can't observe, reproduce, or prove.'

'Life is probably more of an out-of-body experience, I guess,' she said. 'But aren't you curious?'

'I can only verify the biochemical processes that occur at the moment of death. The collective firing off of synapses, the death of brain cells from oxygen deprivation. If you're looking for an explanation for the light at the end of the tunnel, that's it.'

'In your opinion,' she clarified.

'That's what you asked me for, isn't it? I'm sorry if it's not what you wanted to hear.'

'I guess we all find out, eventually, who's right. Who's wrong.'

'Perhaps, but there's no rush, right, Miss Fremont?'

The more they spoke, the more she hurt. Couldn't be the pain meds wearing off yet; she'd just been shot up with a ton downstairs. Agnes thought she might even be bleeding, but didn't dare expose the bracelet in front of him. Exactly why, she couldn't say. Anyway, the boy had been so secretive about it and she didn't want to get him in trouble.

'Are you all right?' He nodded to the nurse to note her distress for the record.

'I'm fine. Really. I can do this.'

'We can wrap this up . . .'

Agnes swallowed hard. 'No. So you're saying we're like any machine, a car engine or a computer breaking down suddenly.' She saw a wry smile on the psychiatrist's face. 'Is that what you think?'

'Yes.'

'That's not very romantic.'

'No,' he replied. 'But it's honest.'

'Then why work in a Catholic hospital?' she asked. 'Isn't that hypocritical?'

'It's where I'm needed right now.'

The pain of her wrists was searing and Agnes couldn't continue even if she'd wanted to.

Frey made a few notes in her file and closed it, handing a prescription order to the nurse.

'Are you going to let me go?' Agnes asked, returning to the matter at hand. 'Or is my mom going to commit me?'

'That's a bit drastic.'

'You don't know my mom.'

'I expect you will be released tomorrow, but I will need to keep you overnight,' he said, eyeing her wrist. 'For observation.'

'Like one of your experiments?'

'You wouldn't be the first.' He extended his hand almost to force her to reach for his. 'Nice to meet you.'

Lucy rubbed her eyes, tossed her keys on the table, kicked off

her spiked heels, crawled on to the couch on her belly, and logged on to her laptop. She adjusted the contrast on the screen to see it more clearly and pulled it toward her. The web address appeared as she typed it. She hit enter and waited anxiously for the screen to change. She'd been stealing wi-fi from another tenant's unsecure account for ages, and access was not a guarantee. Since she'd been on her own, she'd got good at cutting corners and funnelling all her disposable cash into her outward appearance.

'No passwords make for good neighbours.' Lucy chirped silently as the website loaded, filling the entire screen. There it was on the home page. Just as Jesse said.

Breaking now: LUnaCY

Has LULU really lost it? Her mind, that is? Downtown Party Girl LUcky LUcy Ambrose sure did live up to her moniker last night as she was carted from just-opened Brooklyn burlesque hot spot BAT in the wee hours by EMTs and then transported to the Perpetual Help Hospital in Cobble Hill. The pAArty girl was at the club in the VIP room celebrating hAArd at their Halloween couture costume benefit, and what happened next was downright whorrifying! Those close to her say she was found classy smashed, passed out on the floor of the MEN'S bathroom and that she received treatment on the

scene. She was released from the hospital this morning for an undisclosed condition. The NYPD were dispatched to Perpetual Help to interview her. Neither the celebutante nor hospital spokesman were available for comment.

Status: DEVELOPING!

Click HERE for an exclusive photo gallery of LULU arriving at the club earlier that night.

As she scanned the page, she nodded approvingly. The photos were good, which meant mainly that it was big. And they'd got a clear shot of her new shoes and bag. That was money. And placement, which meant more free stuff.

'That will travel,' Lucy said matter-of-factly, uploading the link to all her websites. 'Heart it, bitches.'

Lucy began to click through all the other gossip sites. And there it was. Despite it being her best coverage to date, she had a sick feeling in her stomach. Even her favourite pastime – judging others – wasn't comforting her. She'd had an epiphany while thumbing through the plethora of tabloids that had piled up on her duvet. Rather than just flip through the pictures of stars at awards shows, on vacation, clothes shopping, eating lunch, and getting jealous, Lucy slowed down and spent an extra second staring at each photo. The longer she looked, the uglier they became, and the more enjoyable the experience became for her.

She measured her life in hits, and followers and status – of both the actual and online varieties – was everything. Not one to wring her hands over anything, she had taken shamelessness to new heights, crashing book parties, record parties, movie premieres, department stores, fundraisers for even the most obscure diseases, attending the opening, as they say, of an envelope. It was a time-tested technique that could barely be held against her, but it was the fact that she got so much coverage that irked everyone, especially on BYTE, the most influential and widely read blog in town. Thanks to her.

She thought back to how BYTE began as a vile little online journal authored by Jesse Arens less than a year earlier to settle perceived slights with his enemies, a snotty clique of blue-blooded party-hopping private-schoolers of which Lucy was a charter member. As was he, for that matter. But it didn't take off until Lucy came on board, involuntarily at first. Jesse knew that Lucy was not nearly as well-to-do as the others in her circle, that she blew her 'allowance' from her absentee father at the beginning of the month, and then, at the end, was hard up and desperate for cash and attention. He also knew her secrets, her mother's backstory – a source of huge embarrassment for Lucy, and one she did not want shared.

In an effort to avoid an all-out personal tabloid assault by the release of the humiliating details, Lucy complied. She would secretly provide him with embarrassing information about her high profile friends, and he would see that every little move she

made, everything she said, ate, or wore, would be covered. The more exclusive the info, the more widely read was BYTE, the more famous 'Lucky' Lucy or LULU became in turn, which translated into free stuff, gift bags, and coveted invites for her. The 'lucky' moniker came from the fact that nobody could quite figure out what she'd done to merit so much notice. With little more than guts and ambition, she'd mastered the fame game. Lucy's deal with the digital devil had paid off.

Fame could bring many things: personal appearances, sponsorships, free travel, clothing, accessories, carte blanche at clubs – but there was an even bigger thing that it couldn't bring her. As she brushed the screen gently with her fingertips and spun through the backlog of personal emails on her smartphone, there wasn't a single entry from anyone she knew asking how she was doing. They had to know, had to have seen the hospital coverage. Not one relative or girlfriend, not one ex-boyfriend, few though there were. Actually, she didn't have friends anymore, just competitors, sacrifices, distanced from her peers both by her own sudden fame and the means by which she'd achieved it. It was harder to betray people you were close to, even for a media mercenary like Lucy. Especially lately, when her onetime BFFs were becoming increasingly suspicious of her.

Truth be told, she didn't miss them until she found herself in the ER and found out firsthand that no one genuinely missed her. No one besides Jesse, but his motives weren't exactly pure and always came with strings attached. The more frantically she searched for some online sympathy, the more depressed she became. Then the mobile phone rang. She checked caller ID and wasn't sure if she should answer, and then she did anyway. 'What?'

'Didja see it?' Jesse asked.

'How could I miss it?'

'We did it again. The site is almost crashing from the traffic.'

Lucy fought back the sick feeling that began brewing in her stomach.

'Where are you gonna be in the next hour?'

'In bed.'

'I'm coming over.'

'Ewww. No. Pig.'

'Not for *that*. For a photo call. I need a picture. The premium subscribers want some exclusive content. To see how . . . you look.'

Lucy was used to being treated like this. As a thing. Mostly she didn't mind, but tonight things were different. 'Can't you wait until the body is cold?'

'Not on BYTE. We only run hot.'

Even our verbal sparring revolves around branding, she thought.

'Wear something sexed-up, you know, heels and boxers, but maybe no makeup,' he said, art-directing her as he usually did.

'You're so gross,' she said, douche chills running up her arms and legs.

'Don't be so self-righteous, Lucy. Nobody put a gun to your head.'

'I wish someone had,' she said. 'I'll send something tomorrow.'

'I need eyeballs and advertisers,' Jesse insisted. 'Now.'

Lucy crossed her legs and stared at the chaplet. The open eye carving on the charm freaked her out a little, like it was looking right at her again. She looked at it for a second and then turned it around so that the eyes were facing away from her. 'Don't ever speak to me like I'm your bitch. You're the one that needs me. More people read what I write on my shoe than read your blog. Last word, loser!' she screamed, slamming the phone back in its charger cradle.

The phone rang immediately.

'What's got into you?' Jesse asked.

'Don't you get that all this is really disgusting?'

'I'm not a priest, so don't waste your time confessing to me.'

'I'm not looking for your forgiveness, dickhead.'

'We have an arrangement, Lucy.'

'It's for ever, Jesse. It never goes away. Their grandkids will be able to search it.'

'And?'

'And I have to live with these people, look them in the eye. They know it's me. I see the look of betrayal on their faces when they read this crap on your site.'

'Not crap,' Jesse admonished. 'Content. That you provide. Besides, you dropped out. You barely see these people except

for a few hours across some sticky leather banquet.'

'I need a break.'

'You can't cash cheques without consequences, Lucy.'

'I'm not asking you, I'm telling you. Jesus, Jesse,' she said, revolted by his desperation at pimping her out.

'If we don't get the picture in the next hour, the buzz dies,' he said. She could hear the desperation in his voice.

'It's always the next thing – the next shot, the next tragedy, the next failure, the next high. Always chasing . . . something.'

'Just remember what's at stake.'

'You mean like the reputations of people I grass on for a slimy item?'

'Their reputations,' he began. 'Or yours.'

The nurse escorted Agnes out and handed her a plain white paper cup with a mint green pill.

'Take it,' the nurse demanded.

'No more therapy or anything?' Agnes asked.

'This is therapy.'

Agnes placed the pill on her tongue. Stuck it out at the nurse and then washed it down with a swig of metallic-tasting tap water. Normally, she would be reluctant to take such a medication. She only took holistic remedies, unless she was really ill. But now, she hoped that this pill would help her to stop thinking of Sayer, or anyone else she'd ever fallen for. She wanted to be numb.

'Open,' the nurse ordered.

Agnes opened her mouth to show the nurse that she did indeed swallow.

After documenting the proof on her clipboard, she handed Agnes a loose-fitting bleached ultrawhite psych ward top and white scrub pants and then led her down the corridor.

Once there, she was stripped down.

Bare.

All except for her bandage and her concealed bracelet.

A maze of tiled and mildewed shower rooms beckoned, each with open stalls, steamy windows, oversized showerheads, and ceramic flooring, slightly bevelled toward the centre to promote proper drainage. In the entry room, there was a little sitting area, also tiled and peppered with drains and a long, wooden, locker-room bench.

She couldn't decide whether it looked more like a condemned day spa or the funeral home that she worked at for one unforgettable summer job. While there, it was her responsibility at the end of the day to pull out the hose and wash the hair, nails, flakes of skin, powder, gauze, and whatever else was mixed in down the drain – all of it swirling together with the bright orange embalming fluid, transforming it into a melting creamsicle of runoff. She only worked there for one summer because the owner, the undertaker, killed himself. Agnes found that somewhat comforting in a strange way and it had given rise to her preoccupation with life and death that she'd shared with

Frey earlier. The mortician worked with the dead, after all; maybe he had some inside info that helped with the decision.

Then, the washing.

Agnes was showered. It was undignified, but like so many undignified things, it felt kind of good. The water was cool, not brisk enough to snap her completely out of the drug-addled stupor she was in, but just enough to remind her that she was a human being – flesh, blood, and five senses. She was suddenly alert enough to cry; warm tears were birthed from her eyes, free falling, mixing seamlessly with the water, until they hit the ceramic tile and disappeared down the rusted drain. She wanted to go with them.

Agnes dried off and put on her hospital issued 'outfit'. There were only two occasions where one could pull off this all-white ensemble – being committed to a psych ward and one's wedding day. She was then taken to a tiny, boxy room with no windows and a roommate.

The place was unremarkable, impersonal, resembling a dorm room that belonged to someone who never received care packages from home. The only thing hanging on the wall was a faded picture of what looked to be a religious icon.

Agnes studied it closely, losing track of time and the fact that she wasn't alone.

'Saint Dymphna,' her roommate said in a weak tone. 'The patron saint of nervous disorders and the mentally ill.'

Agnes looked at the girl lying on her bed facing the wall.

'She was murdered by her father,' the girl said. 'See, he was a pagan king and her mother was a devout Christian. When Dymphna was fourteen, her mother died. Her father loved her mother so much that he went totally crazy after her death and tried to get with Dymphna 'cause she reminded him of her.'

The girl closed her eyes and mustered the strength to continue. 'She ran away. And, when he found her . . . he drew his sword. And then he . . .' She paused and swallowed. 'CUT off her head. She was sixteen. Like me.'

'You sure know her story well,' Agnes said.

'I'm Iris.'

Iris turned around to face Agnes. She was sickly-looking and sunken-eyed.

It hit Agnes that Iris knew Dymphna's story all too well.

'I'm Agnes.'

'So, Agnes, why are *you* in here?'

After looking into the vulnerable girl's eyes, Agnes put her arms in front of her and exposed her bandaged wrists.

'Yeah, me too,' the girl said.

'Why did you do it?' Agnes asked.

'Doesn't matter. No one believes me, anyway.'

The girl turned back over in bed, again facing the wall.

'I will,' Agnes said, surprising herself with the certainty of her reply. *Maybe it's the pill, or maybe it's something else,* she thought.

4

12:51

'Touché, bastards!' Cecilia yelled, a slim silhouette wielding her guitar from the darkened wooden stage at the Continental bar on the Bowery.

Cecilia was killing.

As usual.

It was her night to headline. Thursday. The midnight show.

The emergency-room detour of the previous weekend was a distant memory and the only ones who appeared to be gasping for breath now were the awestruck fans before her. She held them mercilessly, musically, by the throat.

The Vari-Lite rig flicked on. Incandescent beams shone around her head and shoulders like a fractured, multicoloured laser light halo.

The PA system crackled expectantly.

The audience, anxiously awaiting her surround-sound sermon.

There she stood.

Silent and powerful. A vanguard vixen vision in white.

A blank screen ripe for whatever the audience wanted to project upon her.

With her don't-mess-with-me fashion and her weapon of choice, CeCe was ready for the jaded hands-in-pocket hipsters that were gatekeepers on the New York club scene. She accepted the challenge.

And she certainly looked the part. Over her head, she wore a sheer, white, netted veil tucked close, obscuring her face even to those at the edge of the stage. Her hair was pinned up in a messy, romantic do. Her thin, long neck was bare. She wore a white peekaboo kevlar vest, strapped tight with Velcro bands. Her pants were white McQueen 'thrift score' leggings, made of vinyl, that laced up the front. A chainmail epaulet dangled from her bare shoulder with a single-strand sash made of old rhinestones crossing her torso. Her nails were painted white with some type from a book faintly visible – she dipped them in surgical spirit and pressed a cheaply printed Bible that Bill had acquired over them so that words would transfer to her nails. Her eyes were dark, smoky black and grey, and her lips glossed in a flesh-coloured hue.

Cecilia stared blankly toward the back of the long, narrow room as she surveyed the crowd in front of her from the drum riser, legs spread, Fender guitar slung low around her waist, arm stiffened and extended straight outward as if drawing a bead on the audience. It was an aggressive pose, and one she thought worth striking.

Beaming. Beautiful. Badass.

People didn't so much attend her weekly shows at the Continental as loiter around them. She drew a mixed crowd and she was proud of that. Lurking in the dingy room where a few neighbourhood regulars, slumming private-school students, stylists for big-name musicians who were there to 'borrow' her look, cheating boyfriends, bartenders with arms folded, an overly enthusiastic gaggle of girls packed unnecessarily tightly at the lip of the tiny stage, and the four or five guys in back who'd come mostly to perve on her. Lots of people had come to see her tonight, but not the one person she was hoping to see. She knew she had no right to expect he would turn up, but she was disappointed anyway.

She looked out over the heads of the gathering, breathing the stink of her own sweat mixed with splintered floorboard marinated in spilled beer, saliva, smoke, and ash from cigarette butts long since stamped out before the city smoking codes changed. Pretty much a typical Thursday night, except for the new accessory she was sporting: The emergency room chaplet she'd been given was worn around her bicep, twisted like a

tourniquet, matching her stark white ensemble with the unusual charm dangling perpendicularly from it.

For her, the applause was beside the point. It was about communication. It was the look of adoration in their eyes she'd sought. That she needed. Their respect, not their approval, that turned her on. That's what inspired her to begin with, the same compulsion that had driven her musical heroes and the people she admired. To tell the truth. To reveal to people what they already knew deep inside. To shake them up.

Sebastian was a total stranger but he got that about her. And she got the same vibe from him. She wasn't into playing it safe. If anything, her goal was to put some risk, put the unexpected, back into music and into life for that matter.

In the end, she just wanted to cut through the bullshit, on stage, at least, if not off, where she'd fashioned a persona that resembled both a wounded soldier and a sharp blade, but more a shank than a rapier. The suggestion of violence, disruption, thinly veiled and always present.

She wasn't afraid to show her lady balls.

To be hard.

To be intimidating.

The warrior queen of her own private dystopia.

As she held fast both her dramatic pose and the audience's attention, she looked out past the bright lights and into their eyes. It was mesmerizing.

She took the time to stare down each and every one of them.

Surveying the crowd for one in particular. Sebastian. But, he was nowhere to be found. A no-show.

She noticed all of them.

Watching her.

Watching for what she would do next.

The bartenders unfolded their arms.

The girls stood still.

The guys, waiting. Patiently.

For her.

For her to make a move.

She slowly opened her hand, keeping eye contact with the crowd, and let her guitar pick fall in front of her, off the stage. The lonely, lost eyes, out on a Sunday night, looking to her for something. Something she realized she couldn't give them. Not tonight.

'What the hell is going on?' a guy in the crowd yelled. 'Play for us!'

'Cecilia, play for us!' the crowd began chanting in unison.

If I can't play to him, she thought, *I'll play for him.*

She slyly slid the chaplet over her wrist and wrapped it tightly around her hand, the most gorgeous set of brass knuckles anyone had ever seen, the sword charm suspended just low enough for her to grip it, like a pick, between her thumb and forefinger. She cranked her guitar up and tore into a wailing solo, channelling all her feelings into a wordless maelstrom of sonic aggression, the gold charm slaying the steel

strings and feeding back relentlessly into the amps and out into the audience.

CeCe attacked the fretboard, bending notes with such passion that she nearly pulled the instrument out of tune. The pointed end of the sword charm dug deep into her hand. Drops of blood ran from her palm down her fingers to her cuticles and on to the pick guard and the whammy bar. Without uttering a word, she'd said everything she needed to say to the stunned gathering.

Spent, she turned and faced the drummer, on the verge of tears, and mouthed, *I can't.*

But she already had.

CeCe bolted from the stage, guitar in hand, and headed straight for the backstage cupboard that doubled for a dressing room. She grabbed her bag, squeezed it to make sure her wallet was still inside, looked indifferently at herself in the tiny cosmetic mirror on the door, and started for the exit.

'Where the hell do you think you're going?' a gruff voice quizzed. 'I paid you for an hour show.'

'You didn't pay me, Lenny,' Cecilia reminded him. 'It was a door deal, remember. I keep the cover, you get the bar.'

'What bar? Those freaks you brought in were underage. I don't make money selling ginger ale.'

'That's your problem.'

'Now it's your problem. Don't come back here.'

'That's the idea.' Cecilia wasn't sure what had come over her.

'I was doing you a favour. Giving you a night here to showcase. Build something. A following.'

'A favour?' she huffed. 'You mean like the weekly photo shoot of me changing that you tried to arrange from the camera you have planted in the bathroom? You just want to get in my pants.'

'No thanks, honey.' Lenny wagged an arthritic finger. 'I'm a little too scared of what I might find when I get in there.'

'Pay me,' Cecilia ordered, holding her bloodstained hand out.

'Ha. You're like all the others. You screw a guy and then you want to get paid.'

CeCe stood there, waiting for Lenny to grease her palm. He grabbed her wrist and, instead of paying her, he stuck out his tongue and licked it, blood and all, and spat at the floor, cursing her. 'You're not getting one dime from me after that shit you just pulled out there.'

'Keep it,' she said, wiping any trace of spittle and plasma from her hand on to his shirt. 'And the herpes.'

Cecilia stalked off, noticing a pale and familiar face in the smoky darkness. Ricky Pyro. An up-and-coming Goth-punk front man and druggie scenester. It certainly wasn't the guy she was hoping to see. He was much different from Sebastian, even though she'd known Ricky for a long time, and Sebastian only a moment. But, oddly, Ricky was more of a stranger to her. Her pet name for him was 'sociopath'. He was out for himself. No

mystery. No manners. Crass. The complete opposite of Sebastian. Ricky was a fellow soldier on the music strip and a sometimes booty call. They had a history and not always a good one. She packed up as she bitched to him. 'You saw all that, right?'

'Yeah, I saw it.'

'Showbiz.'

He nodded in agreement. 'Short yet frickin' amazing set.'

'I gotta get out of here. You on next?'

'Yeah.'

'What are you calling the band tonight?'

'Pagans,' he replied, sticking his hand in his pocket and looking her up and down.

'Sounds familiar. Better call your lawyer,' she joked, knowing he was so broke he used to book his band pretending to be his own agent.

But then again, so did she.

'That band was *The* Pagans, smart-ass,' he corrected, pointing out a distinction but not a difference. 'They were a punk band. I found the lead singer. He's, like, a caretaker now or something. He said we could use the name if we sang one of his old songs every night. He still owns his publishing. Business, ya know.'

'Must be a valuable catalogue. Which song?'

'"What Is This Shit Called Love?"'

'Charming. Break a nut. Oh, and thanks for getting me to

the hospital the other night.'

'Hospital?'

'Never mind,' she said, rushing for the door.

'Where you headed?'

'Don't know,' she called back as she reached the door, the silence from the outside getting sucked into the roar inside. 'Oh, and by the way. I'm feeling better. Thanks for asking!'

'Hit you up later?'

'Nah,' she said, looking over at his groupies, who would kill to be with him. 'Don't ever fall for me, Ricky.'

'Too late,' he replied.

Then she looked condescendingly over to his band members. 'By the way, no matter what you call them, they still suck.'

'Not as good as you do,' the drummer shouted.

CeCe pushed the bar on the back door and walked out into the alley where a few of her fans – the diehards – had gathered. Her 'apostles' she called them, all sporting her look, with varying degrees of success. She appreciated them, their loyalty and devotion most of all, but right now, even they were not enough.

'What happened?' one shouted as she rushed by them. 'Everything OK?'

'I'm good.' She grinned unconvincingly, like someone about to vomit, and kept walking.

'Sick bracelet,' another girl called out. 'Where'd you get it?'

'Some guy,' she answered, preferring to keep the details to herself.

She held up her arm as much to show off the chaplet as to wave goodbye. The girls turned wide-eyed, covered their mouths, and giggled silently, devouring the piece of inside info they'd just been tossed. She was rude and they didn't deserve that. *They deserved an explanation, but what was there to be gained by preaching to the converted, to her followers,* she thought. Whatever she said they'd just nod their heads, listen attentively, frown sympathetically, and agree with every word. She needed some criticism, some perspective.

Maybe she should have just admitted to them that all that bravado and empowerment talk she put out there was just a load of bullshit, a stage persona that she put on and took off the way she changed her outfits or boyfriends. That the club owner was a pervert who she subtly encouraged to keep her weekly gig, that she barely made cab fare to and from her apartment from her ticket and download sales, that she'd allowed herself to be used by every Strokes wannabe in a leather jacket and skinny jeans from Williamsburg to the East Village, and that she'd finally had enough. She was still coughing up dirt from the previous weekend's puddle if she needed any further proof. If nothing else, she was comforted by the knowledge that she'd given them an interesting status update for their fan pages.

Frauds, liars, cheats, users, perverts, wannabes, and worse. She let them all in, bit by bit, until it seemed almost . . . normal.

Until she felt comfortable, with them and with herself for choosing them. Until she almost needed them. The height of self-delusion, she knew, but it made it much easier to get through the day – and night – most of the time. Sebastian seemed like he might be the antidote to all that. But then again, maybe not. He couldn't even be bothered to come.

'I know how to pick 'em.'

She suddenly felt a hard thud against her chest that startled her out of her own pity party.

'Oh, I am so sorry!' a sweet but shaky voice intoned.

'Watch it!' CeCe barked, moving around the person who'd just body checked her.

'Would you sign this for me?' the girl asked sheepishly, holding out a show flyer with Cecilia plastered all over it. 'If it's not too much trouble.'

Cecilia froze and gritted her teeth. It was the last thing she wanted to do right then, but she could still remember when nobody cared. Her ego kicked in. 'Sure.' CeCe grabbed the neon pink and green punk-style poster from the girl's trembling fingers. 'I see they advertised me tonight,' she said, realizing that Lenny needed her much more than she needed him. 'I never get to see these.'

'I'm sure your fans rip them down and have them hanging in their rooms.'

Cecilia shot her a look.

The girl realized that *she* was one of those fans.

'What's your name?' Cecilia asked impatiently.

'Catherine,' the girl said nervously, unable to disguise her excitement. 'I'm from Pittsburgh too.'

Funny thing about New York City, Brooklyn in particular, Cecilia thought. *If you're living there, you're from there.* They say that after ten years, you're considered a native, but it really didn't matter how long. You were instantly absorbed in it and by it. Your slate was wiped clean. Pittsburgh was already a very distant memory for her. Another life.

'What are you doing here?' she asked, her eyes focused on her hand as she signed her name.

The girl just shrugged quietly and smiled broadly. 'Same as you. Trying to be somebody. I met this New York photographer online who said I should be modelling, and some guys in Ricky Pyro's band said maybe even make an album.'

Cecilia bristled a little at the mention of Ricky's name and a worried look spread out across her face. As she picked up her head to look the girl straight in the eye, Cecilia could see she was young, maybe a bit younger than Cecilia was, clear-eyed and clear-skinned. Pretty and unassuming. Cheerful in an innocent, nonirritating, way. 'Real' would be one way to describe her. Cecilia saw something of herself in the girl. Herself about a year ago. Disillusionment hadn't taken long to set in. She was tempted to say something, but didn't, feeling it wasn't her place.

Catherine continued on almost breathlessly. 'Ricky said we

could video the session and upload it online and maybe get a few bookings or an audition for a talent show on TV.'

'Yeah, well, don't hold your breath waiting to spin the big prize wheel.'

'I just thought I should try everything.'

'Catherine,' CeCe said sternly. 'Life is not a game show.'

'You know there are still a few kids who hang around outside your house,' Catherine said enthusiastically, as if that small-town tidbit would mean anything to her. 'I guess they were fans of your first band when you were, like, fifteen – I'm sorry I don't remember the name.'

'The Vains,' Cecilia said, the slightest smile crossing her lips as the memory of her very first all-girl psyche-pop trio crossed her mind. 'We did all right for a minute. Before your time, huh?'

Catherine smiled back sheepishly.

'Why'd you break up?'

'The usual. Backstabbing bandmates. Domineering boyfriends. Out-of-control egos. So I split,' CeCe said almost wistfully. 'Mostly I just didn't think they were as into the music as much as me. And here I am.'

'I guess it's really hard to know what you want at such a young age,' Catherine said sympathetically. 'Or ever, for that matter.'

'Really? I knew what I wanted to do at five years old,' CeCe shot back harshly, never one to coddle wafflers. 'If it's in you, it finds you. Or you find it. If it doesn't . . .'

Catherine was stung. CeCe's diatribe felt a little too personal. More like an attack. But it was inspiring also, Catherine thought, in its own way. CeCe bought the rock-and-roll myth. Catherine could see that. A true believer. She was born to do what she was doing. She just knew it. And no one could convince her otherwise. Despite the self-assuredness in what CeCe said, however, the look of hurt in her expression also spoke volumes.

'Your parents don't seem to like those kids hanging around. The window blinds are always pulled down and they never speak to any of them.'

'No surprise there,' Cecilia said uncomfortably. 'They don't speak to me, either.'

'Oh,' Catherine said, sensing she might have hit a nerve. 'Don't they approve of what you're doing?'

'Approve?' CeCe said, her voice rising and nose crinkling up like she'd just smelled raw sewage. The word almost gave her the chills. Whatever the opposite of approval was, that's how her parents felt about her choices and how little support they gave her. They had provided a nice house, nice clothes, nice things. Everything but what she craved. It's why she ran away. She'd stopped seeking their approval the minute she got off the bus at the Port Authority. The fact that Catherine even used the word told Cecilia everything she needed to know about the girl. She still measured herself by her parents' standard. Naïve. Dependent. Still had their voice in her head. That could be a dangerous thing in this town. Pleasers were

eaten alive and spit out like rat guts on the train line.

'Sorry. I didn't mean to pry,' Catherine said.

'It's cool. It was a lifetime ago, y'know. I'm over it. I get all the approval I need from this,' CeCe said, nodding at her guitar case.

Catherine could see that CeCe had exhausted whatever patience and politeness she'd mustered and was pretty much done with the memory lane chitchat.

'So, any advice?'

Cecilia paused, weighing her words.

'Go home, Catherine,' Cecilia advised with a tight smile as she pulled a pint bottle of vodka from her coat pocket and raised it in a faux toast. 'Just go home.'

5

Stations of the Lost

Agnes felt like a car alarm going off after midnight as she walked down the hallowed corridors of Immaculate Heart Academy, the bandages wrapping her wrists her siren. The burden was almost too much to bear, even more than the seeping wounds that threatened to stain her history book through her dark blue school uniform sweater.

Being back in school was humiliating, but it was still far preferable to her than being at home. Nevertheless, the cuts she was expecting from classmates were certain to be deeper and more painful than any she'd inflicted on herself.

'Accessorizing?' came the sly whisper from a two-dimensional blonde traipsing down the hallway, swirling her finger in a circle and eyeing Agnes's wrists. The more they commented, the more she hiked up her sleeves, defiantly offering herself up to their ridicule.

'Love your stitch bracelet.'

She was pelted. With words.

'Sadster.'

'Next time, try harder.'

She took it. Each tongue-lashing. Closing her eyes briefly after each one, recovering, and then walking forward.

'Choose Life!' another mocked, holding her comparative lit book up like a fevered preacher bangs his Bible.

'Classholes,' Agnes mumbled under her breath. She kept walking, keeping her focus forward. Taking everything that they threw at her with strength and dignity. There was a certain pride in being willing to die for something or someone, she told herself. It made the berating a little more bearable, anyway.

Her friend Hazel came up beside her. 'Guys – can't live with 'em and can't die for 'em.'

'Not now, Hazel.'

Agnes smiled. 'I'll talk to you later.'

'Let's hope so!' Hazel said, then burst out laughing at her own joke.

Agnes continued down the hall; she watched everyone watching her. No one approached her. She felt betrayed.

It was hard for her to fault any of them though. Not that she was particularly forgiving, because she wasn't. It's just that

these weren't exactly enemies. Not friends either really, but more than acquaintances. People she hung out with after school or at parties or did group profile pictures with, tongues wagging outward suggestively, giving some unseen someone the finger. Poring over horoscope books and studying numerology, as it pertained to certain guys and whether they were liked by them or not. They were part of her crowd and she was part of theirs, whatever that meant. Fun but numb inside, all of them. She wouldn't have expected much sympathy from them even if they knew how to express it. She knew what they were like and what she could be like, from time to time. It just sucked when the tables turned. Bad.

The bell rang announcing the next class. She was saved, she thought, feeling more as if she were in a boxing ring and not a high school hallway. She didn't expect much quarter and didn't get any. Protect yourself at all times, as they say. She'd been beaten down but threw her guard up as she saw him coming around the corner. She turned back around and hoped the adrenaline pump inside her was good for a second whirl.

'I can hear you rolling your eyes,' she said, feeling Sayer come up behind her.

'Hey,' he said, trying to act concerned.

'Been crying?' she mocked, noticing his red eyes and knowing full well he was stoned.

'How are you?' Sayer asked.

'More to the point, how are you?' Agnes responded.

Sayer was slightly built and long-haired, he was generally dazed and nervous-looking with a toothy perma-smile as if he were almost about to be caught doing something wrong in mid-laugh but wasn't exactly sure what. His natural demeanour suited this situation perfectly. Her nonchalance was totally unexpected. He thought he might get read the riot act, but Agnes seemed to be offering a peace pipe.

'I'm OK,' he answered.

'Oh, that's a relief. I assumed you must have broken your fingers or your legs or something.'

She clung to the burning heart charm under her bandaged wrist and outlined it with her finger as she talked to him.

'Huh?'

'Yeah, otherwise, I thought for sure you'd come by for a visit or call or even just text,' Agnes went on. 'Then it occurred to me it must be solar flares.'

'Solar flares?'

'You know, screwing with the internet. I mean, it had to be something pretty drastic for you to not come see me or even ask how I was doing, right?'

'Opening up your wrists is pretty drastic, Agnes,' he half whispered, topping his insensitivity off with a nervous giggle. 'It was, like, scary. I didn't know what to do, or what to say.'

'So you did nothing,' she said. 'You said nothing.'

'Not exactly nothing,' he said. 'I was thinking about you the whole time.'

'So I'm supposed to be telepathic now? Thinking about me? When? Between bong hits and sluts?'

For the first time, she was able to see him for the selfish, dishevelled, stupefied, and unreliable stoner her mom so vehemently disapproved of. The pointlessness of the conversation took her totally out of body and she began to beat herself up for being so stupid and impulsive, for her moments of weakness or rebellion, but if any good had come of this self-destructive episode, it was that the brain fog from this relationship had lifted. Thank God she hadn't slept with him. At last, something she and her mother could agree on.

'Did it hurt?' he asked slowly, running his finger along his own wrist for emphasis.

'Not as much as it does now.'

'I guess I'm a pretty lame excuse for a guy.'

'Just *some* guy?' she said in a tone that parents and lawyers often use when asking a leading question. 'You were supposed to be *the* guy.'

He wasn't great at thinking on his feet, and her sarcastic inquiry was met with contrite silence.

'I'm sorry, OK?' he whined, the most authentic emotion she could ever actually remember getting from him.

'That's it?' she hissed. 'You cheated on me!'

'I never said we were exclusive.'

'You knew how I felt about you.'

'It was just too much pressure, y'know. All the love stuff,' Sayer said. 'I just wanted to have some fun.'

'Does this look like fun?' Agnes screamed loudly enough to stop the between-class traffic clogging the corridors, holding her bandages up to his face.

Sayer just hung his head.

'It's not worth it,' Agnes said, turning her back on him and rummaging through her locker. 'I guess you were just an excuse. For me.'

'Forgive me?' he asked, reaching for her shoulder, mustering up his most concerned face. 'Please.'

Startled by the sympathetic gesture, she looked him over and honestly thought about it for a second. He was just doing him. He was sorry, at least as sorry as it was possible for him to be. She could see that, even in his blank expression and glassy eyes. But he had now entered 'what was I thinking?' territory in her head. The worst place for any guy to be.

'My mother was right about you,' Agnes said, almost choking on her words.

'At least you finally admit it. We both know, this was never about me.'

'Don't turn it around,' she said, tears beginning to flow more from embarrassment than hurt. 'You used me. I believed you.'

'No, actually, I didn't get the chance to use you, remember?'

'So maybe if I would have slept with you, you might have

cared? What a joke,' she nearly growled, gripping his arm with force.

He shuffled around, pouting in place with his head down for a second like a little boy, waiting for his time-out to be over. She released his arm and pushed him away from her.

'I almost died for you,' Agnes said.

'I almost waited for you,' he said.

As if they were of equal importance.

Lucy was immediately ushered into the VIP area, as usual, at Sacrifice, the afterhours DUMBO club. Both bridges – the Brooklyn and the Manhattan – illuminated the dark space, creating auras around the celebrity guests and patrons. She was wearing rhinestone drop earrings with several gold spikes radiating out of the bottom of each. Her hair was freshly coloured blonde – sleek, straight, and shiny. She was wearing a short grey couture tunic dress with fox fur sleeves dyed royal blue. Her suede stilettos were dyed the same blue suede with gold spiked heels to match the ones coming out of her earrings.

It is amazing, she thought, *how quickly you can become accustomed to A-list treatment, whether you deserve it or not, or to ultimately losing it.* Everyone did at some point. It was like death. Always looming and eventually your fate. Even more amazing was the short ride from getting it, to demanding it, to needing it. It was as addictive as any drug.

As she looked around for someone she really knew well, there were few hellos. Just stares from underage insiders with fast-food opinions, Botoxed curiosity hounds and surgically rerouted Joker faces with etched bellies, unnaturally arched brows, and swollen lips framing tight, twisted-up smiles impossible to discern from frowns. Digital attention-seekers all, with a million questions they were dying to ask, the answers to which they were dying to sell to the highest bidder. It was a cage match of ambition more intense than the climb up any corporate ladder or high school hierarchy. A bloodsport that smelled more like expensive perfume than perspiration.

The competitiveness was palpable, viral. She recognized it in others because she was one of them, one of the afflicted. Riding any wave that would take them to the golden shore of their Fifth Avenue fantasies. It didn't matter whether they caught a clean one in or tumbled and crashed on the sand, they were there just the same. Different day, same night. All the same.

Jesse was ensconced in his dimly lit booth, alone, by choice, observing this mini-universe unfold like a pocket-sized Hubble telescope. He was perched in a primo spot with a bird's eye view – the lit-up city and bridges, his backdrop, and an even more appropriate waste disposal barge passing behind him down the East River. He was dressed all in black, as usual, which made it easier for him to disappear into the background, except for his eyes, which were always watching, and his hands, which were always typing, looking like the Invisible Man in

reverse. She caught his eye and turned away just as he raised his finger to his brow and pointed at her in some kind of obnoxious salute. She wasn't sure whether it was a creepy acknowledgement that she'd arrived or that he was there. Either way, he was the last person she wanted to see.

A high-pitched but aggressive voice Lucy didn't recognize cut through the thump of the DJ's bass speaker, coming at her from her blind side.

'You bitch!' the apoplectic socialite screamed, slapping at the air around Lucy's head. 'You ass-covering sellout!'

Lucy had good peripheral vision and even better survival instincts, and easily sidestepped the raging junior leaguer. But the girl was quick and determined. She turned around and caught a few strands of Lucy's locks in her manicured claws, tugging her hair over her eyes and her head forward. She couldn't see a thing, except for the girl's copper glittery stilettos driven into the stained red indoor/outdoor carpet beneath her, illuminated by electronic flashes from cameras and mobile phones. Lucy grabbed for the girl's legs and took her down at the knees, driving her on to her back to woots and screams, mostly from the guys who took all the panty shots as fan service. Oddly, of all things, Lucy was most worried about her bracelet. That it might get damaged.

Security arrived before a full-on girl fight could break out, and the two VIPs were involuntarily separated. Lucy finally got a good look at her adversary and recognized her as the actual girlfriend of Tim, the guy she'd been grassing on to Jesse. The one who was with Sadie at the hospital. But how could she, this dim-witted piece of eye candy, possibly connect her to it? How could *she* know?

Lucy shot Jesse a knowing and condescending glance. *It was him. Had to be.* Payback for her ingratitude and warning of what he had in store for his rebellious protégé/fetish. He glared back for a second and then returned to his phone, typing feverishly. She pulled herself together and sat down. A few stragglers ambled over for a chat.

'What circle of hell did she escape from?' one said. 'Who cares anyway, right? That will move.'

'This was a total borefest until now,' another one said. 'Did you see Jesse over there? He got the whole thing.'

'You should get in touch with the hair extensions company,' a third snarked. 'Xena over there couldn't rip them out of your head.'

Stunned equally at the vicious attack and the calculating indifference of the brain-dead bar junkies surrounding her, Lucy stared blankly ahead, trying to process the new low she'd just sunk to.

'I'm good, thanks,' Lucy grumbled sarcastically, noting that no one bothered to ask if she was OK.

She hadn't even had a drink and the room was already spinning.

'We saw the BYTE item from last weekend,' they said

following her. 'So cool that you wound up in the ER. It's so . . . effective.'

'I would have bulk-mailed my contact list once I got to the hospital though,' another strategized out loud.

A year ago, this might have been her, she thought. Irritating, clipped, vocal-fried commentary on the minutiae of social climbing by couture ass-kissers. She was just like them – except, she sort of wasn't any more. Not since the hospital. Calculated, cunning, self-interested, and self-absorbed, yes. But not conscienceless. She preferred to think of herself as a flower among weeds. A single bloom, a standout, rising high above the fields of cheatgrass except that, like all flowers in a patch of thistle, the weeds were beginning to choke her off.

She'd become their idol, the one who lit the way for all the other attractive and ambitious, but otherwise unremarkable, Big Apple celebutantes. Their very own Statue of Celebrity, her torch of notoriety shining brightly from VIP rooftop lounges citywide. For a fee, of course. It wasn't much of a legacy, she'd come to see. 'Bring me your entitled, your selfish, your huddled attention-starved masses, yearning to be famous . . .' She'd lifted her lamp beside the golden door, but more and more, she felt the light inside of her going out.

'Excuse me, Lucy,' another voice called from behind her, and she immediately tensed up, ready for another sucker punch.

'Oh, Tony.' Lucy sighed at seeing a friendly face and hugged him. 'Thank God.'

'Listen, Lucy.' The burly bouncer pulled her arms off his neck, leaned in, and spoke as confidentially as possible in such a public place. 'I can't have dis goin' on here. I heard da cops are involved in da t'ing from last weekend and I don't need any more trouble dan I already got. The owners are goin' apeshit.'

'You've got to be kidding me right now,' Lucy said, stunned.

'I'm askin' you as a friend not to come back here. At least not for a while.'

'I was attacked. You're lucky I don't sue you.'

'Don't make me ban you, Lucy.'

'Ban me? I put this shithole on the map. Without me you couldn't find this place with MapQuest, unless of course you're underage,' Lucy said, looking around the room. 'Sure you're checking IDs tonight, Tony?'

Tony stayed calm but firm in the face of her threats.

'Don't bust my balls, Lucy. Maybe all press is good press for you, but not for me. I'm sorry.'

She knew then that it was everyone for themselves and that even thank you cards came pay-on-delivery in this world. She grabbed her things. But, before she could escape, Jesse slithered up beside her for a chat.

'Nice work,' he said, brushing away the shaggy fringe from his layered mod do. 'If I didn't know better, I'd have thought you set that little fight-club moment up yourself.'

'Are you accusing me of social climbing?' she fumed, getting right in his face.

'You *are* a social climber, my darling.'

'They only call you a social climber if you're not good at it,' Lucy said, starting for the front door, checking her phone for what would be the last time, as she exited.

'I deserved that,' she said to Jesse. Without missing a beat, a breaking-news alert popped up on her phone, complete with unflattering photo and nasty comments from 'people who saw the whole thing'. The only redeeming detail about the entire sordid episode was that the chaplet earned its own photo inset as a hot new trend she was kicking off. She stared at it for a while, felt for it on her wrist. Smiled. And then tossed her phone into the street.

6

Fairy Tale of New York

'It's not often that I have something to give,' the old man said, holding out a brown bag scarred and wet with whiskey stains for Cecilia to take.

'Thanks, but I've had enough,' she said.

'Open it,' he demanded in his raspy voice.

Cecilia went to the rooftop of her fifth-floor Williamsburg apartment to see him and give him a sandwich and a bottle of vodka after every gig. For her it was always part of the deal. He was a squatter, a thin, old guy in his seventies, who always wore a suit and hat, who made his home there on the tarred roof under the stars, while writing his beat poetry and hallucinogenic novels.

Cecilia opened the bag that was being offered to her. She slowly pulled out a length of hypodermic needle casings strung together meticulously on a piece of black wire.

'It's a necklace,' he said. 'Didn't have enough to make a chandelier.'

'Thank God,' she said, relieved, putting it around her pale, long neck. 'Recycling?' Cecilia asked, tying it in the back and fixing the needle casings so they all pointed down in a V formation. 'Don't tell me you're going green on me?'

It was sure to be the envy of every wannabe fashionista from Smith Street to the Bowery. But to her, it was the kindest gesture from a friend, made just for her with his own two hands. With the only thing he had.

They'd met several years ago; she would pass him every day on her way to the subway and routinely hand him what was left of her egg-and-cheese bagel. A one-time punk poet who'd fallen on hard times in his middle age and who would willingly trade you a quip from Jim Carroll or Billy Childish, or personal stories from the Chelsea Hotel or the Beat Hotel in Paris, for what he needed that day.

It wasn't just the daily word of wisdom for her that tipped him off as a writer. It was the dilapidated vintage Royal typewriter, his prized possession, that he positioned in front of himself, turning the pavement into a desk of sorts. All the keys seemed to work, but it had no ribbon or paper, which was to her more profound than anything he might have said or written. The lack of ink didn't stop him from banging away, however, typing his thoughts into the ether as if he were composing out loud or dictating to an imagined Girl Friday from deep in his past. Whether it was drugs, mental illness, or just plain determination, she found it, and him, inspiring.

More than any preacher, spiritual figure, or self-help guru, he spoke to her soul. A maestro, playing his typewriter like an instrument, performing his thoughts. As a musician herself, she could relate. He needed to write, but he didn't need anyone to read it. A confidence she strived for but had yet to attain. She would bring him paper and ribbon when she could get it and catch what she could.

He looked sophisticated, like a William Burroughs doppelgänger, sitting there in his baggy suit, elegant even, despite the fact that his trousers and jacket swam on him. He was so gaunt, given his proclivity for drinking his meals, that she was sure her sandwiches were the only solid food he got. Not that she was one of those 'pay-it-forward' types. She hadn't been on the receiving end of much kindness or generosity to transfer anyway.

Besides, she'd met plenty of those and there was something so unnervingly self-serving about them. Do-gooders willing to volunteer or donate but not if it hurt, not if it really required some effort or compassion, and only as long as someone was watching, as long as there was credit to be taken in exchange for their largesse.

They became closer the night he was attacked by some street thugs and she offered him her rooftop. It didn't belong to her, but it was something she could let him in on. She'd been taking him sandwiches, and vodka, and an endless supply of paper ever since.

Cecilia handed Bill a bottle of Stoli that she'd carried from the gig. He looked sick, his eyes hollow and desperate, and she knew he needed a drink. But he would never come out and ask her. Not her. Then again, he didn't need to.

'That shit's like drinking poison, you know,' Cecilia said, as she kicked a few needles out of her way to get to him.

'No, Night Queen. Anger is like drinking poison . . .'

'And expecting the other person to die.'

'That part sounds more like jealousy to me.'

'You're a smart man,' she said, unwrapping his sandwich to make sure he ate something.

'No, I'm just a junkie with a typewriter.'

'OK, then, you're a dangerous man.'

She sat there in the dark, next to a smoke stream of sandalwood incense, strumming her guitar for him until he ate. Then they sang the parts of 'Fairytale of New York'.

She watched as he began to nod off, bottle still clutched in his hand.

A junkie lullaby.

It was the same every night – Cecilia covered him up with a spare suit jacket that he carried around, finished smoking his lit

cigarette, took the poem he wrote out of his typewriter, and then made her way over to the steel reinforced door and down to her apartment. She would read his work at night and return it before he woke up in the late morning. He was writing for her, anyway. He would never sell his soul, but he would give it freely, lend it to someone who needed one. To her.

That particular night, as she reached her floor and rounded the corner, she could see the sign on the door.

She was marked.

She'd seen the signs on the doors of others and knew exactly what it meant.

NOTICE OF EVICTION

The Landlord has legal possession of these premises
pursuant to the Warrant of Civil Court.

She leaned her guitar case against the stack of thirty-gallon rubbish bags that had been piling up outside her door, pulled the old filament lightbulb hanging overhead toward her, reached for her key, and tried in vain to slip it in the lock. She didn't have a prayer that it would fit, and after a few frustrating seconds of recapitulating the stages of grief, she gave up. It wasn't her life that flashed before her, but a series of special-delivery envelopes from her landlord that had been turning up in the past few weeks. Letters that were piled, unopened, fifteen centimetres high on the kitchen counter next to her beloved vintage hand juicer and a terrarium made from a broken liquor

bottle that Bill gave her last Christmas. It was filled with moss, a cigarette butt, a wad of chewed-up gum, an old subway token, and a switchblade, all orbiting a tiny plastic baby figurine – a cupcake topper for a baby shower that he scavenged out of a bakery dumpster. He called it 'Street Life.' She joked that she could sell it for a hundred bucks to a Bedford Avenue boutique. But she never would. Not for a million. Not even now.

Cecilia collapsed into the door, banging her head against it just hard enough to hurt, hard enough to remind her of how bad things had got, hard enough to press a teardrop from her heavily mascaraed eye.

Besides not having a place to sleep or shower, the thing that upset her most was the element of rejection she was suffering and that it was her own fault. She was used to getting thrown out of apartments late at night, it just wasn't usually her own. The other thing was something much less self-involved but just as urgent. She grabbed her guitar, slung it across her back, as two black tributaries meandered down her cheeks and flowed together to form a liquid soul patch under her chin as she read what Bill had written.

> Our Lady of Sorrow
> No hope for Tomorrow.
> No soul left to Borrow.
> Your hands hold Tomorrow.

Cecilia smiled through her tears momentarily and walked outside with her guitar strung across her back. She nodded goodbye in the direction of her friend on the roof, and hailed a pedicab.

'Don't ever speak to me again!' Agnes yelled at her mother, her eyelids now in the shape of half-moons. Her mind was a raw, open sore, and Martha would scratch and scratch at it relentlessly, trying to bust it open any way she could.

'Why? Because I was right? Why are you so afraid to hear the truth?'

'It's *your* truth, Mother.'

'The truth is the truth, Agnes.'

Sounded familiar. Agnes began to wonder if her mother and the doctor were conspiring and, just as quickly, refused to give in to paranoia. 'I broke up with him. What more do you want from me? Do you want me to grovel, beg for your forgiveness for straying from The Path?'

'Don't get hysterical, you'll bust one of those stitches.'

'Oh, so now I'm crazy and can't make my own decisions. Nice, Mother.'

'What do you mean "*now*"?'

'I hate you.'

'Why you would go to such lengths, I'll never understand,' Martha said, trying to fix Agnes's bandage.

'No, you never will,' Agnes said. She pulled her arm away.

'I'm not afraid for my future. Not afraid to follow my heart.'

'How naïve. You're young. You'll figure it out.'

'You are so bitter. No wonder Dad left.'

Martha was livid. It was the most hurtful thing Agnes could have spat at her. And it was too late to take it away. But Agnes was actually relieved to release the elephant in the room. The ice rattled in Martha's cocktail tumbler. 'When I married your father—'

'You weren't married, you were sacrificed,' Agnes cut in. 'Isn't that right?'

'Don't talk to me like that. I am your mother.'

'Technically.'

'The Harrison boy is perfectly nice. Good family, the best schools, polite, well-spoken, SATs through the roof. He's got everything you need to make it in life. Not like that *Pineapple Express* understudy you were dating.'

'Oh, please, Mother. Don't start with the matchmaking again. It's lame.'

'Because you are doing so well?'

'"That Harrison boy"? You don't even know his name. What is this, 1950? Besides, I'm sure he's looking for one of those "dress for success" types who's a whore in the bedroom, just like all those other future Wall Streeters.'

'Don't you dare speak that way to me!'

'Oh, but you can treat me like that, I just can't say it out loud. I get it. I am nothing like that. Like him.'

'Opposites attract,' Martha spat back.

'I'm sixteen, Mother. I'm not looking for a Trump.'

'Would it hurt you to fish in a less polluted pond? Or do something with that hair falling all over the place. Throw some heels and makeup on. Sharpen up a little, for God's sake.'

'How about a goddamn geisha getup? I know there is something better out there for me. I don't need to have a master plan drawn up.'

'You don't need to because I do all the heavy lifting. I make the sacrifices, so that you won't have to.'

'You're my mother! Do you need a medal?' Agnes screamed, frustrated at the level of selfishness.

They each took a breath.

'When I find it, I will know it. Instantly. It won't take an audit to convince me,' Agnes continued.

'Find what, Agnes? You obviously don't have a clue what you are looking for, flitting from loser to loser like some kind of serial romantic.'

'Love, Mother. Real love. A heart and a soul. Not a wallet with feet. Simple as that.'

'Please,' Martha pleaded. 'Not another lecture about love at first sight, Agnes.'

Agnes stared her mother down. Both dripping resentment.

'You know how you explain love at first sight, Mother?'

Martha sighed. 'No, how?'

'You don't. That's how.'

'Real love.' Martha just laughed derisively, practically gargling the words. 'Don't be so high and mighty.'

Agnes grabbed at her ears, trying to block out the scepticism, the rigidity, her mother cutting her down to size. She almost felt herself transported back to the therapy session with Dr Frey, except this conversation was a bit more unprofessional.

'You were the one who insisted on Catholic school.'

'And I expected better results for the tuition I'm paying!'

Always back to money, Agnes thought. *And guilt.* She was a failure to her mother and her mother was a failure to her. She pursed her lips, trying to hold back the bile that had been building for months – actually years – and then exploded.

'Can't you see? I don't want to wind up like you and your Franken-Forty so-called friends. Drunk by dinnertime, blow jobs for Botox, and sleeping with their divorce settlements under their pillows.'

'Annulment!'

'So as long as the Church approves, it's OK? You hypocrite.'

'Watch your mouth, young lady! You don't know who you're talking to!'

'And neither do you,' Agnes said. She stormed off to her room and slammed her door, almost breaking the glass doorknob and the mounted antlers that hung above it. Her room was her sanctuary. Her cocoon. It was as Zen as she could make it and exactly what she needed right then. Flooded with light, the high ceilings, dark wood floors, and blush walls were

a direct contrast to the harshness of the conversation that had just taken place in the living room. Colourful scarves were draped over her lampshades just centimetres from catching fire, exactly how she liked it. A vivid kilim rug – upholstered footrest and a bottle-green leather wingback chair, large coffee table books stacked up with cushions thrown on top for seating on her lush sheepskin rug, burlap feed-bag pillows, a huge cement pot filled with succulents in every shade of green, incense holders, and an impressive collection of extraordinary silk robes and caftans.

She switched on her Moroccan lantern, lit a stick of incense, grabbed her favourite heirloom Afghan blanket from her bed, and wrapped herself inside it as she sat down at her desk – an antique door that she had propped up on trestles. Her enormous grey Maine coon cat, which she named Elizabeth of Hungary, jumped up on to her lap. She stroked her back and stared at her curiosity cabinet filled with her collection of beautiful, rare things that she'd collected over the years – an antique wooden hand that she used to hold her vintage necklaces, a collection of antique thimbles, vibrant glass-winged butterflies, once alive and free, pinned to a board. She, like her mother, loved to collect beautiful things. She often felt her mother counted Agnes as one of her pretty possessions. And she was done with being part of her mother's collection.

Agnes held her head and began to cry. She knew that her mother was right. Not about everything, but certainly about

him. Right then, she wasn't sure what hurt more, her arms or her ego. They were both so badly bruised.

She pressed a fingernail into the least healed portion of her wound, bit her lip, and forced a wince. In a way, having an open gash was convenient, more so than the tiny little injuries she'd been inflicting. Now there was a big enough target to deliver the sufficient dose of pain and discomfort she felt she deserved.

She didn't cut, or pick, or break her fingers and toes as a general rule. She punished herself by refusing to be herself. Denying herself. To go along with the life her mother had plotted out for her. Until recently. She'd begun choosing guys and friends on her own, letting her hair grow, literally. Not happier, necessarily, but freer.

Her mom just put it all down to hardheadedness, a phase she was going through. And there were times that she, Agnes, felt that way. But this wasn't one of them. Her mom was too rigid, too angry over her divorce and the fighting and scratching she had to do to rebuild her life, or as her mom liked to say 'repositioning herself'. She couldn't be heard any longer. Where once she felt like her mom's 'prized possession', she had lately become just another obstacle, an insubordinate ingrate.

'I have no idea what to do.' Her mom's voice seeped through the door and into her room. 'She's ruining her life. And mine.'

Agnes scrolled through her smartphone playlist for one of her favourite songs, 'Summer Lies'. She popped the phone into

her speaker dock, pressed play, and dragged the volume bar as far as it would go. It had special meaning for her after the whole Sayer thing, but more importantly, it could drown out the hurtful conversation going on right outside her door.

> *All the sweetest things you said and I believed*
> *were summer lies*
> *Hanging in the willow trees like the dead were*
> *summer lies*
> *I'll never fall in love again.*

Whichever neighbour or relative her mother had chosen to bitch to over the phone, it was the last straw for Agnes. She knew she couldn't stay there any longer. She stared out her bedroom window for a while, watching a car parked across the street disappear in the twilight, giving up a precious spot on their busy street for a different destination.

> *I whispered too but the things I said were true*
> *and I gave up my whole world for you*

The sudden touch of the sheer curtains blowing away from the sill and lapping her cheek seemed to her like the billow in a sail that had just caught a breeze and was ready to leave port.

> *I pine and wane, pale and wan, never knowing*
> *when it's dawn, curtains drawn, hiding in my room,*
> *wasting away, cutting myself.*

The song was over. She opened the window, fastened her bracelet tight under her bandage, and climbed out into the garden of her Park Slope ground-floor apartment, hopped the fence that bordered her yard and her neighbours' and . . .

She was gone.

7

Souled Out

'Drizzle is such a limp dick,' Lucy bitched, opening up the driver's side of the cab parked in front of the club and nudging the driver over on to the passenger side. 'Either rain or not!'

'What are you doing?' The club was a regular pickup for him. He'd seen her come and go. He'd heard stories. He knew.

'Driving!' She slammed the door and peeled away. Tyres spinning and squealing over the slickened cobblestones in the DUMBO district toward Furman Street and Atlantic Avenue. At first all he could see was the anger in her eyes, but now the liquor on her breath was making its presence known as well.

'Miss, I can gladly take you home.'

'I don't want to go home. There is nothing there for me but my laptop, and I can't face it. You understand?'

'But it's very late and the storm is coming.'

'You have anything better to do?' Lucy slurred, licking her lips seductively. It was just a tease, more tactical than sexual, but enough to keep him in line, as she knew it would be.

The mist was coalescing now into fine droplets, obscuring her view of the road ahead just enough to irritate but not enough to give her pause.

'God's tears, they say,' the cabbie said without missing a beat.

'What?'

'The drizzle,' he said, looking Lucy up and down, focusing on her exposed long legs.

'Who says that, exactly? I forgot to vote in that online poll.'

'People say, I guess.'

'Well, I say, maybe they're right.'

'Where are we going?' he asked, clicking the meter and then sliding his hand over to her knee. She didn't have a car in the city, and so when she needed to get somewhere, she would just drive herself by taking over someone's cab. Usually it worked out because of her strong sense of entitlement, her looks, and the domination fantasies held by the perverted cabbies, most of whom had religious statues on their dashes.

'I'll know when I get there.' Lucy sped on down the increasingly slickened Henry Street, drunkenly weaving around

potholes like a bat out of hell, oblivious until now to the urgent weather alert blaring every eleven minutes from the talk radio station. According to the warning, this storm was going to be biblical.

A massive nor'easter, which has already been named the Three Days of Darkness, is brewing along the North Carolina coast and bearing down on the entire tristate area. A severe storm warning is in effect for the next seventy-two hours. Expect dangerous periods of gale-force winds, torrential rain, hail, dangerous lightning, and street flooding. A tornado warning is also in effect for portions of Brooklyn and Queens through late Saturday night. NYPD is imposing a midnight curfew with widespread power outages from wind and water damage expected. Subway and bus service has been cancelled. Coastal evacuations and widespread road closings are possible. Check flashlight batteries, charge all electrical devices, stock bottled water and wherever you are, plan on staying for at least three days. Travel will be treacherous.

'What day is it?' Lucy asked.

'Thursday night,' he answered, then quickly corrected himself after checking his watch. 'It's Friday now, actually.'

'Three days. There goes my weekend.'

'A lot can happen in three days.'

'It better.'

Police, fire, and emergency services have been reassigned from regular duties. Expect 911 response time to be delayed. Stay tuned to this station for updates . . .

'Storm of the Century. Three Days of Darkness. Blah, blah . . .' Lucy whined. 'That's not a weather report, it's a prophecy.'

She reached blindly for the power button on the car radio and pressed it, silencing for the moment the panic merchants that passed for journalists.

'This shit doesn't happen in Brooklyn,' Lucy said. 'So inconvenient.'

The driver was aghast at her self-centeredness. 'I'm not sure who you call for an apology, miss.'

'Why do storms always "brew" anyway?' Lucy ranted, more for her own benefit than the jittery cab driver's. 'Can't they just say, "It's going to rain. Stay inside"? It all has to be so mysterious . . . so goddamn witchy.'

'Ratings,' the cabbie said in a thick eastern European accent that made his *Hollywood Insider* analysis both funny and sad all at once. 'Storms sell.'

'Uck,' Lucy groaned, disgusted how far showbiz trickled down into the culture, right into the seat next to her, in fact.

Trickled like warm pee down the side of a building. Just like drizzle.

Lucy hit the gas, suddenly in an imagined race with not just the storm, but her life. It was fair, she felt, since neither she nor the weather announcers on the radio seemed to know exactly where they were going. For just a second, she imagined herself one of those desperate Midwestern tornado jockeys who risked their lives chasing storms, and for what? A few seconds of cable coverage on some weather channel. She could gin up twice the attention just by flashing a bra strap at the deli.

'Suckas.' She laughed, pursing her lips tightly to keep the condescension inside.

The sudden pickup of the windscreen wipers, together with the wind and rain, wiped the smile quickly from her face, along with whatever expression the cabbie was wearing. She strained to look up through the glass. It was dark and getting darker, deep greys, purples, and blackish greens swirling above, looking to Lucy almost exactly like El Greco's *View of Toledo*, the city lights obscured by clouds. It was as if she were staring directly into the eye of the gathering storm. The air was suddenly charged, electric. They could feel the clouds filling and the tension from their heavy breathing found an inconvenient home on the inside of the windscreen, fogging them in, no matter how much she wiped at it with her couture coat sleeve. It was eerie, to say the least, and the cab driver was becoming more and more anxious.

'Enough. You're drunk. Pull over or I'm calling the police,' the cabbie insisted, keeping his eyes warily on the road now and not on her, nervously clenching the handle above him.

'Save your minutes,' Lucy replied, dodging the hurriedly parked cars poking too far into the street and the few pedestrians that were still out and about, and gradually slowing down enough to notice the empty streets. 'Where is everybody? I mean, it's just a little bad weather. It's not like the world is coming to an end or anything.'

The streets in Brooklyn Heights leading to Cobble Hill were deserted. It was as if the whole borough had sought shelter and gone into hiding. Strollers and French planters were pulled into the yuppie-owned brownstone apartment blocks while weathered religious statues, parked in the patches of grass and cemented over courtyards in front of old Italian ladies' homes, were covered in plastic and prayers. It was more than unsettling.

'Most people heed desperate warnings,' the cabbie said impatiently.

The stress of the evening – the fight, Jesse, all of it – began to tire her. Whether it was the alcohol, the ineffective windscreen defogger, the liquid air freshener on the dash, or the persistent rainfall that had made her bleary-eyed, she didn't know.

Until suddenly she did.

A massive Gothic-styled building of blue-grey stone in the early stages of renovation, and the length of scaffolding and

steel trusses running up all sides of it almost gave the appearance of being on crutches caught her full and undivided attention. The shredded protective black netting encasing almost the entire structure, from ground-floor entrances to the single soaring spire, snapped loudly in the wind, like loose bandages. There seemed to be an incredible amount of sculptural detail on the church exterior hidden behind all the metal and wood that was almost impossible to discern under the circumstances. Angels and gargoyles sprouting from the shrouded architecture, beckoning her, warning her.

Then she saw it.

Or, it saw her.

Two eyes carved into the masonry, peeking out through the torn mesh.

Her two eyes.

Her charm. The one dangling off the bracelet around her wrist.

Staring back at her.

'What is this place?' she asked.

'The Church of the Precious Blood,' he said. 'Used to be, anyway. Apartments soon.'

She jammed her heel on the brake and skidded on the rain-soaked road to a screeching halt. The cabbie went headfirst into the dashboard, and Lucy slammed her forehead into her hands on the steering wheel, specifically the charm on her bracelet, which opened a small cut at her hairline, beneath her widow's

peak. Somewhat in shock, unsure if what just happened had really happened, she scanned for injuries through blurry eyes and turned her fractured attention back to the insignia on the church facade.

'Are you OK?' he asked her before he even knew if he was OK himself.

'I don't know,' she said. Unable to focus on her physical problems, preoccupied by what might be her mental ones.

She took off her prized Pucci scarf. The vintage one she would never let her friends borrow, the one that became her staple in the rags.

'Here, take this and apply pressure.'

'I couldn't,' he said, refusing politely to wipe his blood on such an obviously luxurious and expensive accessory.

She pulled the scarf back.

The driver reached again for his brow.

'Well, you're not taking it.' She wrapped it around her two fingers, leaned over toward him, and began blotting his wound gently with it. He looked at her, surprised at her compassion. 'I'm giving it to you. Your blood is already on it.'

He accepted her generous gift reluctantly but shot back a look of concern rather than gratitude. Blood had begun to pool at her hairline and run down toward her eye socket.

'You're injured too,' he said. 'Let me call an ambulance.'

'No.' All the questions she'd be asked, the explaining she'd have to do, the excuses she'd need to make were not worth the

attention she'd surely receive. Not tonight. 'Let it bleed. We learn to live with a little pain, you know?'

'I can't let you out here,' he said, the sky looking as if it were about to close in on them.

'I'll be OK,' she assured him. 'I'm sorry that I hurt you.'

Lucy got out, threw all the money she had in her wallet into the backseat, hoping it would compensate for any damage. It felt good to get rid of it anyway, the only thing that she worried about as much as her public profile. The cabbie slid back over into the driver's seat and the car rolled away silently, except for the sound of hard rain suddenly pelting the cab like a never-ending spray of bullets. She watched his red rearlights disappear down into the night like two evil eyes in the dark. He didn't bother to switch the fare light on his roof back on. She was his last for the evening. Anybody else looking for a lift from him was out of luck.

She tucked her chin down, pulled her collar up, and fastened her trench coat tightly across her chest as she expertly leaped in her heels over pools of water and bolted for the aluminium-and-plywood covered walkway across the street.

The covered walkway extended around almost the entire church, and offered little protection from the elements raging around her. It was a whole block long on all sides, obscuring her view of everything but the black iron fencing along the perimeter of the church grounds. She followed the fence about halfway down the side street until she came upon a flight of steps with an ornate wrought-iron railing on either side, riding up to huge wooden double doors, closed shut. The tall windows on either side were boarded up and affixed with NO TRESPASSING stickers.

The doorway was too high and too dark. She lifted her wrist and tried to catch whatever beam of streetlight might find its way through to her, but it was useless. The storm was becoming increasingly more violent. Branches were being tossed like twigs, and windows, under assault from the wind and dropping barometric pressure, were beginning to crack into shards like boiled sweets. The thunder began to rumble and the first flashes of lightning strobed the sky. She felt like prey being stalked by it. Targeted. Hiding under the walkway covered by metal around a building surrounded by steel in an electrical storm was a death wish, Lucy thought.

She needed to get inside.

If a storm like this had ever blown through Brooklyn, she couldn't remember it. The streets of Cobble Hill were by now completely barren, and lights inside and out were beginning to blink spastically on their way to going out. The power grid was clearly overmatched by the weather gods. Some of her favourite haunts, patisseries, and boutiques were already starting to suffer some damage with cracked windows and signage, like the ALWAYS DIGNIFIED funeral home advert, flying recklessly down the street.

She turned with her back to the doors and looked down

from the makeshift portico at the deluge running along the pavement. Where were all those paparazzi tailing you when you really needed them? she wondered. She was drenched and cold, but her heart was racing and her palms were sweating. She should have listened to the cabbie. Getting home would not just be a problem, it would be impossible.

Fortunately, Lucy had her weekender bag with a spare outfit in case a pretender aiming at her pedestal attempted a sartorial sneak attack and copied her look. 'Shoot first' was her motto, and it had served her well. She had never been the loser in a 'Who Wore It Better' spread, and she was determined never to be. Fashion emergencies were rife in her world and she always planned ahead, right down to the just-add-water miniature bath towel from her local dollar store.

She stepped back carefully and looked over at the windows once again, this time noticing a faint glimmer sneaking through the gap between the granite blocked wall and the plywood. Intrigued and intimidated, she pulled harder on the handle, to no avail. Thunderclaps, louder than before, louder than she'd ever heard, rocked her almost out of her shoes, and a sudden gust of wind threw her against the doors with enough force to jar them open and let her slip her head in.

The tiny glow was extinguished.

'Hello?' she asked, her shoulder now throbbing along with her head. 'Is there anybody in here?'

It was nearly pitch-black inside, and each movement she

made was almost deafening. Like a blind person, she edged forward into the unfamiliar territory, arms outstretched, feeling ahead for something inside to bump into, to guide her. Through a darkened vestibule and second entrance into the church proper, she stopped. It felt like an opening to a cave. No sense of how high or how deep it went. It was cool, dry, and quiet, like she'd hit the mute button on the tempest growing outside. The space was oddly fragrant with the vaguest hint of decomposing fruity floral scents hanging in the air, like a wine tasting at a funeral home.

The sudden pall of silence was heavy and uncomfortable, just as her clothing had become. The lightning continued to flash, each burst exposing bits and pieces of the abandoned interior. She found herself in the midst of more scaffolding and other remnants of construction that'd been abruptly halted. Not just hammers and nails and tarps, however.

She saw things in slices. Like a slide show of random horror.

First bolt: a distressed statue of a cloaked woman stepping on the head of a serpent.

Second bolt: a splintered crucifix.

Third bolt: an elaborate fresco painted across the vaulted ceiling – angels crying, blood, bludgeoning. Supernatural suffering.

Everything felt out of place.

She was disoriented, looking up, feeling like she was part of the otherworldly mural, surrounded by empty pews and

boarded-up stained-glass windows. It was the feeling she got as a little girl going to church surrounded by gruesome statues spearing demons, and angel wings flapping in stone – all ingredients for her lifelong nightmares.

Lucy was shaken and reached desperately for a metal holy water font beside her for support. It was empty, long since dried out, and only now refilled by the runoff from her designer blouse. She grabbed on to it. Trying to keep her footing, but her soles were slick and gave way, sliding out from under her. The plaster split under her weight and the bowl came right off the wall, dropping along with her to the marble floor.

Lucy fell.

She hit the ground hard, forehead first, and lay there for a while – how long she couldn't be absolutely sure. She was dizzy and moaning quietly but present enough to wiggle her fingers and toes.

She reached for her head to make sure it was still in one piece and felt something wet above her brow and realized instantly it wasn't from her rain-soaked hair. She put her fingers in her mouth and licked, sitting up slowly. The trickle of blood from the steering wheel had turned to a river running straight into her eye.

'Blood alcohol level?' she slurred. 'Shitfaced.'

She couldn't see a thing. For a second she wished she had her scarf back, but she knew there was no point crying over

spilt Bloody Marys. Which sparked another childhood fear. She tried not to repeat 'Bloody Mary' three times in her head, because that childhood game of looking in a mirror and doing so and having an image of the Virgin Mary appear in blood seemed like a real possibility now.

'Why did I quit smoking?' she groaned regretfully, fumbling in the pitch-black church through her pockets and her purse for her flint lighter – the one that led her through numerous dark VIP rooms. She'd almost given up hope when there it was, at the bottom of her handbag. Lucy popped the spring-latch cover and flicked. The thumbwheel sparked against the flint and the wick burst aflame.

'A miracle.' Lucy laughed to herself.

She blotted the gash and cleared her eye as best she could with her coat sleeve. She remained still for a while in the dark to get her bearings. The storm outside was deepening, reaching through the walls now, even into this fortified and forsaken space, stirring her back into reality. Her first thought was that this must be some vendetta for past sins, after all she hadn't set foot in a church for years, and she was drunk at that. She got to her knees and then slowly to her feet.

'OK, we're even,' she said, looking upward. Her dulled senses adjusted gradually. There was just enough light to see a few feet in front of her. Raising the lighter, Lucy managed to discern the first few of a long row of pews, and to her left a large, freestanding wooden structure that looked like the most ornate cabinet she'd ever seen. And then it dawned on her – it was a confessional.

Using the long bench for both support and navigation, she shimmied toward it and rushed inside it like a child pulling up her bedsheet, looking for cover and comfort.

She placed the lighter down on a carved ridge shelf and slammed the door shut, looked around at the dark wood etchings, meticulously done, and took a seat on the crushed red velvet cushion. It was a place out of time.

The only nod to modern life was a dusty sign that read: PLEASE TURN OFF ALL MOBILE PHONES, SMARTPHONES, AND OTHER ELECTRONIC DEVICES. She laughed nervously. It made a weird kind of ironic sense to have a sort of preflight instruction affixed to a booth where an otherworldly conversation was about to take place. Preparing yourself to be skyrocketed to forgiveness.

'I need to change.' She wrung out the blue fox fur sleeves on her dress and kicked off her soaking-wet blue suede stilettos, desperately trying to stay in the moment.

She opened her satchel and started pulling out dry clothes – a fitted beige trench coat, a pair of deep garnet crushed-velvet peep-toe platform pumps and a garnet fedora to match. She began to undress, peeling the damp outfit from her body until she stood only in her pure white silk slip. Free from her couture armour, she was quickly overtaken by the fact that she was entirely alone, the paps, wannabes, and haters that trailed her,

all gone. Left only with her innermost feelings.

A girl in a box.

Her head and her life, both spinning. Weighing on her. Hurting her. Drowning her in a deluge of misery.

The flame from the lighter, which had been slowly fading, petered out completely to a puff of smoke.

'Great,' she fretted, banging her hand angrily against the side of the antique wooden booth, the chaplet on her wrist scratching at the panelled interior.

Alone.

In total darkness.

Finally silent, with just her conscience.

Lucy broke down sitting in that confessional. Drying blood mixing with mascara, charcoal-coloured trails streaming down her porcelain face. Wiping bloody tears on her pristine slip. Alcohol still on her breath. She wanted a shower, dry clothes and a warm bed.

'Somebody,' she moaned out loud. 'Save me from all this bullshit.'

'Save yourself,' came a muffled, disembodied reply through the shadowy confessional screen.

'Shit!' she screamed, the burst of adrenaline sobering her up instantly. She braced herself, felt her face flush and the muscles in her calves and thighs slacken as she prepared to run for it. She couldn't move but knew she had to. Lucy stiffened her back and her knees in the narrow booth and kicked the door

open. She catapulted out of the box, still clutching the shoes from her bag – her trench coat, fedora, and weekender left behind in the confessional, along with her shame. In her desperation, Lucy slammed her knee into the edge of a pew and fell to the floor. Another scream tore from her throat. Almost instantly she felt a presence above her.

A human one.

A male one.

She felt a hand grab her arm and another wrap around her mouth and press tight. 'Shhhhhhhh.'

Lucy struggled, but a knee in her back kept her down and under control. She couldn't bite or scratch or fight back in any way. No sooner was she contemplating the worst than she felt his grip tighten, not to subdue her but to hoist her up. She nearly flew to her feet as if on wires. Lucy still could not really see his face, though she was staring directly into it. All she could discern were his hazel eyes, which appeared to glow. He removed his hand from her mouth.

'Don't you know who I am?' she babbled nervously. 'People will be looking for me.'

He took her in between lightning flashes as she stood there scared, wet, defiant. Her beautiful blonde hair lay dripping on her bare shoulders, lips pursued defiantly but quivering. It amazed him that she was still clinging to her shoes, which matched her blood, the same way a mother would hang on to a toddler to escape a burning building. Her gorgeous blue eyes

captivated him. It was as if he were talking to someone whom he only dreamed of.

'Look,' she said, her speech a breathless staccato as she tried to wiggle out of his grasp. 'I don't know who you are or what you are doing here, and I don't care. Just let me go and we'll pretend this never happened.'

Lucy worked her wrists up under his chin trying a Krav Maga move she'd learned from a bodyguard friend of hers to break his grip, when unexpectedly, she felt his hands loosen around her arms. He seemed to her to be looking down her slip, but it was the bracelet on her wrist that really caught his attention. She backed away from him but thought better of running, still not certain she could easily find the exit and hoping to calm him down before anything really bad happened.

'Are you done?' he asked.

'You tell me.' Lucy was feeling even more frightened when it occurred to her that maybe he'd followed her here. Maybe he was some kind of celebrity stalker waiting for an opportunity to get her alone. To get a front-page box for killing a socialite. She'd seen that movie. A few of them. But she also had to consider that, if he wanted to kill her, she'd probably be dead already. 'What do you want?'

'Same as you.'

Lucy heard the scratch of a match head along a striker, then the incandescent burst of phosphorous, and both the stranger and the path were revealed, at least in part. He walked toward

an elaborate iron candle stand.

He lit the first votive.

It illuminated through the rose-coloured glass holder. The candle threw more shadow than light but there was just enough for her to see him, or at least his silhouette cast against the wall of the side altar.

She got a better look. He was young, probably not much older than she was, she observed, but there was nothing boyish about him. He was drop-dead gorgeous, with sharp features and a strong chin. Classic looks that fit in perfectly with the classical stylings of their surroundings. He was wearing black jeans and a tight black V-neck sweater that looked like it was almost shrink-wrapped on him. His dark brown hair was thick and sexy, like a lead singer of a band – well-coiffed in the messiest way. And his eyes. Those hazel eyes that pierced the darkness, were even more entrancing in the candlelight. If she was going to be trapped with someone for three days, she could do worse.

'You need to change?' he asked.

'Oh, that was the whiskey talking,' Lucy said, embarrassed at being overheard in such a vulnerable moment. 'I just needed to get out of the storm. To change, you know.'

'Yeah, I know.'

'Guess this is the place to be tonight, huh?'

'For us it is,' he replied with a smile. 'What's your name?'

He didn't know her. A good sign. She thought about lying to

him but she hadn't needed to introduce herself in quite a while. And she liked it.

'Lucy.'

'Sebastian,' he replied, pulling up his sweater to the elbows and extending his hand.

She noticed each of his exposed arms sported a full sleeve of black ink from his bicep to his forearm, but it was the tattoo around his wrist that really got her attention. That gave her pause at first, and then set off a full-fledged panic.

It was a tattoo of an arrow, in the same style as her bracelete. It was intricate – the shaft wrapped around his wrist with the head and the neck meeting on his palm side. Almost touching.

Lucy took a big step back and grabbed the pew once again, so flustered that she lost her footing.

'What is that?'

'A reminder,' he answered.

She was shaking as her skin turned not just to goosebumps, but bubble wrap. 'I'm out of here.'

Sebastian didn't try to stop her. If she wasn't so afraid of him right then, she might have even supposed he was letting her go. She backed away and tentatively toward the door she'd come in, but she might as well have been trying to navigate a caved-in mineshaft. She slipped to her knees and started to cry.

Lucy fell the second time.

Overcome by both the throbbing in her skull and the realization that she might have just made the biggest mistake of her life by entering the church. One thing she was sure of, she couldn't stop. As her sobs intensified, she felt his hands on her once more. A firm but gentle grip under each armpit and suddenly she felt herself lifted back to her feet again, facing him.

'Get up,' he said as firmly, staring directly into her eyes.

'Don't hurt me, please.' Nearly naked, bruised, bleeding, and distraught, she did something totally out of character. She didn't fight. She resigned herself and prepared for a forced kiss or much worse, for whatever was to come. He raised his arm, causing her to flinch. Then he proceeded to dry her tears with the sleeve of his black pullover. She grabbed him and held him tight for a second, then pulled away, not exactly sure of what had just come over her.

'Looks like you took care of that all by yourself,' he said, brushing her hair away from her face to get a clearer look at the cut.

Lucy hung her head, looking downward, crisscrossing her arms around her chest both to warm up and to hide. He could see it was all she could do to keep herself from convulsing in relief. He took his sweater off.

'No, please!'

He stopped. Looked at her. And gently wrapped it around her shoulders.

'Go,' he said, gesturing toward the confessional.

'Where?'

'Change.'

8

Rebel Resurrection

Sebastian tuned into the angry sounds of the storm outside as he waited for Lucy to come out of the confessional, certain she would be filled with questions. Questions he wasn't yet able to answer. Answers she wasn't ready to hear.

A rumbling outside the church door, definitely not from the gale-force winds as far as he could tell, startled him. Three loud thuds announced a visitor – unwelcome or not, he didn't know, but Sebastian was ready either way.

A soaking-wet silhouette slipped through the doorway, its image flickering in the bolts of lightning that were striking ever more frequently.

'Damn!'

He recognized the voice from the emergency room.

Cecilia.

Still, he didn't say a word.

She pulled the door shut behind her, shaking the rain off. The darkness before her was thick and intimidating, but no more so than the wuthering wind outside. She peeled off her black ostrich-feather coat, which was drenched and weighed a ton, and stripped down to a vest top she was wearing underneath. Her black leather panel leggings clung close to her body. She looked the part of a rock-and-roll renegade – dark kohl running eyeliner, glittery midnight-blue shadow, and nude glossed lips.

'Anybody home?'

She wasn't hoping just *anyone* was.

She was hoping *he* was.

A spark in the distance surprised her. She wasn't alone. She thought about removing her Fender from its case for protection. On stage it was an affectation but now, it might be a matter of life and death. She fumbled for the latches on the case, eyes on her shadowy target.

Sebastian raised a woodstick he'd lit from the first votive head high, silently revealing himself to her. She could barely make him out in the dim light from that distance, but she felt his presence, just as she had in the hospital room, and relaxed just a little. Her disappointment from earlier in the night was

totally gone. Replaced by disbelief of the best possible kind. *It's magic*, she thought. *Answered prayers.*

As she approached him, she could see that he was bare from the waist up and everything she'd imagined.

He lit a second votive flame from the first.

'This is a surprise,' she said.

'Is it?'

'Well, I was hoping, I thought, I might see you.'

'You hoped.'

'Sort of.'

Sebastian chuckled. 'How did you find me?'

'I remembered the smell of frankincense from some gigs I played here. I'll never forget 'em. Best gigs I ever did. You smell exactly like this place. That and the charm on the bracelet you gave me. The exact sword that's etched above the door. A sign, I guess.'

'A good one or a bad one?'

'We'll see.'

'I'm glad you're here.' He couldn't help but notice that she looked like a supermodel who had just been hosed down for a high-fashion shoot. Whether in a sickbed or soaked to the bone, he thought, Cecilia had undeniable natural beauty and edge. 'How are you feeling?'

'Wet. Unemployed. Homeless . . . you know, better. So, this is what you were in a massive rush to get back to the other night?' she asked.

'No, I haven't been here long,' he said. 'But it's safe. Mostly. I come here sometimes.' Sebastian walked toward her, wearing only his jeans. His long, muscled arms accentuated by the candlelight, keeping his eyes fixed on hers all the while.

'Slow down, sailor,' Cecilia said worriedly, but only half joking.

He smiled, balled up an altar cloth, and tossed it to her.

'Dry off,' he said.

'Tease,' she jibed, turning away and wiping the droplets of cloudburst from her face, neck, and arms.

Cecilia stood there for a moment, gathered herself, and pulled a Clove cigarette out of her wet bag and tried to light it with her soaking-wet matches. Sebastian took it away from her, put it in his mouth, leaned over the candle, and lit it for her. He slowly took a drag, inhaled it, closed his eyes, took the cigarette from his lips, and held it to her lips, gently rubbing it from side to side until she relaxed and let it in. He tilted his head upward and exhaled. He wore the satisfied look, she observed, of a man who'd been trapped on a desert island or a maximum-security inmate with his hour outside.

'Amazing how quiet it is in here,' Cecilia said, straining to see as much of the space as she could. 'You can barely hear that insanity outside.'

'Yeah, it's peaceful,' Sebastian agreed, looking completely at ease to her.

'So now we know why *I'm* here, but what about you?'

She stepped in closer to him, removed the cigarette from her mouth, and brought it to his lips, waiting for his answer.

Lucy was taken aback at the sound of chatter outside the confessional booth and cracked the door. She peeked out and saw Sebastian with a stranger and watched for a while. She was curious at first, then jealous, and suddenly, furious.

Lucy charged out of the confessional loudly, holding Sebastian's sweater, drawing as much attention to herself as she could. Cecilia barely knew this guy, but her face flushed as if she'd been caught cheating, or had caught him.

'Oh, so *this* is what you're doing here,' Cecilia said.

'What's going on here?' Lucy huffed as she sidled in closer to them.

'It's not how it looks,' Sebastian tried to explain to both of them before CeCe cut him off.

'Sloppy seconds taste terrible, don't they?' Lucy snarked.

'Only on a cheap date,' Cecilia replied.

'Honey, there's nothing cheap about me.'

Sebastian didn't say a word.

'So, not only do you cruise hospitals, but you cruise churches, too?' Cecilia said, stomping out her cigarette and gathering her things to leave. 'Classy.'

Sebastian moved towards her, but Cecilia backed away. He couldn't get a word in edgewise as she rambled on angrily, dropping her matches and then her cigarettes in her haste.

'The confessional?' Cecilia sniped. 'Definitely rock-star points for creativity, though – baring your body and soul. Screams "hot and steamy" to me.'

'Who the hell do you think you are?' Lucy snapped.

'I didn't know you went trends gender,' CeCe said with a laugh. 'And just out of the closet, too. I bet you don't even know her name. Oh, but then maybe you got it off the clipboard on the edge of her hospital bed. Like mine.'

'Hospital bed?' Lucy asked. 'Wait, what's going on here?'

Coming closer, Lucy got a better look and was surprised. This girl didn't look like the jealous type to her. She was cool and gorgeous and, judging from her outfit, tough.

'You know each other?' Lucy asked, her heels clicking louder against the marble floor the closer she got.

'From Perpetual Help,' CeCe explained. 'I was there last weekend. No big deal.'

'So was I,' Lucy chimed in.

Lucy rolled up her cardigan sleeves and Cecilia spied her chaplet.

Cecilia shot Sebastian an angry, disgusted look.

'You got one too?'

'Found it on my nightstand in the ER,' Lucy admitted.

'I really thought I'd seen it all,' CeCe huffed. 'This guy was fishing. In the ER, no less! Spread a few lovely little parting gifts to see who he could reel in. I mean, I was only kidding when I

asked if you had a thing for sick girls.'

The girls looked at each other, feeling humiliated, shaking their heads in unison, as if to acknowledge their astoundingly bad judgment when it came to guys. They made a good team, he thought, even if they had suddenly turned on him.

'I didn't drag you here,' Sebastian said, pushing back. 'Either of you.'

'No, you just planted a few seeds,' Lucy said, feeling deceived as well.

'Don't turn this around,' Cecilia interjected.

'You came of your own free will, didn't you?' Sebastian said. 'And you can leave of your own free will.'

'Good idea. There are other skips to crash in. With smaller rats.'

Cecilia was hurt. Lucy was crushed.

'I thought this was special!' Lucy shouted while removing the chaplet, and then threw it back at him.

Cecilia followed, taking off her chaplet and tossing it casually to Sebastian. 'This was a big mistake. Let's go.'

Lucy paused, giving him one last chance to explain, but he didn't. She joined Cecilia, reluctantly.

'They are special,' he called after them in the darkness. 'You are special. It wasn't a mistake.'

They stopped and turned.

'They brought you here. Both of you. Here,' he said. 'To me.'

'What are they, freakin' homing devices?' CeCe remarked.

'The charms, they're called milagros. That means miracles,' he said, handing them back to their respective owners. 'They are used to ground you. Heal you. Lead you home.'

'Well, fail!' Cecilia said, throwing up her arms. 'I'm not home. I don't have a home!'

'Why don't you just listen for a second,' Lucy snapped at Cecilia.

'I ain't into threesomes,' Cecilia said, pissed at Lucy's indecisiveness. 'Have fun.'

Lucy grabbed her arm. 'It's going to get really bad out there. Let it pass.'

Cecilia felt a bit of reverse psychology at play in Lucy's tone. Like she didn't really mean it. Lucy wanted her out of there. She wanted Sebastian to herself.

'Pass? You mean like a kidney stone? No, thanks.' Cecilia huffed, breaking Lucy's grip and eyeing Sebastian. 'I didn't come here to play Bachelor. Besides, it couldn't be any worse out there than it is in here.'

Cecilia grabbed her guitar and her heavy coat and made her way through the darkness to the door. She opened it and was almost immediately blown backward by an angry gust that nearly blasted the enormous wooden door from its hinges. She could barely see, but what she could make out was horrific. The sheet metal and scaffolding rattled and groaned in the wind and large branches snapped from tree trunks, littering the street,

crushing parked cars beneath them, blocking the pavement below the stone staircase and down the brownstoned block farther than she could see. The downpour had already overwhelmed the sewers, flooding over kerbs and into cellars. Plastic supermarket bags, wrappers, and rubbers clogged sewer drains as the smelly contents of overturned dustbins floated by under the straining street lamps. To CeCe, the entire area had the noxious odour of a dive-bar bathroom.

She held tightly on to the side of the large arched doorway and braced herself; the brutal wind pushing against her cheeks, turning her face into a virtual skull mask and her arms and legs into reddened ripples of wet, quivering flesh. The decision about whether to stay or go was moot.

'Shut the door!' Lucy shouted. 'You're letting it in.'

The door that had proven so difficult to open when they first arrived was now proving equally challenging to close. Lucy rushed to the entrance and got her back into it as well, the sudden pressure drop of the thickening storm spiking the pain in her head.

Cecilia and Lucy pushed against the gusts, but not before a high-pitched whimper found its way through the ungodly din and reached their ears.

'There's something out there,' Cecilia said.

It was coming from right near the doorstep, as far as CeCe could tell. A stray cat trying to survive the storm on the steps? she wondered. She braved the impossible wind and poked her head outside and around the door and cried out in shock.

'Son of a bitch!' CeCe yelled.

'What?' Lucy screamed. 'What is it?'

Cecilia was dumbfounded.

It was a girl, barefoot, weeping, face buried in her hands, her long auburn hair barely contained inside the lambswool-lined cowl of her poncho. Both were drenched. She was curled up in a ball, shivering from cold and from fear. Crashed and washed-up, like debris from a shipwreck, in the doorway.

Cecilia stepped out and was instantly blown back against the church door. She knelt and reached for the girl, who tightened her pose, making her difficult to move. She was nearly catatonic but still resisting, immovable, as if she were nailed to the spot.

'C'mon,' Cecilia begged. 'You will catch your death out here.'

Lucy stood unsteadily in the vestibule, frustrated, watching the one-sided negotiation.

'Hurry up!' she screamed. 'If she wants to be stubborn, let her. I'm closing the door.'

Cecilia turned back, looking to Lucy for help, nodding her over.

'Weren't you just leaving?' Lucy reminded her.

'I can't do this alone! . . .' Cecilia yelled, realizing she didn't have a name to go along with the urgent request.

'Lucy. My name is Lucy.'

'Cecilia,' she replied warily. 'Please, Lucy. Help me.'

Lucy reluctantly complied, edging over with her back to the door as the two girls fought the elements and the girl, standing her up, and dragging her into the partially open doorway, where they huddled.

'You'd better be appreciating this,' Lucy raged at the stranger, holding both girls tightly. 'This outfit cost more than your house.'

As Cecilia and Lucy tugged at the girl, her sleeves rode up, revealing bandaged wrists and a bracelet. A bracelet almost identical to theirs. The two of them stared at each other in disbelief.

'It's OK,' Lucy said to the girl, showing her own chaplet.

The sight of it seemed to calm the girl.

'I saw it,' she said quietly, 'outside.'

'I know,' Lucy replied.

An unexpected flash of lightning, an earsplitting crack of thunder, a torrential downpour and explosion of darkness suddenly assaulted them.

'Blackout!' Cecilia shouted.

'I can't see a thing!' Lucy screamed.

The three girls teetered at the edge of the staircase, completely disoriented by the fast-changing conditions, and nearly carried one another over the railing. Cecilia was losing her grip and Lucy her balance. A second before they tumbled, Sebastian reached out for them with both hands, steadying them, and dragged them inside. He looked up at the greenish black sky showing through the rent overhang and kicked the door closed.

Sebastian ran to them and immediately attended to the stranger, walking her gently to the votive stand where the flames of the other two red glass candles were still flickering.

'You're OK,' he said, taking her hand in his.

He lit the third votive.

'Thank you,' she whispered to him.

'What's your name?' Cecilia asked.

Sebastian pulled the girl's cowl back and brushed the long, wet hair from her pale, luminous face. Her skin almost gave the appearance of being lit from within.

'Agnes.'

Lucy helped her off with her shearling poncho and replaced it with her now-dry trench coat. She was raw and battered by the night, wincing at even the most delicate touch.

'Are we going to die?' she asked through tears.

'You are safe here,' he promised her, smiling.

Overcome with relief and regret,

Agnes wept.

9

Tame the Tongue

'Tell us what's going on,' Cecilia said as the candles blazed, all three of them and Sebastian, cold and wet, huddled around the votive stand as they might a campfire, listening to the horror outside the church walls. Strangers, but oddly not.

'That's a big question.' Sebastian studied them silently as the storm raged all around them, taking each of them in, their looks, their style, personalities, their quirks, strengths, and vulnerabilities. Cecilia nervously drumming on her thigh, Lucy obsessively examining each cuticle on her fingers, and Agnes huddled with her knees up, her shiver beginning to subside.

'We have time. Three days, in fact, according to the weather dudes,' Lucy said. 'If we don't kill each other first.'

Agnes and Cecilia looked over at Lucy, signalling that could be a distinct possibility. Without a change of clothes and any real food except for the junk food crap that Sebastian had in his backpack, all bets were off.

'Three days,' Sebastian echoed. 'That will be enough time.'

'Enough time for what?' Cecilia prodded.

'For you to understand.'

Cecilia was spooked. 'Now I'm not sure I really want to know.'

'I do,' Agnes said quietly.

'I'm really appreciative of the gift, but where did you get these bracelets?' Lucy asked. 'I've never seen anything like them.'

'They were given to me,' Sebastian said.

Lucy was sceptical that the boy in front of her came from such a moneyed line. He'd have to be from royalty, aristocracy of some kind, to receive such an inheritance. 'Passed down to you? These are like, ancient, museum quality.'

'Why give them away?' CeCe pressed.

'Because they aren't mine.'

'OK, they were given to you, but they aren't yours. I don't get it. Is this some kind of Robin Hood thing?' Lucy asked.

'That's all I can tell you right now.'

Sebastian sat back and leaned his head against the wall behind him. Their view of him was still distorted by the light and shadow from the flickering candles and lightning

flashes, but they could see he had become suddenly pensive, the expression on his face pained. All of them were curious, but none of them dared pry any further. They were safe. For the moment.

Agnes looked up at the burst of light flashing through the apertures where stained-glass was once fitted. The bolts were more frequent and violent now, and the thunder was getting louder. 'Did you know that you can tell how close a storm is by counting the amount of time between a lightning flash and thunderclap?'

'I don't need to count,' Cecilia answered.

'It's close,' Sebastian said.

'So beautiful,' Agnes said, looking upward. 'A living lava lamp.'

'Cosmic. Literally,' Cecilia noted, in appreciation. 'You couldn't buy a light show like that with all the money in the world.'

Lucy disagreed. 'Probably could, if you ask me.'

'Nobody asked, buzzkill,' Cecilia huffed.

Lucy wondered aloud as arcs of electricity crackled overhead and spread outward against the starless sky, lighting it up like a mad-scientist laboratory. Streaks of cool white, red-orange, and phosphorescent blue blinking as they enervated the canopy of clouds.

'Looks like a spiderweb to me,' she said. 'A trap.'

'That's comforting,' Cecilia said.

'Or a CAT scan,' Agnes continued. 'Veins and arteries of the sky. A CAT scan of heaven.'

'So romantic.' CeCe laughed.

'Thanks,' Agnes replied, without the least bit of irony.

Lucy suddenly felt the downy hair she resented having to bleach begin to stand on end. She looked up and around, as if for a ghost, and then to the others for verification that something had changed inside the room. She watched them open and close their jaws in a futile effort to fight the sudden pressure drop in their ears, and she did likewise. Lucy reached for her brow and Agnes for her bandaged wrists, the swelling becoming infinitely more painful. The air was electric and they tingled like antennae.

Wave upon wave of thunderclouds broke directly over the church, heaving grapefruit-size hail down without and within. The temperature in the building dropped almost instantly and the girls curled into tight balls, under assault from the frozen sleet, which was falling down around them.

A fierce rattle hummed through the building. They could feel the vibrations creep up their feet and into their legs. Another thunder crack and they shuddered, instinctively reaching their ears. The candle flames waxed brightly, fed by the influx of oxygen, then waned almost to nothing, nearly extinguished in a fusillade of wind. One more lightning strike, stronger, brighter, and closer than before, was followed by the distant sound of shattering glass that almost seemed to come from

behind the altar. And just as quickly as it came, the hail expended itself, replaced by a hard and cold rain.

'Wait here,' Sebastian ordered, leaping to his feet. 'I'm going to check that out.'

'I'll come with you,' Cecilia said.

'No,' Sebastian said firmly, taking them aback.

'I want to help you.'

'I'll be back.'

'Be careful,' Agnes called after him.

Sebastian disappeared into the darkness. They could hear him walking and then lost him in the sounds of the stormy night. A door creaked at the front of the church and the familiar sound of a latch catching and then silence. He was gone.

'Help him?' Lucy scoffed, mocking Cecilia. 'You were just looking to be alone with him.'

Cecilia rolled her eyes and changed the subject. There was more joke than spite in the comment and there was a noticeable thaw in the chilly distance between them.

With Sebastian gone, the girls felt more compelled to speak their minds, the dark, the cold, the uncertainty scratching at their stubbornness, wearing on them like a hair shirt.

'Do you think he stole these?' CeCe asked, fondling her bracelet.

'I don't really care,' Lucy said. 'I love it.'

'OK, but why us?' CeCe asked. 'We don't know one another or him.'

They each gave it some quiet consideration until Agnes piped up. 'But what about what he said? About them leading us here? I don't know about you guys, but I've never been to this church before in my life. And suddenly, it seemed like the exact right place to go.'

'Maybe he's a freak,' Cecilia said. 'Probably just gave these out to the first three chicks he came across at the hospital.'

'You don't really think that,' Agnes said.

'People do all kinds of crazy shit,' Lucy responded.

'Like sneaking into churches at night?' Agnes quipped.

'Why are you defending him?' Cecilia asked.

'I'm not,' Agnes said. 'I just don't see why we shouldn't believe him.'

'Why?' Lucy barked. 'How about he's a total stranger, for a start.'

'That doesn't make him a liar. I don't know you, either, but I'm listening.'

'He's not being up-front, Agnes,' Cecilia challenged. 'I mean, what's he doing here? Really?'

'Why don't you ask him?' Agnes answered. 'I'm sure there's no great mystery.'

'I might give him a pass on that one for now,' Lucy countered. 'We don't even know why *we're* here.'

Agnes raised her arm and brandished her chaplet proudly, like some fresh ink. 'This is why.'

'Do you just believe everything a guy tells you without

questioning anything?' Cecilia asked.

'I'm just saying, maybe they are really meant for us.'

'And I'm just saying I'm here for – what was it, three days?'

'Three Days of Darkness,' Lucy said, mocking the weatherman from the radio.

'Ye of little faith,' Agnes said sharply.

'Ye of little maturity,' Cecilia spit back.

They both looked at each other, overtired, oversensitive, and over the conversation for the moment.

'Anybody know what time it is?' CeCe asked.

'No idea,' Lucy said. 'Very late. Or early.'

'Whichever, I can't sit any more,' CeCe said.

'Let's check this place out,' Lucy suggested.

'Sebastian said to wait here,' Agnes said.

'Suit yourself.' Lucy grabbed a handful of long tapers that had been left in a small pile on the floor near the votive stand. She offered one to Agnes. Agnes took it. They each lit theirs, fitted it with a foil bobeche, and walked slowly from the side altar at the back down the centre aisle of the Church, wax dripping down the side with each step and hardening as it hit their knuckles. The light was just enough to guide them, for them to be able to see one another, but not so much as to draw attention from the world outside, if there was even a world left. The flames blew sideways despite their best efforts to shield them, useless against the stiff breeze that had managed

to make its way through the broken windowpanes.

There was little to see. Lucy, Agnes, and Cecilia placed their tapers in the candleholders at the foot of the altar. CeCe lit a cigarette off the flaming stalk and inhaled.

'It's like an end-stage cancer patient, you know,' Cecilia observed the surroundings, exhaling billows of smoke upward as she spoke. 'A shell of something that was once so alive.'

'With a Do Not Resuscitate order,' Lucy nodded, waving the smoke away.

Streams of rain water dripping through the damaged roof got Cecilia's attention. She grabbed a few rusted holy water buckets stacked up next to the marble altar rail and handed them to Lucy and Agnes to place under the leaks.

Agnes chaffed a little at the analogy, her own brush with death still fresh in her mind. 'It's not something to joke about.'

'No offence, but you get my point, right?' Cecilia groused. 'This place was dying way before the developers bought it.'

'When you needed shelter from the storm, you came here. You get *my* point, right?' Agnes said.

'No need to get all self-righteous,' Lucy sniped. 'Agnes is right. We all know why we're here, whether we want to admit it to one another or not.'

'Speak for yourself,' CeCe said. 'Why are *you* here?'

The tiff brought them right back to the earlier conversation they'd been dancing around. Sebastian argued that they were there by choice, but were they? The chaplets said otherwise.

'Same reason you are,' Lucy said tersely. 'Not a lot of other options right now.'

'Is that right? You don't look like much of a couch surfer to me,' CeCe observed.

'Spoiler alert,' Lucy said. 'That's because I don't sleep around.'

'Sucks to be you,' CeCe shot back.

'Slide to unlock, huh?' Lucy cracked, swiping her imaginary touch screen sarcastically with unfettered ease.

Agnes eyed Cecilia sympathetically and shook her head.

The voices were getting louder as the argument descended ever deeper into pettiness. The vaulted ceiling captured the cacophony and ricocheted it back to them, amplifying the angst until their own voices became so echo-delayed and distorted they could barely understand one another.

'What are you looking at?' Lucy barked at Agnes, her irritation overcoming whatever sympathy she initially had for the girl. 'You've been staring at me since you got here.'

'Nothing,' Agnes replied sheepishly. 'You just look familiar.'

'Yeah, you do,' Cecilia concurred. 'In fact, I think I know you.'

'Believe me,' Lucy assured her. 'You don't know me.'

'I mean, I know *of* you.'

Lucy was mortified, the blood draining from her face like an underage clubhopper busted for flashing a fake ID. She braced for attack.

'Usually so meticulously groomed, well-dressed, and

imperious-looking.' Cecilia scrutinized her. 'Mascot of the rich and shameless.'

Lucy stood her ground, taking the punishment like a shock absorber. Glaring silently back at CeCe. A little mocking was nothing new to her.

'Oh, I'm sorry, aren't I allowed to look you directly in the eye?'

'Wow,' Lucy chided in faux disbelief. 'I never knew you could make toxic friends so fast.'

'Friends already?' Cecilia sniffed. 'Maybe in your world.'

'Hard to believe that such a skinny slut can stand up straight with such a big chip on her shoulder.'

'I haven't got any complaints,' CeCe huffed. 'What's your excuse?'

'What's that supposed to mean?' Lucy hissed. 'I have guys lining up, for your information.'

'Photographers don't count,' CeCe countered. 'They're paid to line up for you.'

'I don't need to pay for my dates,' Lucy bristled. 'And they don't pay me, either.'

'No, you use each other for the photo, sell the rights, and split. You don't date. You fundraise.'

'I'm proud to sign my cheques on the back. Not the front.'

Agnes was mystified at how venomous the bickering had turned. Just like the fights between her and her mother. She knew full well where this was headed.

Cecilia wouldn't let it go. 'Well, you look nothing like your pictures, but I won't hold it against you in this weather.'

Suddenly, it dawned on Agnes as well. She gasped. 'Lucky Lucy.'

'Brooklyn's very own Miss Teen Famewhore,' Cecilia scoffed.

'Like it or love it,' Lucy shrugged, gladly embracing her reputation. 'You can take your finger off the jealous button now.'

'Hardly,' CeCe said, dropping her cigarette to the floor. 'But at least you're self-aware.'

'Bitch,' Lucy said.

'God, when will they legalize medicinal murder?' Cecilia said out loud to herself, while looking up to the heavens.

'You're making my head hurt!' Agnes was wearing down and it was beginning to show. They all were.

'Stay out of it, Rapunzel,' Cecilia said, a little irritated at both her long mane and her faux-bohemianism.

Lucy's wasn't the only familiar face to Agnes. The longer she listened to CeCe peck at her, the more she realized Cecilia had a familiar face as well.

'And I know *you*,' Agnes said to CeCe. 'You opened for that band at my school a few months ago.'

'That can't be true,' Lucy cracked. 'You are an artiste. An indie goddess. An original.'

'It was for charity,' Cecilia explained sheepishly.

'Rockin' the school gym,' Lucy snarked. 'How desperate.'

'I rock anywhere I am,' Cecilia quipped.

'Something we have in common, then,' Lucy said.

'No, I actually *do* something.'

'Stop,' Agnes demanded. With points scored on each side, Lucy and Cecilia finally took Agnes's advice and took a deep breath. They each plunked themselves down in separate pews and stared at the burning wicks, seated near to one another but each left alone with her own thoughts. All thinking the worst was yet to come, as the tension between them was growing, like they were passengers stuck in a stalled lift. 'We're all just tense. Let's be silent. Be still.'

'I was just looking for a way out,' Lucy blurted. 'That's really why I'm here.'

'I get that you're hiding,' CeCe said.

'Who isn't?' Agnes agreed. 'But there are other places to disappear.'

'Doesn't everybody look to hide in a shuttered church with a hot guy?' Lucy replied, trying to tamp down Agnes's magical thinking.

The sudden sound of banging, nails being driven into wood, startled them and ended the conversation for the moment.

'Sebastian?' Cecilia called out to no reply, just more hammering.

'Actually, there is a long history of people seeking sanctuary in churches. To avoid persecution,' Agnes cut in. 'Brooklyn is known as the Borough of Churches.'

Cecilia and Lucy just looked at her sceptically.

'Makes sense,' Lucy added. 'I'm constantly feeling persecuted.'

'You and your first world injuries,' Cecilia pushed back, lighting another cigarette from an altar candle. 'It still doesn't answer the basic question. Why were we all drawn here, to this place, with him, specifically.'

'I guess the honest answer is, I don't know,' Lucy said. 'I'm not religious or anything. I don't even say "God bless you" when someone sneezes. What about you?' she asked Cecilia. 'And yelling "Oh God" early on a Sunday morning doesn't count as religious.'

'I am a total ecclesiophobe,' CeCe responded.

'Wait, you're afraid of churches?' Agnes asked.

'For good reason, I'll bet,' Lucy added snidely.

'I just prefer preaching to come from an amp, not an altar.'

'So postmodern,' Lucy scoffed.

CeCe ignored her, lost momentarily in thought. She wasn't feeling at all uncomfortable, to her surprise. 'The majesty, the rituals, the history, the art. A lot of it is really cool,' she went on. 'I get it. But it's hard for me to really believe in anything I can't really feel.'

'I don't go to church much, mostly because my mom makes such a big deal out of it,' Agnes admitted. 'But I do go to Catholic school.'

'Those are the worst. I'd drop out if I were you,' Lucy snarked. 'Oh wait, I did drop out.'

'My mom thought it would be a better environment for me.'

Lucy translated. 'More disciplined, she meant.'

'Is that so bad?' Agnes asked.

'You tell me,' Lucy answered, pointing to Agnes's wrists. 'How's it working out for you?'

'My parents tried that on me, too, but I told them I would run away before I went,' CeCe confided.

Agnes admired her backbone. 'So they made you go?'

'No, I ran away,' CeCe said. 'Public or parochial school wasn't really my main issue. Going to school at all was.'

'So here we are: a squatter and runaway, a dropout, and a would-be suicide. Four sinners in a giant church, and none of us knows why?' Lucy summed up. 'Is that it?'

'One of us knows why,' Cecilia croaked, her voice getting hoarse from the dusty dampness.

'Knows what?' Sebastian said, emerging from the darkness.

'Eavesdropping?' Lucy asked.

'No need,' Sebastian said. 'I'm surprised they didn't hear that catfight outside.'

'So, what was it?' Agnes asked.

'A huge tree snapped in half, pushed through one of the windows. Glass everywhere. I did the best I could to board it up. You can't keep it outside for ever.'

'The storm?' Lucy asked.

Sebastian was once again silent.

'We were just asking each other how we all wound up here,'

Agnes added calmly. 'None of us has a clue.'

'How about you?' Lucy asked.

Sebastian sat down in their grouping.

'Me and this place go way back,' he began. 'I was an altar boy here when I was a kid.'

'Overshare!' Lucy gulped.

'Nothing like that,' Sebastian pushed back. 'I learned a lot about myself here.'

'Is that why you know your way around so well?' Cecilia asked.

'Sort of,' he said haltingly. 'My grandmother raised me and used to bring me here on Sundays. When she died a few years ago, I stopped coming.'

'Did you lose your faith or something?' Agnes asked.

'No, I think maybe some other people lost theirs.'

'Have you been on your own since then?'

'I got bounced around to a few foster homes in the neighbourhood, but that didn't last long.'

Sebastian was clearly uncomfortable revealing details of his personal life.

'Well, we're all here now,' CeCe observed.

Agnes was settling down but Sebastian could see she was still pale and shaky. 'Are you OK?' he asked gently.

'No,' she said.

He walked over to her pew, helped her up, and moved her to the back of the church where he sat down next to her, leaving

Lucy and Cecilia alone together.

'That was convenient,' Lucy whispered to CeCe as Sebastian led Agnes away. 'She's really working that whole little-miss-vulnerable thing, and he's totally falling for it. Well, he doesn't know what he's missing.'

'His life is really none of our business, and vice versa,' Cecilia whispered. 'Once the storm passes, we'll go back to our lives like none of this ever happened.'

'Yeah, but all I'm saying is the altar-boy thing sounds a little shady,' Lucy pressed. 'I think he lives here and he's too embarrassed to say it.'

'So what if he does?'

'I hate wasted potential. He's smart, cool, amazing-looking. The sky is the limit,' Lucy said.

'Not everybody wants what you want. Maybe he's got other plans for himself. Better things than just getting his picture in the paper or on some blogger's home page.'

'Like what? Playing dives and pretending to be happy?' Lucy railed snidely. 'We live in a headline world and he's a headline guy. In fact, he kind of reminds me of myself. The things I like, anyway.'

'Are you bipolar or something?' CeCe rasped.

'Tell me you don't feel that way too?' Lucy asked. 'He's sensitive with Agnes, inspiring with you, reassuring with me. He doesn't even know us but he knows what we want. What we need.'

'Your theories are making me tired.' Cecilia yawned, standing. 'Besides, why do you care?'

'I don't really . . . But I do,' Lucy said. 'Don't you?'

Cecilia went silent as they walked toward a pew at the front of the church, sneaking peeks back at Sebastian comforting Agnes.

'Yeah, I guess I do,' she admitted.

'Whatever. It will be a good story someday,' Lucy said, putting her promotional cap on, as she was trained to do in difficult situations. 'Maybe he's just a religious fanatic or a Bible-basher or something.'

'I really hope not.'

'Why?'

CeCe flashed a smile.

'I don't do Bible-bashers.'

'I bet you do.' Lucy laughed.

'We're in a church for Christ's sake,' Cecilia said, feigning indignance.

'Look who's talking,' Lucy reminded her.

Cecilia felt her knees buckle slightly. 'I don't know what it is but my head is spinning. I need to chill for a while.'

'OK, yeah,' Lucy agreed, her head still smarting. 'I'm not feeling like myself either.'

'I think you need some sleep,' Cecilia said. 'We all do.'

Cecilia's Dream

*C*ecilia rose just before dawn.

She was alone.

Dressed in an elaborate garnet-encrusted bodice and long, off-white, intricately ruffled gown, the entire ensemble sacked loosely in black chiffon. Her hair was teased a little, held in an updo by a supple, thorny vine. Her lips were white, like her skin, slightly powdered over. Her cheeks were etched in a deep rose colour and her eyes were smoky and dark. She looked like a work of art more palette than person.

The first wave of panic since she arrived surged through her, flooding her arteries with adrenaline and setting her heart racing.

'Lucy,' she called out. 'Agnes?'

And finally, 'Sebastian.'

'Over here,' he said.

She turned her head in the direction of the altar and saw him.

The beams of light breaking through and into the nave actually made it harder to see from that distance. She needed to get closer.

'Don't move,' she said, edging herself out of the long pew toward the centre aisle of the church. 'I'm coming.'

She paused, unsure whether to genuflect, bow her head, or just keep moving, it had been so long since she'd had to think about it. She did a little of all three – bending a knee, lowering her chin a touch, and slouched forward toward the altar. It was a far cry from how she'd pictured her wedding as a little girl.

Back then, her gait was slow and steady, in waltz time, her white-satin-and-bead gown flowing, the pews full, silk streamers hung into the aisle, bouquets of roses and peonies wrapped with fresh Irish bells adorning every square inch of the church. Waiting for her, of course, was the perfect guy. She could never actually see his face, but he cut a handsome figure nonetheless. Tall, tuxedoed, trim, she imagined him walking right out of a fairy tale when she was younger, these days walking off the cover of Rolling Stone would do just fine.

How different her life was turning out. Instead of a charming prince to cuddle, it was an endless parade of sketchy pervs, all take and no give. Their appeal to her soon became their utter predictability. They got what they came for, and she got what she asked for. A vicious circle of boredom, guilt, punishment, and self-hatred. Expect nothing and you will never be disappointed, she'd heard it said. Cecilia was never disappointed.

She admired her dress, feeling like it was made just for her, but

when and by whom, she had no idea. She felt like a goddess. As she approached the altar, she stared down at the two marble steps preceding it and looked up again at Sebastian, who was standing near the lectern, a harp behind him. A sudden bout of vertigo struck her and her ears began to ring, as if she'd been hit in the head. She felt unsteady, slowed.

'I'm waiting . . .' he said. 'For you.'

'Where are the others?'

'We're here,' he said, reaching out his hand for her.

'I don't know. It doesn't feel right.'

'The altar or me?' he said, his piercing eyes catching hers, burning through her resistance.

'Is there a difference?' To her, they felt like one and the same. A sacrifice.

'Don't be afraid,' he said reassuringly, reaching now to her with both arms open.

She lifted her leg from the floor and placed it on to the first step. She was finding it hard to breathe. 'I feel like a child. Why is this so hard?'

'Because it's right.'

She bowed her head and gently began to sway it in time to the sound of the harp which was just beyond her reach. 'I hear music.'

'What is it?'

'A love song. Do you hear it?'

She began to mumble, then hum, and then sing softly as if channeling an invisible karaoke machine. It was an old habit. A

chant to prepare her heart for battle.

'I do,' he said. 'Blues?'

'Johnny Cash,' she said. 'Hurt.'

'Sing it for me.'

'No. Too sad. The saddest song I ever heard.'

'The happiest.'

'Is there a difference?' She moved her other foot up on the first step and then the second, music blaring in her head. She walked into his arms and pressed her ear against his chest. It was muscled, hard, unlike the guys she'd usually 'dated'. She rested there in his warmth for a while and felt his hands roll over her back, which she was always self-conscious of. All those years of dance as a kid, she supposed. Her spine was an outie the entire length of her sway back, a ridge of bony angles pushing up through her skin. Reptilian. At least that is the way she always described it. Ugliness inside trying to get out, and if not out, then to make itself visible. A warning. A way to keep love at arm's length. Like a peacock showing its colours or a cobra baring its fangs.

'You are so beautiful,' he said.

She was embarrassed, both by the tenderness of his words and the depth of her own self-loathing. She'd heard those words before, from overenthusiastic fan girls spewing random compliments or smarmy one-night stands trying to make nice before asking her to leave. She'd heard those words, but never listened, until now.

'I don't do love,' she whispered, looking up at him quickly for a reaction and then returning to the nest she'd laid in his chest.

'Because love has never done you,' he said, reaching out to hold her.

'Please, don't.'

Sebastian reached inside a glass reliquary box and pulled out a plain platinum wedding band.

'The choice is yours,' he said, placing the ring on her finger and holding her tighter. 'Not mine.'

'Love is never a choice. Is it?'

He reached firmly for her face and turned it up toward his for a kiss. Their lips met, and joined in a gentle collision of confusion and desire. She felt the sharpness of his stubbled chin and cheeks rubbing against hers; it hurt and she liked it. Cecilia felt a peace she had never known and all at once, an angst she had never known, either. The harp song grew louder. She felt like a string being plucked, vibrating in tune.

Her heart was beating even faster now, dangerously so, and she felt the blood leaving her head. Her hands went numb and her knees weak. Is this love, she thought, a panic attack, or something else?

'I'm not ready,' she gasped through purpled lips.

'Is there a choice?' he asked.

Cecilia often thought love might kill her, but this was different from anything she could have imagined. As if her heart were too full, not broken.

'I'm dying,' she said, reaching for his hand, which was now squeezing ever tighter around her slender throat. 'You are killing me.'

'Don't be afraid,' he whispered again in her ear, tightening his grip.

'I have no faith,' she gasped, 'in love.'

'You look so beautiful,' he repeated again. 'So. Very. Beautiful.'

Cecilia continued to struggle but was weakening fast. She felt helpless to stuff back in the life that was leaving her body.

Her eyes were bulged wide and fixed on an illusionistic mural painted brightly on the ceiling. Angels and a blue open sky above, which seemed to come to life as she was dying. Then she fixed her eyes on his. He was looking at her so lovingly. So passionately. Like she'd never been looked at before.

'I love you, but I must not think of you.'

She felt clean again.

Her dress turned to pure white satin. Like her skin. The thorny vine that wove through her hair sprouted delicate, tiny, red spring beauties. Just like she always dreamed it would as a little girl.

As her chest heaved and her last breaths left her, her arms dropped limply to her sides, a stream of garnet blood began to colour her powdered lips as black beauty roses formed a bed around her feet. The music stopped. Her consciousness faded to darkness and then suddenly a burst of white.

Never feeling so alive, she uttered her final word.

'Sebastian.'

10

Love Vigilantes

Agnes was sick.

And scared.

She was afraid of the dark and always had been. It was irrational, she knew that. Hadn't really slept alone until she was fourteen, and even then only with a nightlight and the bedroom door cracked open. That was probably one of the reasons why her mother felt so justified in interfering with her life. At sixteen, she was not just young, but still very much a child in her mother's eyes. She was stubborn, but not independent.

Lucy and Cecilia were asleep in the pews around her. Sebastian had yet to return. She felt surrounded, but alone. 'Swallowed' described the sensation of being enveloped by the darkened nave. The reality of what she was doing began to pour in like the rain through the leaky church roof.

Her mom was going to freak when she came into her room to get her up for school and found the bedroom empty and the bed made, bedspread pulled over the top, and sheets tucked tightly. What would she do next? Call all her friends most definitely to drum up support, and attention for herself, but then panic would certainly set in. She was her mother's life.

The thought of her mother's angst brought out her own neuroses even further, and she began picking obliviously at the tape holding her bandages on, when the sound of a few footfalls behind her and a hand on her shoulder sent a shockwave through her entire body.

'Are you OK?' Sebastian whispered.

Deep in thought, Agnes was startled, frightened. Instead of pulling away, he leaned in waiting for her response.

'Yes,' she said, but her eyes told another story. 'I just can't sleep.'

Sebastian reached for the bare skin on her arms and then brushed his hand along her forehead. She was burning up.

'Do they hurt?' he asked, sliding his hand from her shoulder down along her arm.

'No,' she said again, this time with more conviction, but quickly reversed herself when she saw the scepticism in his eye. 'Yes.'

'Come with me.' Sebastian reached out his hand and gently

helped her up. Agnes was in her bare feet, wearing a soggy Hippie Gypsy crinkled tiered peasant skirt that went down to her milky-white ankles – each tier a different shade, resembling a snowfall in the city – the first tier was pure white, the middle tiers were degrees of grey, until eventually the bottom tier, which was the soft black color of soot.

He led her down the side aisle toward the front of the church, through a door and into a small room behind the altar. It was cool and the air was heavy with the aroma of sandalwood, balsam, and rose. Agnes had a good nose for aromas and prided herself on her ability to pick out even the most obscure scents for the personalized fragrances and soaps she made for her friends as birthday gifts. The one scent she did not pick up, which permeated the rest of the building, was the odour of her own decay.

Sebastian struck a match, lit a taper, and stood before a large wooden cabinet with drawers and double closets, one on each side. It was traditionally styled, antique, though it was hard to see completely in the dim light. The sort of oversized piece that Agnes and her friends might scour the Park Slope flea markets for ages to find. He turned the candle sideways so that some wax would drip from the wick and form a molten puddle on the wooden countertop. He forced the bottom of the taper into the hot wax and held it for a few seconds while it fixed itself, holding the candle upright.

For the first time she was able to see the room they'd entered.

A large gold crucifix hung above the cabinet and colourful robes of purple, green, and white were suspended from hooks behind the door. There was a kneeler and several ornately carved chairs with deep burgundy velvet seat covers. She noticed two doors, a larger one next to the cabinet that led to a small bathroom and a smaller black one in the back wall. Strewn across the top of the cabinet were boxes of taper candles, votive candles, brass snuffers, incense packets, and chained bronze urns, glass and ceramic casters, gold cups and plates unlike anything she'd seen before. A bookstand with a leather-bound and gilt-paged prayer book, open, with multicoloured satin bookmarks dangling from select pages. Agnes was awed and more than a little uncomfortable.

'Where are we?' Agnes asked.

'It's called a sacristy. Like a man cave for priests.'

'Looks more like an operating room, I think,' Agnes said, eyeing all the tools of the Episcopal trade on display.

'Speaking of which . . .' Sebastian grabbed for the closet door and pulled it open.

The aromas wafted upward and became even more intense, almost overwhelming to her. He reached for a glass cruet from among several on a shelf, stood up, turned toward her, and removed the stopper.

Agnes turned effortlessly toward him like a delicate figurine inside a music box.

'Give me your arms,' he said tenderly.

'Why?'

'It's OK,' he said, smiling concernedly, and held out his hand to receive hers. 'I won't hurt you.'

She raised her slender limbs and held them straight outward, wrists facing up, almost offering her wounds to him. Sebastian's eyes fixed on her chaplet.

'He gave this to me,' Agnes said. 'Just like you asked.'

'He's a good boy,' Sebastian said as he gently pulled at the wrapping on her wrists. Slowly, he removed the tape and then unwound the protective and gauze bandage until all that remained on each wrist was a rectangular absorbent pad, soaked through a brownish red with her blood. More concerning was the tinge of yellow on the pad.

'I think it's getting infected,' she said, wincing.

Sebastian got as good a look as he could by candlelight. The wound was healing but still raw and inflamed. She'd cut deep and there were more stitches than he could count.

'I was supposed to go back to the doctor today,' she said nervously, 'but I got into a fight with my mom and—'

'Do you get along with her?'

'We just see things very differently.'

'Like?'

'I don't know.' Agnes hesitated. 'Love? Life?'

'Is that all?'

She smiled.

'What about you?'

'I don't have an family left,' he said. 'Makes things easier, in a way.'

'And harder too?' Agnes observed, reaching gently for his arm.

Sebastian lowered his eyes.

'I'm sure your mom loves you,' he offered. 'You don't want to take that for granted.'

'I try not to, but everything she does is so planned out. She wants me to be like that, like her, but I can't be.'

'You have to be true to yourself,' Sebastian said, getting right to the heart of the matter. 'Always.'

'Yes!' Agnes said, almost with relief. 'I'm so glad you understand. People make me feel like such an idiot sometimes. I'm almost starting to believe it, to tell you the truth.'

'Don't,' he said.

'If I didn't get out of there, I felt like I would have just lost myself completely.'

Agnes was getting teary, feeling the effects of sickness and sadness weighing on her.

'You're here now,' he said, taking hold of her.

'She thinks I'm weak because I believe in true love. Like the world will chew me up and spit me out or something.'

'I don't think there is anything more powerful. If you can change hearts, you can change minds.'

He was supportive. Open. Not much older, but so much wiser than the other guys she knew at school. Her friends

weren't much better. For the first time in years, she didn't feel so alone.

'It's like she wants to change me, change who I am.'

'You're not the only one who's felt this way. I've been there too,' Sebastian said, holding her hands tenderly in his. 'You can't let that happen.'

'I know. It would be worse than . . .'

'Death?'

'Yes,' she gasped in amazement that he'd completed her thought. 'Death.'

Everything about him was comforting to her. Her anxiety and tension melted away. Her infection, unfortunately, remained.

He could see on her face that the conversation was taking a lot out of her and she didn't look like she had much more to give.

'Let's take care of you, OK?'

Sebastian turned the candle on the wall behind them and grabbed a stole from a hook, which he walked over to the bathroom sink and saturated with cold water. He wrung out the cloth and brought it to her, placing it over her gash and pressing down, first on one arm and then the other.

The cold and wet garment on her skin was more a relief than she would have imagined. She could almost feel the sliced and swollen tissue retract. She closed her eyes and exhaled slowly. 'Thank you.'

'Don't thank me yet.' Sebastian reached for the open vessel of fragrant oil and poured some into his cupped hand, dipped his first two fingers in it and spread it across his fingertips.

He grabbed her wrist.

Held it firmly.

She tensed up.

'Relax,' he said. 'Trust me.'

'I'm afraid,' she said.

'Close your eyes.'

Agnes closed her eyes slowly and took a deep breath.

She surrendered completely to him. She was at his mercy.

Sebastian wiped the oil from his fingers on to her wound.

He was inside of her.

Agnes quietly moaned.

He caressed her milky soft skin and held her hand while he worked on her. She was so delicate and . . . touchable.

'No,' she blurted out, pulling away slightly.

'It's OK,' he said, trying to calm her. Stroking her hair. 'This oil has antibacterial properties.' He applied the makeshift salve liberally over the wound and then massaged the inside of her forearms with the oil.

'This feels good.'

'It does.' Sebastian grabbed two clean white linen stoles and slowly, carefully rewrapped her wrists.

Agnes opened her eyes and watched him. His tender technique. He was focused, as if he had something very precious and fragile in his hands.

'Where was it that you got your degree again?' she asked, a little touch of sarcasm escaping her lips along with the smile.

'A joke?' he said with disbelief. 'You must be feeling better or something.'

'Or something.'

Agnes smiled and her gaze turned to the small door at the back of the room. 'Is that another way out?'

'Maybe.'

'Don't you know?'

'I do.'

'But you won't tell me.'

'No.'

'Lucy and Cecilia think you're keeping something from us.'

'They're right.'

Agnes was surprised.

'So, you lied to us?'

'No,' he said. 'I haven't lied. I've told you what I can.'

Agnes eyed the door and then Sebastian once again. She could tell it meant something to him. Even in her weakened condition, her curiosity and stubbornness were getting the best of her. 'What's down there?'

'A chapel.'

She pressed him. 'Is the answer down there?'

'See for yourself.'

'OK, I will.'

Agnes walked over and reached gingerly for the doorknob and stopped. Her grip was weak and the door looked intimidating; she was worried she wouldn't be able to muster any leverage at all from her forearms to turn the heavy knob. That it might hurt if she tried. 'I hate locked doors.'

'How do you know it's locked?'

She stepped back to the door and grabbed the knob this time. She paused, trying to focus all of her strength and willpower into her left wrist. She tried over and over to find the strength, but it was pointless. Sebastian was impressed by her determination. Agnes stopped and backed away again, the look of chagrin on her face like a corner-store gambler with a losing lottery ticket.

'I can't open it,' she said, frustrated but still determined. 'Yet.'

'Try again another time.'

'When?'

'Whenever you're ready.'

'Good advice for opening doors and hearts,' Agnes said.

Sebastian opened his arms to her for a comforting hug. Agnes balked but stepped slowly into his waiting grasp. She turned her head and pressed her cheek against his chest, her long, cascading hair the only chaperone between them. Agnes felt Sebastian's heart beating. It was strong and steady, unlike hers, which seemed to be fast and skipping beats.

He tightened his arms around her and she squeezed around his waist, with strength she had failed to conjure for the

doorknob. It might not have been true love yet, but this, she thought, is what love should feel like. Passion and peace, danger and safety, all at once.

'We shouldn't,' she said, her head staying just a little bit ahead of her heart.

Sebastian didn't budge and she didn't really want him to.

Agnes straightened up and Sebastian fell to his knees. He looked up at Agnes, her long flowing hair falling on her bare shoulders down to her chest, her silk camisole clinging to her pallid skin. She looked statuesque.

Sebastian slowly took her hand.

'Ah, I think the others will be worried,' she said, reluctantly. 'We should go.'

They separated slowly, eyes locked. After an uncomfortable second or two, Agnes tossed her long mane back behind her and cleared her throat.

'May I thank you now?'

'You may,' he said, bowing slightly at the waist and formally gesturing toward the door.

As he bent back, he found himself face-to-face and eye-to-eye with her again.

'Thank you' barely escaped her lips.

He leaned in, slowly closing the distance between them. She leaned toward him expectantly, slowly closing her eyes again.

The pulsing storm outside providing the perfect underscore for forbidden romance.

A first kiss.

The kiss they both felt coming on was interrupted by an earth-shaking crack of thunder.

Like a warning finger wagging from above.

The phone rang. It was the principal. At least a reasonable facsimile.

'Due to the citywide weather emergency and out of concern for the safety of students and faculty . . .'

A school cancellation robo call. Martha picked up the receiver, listened groggily, and hung up. *Was a call really necessary?* she thought.

'Agnes,' she called out. 'Agnes!'

The wind blew hard against the windows, making it impossible to hear or to be sure she'd been heard.

'Damn this weather!' she said, sliding out of bed and heading down the hall to her daughter's bedroom. 'Will it ever end?'

Martha reached the door with the massive, rusted KEEP OUT wharf sign affixed to it that Agnes had dragged back on the train from last summer's Montauk vacation. Martha resented it. She couldn't help but take personally that Agnes would expend so much effort to broadcast her desire for privacy. Especially when it was just the two of them living there.

Come to think of it, the problems between them could be traced back to last summer and the beginning of her relationship

with Sayer, that boy that Martha disapproved of so strongly. *Mothers and daughters at each others' throats. A tale as old as time.* Agnes would come around and it would blow over. Eventually.

'Agnes, that was the school,' she said, rapping on the door to no response. 'You can sleep in.'

The irony of waking Agnes up to tell her she could sleep later was not lost on her mother, and she smiled a little. Though she was a little surprised that Agnes was able to sleep through such an epic storm. Usually she'd wake to find the girl in bed next to her. Her mood and her tone softened considerably.

'C'mon, honey. You're not still angry, are you?'

Martha reached for the knob and turned it, fully expecting the door to be locked, but it wasn't. The door creaked open under its own weight and Martha noticed immediately the windswept curtains. The sill and the carpet below looked soaking wet, things had been blown off of shelves, and the room was freezing cold. She pushed at the door and it flew open wide, like her mouth. The bed was made, unslept in. Agnes's desktop was still on, although toppled over, and her mobile phone sat charging on her turquoise-painted bedside end table. Her clothes were left where they'd landed from the night before.

Martha grabbed the phone and scrolled through Agnes's missed call list. She hit call on a contact name she recognized and moved over to the computer, checking her daughter's email, sent and received, which was still open on the screen.

'Hello, Hazel? This is Mrs Fremont.'

She always used her married name, even though her marriage had long since ended. It was for Agnes's sake. Having the same last name kept them connected in a way, and looked better to strangers, however semidelusional it might have appeared to others who knew better.

'Oh, hi. I thought you were Agnes calling me.'

'Agnes isn't with you?' Martha said, trying to hide the depth of her panic.

'She's not at home?'

'No. Any idea where she might have gone?'

'I thought she might have gone to bed early to rest or whatever from her . . . you know . . . attempt.'

'Thanks,' Martha said worriedly, ignoring the lack of sensitivity. 'If you hear anything . . .'

'Don't worry. She's totally over Sayer. I'm sure she'll be back later. She's probably just trying to piss you off.'

'But the storm and her arms,' Martha complained. 'It's hideous outside; they say they are expecting a tornado. In Brooklyn! And she's not in the right shape mentally or otherwise to be out there right now. Alone. In this.'

'I know. Can you believe it? We haven't had power since last night. Trees are down everywhere. You can't even get down the street.'

Martha couldn't have cared less at that moment. 'It's just not

like her to up and leave like that. I mean, we've had much worse arguments.'

'She's just really fragile right now. I'll text everyone. She'll turn up.'

Yes, but hopefully not in a skip, was all Martha could think.

Sebastian and Agnes opened the sacristy door and were startled to find Lucy and Cecilia standing there, about to knock and equally startled.

'Did you hear that thunder crack?' Lucy said, grabbing her arms in a shiver. 'We were yelling for you.'

Agnes flushed at the momentary awkwardness and flipped her hair nervously over her shoulder, crossing her arms defensively and looking downward.

'We're not interrupting anything are we?' Cecilia asked rhetorically.

'I was helping her with her wrists,' Sebastian said, as Agnes nodded her agreement.

'Cecilia woke up screaming. I'm surprised you didn't hear it,' Lucy prodded.

'Good thing, too,' Cecilia said, still shaken.

'Bad weather or bad dream?' Agnes asked sympathetically.

'Nightmare.' CeCe nodded.

Agnes wasn't sure if CeCe was talking about her actual dream or the compromising situation in which she found herself.

'It's really hard to hear anything in there,' Agnes protested a little too much.

'Yeah, whatever,' Lucy said, instantly distracted by a glittering item poking out from a partially opened drawer she spied in the sacristy. '*What* is that?'

'It's a vestment cabinet,' Sebastian explained.

'No, not the cabinet. Inside the drawer.'

She wasn't absolutely sure it wasn't stars from the blow she'd taken to the head earlier, so she pointed, hoping the others saw it as well.

'Priest clothes?' he asked.

Lucy walked to the drawer and slid it open, revealing a neatly folded pile of the most elaborate garb she'd ever seen. Approaching the cabinet, she spied all manner of majestically embroidered linens in white, red, green, purple, and gold that had been left behind. Sewn with spun silver and gold thread. She admired their beauty even in the darkness, running her fingers over the fabric to feel the heft and detailed stitching. She beckoned the other girls over for a closer look.

'They don't make 'em like this anymore,' she said. 'These have got to be vintage.'

'Holy haute couture,' CeCe added, equally enthralled. 'This is so tempting.'

'Bad girl,' Lucy said, flirtatiously thrusting her chest forward. 'Good girl!' arching her back and recoiling.

'Is there a difference?' Cecilia said, unconsciously echoing her dreamspeak.

Sebastian smiled at her, as if he knew what she was thinking. Like he did in the hospital when they met.

Lucy pulled out the chasuble and swung it over her head and let it fall on to her shoulders and almost to the floor, striking holier poses. A beautiful, hand-sewn image of a young girl, crowned, holding a palm branch in one hand and a plate in the other, took up the entire back of the garment. The care in making and storing such a piece left them to wonder why anyone would ever leave it behind.

'What do you think of my Sunday best, girls?' Lucy smirked, sucking her cheeks in and posing. 'Too much?'

'A wolf in shepard's clothing,' CeCe said as both she and Agnes daintily air-clapped their approval like stone-faced fashion editors in the front row of a fashion show.

Sebastian smiled, carried along by their enthusiasm and the first truly lighthearted moment any of them had experienced since arriving.

'Fashion *The Passion*,' Lucy announced, gesturing at the cabinet like a game show spokesmodel, before throwing gorgeous ponchos to each of the other girls.

Cecilia tossed the heavy, woollen, deep purple and gold garment over her shoulder like a tunic and fastened it at the waist with one of the scapulars that had been hanging from a hook behind the door. She tied Agnes's long hair up in a

ponytail with another and helped her put the vestment on.

'Mother Cecilia!' Lucy laughed.

'And Sister Agnes,' Cecilia said as Agnes slid her arms through the gold accented side holes of the garment and her slight frame disappeared beneath the white cloth.

Sebastian looked on, a little more preoccupied. Agnes looked up at the framed portraits and biblical paintings hanging around them. Images of faith and devotion she had seen at school but had little personal experience with.

'I have an idea,' Lucy said. 'We've got the coolest runway ever out there. Any takers?'

'I'm always up for a show,' Cecilia added.

'The altar?' Agnes asked. 'I don't know. Inappropriate?'

'Sebastian?' Lucy squawked.

They turned to Sebastian looking for his approval but he'd already turned away, staring out a small cracked and dirty window at the deluge outside. He had barely heard the question.

'I guess that's a no,' Cecilia concluded.

'Well, it was just an idea,' Lucy added defensively.

Sebastian didn't react. He was miles away.

'These are heavy,' Agnes said wearily, putting an end to the festivities. She didn't look well. Sebastian took her arm.

'Last call,' Cecilia barked, as the girls relinquished the clerical attire, dropping it hastily and transforming the sacristy floor into a chain store fitting room.

'We should grab some of these,' Sebastian said, taking a handful of stoles and oils to use as bandages and salves for Agnes if needed, with Lucy and Cecilia following suit.

'Thank you for taking care of me,' Agnes whispered.

Sebastian squeezed her arm tenderly.

Agnes eyed the accessories as they carried them back into the church.

'I feel kind of funny about taking this stuff on my account,' she said. 'Like we're stealing from a church.'

'We're not stealing,' Sebastian said. 'I only took what we needed.'

11

The Morning After

'Line one,' the secretary said. 'It's Captain Murphy.'

Dr Frey closed his office door and sat forward in his chair. He took a deep breath and picked up the phone.

'Yes, Officer.'

'Captain,' he corrected.

'My mistake. What can I do for you?'

The relationship between the doctor and the captain was contentious at best, Frey having successfully testified as an expert witness on behalf of defendants to the chagrin of the NYPD and prosecutors on many occasions. It was superficially cordial, but neither was inclined to help the other much beyond what was required professionally.

'I'm surprised to find you at the hospital, Doctor.'

'We are on lockdown and running on generators, and I am needed.'

'I'm practically the only one at the precinct house.'

'I'm quite short-staffed today myself, as you can imagine, and very busy. Are you calling with news?'

'Not the news you are waiting for. I'm calling about another patient of yours that's been reported missing.'

'Who is that?'

'Agnes Fremont. Her mother walked into an empty bedroom this morning after an argument the night before.'

'I see,' Dr Frey said, fingering his files.

'I understand that she was recently admitted to the emergency room there after a possible suicide attempt and was kept overnight under observation, under your care?'

'Yes, that's right. She was released to her mother's custody the next day, and that's the last I've seen or heard from her, I'm afraid.'

'So that was November first?

Frey hesitated and checked his desk calendar as he pondered the date.

'Doctor? Are you there?'

'Yes,' he replied, uncharacteristically bemused. 'She was admitted on the night of October thirty-first, Halloween, and discharged on November first.'

'All Saints' Day,' Murphy observed.

'What?' Frey asked, still distracted. 'Ah, yes, it appears so.'

'In a sinner and out a saint, huh?' the cop joked.

'Are you trying to be clever?'

'Hey, Doctor, if a person with multiple personalities attempts suicide, would you consider that a hostage situation? Now, that's clever.'

'Like I said, I'm very busy,' Frey's reputation for humourlessness was well known. 'Especially so now.'

'OK, any indications she might take off? The mother is beside herself. You know, with this weather and with all that, you know, happened.'

'None.'

'Anything unusual that you noticed or may have discussed with her in your evaluation?'

'No, but I couldn't tell you even if there were. Patient confidentiality, Captain. I presume you know the law.'

The line went silent for a few seconds while the captain pondered how offended he should be by the doctor's comments.

'This is a young girl out on the street, for all we know. If someone out there doesn't get her, the storm will.'

'The relationship with the mother seemed frayed, as I recall. Couldn't she be with a friend? She didn't present to me as a flight risk.'

'Did she have any awareness of what transpired the other night?'

'Not that she discussed with me. Why?'

'She was in the emergency room when that boy, your patient, escaped.'

'So?'

'The video cameras in the building were tampered with so we can't be sure, but our best guess is that he came out of the hospital through the emergency room.'

'And you think they might have had some contact?'

'It's a long shot, but we have to track down every lead. We're getting a lot of pressure to find this girl. I don't want this leaking out and the papers making a connection before we do.'

'I wouldn't be too concerned yet,' Frey said, playing it off somewhat dismissively. 'What is the status of the investigation into Sebastian's disappearance?'

'The status? Ongoing. I assigned a few men to the case who've been pulled off on storm duty.'

Frey wasn't pleased. 'Have you checked the churches yet?'

'First place we looked. Nothing.'

'This is an urgent matter. A public-safety issue. Is your department in the habit of letting killers run wild? New York's Finest, indeed.'

'What is it with you and this kid?'

'I know him, Captain. That's all. Without proper care, he could be a danger to himself and others.'

'With all due respect, Doctor, your lack of cooperation hasn't exactly helped move the investigation forward. He isn't the only suspect.'

'If you want to speak to other patients under my care, in this ward, you will have to follow procedure. I have a job to do and patient rights to protect.'

'One of your orderlies is found at the bottom of the lift shaft, and you are making me get a court order to talk to that bunch of lunatics?'

'These lunatics are human beings.'

'I arrested one of your current patients, Sicarius, myself. He's a soulless, bloodthirsty bastard. What he's doing up there with you in a minimum-security ward instead of in solitary is a travesty of justice.'

'I don't make the laws. Besides, he is medicated, controlled. Hardly any trouble at all.'

'He is a sick bastard. What he did to those little girls. His own goddamn kids. If you want me to guess who tossed your orderly down the chute, I'd put my money on him.'

'I don't want you to guess. I want you to find Sebastian.'

'The kid has no history of violence.'

'The fact that he just happened to disappear the night before the orderly was found notwithstanding?'

'You don't need to tell me my job, Doctor.'

'I wouldn't presume, Captain,' said Dr Frey, condescension dripping from his voice.

'For now, the orderly's death has been reported as accidental. We don't want to panic the city with wild headlines about escaped mental patients and kidnapped teenagers. Especially

not with this weather insanity going on. You understand? We'll find him.'

'The sooner the better.'

'I'll be by to interview Sicarius and a few of the others as soon as this blows over.'

'You'll bring the court order, of course?'

'Thanks for your time, Doctor. If anything occurs to you on the Fremont girl, give me a call.'

'Goodbye, Captain.'

Dr Frey lingered over the calendar and Agnes's file, reviewing his notes, reconstructing his impressions of her and of their meeting. Of the unstable patients he'd seen recently, she was the most stable, her wounds more a mission statement than mental imbalance. Not being one to take unnecessary chances, he decided to take a closer look.

'Nurse,' he called. 'Get the patient log for the ER from last weekend.'

'I don't think anyone is down in records, Doctor,' the nurse advised. 'Is it urgent?'

'NOW!'

Cecilia found it difficult to shake off her dream and began to recover only when the sounds of the street began to make their way through the church walls. Agnes was seated nearby, but not too close. She noticed Cecilia's agitation.

'Can I get you some water?' Agnes offered, ignoring

her own distress.

'I'm OK,' she snapped. 'I just need to be by myself for a minute.'

CeCe got up and walked toward the back of the church and into the vestibule and paused, looking back at Agnes.

'Sorry,' she mouthed to Agnes. 'Thank you.'

Sebastian, Lucy, and Agnes watched and waited for her to approach the front doors of the church, but she disappeared from their sight before she did. They did hear a door open, however, and the scrape of Cecilia's boot soles along a staircase. She reappeared above them, in the balcony in front of a massive pipe organ, like some waifish phantom of the rock opera. She looked down at them as if scanning an audience from the stage, then turned her back and sat on the bench before the keyboard.

She swayed as she touched the keys, which produced a faint sound muted by dust and age, but loud enough for each in the tiny audience below to hear her music. Cecilia broke out into song and a cold sweat. She seemed overtaken, dazed. It was a minor chord plainsong, mournful and bittersweet. A chant, almost, with a lilting, ethereal melody.

It was easy for Cecilia to lose herself, but never more than in this place. Empty and in partial disrepair, it resembled nothing so much as a theatre set in the process of being built, or maybe taken down – she couldn't be sure which – but there was so much more embedded in it.

Lean out your window, golden hair
I heard you singing in the midnight air
My book is closed, I read no more
Watching the fire dance, on the floor

It was a musical arrangement of a James Joyce poem that she loved. It was like nothing she'd ever played in public before or for anyone but herself. Her own music was aggressive, confrontational, but these were the sounds of acquiescence, of resignation.

Full of grace.

'Auditions for choir are next week,' Lucy groused.

The tinge of jealousy in Lucy's tone was obvious, as she eyed Sebastian and Agnes enthralled with Cecilia's performance.

'Let's just listen, OK?' Agnes shot back, irritated by Lucy's pettiness.

I've left my book, I've left my room
For I heard you singing through the gloom
Singing and singing, a merry air
Lean out the window, golden hair

Her voice echoed through the chamber, reverberating through the wooden and metal fixtures placed, stacked, and hung throughout the church.

When she finished, Cecilia stood quietly and made her way back downstairs to the others.

'That was beautiful,' Sebastian said. 'Spiritual.'

'Thanks,' she said shyly.

'Syd Barrett,' he said.

'Yeah,' Cecilia acknowledged. 'A real hero of mine. How did you know?'

All the strongest connections she'd ever made were through music. Who you listened to, what moved you, told her everything about who you were. It was like a secret language. One she felt she now shared with him.

'A legend in his own time,' Sebastian added. 'And a troubled soul.'

CeCe nodded.

'I don't know where that came from,' Cecilia said, examining her hands in wonder. 'I've never played anything like that before.'

'Maybe you're just . . . inspired,' he said, smiling, grabbing her arms tight.

Cecilia's faced flushed and she looked away. She wasn't easily embarrassed or moved by a guy's touch, but this felt different. Especially now. Her dream had frightened her, but it also thrilled her in a way she had never been. She only barely knew him, but she felt herself falling for Sebastian.

Cecilia looked up at him and smiled a little, crossed her arms, which were bare and had turned to gooseflesh from him and the damp interior. She walked over to Lucy and Agnes, where she was greeted with a gentle hug from Agnes and grudging compliments from Lucy.

They were all moved, whether they wanted to admit it or not. They each felt like she was singing directly to them and about them. For them.

'Nice, but it didn't sound like a hit to me,' Lucy said defensively.

'What is your obsession with being the biggest and the best?' Agnes asked.

'I wasn't completely serious, but think about it, why bother pursuing anything unless you shoot for the top?' Lucy spat.

'What about really moving just a few people?' Cecilia said, joining the fray in her own defence. 'I'd rather just reach a few people that really get it.'

'How arrogant,' Lucy chided. 'People that get it? It's your job to *make* them get it.'

'A little sensitive about the whole selling-out thing, aren't we?' CeCe pushed back. 'Art is not a job, or shouldn't be.'

'Please,' Lucy countered. 'If you wanted to be musician, you can do that in your parents' basement or in front of your bedroom mirror. The minute you put your music out there, charge for a download or a ticket at some old-man bar, you are in the music business, you are asking people to make a purchasing decision, to choose.'

'And what are you selling?' Cecilia asked.

'A fantasy,' Lucy said. 'Me.'

'You'd rather be a fantasy?' Agnes asked.

'It's all about the numbers, about outreach. There is only one of me,' Lucy said, 'but everybody has a fantasy.'

'Well, before you hit send, it might be a good idea to think about what you are putting out there first,' Cecilia said.

'Womp. Resentful much?' Lucy scoffed. 'Maybe I'd feel the same if I was playing those toilet bowls you headline.'

'I'm trying to reach people,' CeCe said. 'Not rape people or whore myself out to the highest bidder.'

'Whoring? You must have us confused.'

'Not really, I guess I just prefer to bare my soul than sell it.'

'Well, I say go big, or don't go. Anything else is a bust.'

'She reached me,' Agnes said quietly. 'She played how I've always felt inside.'

Sebastian watched the argument go down and listened carefully to each girl make her case. What they were saying and what they meant to say.

'You need both,' Sebastian said, ending the quarrel by splitting the difference and their differences. 'A message and a messenger.'

The upper-right corners of the hospital files were dog-eared and yellowed from use, the faintest outline of a fingerprint – Dr Frey's – beginning to appear there. Pinching the edges, he had been intently alternating between one page and then the other, searching for some sort of connection, some common thread, a person, place, or thing, in their backgrounds. It was far too coincidental for this girl, he thought, to just up and disappear so soon after Sebastian.

Sebastian. Agnes. Sebastian. Agnes. Sebastian. Agnes.

A quick review and comparison of their report cards and teacher's evaluations didn't reveal anything extraordinary that might attract them; all things considered, they were total opposites. Both young, both smart. And hardheaded. He had firsthand knowledge of that. Similarities ended there, however. Where she was dedicated, hardworking, ambitious, fastidious, he was indifferent, rebellious, self-assured, and disconnected from the world around him, and becoming increasingly so. Manic behaviour had become the norm, along with the delusions and ego inflation often associated with them. If anything, Agnes's self-esteem could use some pumping up.

As he scanned the emergency room admissions, a more important connection suggested itself. Two other teenage girls, about the same age, admitted about the same time.

Cecilia Trent. Age: 18. Height: 1.75 m. Weight: 52.16 kgs. Hair: Br. Eyes: Gr.

No insurance, no personal physician, no next of kin, no phone number. Williamsburg address. Arrived unconscious. Possible drowning. Resuscitated on scene and transported by EMT.

Diagnosis: Acute Intoxication.

He found it peculiar as he perused her blood work results, that he had so much information about this person and yet

almost none at all. He had just literally seen inside her without ever laying eyes on her. 'Technology.'

Treatment: Fluids, bed rest.

Discharged: November 1.

'November 1.'

Unlike the ER docs who'd treated her, he was interested in her mind as much as her body. Putting together a profile from an incomplete bunch of disparate facts was not just a skill he'd developed with years of experience, it was his job. And he was very good at his job. He googled her and quickly found web links to online flyers for her gigs at local bars and clubs around Brooklyn, Queens and the Lower East Side. Dives, he figured, given the lack of info on the spaces. The mobile-phone video clips he streamed from her performances were choppy and dark, not just thematically, but literally dark. She was like an antenna broadcasting her rage out into the ether, a No Wave warrior – not just ready for a fight but looking for one.

Searching for upcoming live dates posted on her fan pages, he noticed that last night's show, which she cut short, was already a subject of controversy. He scrolled down to the comments and read through a string of vicious complaints and put-downs:

Rat In A Cage says:

No show ho! I'm so tired of these arrogant up-and-comers

shitting all over their fans. We won't get fooled again, Bitch! I have comps for next week. Who's comin' wit?

H8ter88 says:
I hope she dies a slow, painful death for punking out mid-show on her fans. Probably had an early date with one of those fat ass promoters she's always sleeping with for Jack money. Just kidding. Love her soooooo much!

FandemoniumGrrl says:
Who wants to bet she plays the stalker-in-the-crowd card on her soon-to-be posted web apology? Wait, it's not me!

MusicKilledMe666:
Two Words People: The. Shitz.

AdultBaby7 says:
My sister's boyfriend's third cousin went to high school with her in Pittsburgh before she dropped out and she says something terrible must have happened for her to cut a show short. Pray for her everybody and check out my new vlog!

With fans like these, he thought, *who needs enemies*, but maybe that was the whole point. Without a volatile mix of love and hate, there can be no passion. And if nothing else, he could see that these people cared. A lot. They were invested in her. There was no medical term for charisma, but wherever it came from, this girl had it by the truckload.

On the last video clip posted of the previous night's performance, he noticed something he hadn't expected to see. Something alarming. A beaded band she wore around her bicep. He recognized it.

He turned his attention to the other 'red flag' on the ER roll. Her name was vaguely familiar to him.

Lucy Ambrose. Age: 17. Height: 1.68 m. Weight: 54 kg. Address: 7 Bridge Street.

'The more adventurous side of the DUMBO district,' he noted.

Contact name and number: Jesse Arens and a 718 number.

Not exactly a poor girl. New building. He imagined her looking out from the back window of her apartment toward the East River at the empty space once occupied by the World Trade Centre towers. The tall buildings of Wall Street, buzz of Tribeca, SoHo, and the Lower East Side, and the bridges, like lifelines, beckoning her.

A quick search turned up several pages of photos and gossip items from the downtown fashion and nightlife sites. One source, more than any other, seemed to be the generator of these cyber file cabinets of coverage, documenting her every move from would-be junior leaguer to A-List party girl.

Trawling through an endless series of gallery openings, charity galas and afterparties, he found the sheer volume of the

coverage was stunning and mainly mind-numbing non sequiturs. Rumours of drinking and drug problems followed reports of endorsement deals with energy-drink manufacturers, downtown designers, and cosmetic surgery practices, until they each seemed to disappear, like puzzle pieces into a bigger picture. Lots of seductive candids and flirtatious dressing, but precious few mentions of one-night stands or real boyfriends or any real friends, for that matter, completed the profile of a girl in a love affair primarily with herself. A narcissist definitely, borderline histrionic personality disorder, probably. Not uncommon, he considered, but unusually fine-tuned for such a young person.

Fame in the ADD Age, he thought. As fine an example of time-lapse digital careerism and social climbing as could be imagined or even wished for. A girl immortalized in pixels for no other purpose than her own glorification. Fame as endgame. The sheer intangibility of it all was breathtaking. But of all the images that assaulted his senses, it was the most recent posting that caught his attention. The image of Lucy picking herself off of the nightlife canvas. But it was not her bravery he admired, but rather the accessory he noticed around her wrist. Nearly identical to the beaded bauble also adorning the musician's arm.

He hadn't actually seen Agnes with one, but she did seem fidgety during her appointment, as if she was hiding something. His scientist's mind led him to only one conclusion.

'It's happening.'

12
Exorcize the Demons
of Your Heart

'Hey, altar boy,' Lucy whispered, waking Sebastian up from a dead sleep. 'I'm ready.'

'Ready?'

'To change.'

They both got up and headed to the back of the church, away from the other two. Neither spoke, but both knew where they were going; guided only by the candle each was carrying. Words were unnecessary.

They stopped in front of the confessional.

'The scene of the crime,' Lucy joked about the spot of their first meeting.

'Not guilty,' he said, raising his arms in surrender.

She reached for the penitent's door and opened it. He reached for the clergy's. They were both careful to close them slowly and quietly. Lucy and Sebastian got comfortable in their respective compartments, unable to see each other until Sebastian slid the wooden door open. Even then, all they could see were silhouettes through the dark metal screen that separated them. It was like a Hitchcockian peep show of the soul. She knelt and moved her face closer to the grille.

'This is kind of hot,' she let slip.

'I'm not sure that is the way this is supposed to start.'

'Why not? It's honest.'

'True. But . . .'

'OK. Confession do-over?' Lucy took a deep breath. And the mood within the cabinet changed. He leaned in closer to the screen and pressed his ear against it. 'I don't want this to come out the wrong way, but is there something wrong with me?'

'I'm not getting you.'

Sebastian barely got his thought out before she steamrolled over it, her frustration, barely kept in check until now, boiling over.

'You're always siding with them. I don't know if it's some kind of passive-aggressive thing to punish me for being ambitious or if you just hate me.'

'I don't hate you, Lucy.'

'People have all these false preconceptions about me. I'm not what they think.'

She was overwhelmed. The bruises, the storm. The tears, like her feelings, began to flow, slowly at first and then in torrents as she hunched over, heaved, and covered her mouth to keep the others from hearing.

'You don't have to change a thing for me or anyone.'

'I mean, we have much more in common. Don't tell them I said that, but it's so obvious, don't you think? I feel like we connected immediately. That never happens to me.'

Sebastian couldn't get a word out but thought it wouldn't matter even if he had. This was a one-way conversation for the moment.

'Besides,' she sobbed, 'I was here first!'

It was a childish rant but winning and heartfelt in its petulance.

'I'm not choosing anyone over you.'

She cleared her throat, a wild mood swing suddenly overtook her. She straightened her back. 'Good, because I still have my pride. I'm not here to play sister wives.'

The ultimatum hit Sebastian hard and hit him the wrong way.

'And this is not a brothel,' he said adamantly. 'Look into my eyes.'

She lifted her bloodshot orbs and matted lashes and connected with his through the small opening, like two lonely prisoners in adjoining cells.

'You are here for a reason.'

'I know I am. I'm here for you.'

He didn't answer.

It was not the validating response she was hoping for. She felt herself in competition now, in this place of all places, just like she was out there, in her everyday life. Lucy had hoped to hide out from the drama, to leave the game for a while, but it seemed to have followed her inside. As in her everyday life, she was determined not to lose.

'I'm putting myself out there for you. I need to know where I stand.'

'I couldn't choose among you. I won't.'

Rejection was foreign to Lucy. She hadn't been with many guys, but it was pretty much assumed that she could have her pick. And not just by her. *Jesse would kill to see me like this*, she thought, but it was a state that no man besides her dad had ever been able to put her in. Sebastian was making her work. Making her think. Making her feel.

'What are you doing to me? I'm not like this.'

'Like what?'

'Needy,' she leaned in and whispered.

'I need you, too.'

'Don't lie to me.'

'Never.'

'I'm confused. I want to trust you.'

'Then trust me.'

She picked up her votive, puckered her lips, and softly blew it out. And relaxed.

'When I was small, my grandmother would light a candle by my bed at night. After she was done tucking me in, she would let me blow it out. If the stream of smoke went down, it meant I was going to hell. If it went up, it meant that I was going to heaven. She made sure that it always went up by secretly blowing, steering it with her breath. I went to bed every night with a smile on my face. I believed her. Just like I believe you.'

Lucy looked down at the extinguished wick and noticed the smoke from it was rising. She could feel his breath blowing it. She moved in and brought her mouth to the screen. Loose and relaxed. She opened it slightly, seductively, pressing her lips against the grid.

He leaned forward.

Lucy shut her eyes.

He took his fingers and traced her lips through the screen.

Her tears fell on to the screen, forming tiny square prisms in their path.

'I'm just so tired of putting on a show.'

'Never apologize for who you are.'

'I hate hiding who I really am,' she said. 'I feel like you know what I mean.'

'I do.'

* * *

The drive to the pastoral residence in Queens was fraught with flooded roads and disabled streetlights, but Frey was determined. It was near closing time as he pulled into a parking space and walked quickly through the pouring rain toward the main entrance. The elderly receptionist had already diverted all incoming calls to voicemail and was gathering her things, preparing to retire to her room to wait out the storm, as the front doorbell buzzed. It was a grating sound, in stark contrast to the beauty of the nightly vesper bells that had just begun to ring out. Her first thought was that it must be something urgent to bring a person out in this weather. A sudden sickness requiring the administration of last rites perhaps, or a doctor making a house call.

'Monsignor Piazza, please.'

'Whom shall I say is calling?'

'An old friend. Alan Frey.'

A very odd time for a personal visit, but the look in the man's eyes told her it was both a matter of some importance and none of her business. 'I'll let him know. Just a moment.'

Frey waited impatiently. Dripping wet from the rain, he parked himself on a rubber welcome mat next to the coat rack and an umbrella stand in the wood-panelled entryway. He wished neither to stain the antique carpet beneath his feet nor leave any trace of his visit, regardless of how transitory. After a short while, a grandfather clock against the wall of the foyer caught his attention. The sense of time passing was suddenly

acutely noticeable to him. The countdown was maddening. He felt like a wrestler pinned to the canvas.

The receptionist excused herself hurriedly as the long, thin shadow of Monsignor Piazza appeared, preceding him into the room. The gaunt old priest limped slowly to the reception area as his waning eyesight confirmed the identity of the unexpected guest. A heavy wooden rosary swung from his hips, keeping time with both his twisted gait and the hallway timepiece, as he made his way across the marble lobby.

Piazza stood before the doctor silently, remembering every exchange between them, as he looked him over. The doctor stared back. The frail man before him had lost much of the regal bearing that had nearly earned him the bishop's seat. His thick white locks had thinned, his back was curved, his arms weak, legs unsteady, his cheeks hollowed, his eyes tired and milky. A spent force.

'Nice place, Father. I'm glad to see you are taken care of.'

'What do you want from me, Doctor?' the priest said tersely.

Frey gestured for the priest to walk with him into the soggy courtyard, protected only by a leafy pergola, as the harsh rain fell all around them. 'You don't still blame me for the church closing down, do you?'

'I blame myself. I lost my church. But I assume you haven't come here seeking forgiveness.'

'It is an urgent matter. The boy. Sebastian. You remember him.'

At the mention of Sebastian's name, the doctor noticed the monsignor's hands begin to shake, ever so slightly.

'He *was* a boy,' the priest said, the tone of regret unmistakable, 'when I sent him to you.'

'Older now, Father, but sadly not any wiser.'

The priest issued a tight smile at the suggestion of rebellion, a certain pride in his onetime charge breaking through.

'Is this the urgent news you have come to bring me on such a dangerous evening?'

'He has done a bad thing. Kidnapping. Murder.'

'I don't believe it.'

'Don't take my word for it. The police are involved and they believe it. But for this storm, they might have him in custody already.'

The priest's demeanour remained purposely impassive. 'Well, whatever it is, I am retired as you see. What would you have me do about it?'

'Do those in our line of work ever really retire, Father? It is a part of us, from beginning to end, is it not?'

'He is your patient.' Piazza waved dismissively.

'He *was* my patient. Now he is a fugitive.'

The statement seemed more an accusation to the priest, as if he might be hiding the boy.

'And you think I know where he is?' Piazza asked resentfully.

'That is what I came to ask you. You knew him better than anyone.'

The priest stared daggers at the sharp-dressed man before him. He had vowed to shepherd his flock, but Frey was definitely a lost sheep. Very lost.

'I should have never sent him to you.'

'I know it's an unpleasant topic . . .'

The priest chafed at the description. 'Unpleasant? A child's life destroyed? Betrayed by those he trusted. Yes, it is most unpleasant.'

'You did the right thing, Monsignor. He was unmanageable. Delusional. In desperate need of medical and psychiatric help.'

'Which you provided so successfully, I see.'

'As successfully as you, Father.'

The priest sat on the stone bench before a grotto centred around a statue of St Dominic, founder of his Order, patron saint of the falsely accused. He placed his face in his hands and exhaled deeply. 'He was telling the truth. But I didn't believe him,' the priest lamented.

'The truth? You are as insane as he is.'

'From the moment I foolishly entrusted him to your care, Precious Blood began to die. Without the chaplets, without Sebastian, the purpose of the church faded and was lost. I was lost. That is when I knew the legends were true. That he was right.'

'Not all was lost though, Father. My property partners and I were able to secure the structure and will soon put it to a much more practical use.'

'That *structure*, as you call it, was built on the graves of holy men with a holy purpose.'

'Yes, well, their mission was derailed, so to speak,' Frey shot back sarcastically.

'Yes, until Sebastian. He understood and tried to make others understand. A herald. But instead of being believed, he was betrayed.'

'These are ravings of that old lady who raised him.'

'She was a holy woman.'

'She was a witch. You said so yourself.'

Monsignor Piazza stood defiantly in her defence and Sebastian's.

'Not a witch. She practiced *Benedicaria*. The Way of Blessing. She passed this knowledge on to him.'

'Knowledge? This is medieval voodoo for the ignorant masses. She filled his impressionable mind with this nonsense. A lonely, orphaned boy wanting to feel special. The shame of it!'

Piazza looked at the physician with contempt.

'She filled him with faith and fire. He could recognize malevolence in others that even I could not. I see that now, and I pray that God forgives me for my blindness.'

'I'm not here to revisit the past with you, Monsignor. I don't have time.'

'Then why are you here really, Doctor? You don't think I'm hiding him in here, do you?'

'Before he escaped, he said there were others. Did he ever

discuss such a thing with you? Did he have friends or acquaintances he confided in?'

'*Others*,' the priest repeated, as if he had just received word of a miracle he'd waited for his whole life. 'As a priest, I couldn't tell you if he had. The seal of confession.'

'This is not the time for antiquated vows, Father,' Frey lectured. 'You care about the boy, don't you? About his well-being. He may not survive this if the police find him first. There may be hostages.'

The priest was rapidly tiring of the doctor's altruistic façade. He had been fooled once before.

'What will be left of him if you find him first?'

'Life is better than death, Monsignor.'

'Not at the cost of your soul, Doctor.'

'I can save him. Save him from himself.'

'Your compassion is most touching. After all, we wouldn't want make a martyr of him, so to speak.' The priest's voice dripped with the wry and combative condescension he had been known for in his younger days. Piazza had got under the doctor's skin. The veneer of civility torn asunder, Frey's frustration now drove him past the point of politeness.

'He is mad,' the doctor opined. 'Illnesses like these are contagious among the weak-willed, the vulnerable, the depressed, Father. Dangerous.'

'Dangerous to whom? You speak of the spread of faith like a disease.'

'All this talk about faith and souls. It is from a different time. Haven't we finally grown past this, Father?'

'I don't know. Have we? You seem quite troubled by something you don't believe.'

'Fairy stories! Lies! Meant to control the mind and behaviour of people for what? For money? Power?'

'Like the drugs you prescribe, Doctor, to alter minds and control behaviour. What do you fear from Sebastian that brings you here? Maybe the psychiatrist should ask himself that question.'

The doctor struggled to keep his composure. 'Show me a soul,' he railed. 'What does it look like? Feel like? Taste like? What does it weigh? Show me a soul and I'll believe you. And Sebastian.'

'Blessed are they who have not seen and yet have believed.'

'Blessed,' Frey mumbled. 'That's the problem, isn't it?'

'For you, Doctor. For me, a solution.'

'That old church was an eyesore, running on fumes for years, Monsignor. No one came and no one will miss it, thanks in large measure to your incompetence. It serves no purpose any longer except as a future apartment block for stockbrokers and their families. On which I expect to earn a substantial return.'

Monsignor Piazza took his argument under advisement and arrived at a different conclusion. He knew now that Precious Blood had retained its purpose, even if it had a congregation of only one. Or four.

'Perhaps you are right,' he said. 'Perhaps not.'

'Look around you,' Frey suggested, pointing out the antique furnishings of the residence. 'Your time has passed.'

'I'll reserve my right to a second opinion, Doctor,' the Monsignor replied defiantly, a sly smile crossing his lips. 'I think we are done. I know you. I know your kind. You will not get what you seek from me. Not this time.'

'The decision to turn the boy over was yours; don't blame me,' Frey said. 'It is too late for regret now.'

'It's never too late.'

The vesper bells ceased. Piazza blessed himself and his unwelcome guest as he departed.

'Don't waste your time,' Frey scoffed.

HEADS
WILL ROLL

For those who see things differently,
The ones who think they know.
For those who want more to be,
Than all that was for show.
Craving excess more and more,
The drug of the trend.
Pain and suffering left empty,
Pray black hearts to mend.
Speaking in tongues of whispers,
Worry what they say.
It's the way you see it,
There is no other way.
Remove the shadows from my sight,
This I pray to thee.
Once I was blind, But now I am me.

LUCY, PRAY FOR US.

LUCY

Patron Saint of the Blind

WATCH
ME BURN

Call me crazy in the head,
I've been called far worse.
But I can't help whom I love,
Evil eyes a curse.
You will keep me from him,
His heart is my heart.
You think this is the end,
But it's only just the start.
So, lock me up, throw it away,
All your hopes and dreams.
Mine, they belong to,
He will burn through me.
Let this bloody tear be a reminder,
When I decided to be free,
You cannot choose whom you love,
It is love that will choose thee.

AGNES PRAY FOR US.

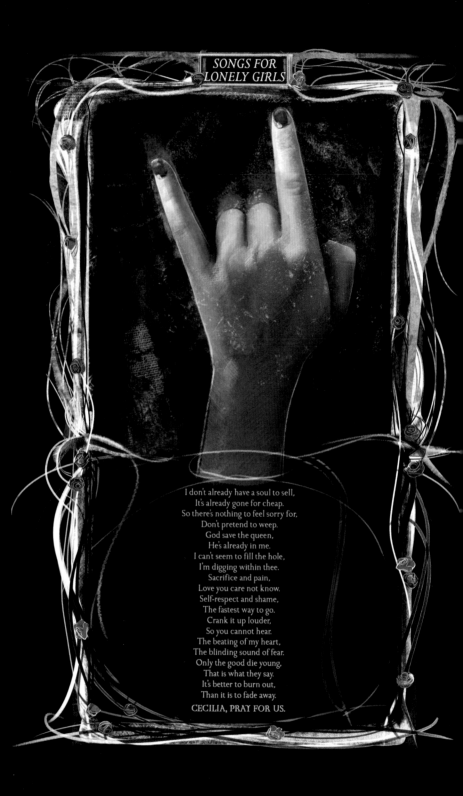

SONGS FOR
LONELY GIRLS

I don't already have a soul to sell,
It's already gone for cheap.
So there's nothing to feel sorry for,
Don't pretend to weep.
God save the queen,
He's already in me.
I can't seem to fill the hole,
I'm digging within thee.
Sacrifice and pain,
Love you care not know.
Self-respect and shame,
The fastest way to go.
Crank it up louder,
So you cannot hear.
The beating of my heart,
The blinding sound of fear.
Only the good die young,
That is what they say.
It's better to burn out,
Than it is to fade away.
CECILIA, PRAY FOR US.

13

The Labyrinth Walk

As the grey light of late afternoon squeezed past the edges of the warping window boards, the Church of the Precious Blood was revealed in all of its decrepit glory. Sebastian was sitting silently in front of the church. Agnes and Cecilia walked the perimeter of the nave and were soon joined by Lucy, who appeared to have an honesty hangover. They stopped to notice odd markings on the wall, fourteen in all, evenly spaced and about head-high, shapes more than anything else but not instantly recognizable until Agnes put it together. These were shadows burned into the plaster walls, bordered now by peeling paint and sawdust, following decades of exposure to the rising and setting sun.

'The Stations,' Agnes said.

'The Stations of the Cross,' Lucy added.

'Stations of the Lost, more like,' Cecilia nodded, noting the missing icons.

'I don't get it,' Lucy said out loud, shaking her head. 'Never did.'

Something they could all agree on.

'A man is humiliated, tortured, and killed for what?' Lucy pondered. 'So a pretend rabbit can crap a basket of chocolate-covered crème eggs and jelly beans.'

'You could say there is beauty in suffering,' Agnes said almost wistfully, calling attention, however unwittingly, to her self-inflicted wounds. 'And sacrifice.'

'You're not comparing yourself, are you? We're not talking curfew fights with your mom or issues with your boyfriend here,' Lucy said, pointing up to the VI standing out from the faded paint around it. 'This is anguish on a whole different level.'

'Talk about carrying the weight of the world,' Cecilia said, scrutinizing each image as they continued walking. 'Puts your own problems in perspective.'

'You think . . . ?' Lucy said.

They began their walk, as Sebastian watched from the head altar, finishing up a makeshift meal for them.

I, II . . .

Cecilia stopped at number two. She stood there in front of an

image of this holy, loving man carrying a cross through a crowd of people. A heavy burden that he so willingly took on. Being lashed and spat on.

III, IV, V, VI . . .

Agnes stopped at number six. She sat down in the pew in front of it. She stared at an image of a beautiful woman, on her knees, in front of Jesus, who was suffering, carrying his cross. She was holding up a gauzy white veil, about to wipe his beautiful face.

'That's all she had. All she could do. And that gave him strength,' she said in amazement.

VII, VIII, IX, X . . .

Lucy was stricken by number ten. Jesus was stripped of his garments. How humiliating it must have been for him, being stripped almost naked, flesh on his cloak because he was so mangled from his journey, stripped of his dignity. As they prepared his cross in front of him. He would die with no worldly possessions.

After a meditative moment of silence, they gathered together again and continued their walk.

XI, XII . . .

'This,' Lucy realized suddenly, at number twelve, 'is what I was talking about. This is big.'

Jesus Dies on the Cross.

'Jesus Christ, superstar?' Agnes chided. 'Is that your point?'

'I did that in middle school. I was Mary Magdalene,' Cecilia said with a shrug.

'Shocker,' Lucy said, then suddenly reached again for her brow and fell backward on to the wall behind her.

'This symbol of the cross is recognizable to everyone for all time. You see it and you instantly know the story. You feel something. You understand,' Agnes said.

'The difference between a flash in the pan and eternal fame,' Lucy said. 'Talk about branding.'

'There's *meaning*,' Cecilia said. 'Everyone can relate to suffering and sacrifice to some degree.'

Lucy felt a sharp shooting pain behind her eye pulse and then spend itself, leaving a path of stars in its wake, like the last gasp of a July Fourth sparkler. Cecilia reached to hold her up, but Lucy waved her away.

'That's a nasty-looking bruise,' Cecilia observed. 'I wish we had some ice.'

'I'm OK.' Lucy staggered into a seat in a pew and stared up at the wall she'd just been leaning against. It had to be a mixture of last night and the Stations. She remembered being frightened by them as a child. It was like some sort of horrific flipbook, watching a man unjustly accused, convicted, humiliated, tortured, and nailed to a cross. It all seemed so inevitable, a condition she'd been fighting her entire life. In fact, nothing scared her more. 'He was the Son of God. How could he let

himself get sucker punched like that?' Lucy murmured. 'I mean, Jesus Christ already.'

'The fix was in,' Cecilia said. 'He played the hand he was dealt.'

'And he knew it,' Sebastian added, coming up behind them. His face hardened as he stared at theirs. The look of distress was plain. He joined them for the last two Stations.

XIII . . .

Jesus is Taken Down from the Cross. They beheld a gorgeous painting in front of them, of Jesus, now with a gold halo, being caressed by his loved ones. Prayed over. Adored.

'I do love how they take the agony and suffering of the reality and mythologize it in such a beautiful, glorified way,' Cecilia said. 'It's just a story anyway.'

'Yeah, but a good one,' Sebastian said.

'*Greatest Story Ever Told*,' Agnes added.

'So they say.' Lucy nodded.

'One that people were once willing to die for,' Sebastian said.

'And kill for,' CeCe added, noting the other side of the coin.

'Religions are just like people. Some good, some not,' Sebastian said. 'Like everything else. Can't blame Jesus for all of it.'

'There are assholes everywhere,' CeCe said.

'A sermon we can all get behind,' he concurred.

'You know the old priest in *The Exorcist* played Jesus in that movie, *The Greatest Story Ever Told*. I met him at a premiere,' Lucy added.

'Only you would name-drop Jesus,' Cecilia said.

XIV . . .

Jesus Was Laid in His Tomb.

As they reached the last station, Lucy was feeling detached, not from the others, but from her body. She wasn't totally sure if she was there, or anywhere at all. She felt like she was floating, watching the whole scene play out from about three metres above the ground. It happened to her sometimes at crowded clubs, but never in a quiet, laid-back situation like this. It wasn't just Lucy. They were all starting to feel strange. The wind pounded, the thunder rolled and lightning flashed, but it was a less violent sound, coming from the church entrance, that really got their attention. Especially Sebastian's.

'Who's that?' Agnes said, on high alert.

The church door slid open just a crack but it was loud enough for the occupants to hear. The girls instinctively crouched down behind the pews; they did not want to be found. Sebastian remained standing, like a shaft rising from the floor.

'Are you expecting someone else?' Lucy whispered over to him.

'No.'

A lone figure hobbled through the vestibule and into the church, pushed forward by the wind, undeterred by the darkness. Even in the dark, Sebastian could tell the man was slight, frail, probably old, far too old to brave these elements at this twilight hour.

Sebastian kept watch.

The girls could hear the anonymous footsteps approaching.

'Who is it?' Lucy whispered nervously.

The man moved slowly, but confidently, forward. He clearly knew his way around. Sebastian recognized his walk, his outline, even in the candlelight.

'Father Piazza.'

He stopped and turned his head from side to side, up and down, peering out into the darkness. Looking like someone who'd returned to his hometown after many years, only to find it changed, altered, but not completely beyond recognition. Just enough of it remaining to reminisce over or mourn for. He hadn't been back since the church had been deconsecrated and his parishioners scattered to other churches, not even to see it from the outside. But now he had to come, even in such a horrific storm. Risking his own life if it were the last thing he ever did. Piazza recalled his tepid effort to save the church and the congregation from the developers and his relief that he had failed. He was preparing for retirement after all, and even the diocese was in no mood to increasingly subsidize yet another money-losing facility. Sebastian had been the last piece of

unresolved business for him. He loved the boy and tried hard, along with the city caseworker, to find a good home for him in the community. Time after time, he tried. Time after time, he failed. Sebastian was becoming *increasingly unstable. Acting out. Talking crazy. Blasphemy.* Making himself unwelcome to even the most sympathetic foster family. Because of depression over his grandmother's death, teenage hormones, or something far more serious, the priest could not be sure. *What else could he have done*, he thought, *but do as he did?* Piazza accessed the network of upper-crust physicians he'd befriended over the years on the boy's behalf. Frey's reputation was impeccable. If anyone could turn the boy around, bring him some peace, it was he.

The monsignor sighed resignedly. His shoulders slumped as he exhaled, continuing down the aisle. The place was a shambles. The hand-cut and tumbled marble and terrazzo floors were covered in dirt, ornately carved and finished wooden pews torn from their anchors and piled up against the side entrances, scaffolds rose to heights only the voices of the faithful had once reached, skids were piled with gypsum board and plumbing in front of empty pedestals where brightly painted statues of holy men and women were once worshipped. Who could he blame for this? For Sebastian?

Only himself.

The old priest approached the altar, step by step, until he reached the centre of the church, where he genuflected, crossed himself, bowed his head, fell to his knees, and clasped his hands in fervent, whispered prayer.

'quia peccavi nimis
cogitatione, verbo
opere et omissione'

'What is he saying?' Lucy asked.

'He's confessing,' Sebastian explained, eyes fixed on the penitent priest.

Piazza halted and beat his chest with his fist one time, the deafening thud of his arthritic hand against his breastbone like a body falling from a building.

'*Mea culpa.*'

And again:

'*Mea culpa.*'

And for a final time, nearly in tears.

'*MEA MAXIMA CULPA.*'

Father Piazza rose and stared straight ahead at the altar and the silhouette of Sebastian before him.

'Sebastian!' he called out with all his strength.

Agnes panicked. 'How does he know you're here?'

'Quiet,' Cecilia said, bringing her hand to Agnes's mouth.

'Yes, Father.'

'Your path is a lonely one made lonelier by my acts.'

'I'm not alone,' Sebastian said. 'I never was.'

Lucy, Cecilia, and Agnes rose from behind the pew. Confused by the exchange, but no longer feeling the need to hide. The priest could not see their faces, but the chaplets gleamed around their wrists in the dim light.

Father Piazza was overwhelmed.

'They will be coming for you.'

'I know.'

'I am sorry,' Piazza said, his voice cracking with emotion.

Sebastian let the words echo around the cavernous space until they faded to nothing.

The monsignor raised his shaking hand in blessing, as he had countless times before within the hallowed walls of Precious Blood, and made the sign of the cross.

'Peace be with you,' Sebastian said.

'And with your spirit.' The priest bowed his head to Sebastian, then to the girls, and turned and walked away. A procession of one. Back from whence he came.

'Father,' Sebastian called out. 'Did you forget something?'

'Yes.' The priest stopped, looked at all of them standing there. He would take them and any information about them to his grave. 'Everything.'

14

Immaculate Deception

'That was . . . strange,' Lucy rasped.

'A man praying?' Sebastian shot back tersely.

'You know what I mean,' Lucy pushed back. 'For an old man to come out in a storm like this, it must have been important.'

'Yeah, a matter of life and death,' Cecilia said. 'He really risked it out there.'

'Who is he?' Agnes asked, her curiosity piqued.

'His name is Piazza. He was the pastor here for many years. He just made the most important trip he'll ever make.'

'Did you know him well?' Agnes asked gently.

'I thought so,' Sebastian responded, the hurt and betrayal in his voice unmistakable.

'Are you in some kind of trouble?' Cecilia asked him protectively. 'You can tell us.'

She recalled how wary he'd looked at the hospital when they first met.

'He said people are coming for you?' Agnes pressed. 'Is it the police?'

'It's nothing I can't handle.'

'*We*,' Agnes stressed. 'Whatever or whoever it is, we can handle it.'

'Together,' Cecilia said.

Even Lucy joined in. 'I know people who can probably help. Whatever it is.'

'That means everything to me,' Sebastian said at their willingness to be there for him, and more importantly, their camaraderie.

A melancholy expression of happiness and regret shone from him. Sebastian rubbed at his temples and stood up, putting a full stop on the question-and-answer session. As if he'd received a cue he'd been waiting for.

'Where are you going?' Agnes asked.

Sebastian didn't answer, continuing on his way. They watched him disappear into the darkness enshrouding the back of the church and up the staircase, his boot heels scraping as he went along.

'Do you think all this is about the bracelets?' Lucy asked.

'I think we're about to find out,' Cecilia said.

'I don't want to leave here,' Agnes said. 'Until I know.'

The answer was in Agnes's eyes. It was in all of their eyes. They were committed to staying.

'I think there's one day of darkness left to find out,' Lucy said, recalling the weather report from her cab ride. 'Something's definitely wrong.'

'He looks worried,' Agnes added.

'For himself?' Cecilia asked. 'Or us?'

'Stalk to me.' The familiar greeting was shorter and the synthetic voicemail beep that followed longer than either needed to be, and more abrasive, Jesse thought. He wasn't used to leaving messages for Lucy that went unanswered. Despite their personal loathing for each other, or at least hers for him, they had an understanding. But it had been two days now without a reply and with this torrential storm causing so much damage already and now the tornado definitely coming, he was thinking the worst.

'This mailbox is full and can no longer receive new messages,' came the disembodied robo rap.

Jesse checked the number to see that he'd dialled correctly, which was moot since she was on his speed dial. Stubbornly as ever, he dialled again. Finally, the phone actually rang instead of going straight to voicemail.

'Yo?' came the greeting in a gravelly Brooklyn accent, a man's voice.

The connection was weak and filled with static and delay, making it hard to talk or hear.

'Where's Lucy?' Jesse sat up in his chair and leaned forward.

'Who's Lucy?'

'Who the hell are you?' Jesse asked. 'Where is she?'

'She's right here, loser,' the man said. 'I'll flip her around so she can talk to you.'

A wave of intense jealousy, more than anxiety, swept over Jesse as he pictured his protégé getting off with some Gravesend guido.

'Listen, asshole, I don't know who you are or where Lucy is, but I promise you the cops will be there before you get your jacket on.'

'Take it easy, man, I'm messin' wit you. I found dis phone in da street outside Sacrifice. Grabbed it just before da storm started. I work der.'

'Then I should have your ass fired.'

The air of superiority finally echoed clearly enough through the phone to cause the guy to worry.

'Shit, is dis Jesse? It's Tony. Y'know, Anthony Esposito. Security.'

'You mean the bouncer.' Jesse sniffed condescendingly.

'Yea, it's me,' Tony confirmed resentfully.

Jesse left out 'tipster'. Most of his best stories came from Tony's texts, if not from Lucy.

'That's Lucy's phone you're on.'

'Wow. Lucky Lucy's phone. It was all blinged out, but I had no idea whose it was. The keypad was locked. It looked like a chick's phone, so I figured I'd hang on to it and hold it for piece-of-ass ransom.'

'What did you do with her?' Jesse asked, getting increasingly angry. 'Where is she?'

'How da hell should I know?' Tony said. 'What? You think she's dead or somethin'?'

'When was the last time you saw her?'

'Same as you probably. Few nights ago. The night I found da phone, matter a fact. She ran outta da club and got'n a cab, I think. I don't know for sure. Tell ya da truth, I haven't seen or heard from any regulars since da storm. We ain't friggin' been open. Just waitin' for the finale. Tornado dey say. Can you believe dat one?'

Jesse fixated gleefully on the mental image of all the assholes he wrote about being carried away by a stiff wind, washing up bloated and blue on some rocky coastline far away. All except Lucy, of course.

'Ya dere?' Tony asked.

'Yeah, maybe she's stuck somewhere,' Jesse said pensively, trying to convince himself more than anything.

'Ya know what dey say. No news is good news, I guess.'

'Not for me,' Jesse retorted. 'Or you, for that matter.'

Leave it to this little prick, Tony thought, to screw with his livelihood, his 'rat' money, as he called it. He was already out

two days' pay from the storm.

'Not for nothin', I was just tryin' ta do da right t'ing. I'll leave da phone at da coat check Lost and Found for ya as soon as dis joint reopens. Between us, *capiche*? I'm just not sure when. It's a mess down here. Water damage, broken glass. All kinds a shit.'

'If you hear anything, let me know,' Jesse said, suddenly distracted by his call waiting.

'I always do,' Tony said, gritting his teeth.

Sebastian climbed the spiral staircase up to the old bell tower, two at a time, almost sucked upward by the vacuum building in the stairwell. He was reluctant to leave them, even for a few moments, but he could feel the time running out. Making his way through the scattered boards, beams, and rusting remnants of bronze window grilles that blocked his path, he reached the top and took a deep breath of the murky air hanging about him.

From the belfry, he surveyed the brownstones below through an angry sky as the dark and threatening clouds skimmed the Borough of Churches. The stained-glass had been shattered and unreplaced from the tracery, the steel lattice swayed uncertainly around him, several windows already uncovered by the gale force winds that continued to batter them. Colourful shards from the broken panes littered the floor of the tower and main roof beneath him. The splinters glittered and blinked like

Christmas lights. *Those lights*, he thought, *usually herald a joyous occasion, but not these.*

The tower had been unused for years, long before the building had been closed by the diocese and targeted by the local developers. It didn't even have a bell. *Why bother*, he considered, *calling people to prayer who weren't coming anyway?*

He stood waiting, like a sentry, like some twenty-first century Quasimodo, keeping watch over his decrepit domain and his three Esmeraldas. They were together now. He felt their presence not just around him, but inside of him as surely as he had at the hospital that night. The night he got away from Frey. Got to them. He could have never imagined that would be the easy part. He wanted to tell them everything but knew he could not. But the time was drawing near. Would they even believe him?

Sebastian strained to eye the harbour in the distance and Manhattan beyond, enshrouded in a light fog that was rolling toward him, across the East River to the piers that stretched along the coastline from Red Hook to Vinegar Hill. From this stone-and-mortar perch above, he imagined himself the captain of a besieged vessel, charged with transporting precious cargo to a far distant shore through stormy seas and jagged reefs. Surrounded by enemy ships, unseen but ever present.

Much easier to spy from this vantage point was the design of the church directly beneath him. From the inside, the church simply appeared huge and cavernous. So familiar and like all

other churches in that little thought was ever given to its blueprint. But up here, the purpose was more evident. Transepts stretched outward, like open arms, on either side from the nave, or centre portion of the building. It was in the shape of a cross. The obvious reason, he figured, was so that God could see it from heaven, but he had another sort of surveillance in mind just then. They were coming for him, and soon. That, he was sure of.

It would be so much easier to just end it right here. To take a dive. To just spread my arms wide, close my eyes, and tip over gracefully, he thought, *like one of those novelty-shop birds that endlessly nosedives for a drink of water.* The bird, however, continued dipping. He wouldn't be so fortunate. Not that he hadn't considered it often throughout the endless days he'd spent locked up in Dr Frey's asylum, demoralized, disbelieved, watching from the 'penthouse' windows as the scaffolding went up around Precious Blood. But even then, he knew he didn't have the luxury of suicide, and with so much at stake, his own suffering hardly mattered. He'd accepted that when he'd accepted himself. He still had much to do. Much to tell them about who he is, who they are, and why they were there. And nothing and nobody was going to stop him. He felt he had little choice in the things that had happened, but he had at least that much. He had his spirit.

Sebastian watched for a long time, hoping for his mind to empty along with the streets. Freeze-framed memories as jagged as the glass at his feet replayed and sliced at his conscience, haunting him, driving him to his knees. He was so overcome, he could barely feel the fragments cutting holes in his jeans and grinding into his skin. Time had become so fluid. It might have been weeks ago or hours. He saw himself dragged into the psych ward, restrained, sedated, evaluated. Involuntarily. Like a frog specimen in biology class, poked, prodded, and about to be shocked in and out of consciousness. Erased.

He relived it every time he closed his eyes. An endless loop of misery. The cuffs, the interrogations masquerading as therapy, the stark white room, the ECT machine, Dr Frey's poker face, the orderly's powerful grip.

'*Am I keeping you from something?*'

'*Yes.*'

'*Do you know why you are here?*'

'*You're the doctor. You tell me.*'

'*Mania, delusion, depression, paranoia.*'

'*All lies.*'

'*Denial.*'

'*I don't belong here.*'

'*Where do you belong?*'

'*With them.*'

'*With who? The priests? Father Piazza?*'

'*No, he didn't believe me either. You know that. He sent me here, didn't he?*'

'*He just wanted what's best for you. As we all do.*'

221

'You mean what's best for you.'

He remembered how Dr Frey's face tightened. He wasn't used to being challenged, let alone doubted. His irritation was palpable, unlike the calm and cool demeanour he regularly wore as he strolled through the hospital corridors and awards dinners. He was used to being treated with respect, with deference. He'd earned it. Degrees in medicine, psychology, sociology; he was a scientist, as credentialled as they come. And a humanitarian. He barely had enough shelf space in the lobby for the honours he'd been granted. Sebastian was paraded by them with the other patients every day. Taking Frey's victory lap for him. The first stop on the psych ward tour.

He had not been in much of a mood to take any lip from this punk kid with a messianic complex. He had tried to maintain the analytical cool for which he was renowned, but Sebastian was getting to him.

'You arrived with only these three sets of beads when you were placed here. Removed from the old chapel beneath Precious Blood.'

'Souvenirs. The place was shutting down. What's the problem?'

'Stolen property. Isn't that a sin?'

'I didn't steal. I took only what I needed.'

'Needed?'

'They took them away from me. Afraid I'd hang myself, or stuff them all in my mouth and suffocate.'

'You don't present as the suicidal type, Sebastian.'

'Then give them back.'

'Why do you want them so badly?'

'Why do you care?'

'Perhaps it will help me to understand you better.'

'Haven't they told you, Doctor? I'm the spiritual type.'

'So I've heard.'

'Is that an illness now?'

'All depends, Sebastian.'

'If you want to help me, let me have them. Might just chill me out. Isn't that what you want?'

'We could change that if you wouldn't continue to refuse medication.'

'I'm fine with who I am.'

'And who are you?'

'You wouldn't believe me if I told you.'

'Try me.'

The orderly was taking notes for some reason but not for Sebastian's official medical file. Frey was keeping two sets of records on him.

'Not enough in there to condemn me yet? To lock me away for good?'

'I'm not here to judge you. The courts made their decision.'

'On your authority, your testimony, Doctor.'

'And Father Piazza's. He referred you here to begin with.'

'Had me arrested and committed, you mean. At your recommendation.'

'For your own good.'

'You've got people everywhere, haven't you? Even the clergy.'

'He knew you as a boy. Saw you steal the relics from the chapel, Sebastian. Need I go on?'

'I wanted to be heard.'

'He heard you. Your ravings. Your delusions. There was no choice but to put you here. I didn't seek you out.'

'No fingerprints, isn't that right, Doctor? You didn't convict me and you aren't here to judge me.'

'More delusions. You are sick, Sebastian.'

'That's how it works, isn't it? No secret handshake, no clubhouse, no uniforms. Just a confederacy of the like-minded in positions of power and those they can use for their evil purpose.'

'Seems you have it all worked out.'

'I know all about you. It was revealed to me. Everything.'

'You've been here three years, Sebastian. Don't you think it's time you shared that revelation with me? Or are you afraid?'

'I'm not the one who's afraid.'

'Unburden yourself and we can stop this. Why don't you tell me?'

'Because you know. Don't try to make a fool out of me.'

'I'm not here to mock you.'

'No, you're here to eliminate me.'

'No, to help you.'

'It doesn't matter. There will be others.'

'Others? Who? Where?'

'Closer than you think, but why would I tell you?'

'You can talk to me. Anything you say will be kept in confidence.'

'Forgive me for not believing a damn thing you say.'

'The doctor-patient relationship is sacred, Sebastian.'

'Sacred? That's funny. Father Piazza said the same thing.' Sebastian's face twisted up in loathing at the very thought.

'You'll feel much better when this is over.'

'Do you always do these procedures so late at night, Doctor? On a weekend, when no one is around? With a patient in street clothes?'

'Take hold of him.'

'Why are you so threatened by me? Is it because you believe me? Is that it?'

The doctor nodded at the attendant to begin.

'Is this your idea of treatment?'

'We've tried everything else.'

'Trying to get me closer to God, Doctor?'

'No, to sanity, Sebastian.'

Sebastian could still feel the struggle. His muscles flexed, cramped, as he remembered being dragged, inch by inch, toward the table. The restraints hung loosely, waiting for arms and legs. The IVs were bloated with anesthesia and hungry for his veins. The rubber bite plate sitting on the metal tray next to the stretcher sat idle in anticipation of his clenched teeth.

'You'll need more than one guy to help you.'

The arrogant smirk on the orderly's face suggested otherwise.

'Sicarius is nearby if I need him.'

'On a leash?'

'Sedate him.'

'*Relax. Just a little pinprick and you won't remember a thing.*' The orderly approached Sebastian, who evaded his grasp. Sebastian spun him around facing the doctor and put him in a vise grip headlock. The orderly struggled and gagged, flailing his arms, his face turning red, then purple, and then a ghostly white as Sebastian continued to apply pressure with all his strength. Sebastian stared directly at the doctor, who did nothing, as the lackey was on the verge of unconsciousness. A final silent squeeze of Sebastian's arm, and the orderly slipped helplessly to the floor.

'*Well done,*' the doctor said. '*Now you are not just psychotic, you are a murderer.*'

'*He's not dead.*'

Sebastian rushed at Frey and slammed him against the wall, pinning him there with his forearm pressed hard against the doctor's throat. He didn't resist.

'*Is it my turn now?*' Frey taunted.

'*The chaplets,*' Sebastian demanded.

Frey handed them over.

Sebastian reached into the doctor's pocket and took his keys and removed the battery from his mobile phone. He stepped out quietly and locked Frey in the treatment room.

'*Go ahead and scream for Sicarius now,*' Sebastian shouted. '*Him, I will gladly kill.*'

'*Does killing evil make you yourself evil?*'

'*That's just what I'd do. I'm not the judge.*'

'*I'll see you again, Sebastian,*' he said through the thick glass window of the metal door.

'*God help you if you do, Doctor.*'

He could see Jude's sweet face poke out of his room, startled by the unusual late-night commotion. The boy was clearly frightened for him. They'd got close in the time they'd both spent on the ward, despite the age difference. Sebastian had become like a big brother. He pointed in the direction of Sicarius's room, a silent warning, but Sebastian waved him off. If Frey had intended to bring out the big gun, it would have been done already.

Sebastian kissed one of the chaplets and tossed it to Jude.

'*Give it to her for me,*' Sebastian said. '*And be careful.*'

The boy nodded, not needing any further instruction.

'*You. Be. Careful,*' Jude said haltingly, his eyes squinting and lips trembling.

'*I won't forget this,*' Sebastian said, rushing for the stairwell. '*Remember everything I told you.*'

Jude smiled and pulled his head back inside his room.

A giant wind gust followed by the loudest silence he'd ever heard knocked Sebastian back into the moment. The air around him crackled and his ears clogged painfully and then popped, sending him sprawling off balance to the deck of the tower.

He rose slowly to his feet, fighting a stiff wind.

However painful the recollection of his captivity, he was proud that he'd got away from Frey. Against all odds, he'd escaped and had nearly fulfilled his mission.

Sebastian raised his fists in triumph, challenging the wind and the rain, daring the lightning to strike him.

The old tower began to quiver violently from the wind and sonic assault from the thunder, shaking loose mortar from between the stones and some of the fairy dust from his memories. At once, he felt a sickness in his stomach. Not from what he'd accomplished but from what he'd missed, what he'd overlooked. Had he really escaped after all or had his hubris in that moment clouded his judgment? He replayed the scene over and over in his mind, trying to make some sense of it. Frey didn't resist. Why? And then it struck him. Hard as the impending tornado bearing down on Precious Blood.

'What have I done?' he repeated, dropping his head into hands, allowing himself a rare moment of doubt and self-pity.

A sudden burning across his arms and legs. The coloured glass, splintered timber, and finishing nails that had been lying at his feet began to swirl upward like a vortex in a hurricane force gust, almost revolving around him like a swarm of hungry mosquitoes. The storm was upon him. He covered up as plywood and planks crashed down relentlessly in the belfry around him, knocking him to the cement floor. It was loud as a battlefield, but the only sound Sebastian could hear was the sound of his own voice, filled with a painful realization. He had put the girls in more danger than he could have ever imagined.

'Oh, my God. Frey could have stopped me. He *let* me go.'

15

Faith Rape

'It's getting really dark,' Agnes said, noting that things got strangely still for a moment. 'Where is he?'

CeCe wondered the same. 'Maybe I should—'

The crashing sound in the bell tower reverberated through the church below as beams weakened from the renovation and from the storm, blew around like toothpicks. The organ began to play, random keys triggered by the shaking and falling ceiling plaster. Torrents of water were breaking through the roof, turning the balcony into an indoor waterfall.

'Tornado!' Lucy screamed, steadying herself as the entire church seemed to roll from back to front, side to side.

Cecilia stumbled to the vestibule and yelled up the stairwell to no avail. Debris and plaster dust from above tumbled down like vomit covering the railing, the steps, and her boots. She sucked in a mouthful of grit and began to choke on it. Plaster dust filled her sinuses and nasal cavity. Red faced and runny-nosed, she yelled up as loudly as she could. 'Sebastian!' She strained to listen for a reply but none came. She was about to race up after him, when Lucy grabbed her from behind. 'Let me go! He might be hurt.'

'You might *get* hurt,' Lucy chided, sensing something desperately wrong.

'I'm not going to let him die up there.'

'We need to stay together. Or we'll die down here.' Lucy looked up and pointed. Huge pieces of plaster were cracking along the vestibule ceiling directly overhead.

'Run!' CeCe shouted, pulling Lucy along through the nave and nearly out of her peep-toes.

All hell was breaking loose outside and in.

A whoosh of wind and the plywood from upper windows began to creak and shake loose. The entire church was transformed into a giant wind tunnel as the twister came ever closer. They felt the oxygen ripped from their lungs. It was breathtaking, literally.

Windowpanes in the clerestory, already cracked and fragile from construction jackhammers, dropped shards of glass over the sills and into the aisles, hitting the floor and detonating just inches behind their heels, turning the onetime house of

worship into a real-time house of terror. Scaffolding swayed in the stiff draft and collapsed like small buildings during a demolition. CeCe and Lucy grabbed for their heads as they raced toward the altar, their calves imbedded with splinters and sharp, multicoloured fragments of leaded glass, covered in grime and dripping blood.

The wind and rain blasted through the open window casements and chased them down the centre aisle almost the entire length of the church. Cecilia motioned to Agnes up ahead, hugging the marble communion rails for dear life, and the girls dived for the relative safety of the pews before any more of the doomed edifice crashed down. Cecilia covered Agnes with her body, protecting her from the falling boards and glass, like a soldier taking a bullet for a comrade.

'I thought I'd be safe here!' Agnes screamed.

'You are,' Cecilia said. 'I got you.'

'I feel like we're under attack!' Lucy shouted back.

Cecilia made the decision to fall back. 'We gotta get out of this place.'

'And go where? For a ride on the cyclone out there? In the pitch-black?' Lucy challenged. 'Are you nuts?'

Cecilia wiped at the warm liquid dripping down her legs and tasted it. It was blood. She eyed Agnes's wraps. 'The sacristy. Follow me.'

They bolted for the sacristy door, Cecilia dragging Agnes,

and Lucy, expensive heels now in hand, fell in quickly behind.

Sisters-in-arms running for cover. Racing the storm and running for their lives. Sloshing through puddled rain and over muddy marble floors. Their bare feet unable to gain any traction on the slippery tile beneath them.

Agnes slipped out of Cecilia's moistened grasp and tripped over a few pieces of wood littering the aisle, landing on her hands and letting out a loud cry.

Lucy stopped and lifted Agnes to her feet in an adrenaline rush of strength, much as Sebastian had lifted her. She was careful not to pull at her wrists.

'C'mon,' Lucy shouted, helping Agnes along.

Cecilia reached for the door and flung it open, Agnes ducked in and then Lucy slammed it closed behind them, shutting the worst of the storm out, at least for that moment. The quiet was a relief.

'Can you move any slower?' Lucy exhaled in frustration at Agnes. 'We should have left you back there.'

'I'm sorry. I did my best,' Agnes said, throwing her matted mane away from her face. 'Thanks for helping me.'

'Hey,' Cecilia called over, signalling Lucy not to push it. 'Chill.'

'No, I'm the one who's sorry,' Lucy offered apologetically.

'It's OK,' Agnes said, leaning her head on Lucy's shoulder.

The physical contact took Lucy off guard. She hadn't let a girlfriend close enough to touch her, let alone console her, for

a long time. If ever. She reached out for Agnes and slipped her hands under her thick mane and around both sides of her face. 'I'd never do you like that,' Lucy whispered.

Agnes kneeled down and brushed her fingers along both girls' legs, feeling for bits of glass, which she picked out gently one by one from each of them. She wiped at the tiny cuts with the gauze from her wrappings. 'Not exactly sanitary,' Agnes said, 'but it's the best I can do.'

Cecilia and Lucy scanned the room from floor to ceiling. Flaking paint, bubbling plaster, water damage, and mould creeping along the walls and ceiling signalled to them that Agnes was more than a little right.

Lucy looked down at the wraps around Agnes's wrists and saw they were looking wet and stained not just with their blood, but with Agnes's own.

'We should probably change those,' Lucy said. 'How are your arms?'

'They hurt.'

Lucy reached for Agnes's forehead as she stood up, to get a sense of her temperature, and noticed her skin felt cool and clammy. She could feel that Agnes was getting increasingly unsteady on her feet by how tightly she was beginning to hold her arm. The November daylight was fading fast as the storm was waxing once again. Without even the cold white glow of the corner streetlamps, still silenced by the blackout, night was falling unchallenged.

Cecilia proceeded to light the votives stacked on the cabinet from her single taper and positioned them throughout the room, turning the walls into funhouse mirrors of flickering shadows.

Agnes appeared flushed and sweaty.

'Let me get a look at them,' Lucy said. 'Cecilia, can you bring that candle closer?'

Lucy rubbed at her eyes, which were blurry now and watery from the dust and mildew. Agnes winced as Lucy untied the knotted fabric holding the wraps on. The black threads that cinched the wounds together were shiny in the light, and the edges of the cuts were still red, raw and oozing. Unhealed. It was in that stage where it wasn't possible to tell if she was getting better or worse.

Lucy made an amateur but accurate diagnosis. 'That's not looking too good.'

'Don't scare her,' Cecilia whispered harshly.

'Maybe you should leave?' Lucy pressed. 'Go back to the hospital.'

'No!' Agnes shouted, mustering every bit of strength.

'She's not going anywhere in this weather. Who even knows if there is a hospital left,' Cecilia said, taking charge. 'Let's just keep the wounds clean and dry for now.'

Agnes ambled over quickly, leaning slightly, arms limp at her sides and exposed to the dank air, as if navigating a balance beam in gym class.

'Don't humour her. This is serious. Her wrists are infected,' Lucy said, grabbing Cecilia's arm. 'People die from this shit.'

'And they also die in tornados!' Cecilia shouted. 'I'll talk to her. Just give us a minute, OK?'

Lucy nodded.

'Do you smell something? Something sweet?' Agnes asked. 'Is it roses? I smell roses.'

Now Cecilia was getting worried. Not that she could smell much of anything, but the only scent starting to come through was the stink of rot from Agnes's arms.

'Maybe some late bloomers survived in the courtyard,' Cecilia said unconvincingly, since it had been far too cold lately.

'I don't want to leave,' Agnes pleaded.

'Here? Or him?' Cecilia asked, turning each wrist under the stream.

'You don't either. I can see it in your face. Lucy's, too.'

'We're all going to have to leave eventually,' CeCe said. 'The storm can't last for ever. Nothing can.'

'Maybe not, but we need to worry about right now,' Lucy interjected. 'That door is not going to hold much longer.'

CeCe wrapped Agnes's arms quickly and tried to think.

The heavy bronze inlaid wooden portal they'd entered through suddenly began to shimmy on its rusted hinges. It was beautiful, solid, a work of art in and of itself – or had been once, until it was allowed to fall into such disrepair. With nothing to barricade it, the door would soon be useless against the

encroaching winds. The flooding rain was already beginning to seep underneath.

They felt trapped.

'We need to keep going,' Cecilia said, a new urgency in her tone.

'To where?' Lucy asked.

'There,' Agnes spoke up, pointing toward the smaller rear door.

'Outside?'

'No, Sebastian said it goes to a chapel downstairs.'

'Underneath the church?' Cecilia asked, wondering if she might be completely delirious. 'Have you seen it?'

'No,' Agnes answered, turning her wrists to CeCe. 'I tried to open it but I couldn't. Sebastian said I should try again when I was ready.'

'No way the storm can touch us down there,' Lucy observed, eyeing the door.

'He said something else,' Agnes added.

'What?' Lucy asked skeptically.

'That the answers were down there.'

'Answers?' CeCe asked.

'To our questions. Why we're here,' Agnes added.

Lucy was getting spooked. She felt Agnes was beginning to ramble, her elevated white blood cell count speaking for her, distorting her reality. And theirs. She was afraid to go down, but the alternative was far more frightening.

Cecilia grabbed a few long candles and lit them. 'Hurry! That door is not going to hold much longer.' She handed Agnes and Lucy each a candle and they scrambled quickly for the door. 'It's now or never. Are we ready to try it?'

'Ready,' Agnes said.

'Lucy?'

'Ready,' Lucy responded.

They each took hold of the large oval knob.

'Pull!' Lucy screamed.

'We can do this!' CeCe wailed.

With all their strength they tugged at it, again and again.

The three of them.

Refusing to stop.

Until it gave way.

'We're safe,' Agnes wheezed.

'We'll see,' CeCe said.

They slipped through the doorway just as the sacristy door burst free of its hinges, hitting the cellar door and slamming it with a horrible thud. They were thrust into complete darkness, darker even than when they'd first arrived at the church.

Lucy lit a small candle that she'd been carrying around with her and handed it over to Cecilia, who stretched her long arms out in front of her.

'Either this is a staircase or it's the biggest walk-in closet ever,' Lucy said. They walked slowly down. The steps were cobblestone and slick from condensation like old cellar steps

in a brownstone. The smell of staleness intensified with each step downward.

With only a tiny flame to light the way, the staircase seemed endless, as if they were descending into a catacomb, the very bowels of the city, of the earth, even. The passage narrowed and headspace shrank, but the deeper they went, the safer they felt. The safest in fact, since they'd arrived.

'All right?' Cecilia said, pausing for a moment.

'Yes,' said Lucy. 'I do my best work in the dark.'

'Too many club nights,' Cecilia swiped, adding a little comic relief.

'Back at you,' Lucy lobbed.

At the bottom of the steps, another wooden door, shorter and squatter than the one above, was gradually revealed in the candlelight, the panels painted in a medieval style – angel-head statues, alert and at-the-ready expressions with child-sized hands supporting cherubic chins, rough hewn from stone rather than cast and moulded in plaster, appeared to guard the entrance on either side. A cross of bone sat above the entrance.

'I don't know about this,' Lucy said, ogling the bleached white cruciform.

'Do you think it's like one of those Wild West warnings? A scalp nailed to the fort door?' Cecilia put on her most ominous voice. '"Come no farther."'

Agnes shed a bit more candlelight on the door and ran her fingers into the groove cut into it.

Carved into the door were the words *Omnes Sancti*. Running along the archway from one side to the other, lettered in faded and chipped gold paint were more words that they could barely see or understand.

'You're the Catholic schoolgirl,' Lucy said to Agnes. 'Go ahead. Make your mommy proud.'

Agnes read the inscription of unfamiliar words, haltingly, phonetically.

> *'Probasti cor meum*
> *visitasti nocte*
> *igne me examinasti*
> *et non est inventa in me iniquitas'*[1]

'What do you think that means?' Cecilia asked. 'I only speak pig Latin.'

'I have no idea,' Agnes offered apologetically.

'All that money down the drain,' Cecilia said, squeezing Agnes's shoulder.

'I'm betting it says something like "Must be taller than this Roman numeral to ride",' Lucy joked nervously, running her fingers along the splintered indentations of the letters like a blind person.

'No,' Agnes said, accessing what little Latin she'd learned in

---

1   Thou hast proved my heart, and visited it by night; thou hast tried me by fire: and iniquity hath not been found in me.

class. 'It's something about a trial, I think.'

'Why would there be a courtroom under a church?' Lucy asked.

'Or a prison,' Cecilia added.

Each felt the bolt of doubt and fear shoot up their spine, like the punishing electric shock from a Skinner box, but said nothing.

'C'mon,' Cecilia said, taking a deep breath. 'Let's not freak ourselves out.'

'Maybe we should wait for Sebastian,' Agnes suggested. 'Who knows what's in there?'

Lucy ignored her and stepped forward to take the lead.

'Seeing is believing,' she said, reaching for the ornate iron handle.

Lucy's jaw dropped as the interior came into view.

'No need to wait for Sebastian. I think he knows where this place is.'

Cecilia slid by her and through the doorway into the room, with Agnes in tow. Their reaction too was silence, turned mute by complete sensory overload.

Unlike the dinginess of the stairwell and church above, the circular room was beautifully lit with station after station of burning votives in opaque rose-coloured glass cups. Semihardened pools of melted wax grew drop by drop on the floor beneath them. The blazing light was almost painful, shining into every crevice of the chapel. It was vibrant and bright, brimming with signs of life and

reminders of death all at once.

Most striking was an enormous chandelier – more of a candelabra – hanging above the centre of the chapel, made masterfully and entirely of human bones. It swayed gently at the breeze of fresh air admitted by the open entrance, candleholders full of melted paraffin bubbled menacingly, straining to contain the overflow and threatening to spill over. Bone fragments of various shapes and sizes were strewn about like broken clamshells on a pebble beach.

Two large monstrances were bookended by a small altar, legs also made from bone, along with two lecterns, each holding an open book.

The front of the altar was bordered by three wooden and velvet kneelers. Behind the altar was a floor-to-ceiling fresco of the Sacred Heart, pierced and encircled by a crown of thorns oozing blood. Four sculptures, veiled with linen sheets tied tightly with twine, sat on marble pedestals before it.

'Not a courtroom or a prison,' Cecilia observed faintly.

'A tomb,' Agnes offered.

They walked in slowly, turning their necks up and around with each step, trying to take in the compact magnificence of the space. It was beautiful but eerie, conjuring a far more intense reaction in them than the larger edifice above.

Heavy leaden stained-glass windows depicting horrific scenes of torture and death, brought nearly to life in the flickering flames, lined the perimeter. Beheadings, beatings, burnings, and worse were ornately rendered in the most beautiful and gruesome detail. In the shimmering candlelight, the windows took on an almost 3D quality, their images floating on the fog as if at the command of a midnight movie projectionist. It was part chapel, part chamber of horrors.

'We think *we've* got problems,' Cecilia said to Lucy, studying the panels.

Cecilia thought it was odd that the perimeter was lined with windows when it was literally impossible for any natural light to sweep through them at that depth.

Lucy walked over to one of the pedestaled figures and unsuccessfully attempted to loosen the knot. In front of the statues on a base of its own, Cecilia saw a gold-framed glass case, the same exact one from her nightmare, misted over and shattered on the front side, through the haze. She wiped the dust and grime away carefully, looking for the rings from her dream.

She rolled the grit around her fingertips for a while, confused.

'What is this place?' Cecilia mused.

'A crypt?' Agnes said, awestruck.

'This actually looks like a place I visited with my father in the Czech Republic,' Lucy said. 'Like an ossuary. A bone closet. It was a chapel constructed entirely of skeleton parts under the Cemetery Church of All Saints.'

'You went there for vacation?' Cecilia asked.

'It was grotesque, but extraordinarily beautiful at the same time, just like this place,' Lucy explained. 'All these bones of

people who died during the Black Death were dug up and intricately sculpted into furniture and religious fixtures by a half-blind monk.'

'It just keeps getting better,' CeCe murmured.

'It was an unbelievable sight, like this. A work of art. A real masterpiece. We talked about it for hours, days, after,' Lucy rambled, the thought of being with her dad forcing out the fear that was making its way in as she scanned the windows that lined the entire perimeter of the room.

Agnes approached the lecterns on either side of the altar and stopped. Both books were open. One book was clearly a Bible; a five-ribbon marker hung from it and she opened the book to the page indicated by the first one. It read *Psalmus*. Frustrated at both her difficulty seeing the pages in the smoky room as well as her inability to read it, she moved over to the other lectern and noted three bookmarkers streaming from that book.

It was a leather-bound and elaborately illustrated tome, sitting inside a wooden case. A tiny key, for a lock, she assumed, sat on the open pages. She'd never seen anything like it and browsed through with the utmost care. It was the first book she'd ever seen that needed protection. *Did it need to be locked up to protect it, or to protect others from it?* she wondered to herself.

'Are those the instructions for this place?' Cecilia asked sarcastically.

'Sort of,' Agnes said, slowly turning pages. 'It's stories.

Biographies, I think.'

Like the markings on the door, the text was in Latin and very old, as far as she could tell. She grasped the book and turned to its front cover.

It read *Legenda Aurea*.

Lucy tried to make sense of a bunch of random items – a life-size wooden box in the shape of a person, like a sarcophagus with eyeholes but without any of the facial detail, carved from wood with a hinged opening, the lid inscribed with more Latin that she couldn't understand:

Mortificate ergo membra vestra quae sunta super terram[2]

She opened it and was shocked to find rows of fine needles and short spikes affixed to the interior. Frightened, she stepped away, afraid to touch the box or even to close it. It was far more scary than sacred to her. But not as horrifying as what she stumbled upon next to it.

A Venetian mirror. Antique and encrusted with soot. Lucy licked the side of her hand and wiped at the mirror glass, able to clear only a small portion of it. Just enough to see the reflection of her eyes, which were red, puffy, and streaked with runny mascara. It was the first good look she'd had of herself since she arrived. She tried to wipe away the rest, but the more she saw, the less she liked it. Hair undone. Flecks of

---

2   Put to death that which is earthly in you.

dried blood still visible on her forehead and nose from when she arrived.

'I look so . . . ugly,' she murmured to herself, uncharacteristically self-critical.

Less ominous but just as odd, Cecilia noticed a rusted toolbox, fireplace tools, timber, and rope were scattered around. None seemed to be modern construction tools or to have come from the church above. They were older. A coal stove, poorly vented, was glowing red and smoking, the source of the hot, sooty murk that pervaded the space. An urn, also full of smouldering coals, sat atop it. It felt like a sauna. Uncomfortably and unnaturally warm and steamy. A place to sweat out impurities. As the grey smoke vented slowly out the partially open chapel doorway, the remainder of the room revealed itself.

The entire room looked to them like a storage unit that had been long ago forgotten.

Agnes stepped off the altar and stared at the floor beneath her.

'See this?' she asked the others.

On the tiled floor, the symbols from their chaplets identical to the ones carved into the door.

'It seems,' Cecilia said, 'we were expected.'

'Jesse Arens?' Frey asked, his voice cutting in and out from the horrible reception.

'Possibly. Who's this?'

'I have an exclusive story for you,' Frey announced anonymously. 'You like exclusives, don't you?'

'Who is this? How did you get this number?'

'There's been a murder. The victim was found at the bottom of a lift shaft at Perpetual Help. A patient who escaped from the psych ward last weekend is suspected.'

'Then call the police. Or the city desk. Homicide isn't exactly my thing. Why call me?'

Jesse was about to hang up.

'Have you seen your friend Lucy lately?'

Jesse felt his body go numb and a sick feeling rise up from his stomach.

'No,' he said tersely and paused. 'Why?'

'A local Park Slope girl, high school student, was reported missing yesterday. A female musician from Williamsburg too. I think your friend may be involved in some way as well. They were all treated in the emergency room last Saturday night, the night the killer escaped.'

'Is this like some kind of "bad things come in threes" occult thing you're pushing?' Jesse laughed tensely. 'Sounds like a stretch, if you ask me.'

'I'm not the superstitious type.'

This guy sounded dead serious, Jesse thought. And nobody else knew Lucy had gone missing, as far as he was aware, besides the bouncer. He was starting to worry.

'I'm asking you again, why are you telling *me* this?'

'Because you love her, don't you? You would do anything to help her, to find her.'

'You don't know what you're talking about. If you know anything, you know she hates me.'

'Don't I? I've seen your posts. Seen the way you write about her in such flattering terms. The way you photograph her. Only certain angles, her legs, her chest, her hands, her lips.'

'Strictly business,' Jesse said unconvincingly. 'Who the hell is this?'

The line went dead.

He chewed impatiently on his fingernails and waited for a call back, but it never came. The name on his caller ID simply said Perpetual Help Hospital. It was a big place. *Could've been anybody*, he thought. Whoever this was, though, had got way inside Jesse's head. Finally, he hit call back and it rang through to a voicemail.

'You've reached the Department of Psychiatry and the office of Department Chairman Dr Frey. For prescription refills, press one. If you'd like to make an appointment with—' The robotic female greeting was replaced with another, more familiar, male voice. 'Dr Alan Frey' it intoned.

'Please press two.'

Jesse pressed two.

16

The Holy Hour

Agnes focused her gaze upward at the walls and the others followed suit. A single word had been recently painted in black over and over in the empty spaces between the ancient Latin phrases originally inscribed in the gilt and plastered ceiling. Swirling. Twisting. Turning.

CIPHER.

'Jesus,' Cecilia whispered in awe.

'Sebastian,' Agnes whispered, voicing what they were all thinking.

'It's like automatic writing,' Lucy muttered. 'Real OCD shit.'

'More like graffiti, I'd say,' Cecilia added. 'Some kind of warning.'

The heat and haze were oppressive. Worse than anything they'd ever experienced on even the hottest and muggiest summer day in the city.

'I'm . . . feeling . . . dizzy,' Agnes said, overcome, as she collapsed into Cecilia's arms.

'Agnes!' Cecilia shouted, dropping to her knees with Agnes draped over her lap like a living pietà.

Lucy rushed to them, checking Agnes's breathing and her heartbeat, feeling her forehead for fever.

'She's burning up,' Lucy said, accusingly. 'She should have left. We should have *made* her go.'

'Wake up. Please,' Cecilia begged, as she stroked Agnes's long hair gently and supported her with the other arm. Agnes complied. She was delirious. Her body stiffened and her head snapped back.

'I think she's having a seizure!' Lucy yelled.

'*Ne discesseris a me,*' Agnes moaned over and over again, spewing Latin as if in a trance. '*Quoniam tribulatio proxima est quoniam non est qui adiuvet.*'

Cecilia leaned back and Lucy's eyes widened. Frightened. She looked up around her and brought her trembling hands to her lips at a sudden realization.

'Now I'm freaked out,' Lucy said. 'Are you thinking what I'm thinking?'

'Don't be ridiculous,' Cecilia scolded. 'She's sick. It's just random.'

'Cecilia,' Lucy stammered, pointing to a section of the wall

above them. 'She's not babbling. She – she's reading.'

'But her eyes are closed . . .' Cecilia's voice trailed off.

'She looks possessed or something. Out of her mind.'

'Possessed? In a church? I—'

Lucy turned toward the door, alarmed by the sound of old hinges grinding and popping. Like barking. 'Do you hear that? Dogs behind the door. Cecilia!'

She ran to the door and pushed it shut. Lucy stood with her back against it for a moment, eyes shut, needing to feel something solid, supportive, while she waited for the growls to fade. Relieved, she opened her eyes, but it was harder to see now. The slamming door extinguished the rows of votives, leaving just three alight, turning the chapel into a virtual cave, illuminated only by the burning wicks. Darkness fell over them like a shroud.

'We might be better off upstairs. Cecilia. Cecilia? Don't you hear me?'

'I hear music.'

'What?'

Cecilia was expressionless, deep in thought. Entranced. The colour drained from her and her skin began to take on the amber hue of the candle flames. She swayed, trying to catch Agnes's beat. Lucy ran for the door and pulled it closed.

'I understand,' Cecilia said in amazement. 'I understand her. "Depart not from me. For tribulation is very near. And there is none to help me."'

They repeated the words together, in time, like a prayer. Agnes in Latin, and Cecilia in English. The sound reverberated around the circular room, swirling.

'Stop it!' Lucy screamed, overwhelmed, grabbing for her face and falling to her knees, the others' chant filling her ears. 'Cecilia, something is so wrong here. What the hell is happening?'

Lucy looked up at the image of the Sacred Heart before her and felt her skin flush and heart begin to race as if she'd just run a marathon. As she tried desperately to calm herself, small beads of sweat began to collect in the pores of her face and scalp, and tumble under their own weight, down her forehead, cheeks, and chin. Black trails of blood seemed to flow from the heart, though she couldn't be sure that it wasn't just the tears streaking her eyes or water damage running through the cracked plaster. The image at the back wall began to undulate on the waves of mist.

'Do you see that?' she asked, trying to refocus through the smoke and glycerin. 'It's beating.'

Lucy was transfixed.

Cecilia laid Agnes gently on her back and stood.

'I see it too,' she said, staring until she'd become too dizzy to stand. Cecilia began to teeter, like a jumper on a narrow window ledge. Turning almost as pale as the bone in the chandelier above, she stumbled backward, slipping and falling into to the iron maiden behind her with enough force that the cabinet doors closed in on her.

She was pierced, back, front, and side, by the small nails affixed to the interior of the cabinet, too many to count, and was forced to remain upright and still. A couple of centimetres forward or back risked unimaginable agony. If this thing was meant to extract repentance or forgiveness, it wouldn't take long, Cecilia was certain. She was frozen in place and in fear.

Trapped.

Numbed by pain.

Trying to remain conscious in the stifling heat.

Holding only a single thought.

We're going to die.

She stood dazed and confused, in shock, staring through the cutouts for her eyes, pupils fixed and dilated at the gruesome scene unfolding before her powerlessly; the chapel awash in blood, sweat, tears, pus, and vomit. Bruised, battered, shamed, and cut, their insides draining slowly but surely out, like dirty oil from a cold car engine.

'Help me,' Cecilia cried out in vain.

Lucy was shaken free from her trance by Cecilia's wail and turned to the cabinet where she was imprisoned and saw it begin to shudder.

Cecilia let out an awful scream as she pushed the door open, calling upon her last bit of strength and sanity, nails piercing both palms front to back.

'My hands,' she moaned, sliding them off the spikes and dropping to her knees.

They twitched and trembled in her lap, blood and sweat pooling in the centre of each palm.

Agnes crawled to CeCe and took her by the wrists, wiping the wounds over her face and hair, the gore drying into a horrible red mask on her face and caking her curls.

She resumed her entreaties with even greater fervour, picking at her soiled bandages, slowly at first, and then tore at them, seeking any relief for the claustrophobia they were inflicting on her, like a prisoner trying to slip handcuffs. The wrappings fell to the floor, filling the room with the foul stench of decay.

Agnes recited:

'*Cor meum tamquam cera liquescens in medio ventris mei.*
Ipsi vero consideraverunt et inspexerunt me.
Concilium malignantium obsedit me.
Sicut aqua effusus sum et dispersa sunt universa ossa mea
  factum.'[3]

Lucy began to gag, choking on the odour. Unable to hold it back any longer, she purged, gushing a bile-filled, watery puke caused partially by the stink of rotting flesh and partially by the pain in her head. She crawled down the short aisle toward the

---

3 My heart is become like wax melting in the midst of my bowels.
   They have looked and stared upon me.
   The council of the malignant hath besieged me.
   I am poured out like water and all my bones are scattered.

altar to find an unstained space, dry heaving all the way.

Finally, Lucy collapsed.

Agnes continued to chant, offering a surreal narration to their torment.

'*Mei animam meam circumdederunt super me.*'[4]

'Lucy,' Cecilia moaned. 'Get out of here. Find Sebastian.'

Lucy heard, but instead walked toward the mirror that had vexed her earlier. She stared at her reflection, at her eyes, which appeared now to glow and made her dizzy once again. She fell headfirst into the glass. One by one, rough shards of mirror pierced her head. She did not move. She stood there and took it.

Another.

And another.

Embedding themselves into her scalp until they formed a halo around her head. She looked at herself in the cracked mirror, blood flowing from her wounds. The reflection in each shard was of her own eyes, looking back at her in the remnants of the cracked mirror.

'Judge not, that you may not be judged,' Agnes whispered.

Lucy reached for her ears.

Agnes crawled toward the votive stand, gazing at the low light of the candle flame and stretched her hand out stiffly

---

4 My enemies have surrounded my soul.

above it, like a curious child over a hot stove. She lowered it gradually, drops of Cecilia's still-fresh blood dripping from her hand into the candle cup and sizzling, until it was perched near enough to the flame to hurt, her long hair near enough to ignite. As the frayed ends began to catch, the acrid smell of burning hair mixed with the rankness of the room.

Through the haze she appeared to Lucy, who was now lying on a mirror bed made of shards, as a pathetic wraith, damned to infinitely repeat a ritual that might one day earn forgiveness for her. Agnes whispered:

'*Dinumeraverunt omnia ossa mea.*'[5]

Lucy mustered the strength to grab her heels and put them on to protect her feet from further injury caused by debris, and hobbled over to Agnes. Before she could grab her hand and hair away from the flame, Agnes turned and faced her. She held her hand up, palm facing Lucy, a silent sign to stop where she was.

'You're sick,' Lucy insisted, hoping to bully some sense into her. 'This isn't you.'

'It is,' Agnes said. 'It's all of us.'

Agnes looked right through her as if she wasn't there. A thousand-metre stare to cover a matter of centimetres.

The room was a split screen of pain and suffering, and Lucy didn't know which way to turn, who to help first when she

---

5   They have numbered all my bones.

couldn't even help herself. She understood how insanity could pounce on even the soundest and sharpest mind, which she always considered to be hers. The closeness of madness was overwhelming and keeping it at bay, a losing battle. Insanity beckoned. She kept telling herself *Deep breath*, to put herself back in her body, but she couldn't manage to take one.

'Seeing is believing,' Agnes mocked and started to giggle, her bloodstained face and hands almost disappearing in the dimness, giving the impression of a headless, limbless torso floating in space. 'How do I look?'

'This is supposed to be a holy place!' Lucy cried. But her pleas were stifled by an explosive pain, the worst of them all. Molten wax from the candelabra rained down, droplets of fire splashing Lucy's eyes, face, and hair. She was glazed, coated, like a mould. She felt as if her eyelids had been glued closed and her eyes cooked into gooey marbles in their sockets.

Blinded.

Suffocating.

Without mercy.

'I . . . can't . . . see.'

Her instinct was to rip it away, but she didn't. Instead she ran her trembling fingers along the cooling ridges of textured mass, the second skin that covered her. She had the sense of moulting, but in reverse. Of being encased, like a wick inside one of the tapers, waiting for a match to ignite her, set her aflame and consume her.

Lucy fell to her knees.

Agnes's recitations became more manic, more urgent. Pleading.

> 'Petite et dabitur vobis quaerite et invenietis pulsate et aperietur vobis.
>
> Omnis enim qui petit accipit et qui quaerit invenit et pulsanti aperietur.'[6]

'Sebastian!' CeCe cried desperately with what little strength she had left.

'Somebody, please. Help us!'

Suddenly, a shrill wail from the other side of the chapel pierced the silence.

'God,' Agnes screamed, as if waking from a horrible nightmare, in desperation. 'Help us.'

Agnes cried out a final time:

> 'Adtendite a falsis prophetis qui veniunt ad vos in vestimentis ovium intrinsecus autem sunt lupi rapaces.'[7]

The room fell silent as each lost consciousness. They couldn't

---

6 Ask, and it shall be given to you: seek, and you shall find: knock, and it shall be open to you.
   For every one that asketh, receiveth: and he that seeketh, findeth: and to him that knocketh, it shall be opened.

7 Beware of false prophets, who come to you in the clothing of sheep, but inwardly they are ravening wolves.

be sure how long it was before they came to. Both time and their suffering seemed to have stopped in that very moment.

A hand beneath her head and another clawing at her eyes awoke Lucy. They were Sebastian's hands. She didn't need her eyes to tell her that. She heard Agnes and Cecilia coughing and calling out for each other as he gently removed the last bits of wax. At least, she thought, they were alive.

'I'm with you,' he said. 'You are with me.'

'Sebastian,' Lucy said, gratefully. 'I can see.'

17
Before the Devil Knows
You're Dead

U p?' the cheery lift operator.

Jesse nodded and stepped in nervously. This lift cab looked ancient to him. Art deco tiling on the floor and walls, deco lighting fixture attached to the ceiling. Polished brass railings. Reminded him of the lift in his grandparents' fancy Park Avenue prewar building, which always smelled vaguely of musty carpet and old people.

Jesse was dripping, his carefully coiffed 'do flattened, puddles forming at his feet. The momentary lull in the storm that had seduced him over to the hospital to meet Dr Frey in person was nothing more than a meteorological headfake. But even the sudden cloudburst that assaulted him as he approached the hospital lobby couldn't dampen his curiosity. He had to find out about Lucy.

The operator smiled. 'Brought the storm inside with you I see. Floor?'

Jesse was put off, suspicious even. He figured the guy was trained to keep it light for the incoming patients' benefit. Which was fine, except he wasn't a patient and wasn't keen to be seen as or treated as one.

'Top.'

He didn't know the exact number and couldn't bring himself to name it.

The operator slid the collapsible gate closed, pushed the car switch forward, and engaged the pulley motor. The cab jerked upward and the operator turned and smiled at him yet again and returned to position, facing forward, watching the lift car pass floor after floor on the way to the top. He felt as if he'd just been caged and both his claustrophobia and paranoia began to kick in. It didn't help matters that he was taking a ride to a psych ward. Jesse grabbed the railing and hung on, counting the floors as they passed. From his neurotic behaviour he wondered if the lift guy would take him for a visitor or a patient. It was late after all, well after hours, and with the storm raging, unlikely that anyone but the most desperate headcases would brave the elements. A visit could wait. An appointment could not.

'Penthouse,' the operator announced, sliding the gate open. 'Have a nice day, sir.'

Jesse exhaled and jumped off quickly without saying a word. He wasn't much for chitchat under the best circumstances and didn't feel the need to exchange niceties with a hired hand.

The lift gate swung closed behind him and he stepped cautiously into the waiting area. The shiny floors and the wet soles of his shoes were not a good match. He extended his long arms outward like wings to balance himself as his feet slid treacherously along the slickened linoleum, laughing nervously to himself that if the operator could see him now, he'd have little doubt about Jesse's mental status. A real live loony bird had just flown into the cuckoo's nest.

There was no reception desk, just an unmanned nurses' station. He looked around for help and caught a glimpse of the inmates in the distance, wandering the corridors.

It was exactly as he'd imagined it. As he'd feared.

Too warm. Colourless walls. Easy-clean floors and countertops. No sharp edges to be found anywhere. Lots of sanitizer. Pens chained to desks. And the smell. Stale and rubbery like vulcanized piss. Worst of all were the dead-eyed patients, sewing imaginary holes, of lifting imaginary packages, staring out windows at imaginary worlds, having imaginary conversations. Mostly with themselves, occasionally at each other.

'Mr Arens?'

'What,' he said, startled.

His jittery rudeness was matched only by the nurse's indifference.

'Dr Frey can see you now.'

He followed the nurse down the hall and into the Chief of Psychiatry's office.

He passed by door after door, each with a small observation window of thick glass reinforced with chicken wire positioned at about eye level. Glancing through each as he walked, all the everyday yet seldom-seen horrors of mental illness were on full display, none of it unsurprising. Men and women in restraints, agitated and struggling to get free, others sedated, unconscious, finding freedom or peace in only their dreams. One thing he had not expected to see was a child. A young boy, his head bowed, hands folded across his waist, sitting completely still as if he were praying.

Jesse stopped.

The boy lifted his head and stared directly at Jesse. Their eyes met. The boy shook his head slightly from side to side and returned to his prayer.

'Let's not keep Dr Frey waiting,' the nurse called back to him.

Jesse resumed his trek toward Frey's office which was now in view. His last few steps took him past several white-walled examination and treatment rooms and finally near a door next to Frey's office that was different from the rest. It was heavier, thicker, made of metal, not wood. The room was dark except for a single amber light that hung from the ceiling. Beneath it

sat a man, big, beefy, and bald. He looked vaguely familiar but shadows fell so deeply into his scarred and pock-marked face that it took Jesse a moment to recognize him.

'Sicarius,' he whispered almost reverently.

There he was. The star of many a boyhood nightmare. As close to a real live boogeyman as Brooklyn ever had. Proof positive, Jesse remembered his parents saying, that monsters really did exist. An infamous child serial-killer who terrorized the borough for months nearly a decade earlier and beat the death penalty rap with a successful insanity defense. Jesse was both appalled and intrigued by his presence.

'Mr Arens!' the nurse insisted.

Her 'can't you read the sign' tone of voice was like a zookeeper's commanding a visitor not to feed the wild animals.

Jesse backed away and finished his walk into Frey's office, still a bit disoriented by what he'd seen. He fidgeted briefly in his chair, pulling the wet clothes from his skin impatiently when the doctor arrived.

'Mr Arens, I'm Dr Frey,' he said, stepping behind his desk and reaching his hand across it to Jesse. 'Thank you for coming, I know it couldn't have been easy to get here.'

Jesse took hold of it only briefly, not wanting to catch any crazy bugs that might be floating around.

'Yeah,' Jesse said. 'On the news they were saying even crime has hit record lows, there are so few people on the streets.

Looks like they keep you pretty busy around here though.'

'Yes,' the doctor said, dismissing the teen's insensitivity. 'Very busy. Mental illness is a silent epidemic, one that doesn't discriminate or stop for storms.'

'Not even for kids or killers,' Jesse said, still disturbed by what he'd seen along the corridor.

'You are observant, as a person in your line of work should be.' Frey complimented. 'The boy, Jude, is prone to sudden violent outbursts. He comes and goes. We monitor him mostly as an outpatient.'

'He didn't look violent.' Jesse noted.

'It starts young,' Frey advised. 'Children. Teenagers. Always best to nip it in the bud when you can. Looks can be deceiving, as the saying goes.'

'Nothing deceiving about the way Sicarius looks.' Jesse parried.

'Oh, he's harmless as long as he's being treated, and he's quite restricted as you saw.' Frey responded. 'I keep him very close by.'

Harmless. That wasn't the first thought that came to Jesse's mind, but Frey was the doctor, a very respected one he'd heard, and he should know best. Besides, the Perpetual Help Psych Ward treatment programme was not the reason for his visit. 'Why am I here, Doctor?'

'As I mentioned, your friend Lucy—' Frey began.

'I hope you didn't ask me here to tell me she's a lunatic,'

Jesse warned. 'First of all, I know that. Second, I'm the only one who can say it.'

'Loyalty is an admirable trait,' Frey said. 'I'm sure it's mutual.'

Jesse was silent.

'As I was saying,' Frey continued. 'You say your friend is missing.'

'A bouncer at the nightclub where I last saw her found her phone in the street. She's not at home and no one has seen her. I'm hoping it's just the storm, but . . .'

'But you have a bad feeling,' Frey said, completing his thought. 'You have good instincts. No wonder you are so successful.'

Flattery. Something to which Jesse was quite susceptible.

'Yes,' Jesse agreed. 'But this isn't the missing persons bureau, so what has that got to do with you?'

'I think I may know what happened to her.'

The doctor reached calmly behind him for a set of files and set them down. He flipped to a small stack of photos and began to explain. Jesse was listening.

'There was a patient here. A young man named Sebastian. A very sick young man.'

Jesse casually examined the picture. It was of a guy, about his age. He was striking, magnetic, with sharp features, deep-set eyes, and faraway gaze. Jesse was surprised he hadn't seen him around but from what the doctor said, Sebastian had other priorities. It was a shame, Jesse thought. A guy with his looks

and presence could go places with the right people behind him. But even in the photo, it was clear to Jesse that this guy was somewhere else entirely in his mind.

'This is a nuthouse, Doctor. Isn't everyone here very sick?'

'Not like him.'

'What are you trying to say?'

'He has certain ideations,' Frey explained. 'I won't bore you with the clinical details, but he is quite dangerous.'

'To himself or to others?'

'Both.'

'This patient escaped from here the other night. We think he got out through the ER. He is still free.'

'Do you mind, Doctor?'

Jesse reached for his notepad. The one he normally used to chronicle the comings and goings of up-and-coming celebstitutes whose story might travel to the mainstream media and weekly rags. This was different.

'Please,' Frey said approvingly. 'It was the same night that your friend came into the ER.'

'Are you saying she was involved in his disappearance somehow? Not likely. First of all, she's much too selfish to help anybody.'

'No, I'm saying that he might be involved in hers. He didn't just escape you see. A man is dead.'

Kidnapping. Murder. Insanity. This was front-page stuff, Jesse thought, as he felt the inside of his mouth dry up and his

throat begin to close slightly. He was inexperienced in this kind of reporting, in fact, in any real reporting at all, but he was starting to feel he might be in over his head.

'And you think he might have Lucy? Why?'

Frey pulled up Jesse's own site and scrolled down to a BYTE bit from a few nights before.

'Do you remember this photo?'

'Of course I remember it. I took it. I was right there when it happened.'

'What do you see?'

'I see two hot chicks rolling around a VIP room.'

'Look closer,' Frey said.

Jesse stared at the image, struggling to find some kind of wardrobe malfunction or up-skirt sneak peek that he'd overlooked when posting.

'I don't really notice anything else but a bracelet.'

'Yes! That's right.'

Jesse was a bit confused. Frey was well-dressed but he didn't seem to be much of a fashion hound, judging from his fairly traditional button-down and khaki outfit. Not the sort of person to pay much mind to a bracelet.

'So? It's nice,' Jesse said. 'I got flooded with emails and texts from girls wanting to know where she got it. Even more so than usual.'

'I know where she got it,' the doctor said.

Frey opened the folder on top of his desk and pushed it

toward Jesse. It contained three photographs, each of a similar bracelet, with different charms dangling from them. One was identical to the bracelet that Lucy was wearing at the club.

'What is it, some kind of devil sign?' Jesse said, pointing to the charm.

'No, quite the opposite. It is a milagro. The kind of emblem you often find hanging from rosary beads or chaplets like these.'

'What's so special about them?'

'I'm not sure but they were special enough to him that he stole them from the old chapel beneath the Church of the Precious Blood.'

A relic thief. Jesse wasn't very impressed. The church had been a construction site for a while. Maybe he wanted a souvenir or something to pawn. It sounded more like a prank to Jesse than some mysterious plot.

'I'm not sure where you are going with this. Lucy's not religious, Doctor. The only appeal of that bracelet to her would be as an accessory. She could have found it on the street for all I know.'

'When he arrived here, we took them from him. Three of them. When he left, they were gone.'

'You think he gave them to Lucy. Intentionally?'

The idea of gifting a stranger with prayer beads was something Jesse had only seen on street corners and music festivals upstate, but then again this guy was crazy.

'Coincidentally, two other girls were admitted to the

emergency room on that night. Both are missing.'

Jesse stared at the photo of the chaplet intently.

'Two and three?' he said, solemnly.

'Precisely,' the doctor said. 'The second girl was reported missing yesterday by her mother. Agnes Fremont is her name. A suicide attempt. I evaluated her myself.'

'And the third?'

'A musician who plays clubs around Brooklyn and the Bowery . . . Cecilia Trent.'

'Sounds familiar,' Jesse said, searching his mental file until her name clicked. 'She's hot. Critics' darling. Dresses over-the-top. She's got a small following I think. Superfan types. I almost wrote something about her once.'

'Her concerts were inexplicably cancelled the past few nights. Odd because she's never missed a show before. No matter what the weather, as I found out. She only lives across the street from the dive where she was supposed to do these shows acoustically. The club stayed open for the locals, blackout and all.'

'Yeah, she's the kind that would play to an empty room if they'd have her,' Jesse acknowledged. 'But then this really is some end-of-the-world shit going on outside. Who could blame her for not showing?'

Jesse was starting to feel uneasy, as if a narrative was being planted in his brain.

Frey pushed the folder with CeCe's picture in it closer to Jesse.

'Does this look like a girl who is afraid of a little rain?'

Jesse balked at the massive understatement. 'A little rain?'

Frey just grinned.

The doctor was persuasive, Jesse had to admit. But then, Frey was the man who got Sicarius off, wasn't he. Jesse stood abruptly and backed away from the desk, a chill running down his spine.

'Why tell me all this, Doctor? This is really a matter for the police.'

'The police are on it but the storm slowed everything down, including the investigation. All their resources are assigned to emergency services. Until it blows over, and then the cleanup begins.'

'And the death?'

'Has been reported as accidental for the time being and buried in the papers by the storm coverage.' Frey said. 'Interested?'

Jesse couldn't help himself. His ego kicked in.

'Interested.'

'This is a dangerous guy and he needs to be found as quickly as possible. Before he can do any further harm to these girls.'

'Yes.'

'Of course, if you attribute any of this to me, I will deny it, so I'm trusting you to keep this confidential.'

'I'm good at keeping secrets, Doctor.'

'Good. I don't think you want to get into a credibility contest with me.'

'Threats? So soon?'

'I'm handing you your future, Jesse. This is the sort of story that makes careers.'

'A regular deal with the devil.'

'Not quite,' the doctor said.

'Just one more question, Doctor,' Jesse asked. 'You said he was dangerous. Delusional. What exactly do you mean?'

The doctor paused for an uncomfortably long time. Taking a minute to choose his words carefully.

'He believes that he's on a mission.'

'Mission? Is he some kind of whacked-out vet with PTSD?'

'Preparing the way,' Frey said.

'What way? For who?'

'Who do you think?'

'No. Way.' Jesse stammered, as Frey's meaning became clearer.

'He believes . . .'

'Believes what?'

'He believes he is a saint.'

18

Virgin Widow

Agnes was draped over Sebastian's arms, the last to be carried up by him. The staircase was steep and his legs and arms were tired. He placed her down gently on the red velvet steps of the chancel, the same as he already had done for Cecilia and Lucy. She was luminous and looked as if she were sleeping atop a bed of roses. She came to slowly. He was the first thing she saw. She mustered a smile.

The three of them were scattered, strewn about the altar, amid the tornado-tossed debris, like sacrifices, as if they'd just crash-landed on an alien planet. Sebastian attended to them. He had a chalice filled with water. He held each girl's head up and brought the cup to their lips slowly. He dried their wounds and wiped them clean.

Things were different somehow. It was quiet for one; the thunder and lightning had subsided. The air was less thick with humidity and mildew. Clearer.

'Where were you?' Agnes moaned groggily. 'I thought you were dead.'

'I'll never leave you again,' he said. 'Drink.'

'You OK?' Lucy mouthed to Cecilia through cracked lips.

Cecilia nodded.

She examined her hands.

They were wrapped in linen.

She clenched and unclenched her fingers. They still worked.

They looked and saw Sebastian. A sight for sore eyes. And then noticed Agnes, who was struggling to get to her feet. She tried to get to her knees but collapsed back down to the floor each time she attempted to right herself, like a child first learning to walk. Sebastian held her under her arms and raised her up.

'Thank you,' she whispered weakly to him.

'Thanks? For what?' Lucy interjected. 'Why didn't you help us?'

'What *was* that?' Cecilia asked, still weak from what had just happened. 'The underground chapel. The bones. This place is possessed.'

The fog in their minds was lifting, like the storm, and suspicion was returning.

'I couldn't tell you before,' Sebastian said.

'I think it's time you told us now,' Lucy answered.

'This church,' he began, 'is special.'

'Aren't they all?' Cecilia said.

'My grandmother told me about it when I was a boy,' Sebastian offered. 'Precious Blood is not just intended to be a holy place. It marks a holy spot.'

'Tell that to the developers,' Lucy said.

'Men died here. Sandhogs, digging the subway tunnels nearly a century ago.'

'So it's haunted,' Lucy shot back.

Sebastian's expression turned deadly serious, the tale he began to tell as terrifying as any ghost story.

'Not haunted, Lucy,' Sebastian corrected. 'Hallowed.

'These were special men. Descendants from a line of caretakers entrusted with the ancient legacy of certain female saints. Girls, about our age, who changed their world by their example and their sacrifice.'

The girls listened intently.

'They dug that chapel with their bare hands. With picks and axes out of rock and sand. An altar and kneelers built from leftover lumber used to keep the tunnel up. Adorned with statues from the old country. It was a place of worship in the truest sense. Built by people with faith, literally from nothing.'

'You could feel something alive, electric down there,' Cecilia said. 'I've felt it on stage. A power all around you. Even in an empty room.'

'What you felt in the chapel was their presence,' he said. 'I've felt it too.'

'Ghosts?' Lucy asked.

'Spirits,' Agnes corrected. 'Souls.'

'It took them a long time to dig the three men out but, the community and the men's families kept a vigil. They prayed day and night. First for their rescue and then for the recovery of their bodies. It took weeks.'

'What a horrible way to die,' Agnes sympathized.

'When they finally got to them, they were collapsed over the kneelers in front of the altar they'd hammered together.'

'They were praying?' Lucy said cynically. 'Maybe they should have been digging, trying to get out instead.'

'They were,' Sebastian answered. 'Trying to get out.'

'But they gave up?' Cecilia asked.

'No, they gave in,' Sebastian said. 'People came for years afterward, climbing down into the subway tunnel to see the underground chapel, to remember the men, to pray, hoping for miracles.'

'Sounds dangerous,' Agnes said.

'It was, and after a while, they raised the money to build this church over it.'

'And those bones?' Cecilia asked.

'I'm not sure I want to know,' Agnes said.

'The bones are their bones. And the bones of those who believed in what they were doing. Holy, some say.'

'A cult?' Cecilia asked.

'Not the way we think of it,' Sebastian explained. 'A cult of saints.'

'Couldn't this just be a story your grandmother told you?' Lucy said nervously. 'Like an old wives' tale—'

'What we felt down there was real,' Agnes interrupted. 'You know it.'

Sebastian was suddenly agitated. Frustrated that he might not be getting his point across.

'She was a *benedetta*,' he said defensively, pacing in front of them. 'A healer of bodies and souls. A woman of faith. She never lied to me.'

Sebastian's discomfort brought the conversation to a halt.

'It just seems really strange that they kept it open after such a tragic accident,' Agnes said.

Sebastian looked at her skeptically. 'I didn't say it was an accident.'

'They were killed? Why?' Cecilia asked incredulously.

'To stop them.'

'From?'

'Fulfilling their purpose.'

Between the events in the chapel and Sebastian's story, it was all too much, especially for Lucy. 'What does this have to do with you or us?'

'The saints whose legacies the subway workers were charged with perpetuating were Lucy, Cecilia, and Agnes.'

19

Pr@y

Jesse raced back to his apartment from the hospital, infused with a sense of power. The kind of power that only comes with secret knowledge. His mind bubbled up with potential, like the hot thin soup in the final moments before the first single-celled organisms clumped up and set life on the road to infinity. For him, this was that big.

He slipped the manila envelope the doctor had given him under his arm, turned the key, and opened the door, looking quickly over his shoulder before slamming it shut behind him. He'd been trusted with secrets before, all the important stuff in blogger world. Who's dating, who's cheating, who's stealing, who's bi, who's Botoxing, who's broke. Not being a real journalist, he didn't feel the least bit compelled to fact check, to seek out multiple sources, to remain neutral.

BYTE was his very own digitized high school diary, a pixelated revenge fantasy fuelled by his wild mood swings, thin-skinned defensiveness, and tech savvy that had set him on the profitable path to mainstream seminotoriety. His business plan was simple: Who can resist obsessing over the pettiness and venality of a bunch of spoiled, privileged, and backstabbing New York City kids? Wisely, he didn't rely on the public deciding on the breakout star, he chose one for them, Lucy, and cast himself as auteur – director, writer, and producer – of her life. And she played the role perfectly, until recently. She thought she could steal the whole damn show.

Jesse reviewed his notes and the girls' files. There were a lot of holes, he thought, which led to a lot of questions. So much about it didn't make sense. Lucy wasn't anyone's dupe, not even his. Why would she allow herself to be taken in by some schizo psychopath?

He uploaded a grainy headshot from their high school yearbook and began to write the item.

HAVE YOU SEEN THIS GIRL? the caption began, in boldface letters beneath the JPEG.

LULU Lost!

LUcky LUcy Ambrose is missing. The party princess has not been seen or heard from for three days and BYTE

hears that the NYPD has been notified. Rumours of a kidnapping or worse are swirling, as an unnamed mental patient escaped from Perpetual Help Hospital on the same night Lucy was admitted and remains on the loose. In addition to Lucy, two other Brooklyn girls, who coincidentally were also admitted to the ER last weekend, have also been reported missing. The tornado rescue operation and cleanup has put a strain on the police, who've been dragging their feet. The Perpetual Help Hospital board has managed to keep the escape and possible kidnappings under wraps until now.

Jesse read and reread what he'd written several times and paused his finger above the enter key, debating for a moment about whether to post the story and share it with the world. He omitted CeCe's and Agnes's names for fear of being sued, knowing damn well that those details would probably get out eventually anyway.

'Send,' he said, pressing the key. 'And wait.'

He kicked back and watched the commenters comment. Likes, shares, tweets, retweets, texts. It was a virtual feeding frenzy. His laptop pinged away with each new mailbox notification. The thread growing, branching out like a spider web.

She's been lost for a while now, said one ambivalently.

Guess that's the end of her 'Lucky' streak, jibed another.

Dibs on her shoes and jewellery if she's dead, posted LucyBFF.

Don't bother, it's all loaners, responded LULUToo crassly.

At least there weren't any Die, *bitch!* posts, he thought, but then again, it was early. Every snide thought was being vented, a veritable dam break of vitriol spewing forth into the electric ether. In the battle between sympathy and schadenfreude, sympathy was running a distant second.

Funny thing, Jesse noted, is that this was coming from the very same people who'd kiss her ass if they saw her at a club, begging to ride her wake through the velvet ropes for a free drink and entrée to the VIP section. All hypocrites. Just like her. Just like him.

Then the ringing phone rang.

'Hello?'

'Jesse Arens?'

'Go.'

'This is Richard Jensen from the Associated Press city desk. I'm calling about your item.'

'And?'

'I've just got off the phone with the Seventy-Sixth Precinct and they wouldn't confirm a thing.'

'So?'

'Can you verify any of this information or point me to someone who can?'

'I don't reveal sources.'

Frustrated, the newsman pressed on.

'Then how do I know if what you're reporting is true?'

'You don't.'

'Listen, kid, you need to give me something. How do you know these girls are tied to this guy?'

Jesse hung up on him in midsentence. He thought about the chaplets and the fact that he'd intentionally left them out of his post along with the names. It wasn't a detail he was ready to share. He was keeping the clue to himself and for himself. There might be more to be milked out of this story if it popped. Like money.

He was very comfortable playing God. Deciding who suffered indignity and who was saved from prying eyes with every stroke of his keyboard and leaving these old media types, who regularly ignored or berated him, twisting was fun to say the least. The call meant the story was out there, and he wasn't about to do their homework for them.

The reporter's question, however, was a good one. All he had to go on was the doctor's story, and who knew what *his* agenda was. These girls didn't know one another, hadn't crossed paths as far as he could tell, lived in different worlds entirely. The only connection, as far as he knew, that could be made to Sebastian was the bracelets. He knew Lucy could be superficial, but what could be so compelling about a bracelet, or about a guy, that would get her to bail on her life, on him? No, it couldn't be voluntary.

He spent a good long while studying the last picture of the fight in the club. He used the touch screen to magnify every bit

of the image including Lucy's body, something he had been in the habit of doing anyway. He stared long and hard at the chaplet and charm trying to unlock whatever fascination it might have held for her. There was something vaguely familiar about it to him, but he couldn't be sure he wasn't just remembering it from the other night.

The phone rang again, but this time Jesse let it go to voicemail.

'Don't bore us, get to the chorus,' his outgoing demanded.

'Mr Arens. This is Captain Murphy from the Seventy-Sixth Precinct.'

Jesse hit talk.

'That was quick.'

'We'd like to have a word with you regarding your story. I'll expect you down at the station tomorrow morning. If that's not convenient, I'm sure I can arrange to meet you at your apartment. Don't keep me waiting.'

Psychiatrists, reporters, investigators. This was all getting a little heavy. He took a look out the window and noticed the weather improving, despite the shitstorm he'd just kicked off. Jesse grabbed his phone and his keys and hit the street to clear his head and his conscience. And to look around.

Martha stood gazing out of Agnes's bedroom window and into the small backyard. She'd barely moved from it in the time since Agnes had gone. For her, waiting meant Agnes was

coming back. If someone is waiting for you, expecting you, then you just had to be coming back at some point. It was only just two nights, but it felt like for ever.

A loud knock at her front door rattled her back to reality. Martha raced to the door hoping it might be her headstrong child returning home. Opening it, the grim expression on the neighbour who'd come calling made her wish she hadn't.

'Did you see it?'

'See what?'

The neighbour was having trouble making eye contact.

'The story on the news right now. I just wondered if you might have heard anything . . .'

Martha grabbed the remote and entered one of the local channels. She had already stopped listening to everything as the cheery CGI bumper for the programme belied the seriousness of the top story. Her heart sank. She felt as if she'd just fallen from a tall building.

'This just in,' the well-coiffed presenter read with the appropriate mix of urgency and seriousness.

Martha watched dumbfounded as video rolled. Three girls and a dangerous, charismatic madman, possibly a murderer. All missing. Unnamed except for Lucy Ambrose. Probably together. A kidnapping? Not so fast. Already it was being turned into a cult thing. Ancient footage of Manson girls intercut with pictures of her daughter's yearbook photo and the two other young girls she didn't recognize. All the details were sketchy but reported as fact.

'I'm sure the police would have notified you . . .'

Martha's eyes were blank. Fixed on the breaking news report.

'If there's anything I can do . . . ,' the neighbour offered as she backed toward the door. Martha was in shock. She couldn't even muster a thank you. She reached for the phone, calmly, robotically, and dialled the police.

20

On the Third Day

S unday morning.

Day of reflection. And repair.

It was still dark inside, but first light was climbing slowly up the outer walls and through the shattered windows.

Outside the church, the buzz of chainsaws and men's voices replaced the rumble of thunder. The sirens of police cars and fire engines could be heard in the distance, making their way down flooded side streets choked with fallen trees.

The storm was finally over.

Lucy, Cecilia, and Agnes sat silently, contemplating what Sebastian had just revealed.

None of them knew what to think.

How to feel.

There was a sound of crunching glass coming from the side chapel. The windows had been blown out, making a way in for an intruder.

A small box-shaped bluish white glow appeared, the size of a smartphone screen, throwing light, and the sound of tentative footsteps echoed through the space.

'Lucy?' a quavering voice called out nervously but loudly. 'Lucy, are you here?'

The voice was familiar to her and most unwelcome. She walked quickly toward the rectangular light.

'Jesse,' she whispered harshly, grabbing him tightly by the arm.

Jesse recoiled, wide-eyed until the look of recognition settled in. The girl looked familiar, but different to him than she had just a few days earlier.

'I knew it,' he said, less surprised than pleased with himself.

'Knew what?'

'That you'd be here.'

'What? Why would you even bother to look for me?'

'Believe me, I'm not the only one looking.'

'How did you find me?'

'It was the bracelet,' Jesse said. 'I knew I'd seen the two-eyed emblem on it some place before. It was from an item I did on the press conference for the condo conversion. I remembered the sculpture on the building. Almost like it led me here.'

The sound of a match striking and sulfur fumes filled the still air, followed by a spark of light from the altar candle. Jesse saw the powerful outline of the imposing figure on the altar, and shook as if he'd seen a ghost. It was the guy in the picture.

'Sebastian,' he mused, the way he had over celebrities he'd written about but never actually seen in person.

Lucy backed away from him, toward the altar, and joined Agnes and Cecilia flanking Sebastian.

'What do you want from us?' Sebastian called out to him.

'Let them go,' Jesse said.

The girls looked puzzled and Cecilia began to laugh derisively at the pale, frail teen down the aisle.

'Let who go?' Agnes asked. 'We're not hostages.'

It was the first time any of them had used such a word, though they were beginning to feel like it. Not hostages in the criminal sense, but cuffed and bound by their heartstrings.

'I know you,' Cecilia sniffed. 'You're that evil little blogger douche. Right, Lucy?'

'That's him,' she said. 'Didn't I tell you I wanted nothing to do with you?'

'He's your friend,' Cecilia said. 'You take care of this.'

'He's not a friend.'

'Look, I know you hate me,' Jesse began. 'But I'm here to help you. All of you.'

'I . . . we don't need your help.'

'We? Are you choosing sides now? This is not a game, Lucy.

He is not who you think he is.'

'OK, who is he, then?' Cecilia scoffed, grabbing a brass candlesnuffer and handing it off to Sebastian as he walked slowly, threateningly toward Jesse. 'You have ten seconds.'

'Yes,' Sebastian said. 'Who am I?'

'He is insane,' Jesse stammered, pointing at Sebastian. 'Delusional.'

With each invective hurled, each accusation made, Sebastian took a step closer.

'He escaped from the mental hospital on Halloween.'

'Did Frey send you?' Sebastian asked, now close enough for Jesse to see the intensity in Sebastian's eyes.

'Send me?' Jesse bristled. 'I'm nobody's butt boy. I was worried about Lucy. He told me what he knew.'

'Told you what he wanted you to know,' Sebastian mocked. 'What else did he say?'

'That you're a murderer,' Jesse screeched, as Sebastian got within centimetres of his face.

'He's a liar!' Sebastian shouted right in Jesse's face, putting the fear of God into him.

The light from the altar candle caught the bell cup on the snuffer as Sebastian raised it shoulder high. It gleamed like a guillotine blade about to do its swift and bloody duty. Jesse swallowed hard. Something inside Sebastian seemed to snap. The girls could see his expression change and harden before their eyes.

'I could split your loser skull.' Sebastian grimaced.

Sebastian took the brass bar and pressed it against Jesse's throat.

'Are you going to kill me now too?' Jesse said, gasping. 'Which one of them is next?'

Lucy had seen two guys she knew fight over her before, but never with so much at stake. She cared about Jesse enough not to let Sebastian hurt him and about Sebastian too much to let him do something foolish.

She came up behind Sebastian and touched his arm, signaling a reprieve for Jesse.

'Don't,' she said. 'Please.'

Sebastian slammed the snuffer to the ground and stepped back. The rattling of the metal against the marble floor had them reaching for their ears.

Jesse exhaled slowly and kept his eyes on Sebastian as he beckoned to Lucy. 'He's crazy, Lucy. And dangerous. You need to get out of here. Away from him.'

'You lie for a living,' Lucy reminded him. 'Why would we believe you?'

'You don't have to take my word for it,' Jesse said, reaching for his smartphone on the floor. 'See for yourself.' Jesse swiped the touch screen and the app for his blog opened. He handed it to Lucy. She read the lead item he'd written, over and over, and followed the links to far more reputable outlets. Agnes and Cecilia came over and read it as well.

'It's all over the place already,' Jesse said. 'Newspaper, TV. Looking for you. And him.'

'Thanks to you, no doubt,' Cecilia said.

'I don't believe it,' Agnes whispered as she and Cecilia finished reading. 'Sebastian, is this true?'

'No, but does that matter?' he said. 'People will believe it because they want to believe it.'

'Who would you believe?' Jesse pushed back. 'Some brooding squatter in an abandoned church or the Chief of Psychiatry at Perpetual Help Hospital?'

'Dr Frey?' Agnes said.

'Yeah,' Jesse said.

'That's my doctor.'

'What a coincidence,' Jesse said, sarcastically eyeing her wrapped wrists. 'His too.'

Jesse had put Sebastian on trial and he railed like a prosecutor seeking to undermine the defendant's credibility. Assembling a case, piece by indisputable piece, until the big picture was undeniable. He was in the right place for a sermon. He moved back toward the doors as he made his charges, just in case.

Sebastian remained silent.

'You were all in the emergency room the night he escaped from the psych ward, and now you're all here. Another coincidence?'

Little by little, Jesse was getting through to them.

'And those bracelets he gave to you? The ones on your wrists.

He stole them. From the chapel. They're ancient. Priceless. Relics of some kind. Do you think *he* could afford them?'

'Shut up, Jesse!' Lucy shouted.

'He's not denying it, so why should you defend him?'

Agnes was nearly in tears. 'Sebastian, is this true?'

'You never did tell me what you were doing at the hospital that night,' Cecilia said, looking to him for an explanation.

'Why *were* you there?' Lucy joined. 'Tell us.'

Sebastian did not speak.

Jesse was emboldened and he felt their resolve weaken.

'I'll tell you,' Jesse continued. 'He was in lockdown. Committed. Refused treatment.'

'Treatment for what?' Agnes asked.

'I'm not a doctor, but I think the medical term is "lunatic." He thinks—'

'He thinks what?' Cecilia interrupted.

'Hasn't he told you?' Jesse said, unsuccessfully attempting to stifle a cackle that rose up and bounced around the walls of the church. 'He thinks he is a saint.'

Lucy rushed Jesse and knocked him against the back wall; his back smashed against the empty holy water font. All the pent-up rage and frustration at him and herself spewed from her. She grabbed him by the balls and squeezed. Hard.

'You jealous lying little bitch,' Lucy said, as Jesse moaned in pain. 'Always sticking your nose in other people's business, ruining lives.'

'It's all true, Lucy. You're brainwashed. Or drugged.'

'Does anyone else know where we are?' she said through her clenched teeth.

'No, no,' Jesse said, breathless and beginning to heave.

'Good. And you won't tell anyone, will you?'

'I swear. I won't.'

'*You* swear? I'm not impressed,' she said, twisting just a little harder.

'Let him go,' Sebastian said.

Lucy stepped back and Jesse fell to his knees at Sebastian's feet, gagging and coughing.

'You're going to let me leave?' Jesse asked incredulously. 'How do you know I won't call the police as soon as I split?'

'I don't,' Sebastian said, handing Jesse his mobile phone, turning his back on him.

Lucy stood alone, eye-to-eye with Jesse, who wiped the spittle and humiliation from his chin. '*He* hasn't done anything. I have decided to open my own eyes.'

Jesse had seen this look of purpose and determination many times before. But never with this intensity. She was different.

'Come with me,' Jesse said, making one last pitch. 'We can turn this cult-bride thing around. You are trending bigger than ever.'

'It's only curiosity,' Lucy said. 'Just get out of here. The sight of you makes me hate myself.'

'You need me,' he said unconvincingly, like a needy ex-

boyfriend kicked to the kerb.

'I used to think so.'

Her rejection turned his insecurity into stone-cold spite.

'You know what? Stay here and play haunted homeless with that murderer. Next thing I write about you will be your obituary.'

'Make sure you use a good picture,' Lucy sniped.

She walked closer to him. Put her face in his. 'I saved your life just now, Jesse. I won't do it again. If you tell anyone where we are,' she said, grabbing him by the balls one last time for good measure and forcing him up on his tiptoes, 'I will kill you.'

He'd longed for her to look deep into his eyes. But not like this.

Lucy turned away from him and walked toward the others as he made his way through the wreckage of the storm, to the exit. She didn't need to see Jesse go. She knew he wouldn't stick around after that.

'Jesse might be a lot of things,' Lucy argued. 'But brave is not one of them. It took a lot for him to come here and say what he did. Now it's your turn to confess.'

His truth spilled out. A truth that was beyond belief.

'You are blessed. Chosen. Each of you,' he said over folded hands. 'It's what led you here.'

'Blessed by who? Dead railway workers?' Lucy asked. 'Is that what you expect us to believe?'

'Look, I'm not here to judge you,' Cecilia continued. 'But mental hospitals and murder don't exactly speak to credibility.'

'Just tell us the truth,' Agnes pleaded, taking his hand.

'The truth is inside you now as it is in me. There is nothing else I can say.'

There was really nothing left for any of them to say.

'No more riddles. No more wasted time. The truth is you're crazy and you've made us crazy too,' Lucy said.

'There has always been something inside. Something that has made you feel different. I felt that too. There is more to this life for you, and deep down you've always sensed that. You don't have to struggle or feel frustrated any more. That is what brought you here. And that is why you stayed.'

The room fell dead silent.

'No, that is why I'm leaving,' Lucy said.

Cecilia agreed reluctantly. 'The storm is over. It's time to go.'

'My mom must be worried sick,' Agnes said sheepishly, letting her hand slip from his. 'Don't worry. We won't tell a soul.'

The three removed their chaplets, collected their things and headed up the aisle like runaway brides. They squeezed through the doorway and disappeared into the glowing light of dawn.

21

Scream Thy Last Scream

Jesse stared at the blinking cursor for so long he felt nearly hypnotized by it. Paralyzed was probably more like it. His voicemail, which he was playing over and over, was filling up with messages from the cops asking for a meeting. The tone was getting decidedly less cordial.

The story was fresh in his mind. He knew exactly what he wanted to say but not if he really wanted to say it. It wasn't the threats from Lucy, although he'd never seen her quite so adamant before. It was just an uneasy feeling he had ever since he'd left the church, a feeling of disquiet and uncertainty. Sebastian was clearly deranged, but deadly?

He definitely got Sebastian's appeal to the girls. Sexy, smart, sinister, misunderstood, Byronic good looks, and a whiff of tragedy around him, he was the entire package. He wouldn't need to drug or brainwash them to keep them around. Jesse had written too many stories about far lesser local ladykillers and their 'way out of his league' conquests to buy that. Especially now that he'd met him, or at least confronted him.

There was always the possibility he thought, that he had not met the 'real' Sebastian. Criminals and lunatics were consummate cons after all, and according to Dr Frey, Sebastian was both. Bloggers weren't far behind, so he could sympathize. It was perhaps the only way in which he could relate to Sebastian. He didn't have the rugged looks or the seductive personality, but he had the desire, the need to get his point across. And of the many tales he'd told about Lucy – true and not – none was more important than this one. The ones before were to give her a life. This one was to save it. So why couldn't he bring himself to write it?

The only thing he could figure was that maybe Lucy was right. Maybe she was contagious. Maybe he was growing a conscience too. Jesse searched his contact list and hit send on his mobile.

'Dr Frey, please.'

Sebastian sat up from the hard wooden pew he'd been lying on and stretched his arms outward. He breathed in and exhaled deeply and more easily than before. The dampness had subsided

along with the bad weather, and the mildewy mist that hung throughout the church like mouldy drapes had dissipated. The place was empty again, as it had been when he arrived. His closest companions were once again the hammers, saws, rats, and roaches that littered the once gleaming and holy space.

He missed Lucy.

He missed Cecilia.

He missed Agnes.

But, the time for wallowing was long gone. He grabbed the chaplets they'd left behind and headed for the sacristy.

Sebastian noted the vestments scattered about. It looked more like the changing room at a trendy Smith Street shop than a priest's preparation room. *Indeed the girls left their mark on this place as much as was left on them.* Pulling open the doorway to the ossuary stairs, he paused and thought of Agnes and her struggle to turn the heavy knob and of the many struggles that lay ahead.

He took the stairs down to the ossuary slowly, experiencing the descent, feeling each step beneath his feet before dropping to the next. He stepped through the chapel door and walked directly under the enormous bone chandelier and to the centre kneeler. *It is as sturdy and solid as the day it was made.* From red dogwood, like the ones that lined the gardens of the church outside, now sick, diseased, and dying. A perfect wood for making weapons or wagons or crosses.

Red dogwoods, weeping dogwoods, pink dogwoods, all

planted to honour the long-forgotten men who died there and the saints they died for. These were special. They bloomed in the autumn, near the start of November. The air was heavy with the scent of incense still smouldering in the metal urn and the dogwood flowers that he'd managed to gather from trees that had fallen through the windows.

Looking up, he gazed upon the name of his enemy. Their enemy. The name he'd scrawled across the chapel walls.

CIPHER.

Frey was winning. There was no doubt about it. All without lifting a finger. Sebastian was on the run. Abandoned. Renounced. Lucy, Cecilia, and Agnes were gone. Lonely as it was without them, he couldn't also help but feel relieved. If they were away from him, they might still be kept safe. It was cold comfort, but it was all he had after what he'd done to them, the danger he'd put them in. He'd done his best. He'd delivered his message as he was charged. Whether they would accept his word he didn't know. His fate was sealed. Theirs was still in their own hands.

Sebastian returned the chaplets to the glass reliquary box that he'd taken them from, bowed his head, and reflected, preparing himself. Instead of finding peace, all he could conjure inside of him was despair. And anger.

'I failed.'

He kicked over the kneelers, screaming at the top of his voice.

'What more do you want from me?' Sebastian raged, toppling

the iron maiden and flinging the other instruments of mortification around the room.

'I've done what you asked. Given my heart, my soul, my mind! For what?'

He stepped on to the altar and reached for the *Legenda* and snatched it from its stand.

'Pain! Rejection! Death!'

He raised the weighty tome over his head and spied the glass reliquary housing the chaplets. About to smash it to bits.

He felt hands on his shoulders. Strong hands. An invisible touch bolstering him in this moment of agony. He felt his lungs empty and chest squeeze, as if he were being crushed in a landslide. He lowered the book and returned it gently.

Out of the haze, on the altar before him, appeared the faintest outline of three figures. Men. They were workers, each holding a tool of his trade. A shovel, a pick, and an axe.

He'd seen them before. They were the ones that told him. About himself. About the chaplets. About the girls. At the time, he gathered it might have been a dream or a nightmare but not any more. It was too late anyway.

'Forgive me for my weakness,' he begged, dropping to his knees, preparing for punishment.

They raised their tools. Not to strike him but to salute him. A gesture of encouragement and respect.

'You have done well,' one said. 'You are an honour to your line.'

'Your time is at hand,' another warned.

'Peace be yours,' said the last.

The shadowy figures went as quickly as they'd come. Sebastian was heartened by their faith in him and strengthened in his faith in himself.

'I am ready.'

Frey was busy, barely noticing the young man already seated in his office and waiting for him, when he backed through the doorway still in conversation with a colleague. Jesse's ego could tolerate rude treatment but not being ignored.

'Oh, I'm sorry,' the distracted doctor said. 'I'd forgotten our appointment. I've just got a second.'

'I've seen them.'

'I'm listening,' Frey answered, slowly sitting behind his desk, eyes focused intently on Jesse.

'That guy Sebastian is a lunatic,' Jesse rambled, averting his eyes from the doctor's gaze. 'Raving. Just like you said. And he's wearing off on the others.'

'How so?' Frey inquired, both his curiosity and his analytical self now entirely engaged.

'Stockholm syndrome. Totally. Wild-eyed. I've never seen Lucy like that. So protective of someone else.'

'Impressive,' Frey admitted. 'I'll confirm your diagnosis for the updated story. Off the record, of course.'

'The police are anxious to know where I've been getting

such detailed information,' Jesse said. 'I'm not sure how much longer I can avoid them.'

Jesse was looking for a reaction.

'Now that you know where they are, it's game over. The police will be satisfied to find them, and you will share the credit. A win-win.'

'You've got it all worked out, haven't you, Doctor?'

'It's not brain surgery, is it?' Frey said straight-faced. A psychiatrist joke. And not a very funny one. The unspoken beneficiary here, Jesse surmized, was not the girls, or the police, or even him. It was Frey. He'd deftly kept his fingerprints off this whole thing but got exactly what he'd wanted. Almost.

'So. Where are they?'

'Here's the thing,' Jesse said, a bit self-righteously. 'I'm not going to tell them. Or you.'

'Why wouldn't you?' he asked. 'If you've seen him, you must know firsthand how dangerous he is.'

'Dangerous to who? I saw Sebastian. Talked with him. He could've killed me if he wanted on the spot. But he didn't. You are the psychiatrist. Why would he do that?'

'He is brazen. Unpredictable. Just because he didn't kill you doesn't mean he isn't a killer. Don't be fooled.'

'Good advice, Doctor,' Jesse answered. 'I won't be again.'

'Are you accusing me of lying?'

'No,' Jesse answered deliberatively. 'I'm accusing you of much worse than that.'

'I hand you the opportunity of a lifetime and this is what I get,' Frey said scornfully. 'Perhaps that's quite predictable from someone with your background.'

'I didn't realize I was being profiled,' Jesse quipped. 'Do tell me about myself, in your professional opinion.'

'In my professional opinion, you are snotty, deceitful, self-serving, untrustworthy, and greedy, Mr Arens.'

'I see you've been talking to my friends.'

'If you're holding out for a payday, forget it,' the doctor said. 'I'm not one of your classmates you can blackmail.'

'Former classmates,' he puffed, proudly confirming his lack of higher education. 'I'm an entrepreneur at heart.'

'It shows,' Frey noted, coldly critiquing Jesse's abbreviated academic career.

'Yes, I am the curious type, among other things,' Jesse responded. 'Curious as to why such a respected physician would risk his reputation and trash his oath to help someone with my, ah, profile as you say.'

'I wanted Sebastian off the street before he hurt himself or the others.'

'How magnanimous.'

The doctor was clearly irritated, but quickly gathered himself. 'Well, no matter. We'll find them.'

'We?' Jesse asked.

'You know, you don't need to trouble yourself with this any further or even worry about avoiding the police, Jesse,' Dr Frey

said offhandedly.

'Why's that, Doctor?' Jesse said skeptically.

'Because they are waiting for you in the lobby. Now, if you'll excuse me.'

Jesse's heart began to pound. He knew instantly he'd been set up. A classic double-cross. No matter if he told Frey or not. His purpose was served. He was going down.

'I can't wait to tell them everything,' Jesse threatened.

'Please do,' Frey said, smiling slyly as he left. 'They might even believe you.'

22

Splintered in her Head

'Mother!' Agnes yelled, making her way through the rubble in the hallway. 'Are you here?' She worried that something had happened to her. That she was injured in the tornado, or even worse. 'Mom!' she called again, desperately. Martha came running down the steps, some of which were completely shot, dodging holes and wayward wood. But that didn't slow her down.

'Thank God,' Agnes said in relief. 'You're OK!'

Martha ran over to Agnes. She looked her up and down, and then slapped her across the face. 'Where the hell have you been? I thought you were . . . do you know what you put me through?' Agnes felt the sting of her mother's hand long after it left her face. 'I can't take any more, Agnes.'

Martha broke down in tears.

'I'm sorry,' Agnes said, cradling her as she cried. For the first time in a long time, she let Martha hold her back. After a few moments, she let go. 'I need a hot shower,' she said before heading to her room.

The phone rang. Martha answered it mid-ring.

'She's home. Went straight to her room,' Martha said into the receiver. 'No, I have no idea where she's been. I don't want to push it right now.'

As usual, the conversation was loud enough for Agnes to hear, but unlike usual, she didn't complain. Compared to what she'd just lived through, a little neighbourhood gossip was a welcome change. It'd been only three days, but it felt like an eternity. Besides, this was just the beginning. She knew what would be coming tomorrow, she thought as she began to slowly peel off her clothes. Curious 'friends' of Martha's would begin peering through the floor-to-ceiling parlour windows or lingering just outside the front porch. Younger kids from school and from the neighbourhood, fascinated by the whole idea of her disappearance, would make things up out of whole cloth. Like how Agnes had been *swallowed by the storm* and that *the girl that had returned home wasn't really Agnes at all but some sort of a doppelgänger or a robot or a zombie* – gossipy ghost stories on autopilot would creep like wild ivy through the neighbourhood. They had before, with much less reason. The truth was

irrelevant, and who would believe it anyway?

'Yes, it's the funniest thing,' Martha said to the caller, 'but her wrist wounds are almost totally healed. Wherever she was, it must have been a safe, clean place. She was well cared for.'

As her mother spoke, Agnes examined her wrists, running her fingers along the fading incisions. There was little to physically connect her to him now besides the scars, her only reminder of what she tried to do to hurt herself and what he did to help her help herself.

'As long as she's back safely and not the victim of some crazy maniac,' Martha said, the relieved mother in her finally coming through. 'Thank you, dear. I will absolutely let you know if we need anything.'

'No doubt you will,' Agnes said under her breath as she turned the shower on and stepped in.

Martha was basking in the attention. The danger passed and she was on her way to wringing every ounce of sympathy and whatever else she could think of out of her circle in exchange for satisfying their curiosity.

Maniac? What an odd thing to say about him.

Sebastian was a lot of things. But not a maniac. No matter what that blogger said. But then how could her mother or anyone else know that? All they knew about him was what the news reported, and from what she'd read on Jesse's phone, the details weren't as important as the headline.

It made her think about all the people she'd probably misjudged.

The phone rang again. Martha had her instructions. No friends. No teachers. No one.

'Agnes!' Martha yelled perfunctorily. 'It's Dr Frey again.'

Agnes didn't respond.

'I'm sorry, she must be asleep,' Martha offered apologetically. 'It's been a long weekend. I'm sure we will be in touch to reschedule when she's better . . . rested. Yes, I will keep you informed. Goodbye.'

Frey was the last person Agnes wanted to see or speak to or keep informed.

Martha had notified the police that Agnes had returned and they in turn had notified Frey. He tried to frighten Martha, telling her that if the reports were true, Agnes might be suffering from *folie à quatre* – a shared psychotic disorder marked by the transmission of delusional belief among people in a weakened emotional state, usually in close quarters. Martha wasn't buying it anyway. Her cynicism came in handy for Agnes every so often.

Frey's call only intensified her thoughts of Sebastian. The things he said. She turned off the water, jumped out of the shower, and booted up her laptop.

'S-A-I-N-T A-G-N-E-S,' she said as she typed.

Pages of entries came up, most of them parish or devotional sites. Several for the *Legenda Aurea*, translated as Golden

Legend, which she scanned and recognized from the chapel. She was right, she thought. They were biographies. Lives of the Saints. Legends.

Agnes. Virgin-martyr.

'Virgin.'

One of seven women commemorated by name in the Canon of the Mass. Born January 28 c.291.

'So long ago.'

Martyred January 21, 304. Age 13. Beheaded and burned.

'Thirteen. My God. For what?'

Refused to marry a member of Roman nobility . . . dragged naked through the streets, sent to a brothel to be repeatedly raped . . . as she prayed, her hair grew to cover her body . . . to protect her . . . then tied to a stake to be burned, but the flames parted away from her . . . finally killed by a soldier's sword to her throat.

Patron saint of virgins, girls, gardeners, rape victims . . . depicted most frequently with a lamb, symbolizing chastity.

Agnes found herself on the verge of tears. 'I had no idea.'

She searched for Saint Cecilia and Saint Lucy and found their stories to be equally awe-inspiring and brutal. Both martyrs. Both among the seven.

Lucy denounced for her faith by her own husband . . . could not be moved or burned when sentenced to die . . . gouged her own eyes from their sockets . . . to make herself less attractive . . . rather than compromise her chastity. Patron saint of the blind.

And Cecilia. They tried to cut off her head, but they couldn't . . . She

sang faithfully for three days as she lay dying. Patron saint of musicians.

Finally, Sebastian. Saint Sebastian. Martyr. Patron saint of athletes and soldiers. Captain of the Praetorian Guard who secretly converted to Christianity. Sentenced to death for converting others.

Agnes was stunned.

Martha knocked.

'Are you OK?'

'Yes, Mother.'

'Can I get you something to eat?'

'No, thanks, I'm not hungry.'

It was all just chitchat. Agnes knew her mother had something on her mind.

'Agnes, what were you thinking?'

It was a fair question and not asked in the judgmental tone she was accustomed to getting from her mother.

'I wasn't thinking. I was feeling.' A non-answer but the most honest one she could give.

'The news reports said you might have been taken in by some kind of psychotic boy with two other girls?'

'I don't know what you're talking about, Mother. Do you believe everything you see on TV?'

'I was terrified.'

'It's over, Mother,' Agnes said. 'I'm here now.'

To her surprise, Martha let it go. No lecture. No fighting. No apology demanded. No guilt trip. Passive-aggression or passive-

compassion? It was hard to say. Maybe the storm had even swept some bad blood away. Whatever the case, it was the best 'welcome home' present she could've received. The truth of her leaving would remain unexplained and unresolved, at least for now.

She flopped down on her bed and found chamomile tea in her favorite garnet-and-gold Moroccan glass that she got on Atlantic Avenue. It was sitting on her nightstand, piping hot.

Thanks, Mom.

Agnes lay there, appreciating the softness of her bedding, cuddling with Elizabeth of Hungary, unable to sleep. She was thinking about the night he had bandaged her. Cared for her. Duped her.

All night, until the dawn, until the rising sun rose over the rooftops and crowned her head with a yellow-orange halo of sunshine . . .

She thought about him.

Cecilia was not only homeless now, but she was also jobless. The club on the Bowery was flattened by the hell storm and Saint Ann's Warehouse had cancelled all shows due to the flood overflow of water from the East River. Lenny, the promoter, was an unfortunate casualty, so there was no following him to another club to get gigs. Apparently, he died trying to salvage however many bottles of cheap alcohol he could, but overstacked the cases in the tiny back hallway and they collapsed on him

like one of those unlucky hoarders on cable. He always said he'd die in that place. Lenny turned out to be a prophet. Even though Cecilia couldn't stand him, he did give her a place to play, a chance, and for that, she was saddened by the news. Maybe because she realized she was the one who probably knew him best. A sad circumstance for them both, she concluded.

That night, the night she left Sebastian, she squeezed into a turnstile with a guy, piggybacking his Metrocard, gaining access, and a bruise on the ass, at the Jay Street station. She played guitar for change and then maintained her routine of buying a bottle and sandwiches for Bill at the corner shop – he liked their cuts of meat and would eat only from there. He was a beggar, and a foodie. An unlikely combination, but then again, so was Bill. The most sophisticated, fey man she'd ever met, always dressed for something. 'You never know when the end will come; or the beginning,' he would say. She grabbed a shower at the YMCA and popped into her staple vintage shop, owned by a girl named Myyrah, an up-and-coming designer, straight out of fashion college, who dressed her for shows. She loved Cecilia's style and often took credit for her design ideas. She used CeCe for fashion shoots, as a muse, and in exchange, Cecilia got handmade, one-of-a-kind clothes. She picked up some things to wear, threw them in her guitar case, and then applied some of Myyrah's makeup before heading directly home, to the roof, to Bill.

'Well, look what the dubious devil dragged in,' Bill said, looking up and seeing Cecilia standing there like a long lost soul mate that he thought he might not have ever seen again. 'Our Lady of Snow.'

He didn't ask her if she was holding, aside from the snow reference, which he knew she'd pick up on if indeed there were anything to give. He was relieved to just see her. For a junkie, that meant everything.

'How did you survive the tornado up here?' she asked, but what she really wanted to know was *how did you survive without me?*

'Cockroaches and junkies,' he said in his slurry, crackled voice. 'Always survive.'

She was comforted by that, as he knew she would be.

'They've been looking for you,' he said stoically, sincerely, concerned.

Cecilia was used to this kind of 'out of mind' talk from him, but what she wasn't used to was his sincerity and intensity when he said it. It was like he was twenty years younger and completely sober. A flash of a man that used to be. Someone who cared for her beyond his exterior and weaknesses. Beyond drugs.

'They won't find you here,' he said. 'I'll make sure of that.'

She gave him his sandwich and then a bottle of cheap whiskey. He barely came up for air, thirsty for the bottom of that bottle.

'Easier to get a camel through the eye of a needle than to get a rich man into heaven,' he said, realizing that Cecilia didn't have any money but still managed to bring him food and drink. It always meant something to him, but now, it meant even more.

As the night fell, she told him everything. She confided in him, every intimate detail of what happened in the church. What they saw, what she experienced, what she felt. About Sebastian.

He hung on her every word. Every detail, as if he were taking a verbal shoot-up through his veins. He dared not ask anything, for fear that she would lose her train of thought and forget a morsel of detail. He watched her lips and felt butterflies in his stomach as if they were two girls talking at a sleepover.

'Why didn't you bring some of that shit home?' Bill asked at the end of the story, insisting that Sebastian had likely slipped the three of them some major hallucinogens like the ones Bill once got on the street right across from the hospital that housed Sebastian in the psych ward. Cecilia felt betrayed by Sebastian, but at the same time, she couldn't help but think of him. She got out her guitar and sang to him.

Every word.

For him.

Lucy signed the contract for a new mobile phone, paid, and walked out of the wireless store activated. Within seconds it was buzzing. Jesse, of course. Leave it to him to christen her smartphone. Her first episode of ring rage since the storm. She hit mute and put it in her bag, determined never to speak to him again. And pulled it back out just as determined.

'What?'

'You're my one phone call,' Jesse said desperately. 'Don't hang up.'

Lucy knew exactly what that meant. 'Where are you? And why are you calling me?'

'House of D,' Jesse said as he was being hurried off the phone. 'You have to get here now. I need to talk to you.'

Click.

'Jail?' she screamed out loud enough for everyone on Gold Street to hear. She growled in frustration, already angry with herself for what she was about to do. But she was within walking distance. And curious. Lucy knew that whatever Jesse did, or didn't do, to get into the House of D, it was serious. Dead serious.

He was an asshole. But he was an asshole who meant well. Sometimes.

She made her way through the DUMBO district just as the subway went barrelling across the Manhattan bridge, on her way from her apartment in Vinegar Hill. Her head pounded as the train shook the inside of her brain along with everything else. She walked by Sacrifice but on the other side of the street. The club was still boarded up and closed down like much of

the neighbourhood. Destroyed, pretty much. As she looked around at the downed trees, flooded cobblestone streets, abandoned vehicles, and dead power cables littering the neighborhood, she realized that the storm that changed her world had truly changed her as well. It wasn't just the infrastructure that had been shredded.

Tony, the bouncer, popped out of the black double doors and noticed her, a lone figure walking across the street. He waved. She put her finger up to her lips, the international symbol for *If you tell, I'll cut your balls off*. He nodded, understanding that Lucy didn't want anyone to know she was around, or alive for that matter. Even though Lucy had a reputation as a cold, ruthless, self-centered narcissist all in one high-end package, Tony was there for her. The keys to her world were relationships – you scratch my back and I'll talk behind yours. He smiled and held up her old mobile phone, to show her that he'd kept it safe and to offer it back to her. She shook her head no. He dropped it to the ground and shattered it with his heel, her contact list, saved emails, and photos never to fall into the wrong hands. She blew him a kiss and kept walking. Uphill.

Lucy was so preoccupied she almost walked by her favourite pizzeria, Paisan's, without so much as a peek in the window. Shelves of every kind of pie known to mankind. She pressed her nose up against the glass and promised herself she'd come back later.

'Hey, Lucy. Where ya been?' Sal, the pizza guy, called out from the service window in a deep gravelly voice.

'In church, Sal,' she smiled, tossing him a wink.

The beefy pie man in the flour-dusted white chef's tunic laughed.

'Now I know you're shittin' me. Time for a slice? On me? You look . . . hungry.'

'To go, OK? I gotta run.'

'Where ya headed?'

'Prison,' she said.

'That's an even better one.' Sal nodded.

He went inside and shortly came out with a piping hot slice right out of the oven.

Lucy wanted to cry.

'Thank you, Sal,' she said, kissing him on the cheek in gratitude for the first time ever.

'Get outta here,' he said, semi-blushing.

Neighbourhood people. She loved them the best. No pretense. No pressure. If it weren't for Sal, she'd forget to eat half the time. She could actually count on him. Like Tony. They were nothing like Sebastian, but he was like them in the most important way. They were for real.

Lucy knew the Brooklyn House of Detention, the House of D, as the locals called it. She, on the other hand, had hoped to call it the 'jail with retail', the first urban brig to feature ground-floor storefronts. But it was not to be. It was an eleven-storey

eyesore at the intersection of Atlantic and Smith, towering over the brownstoned streets and alleys of the rapidly gentrifying neighbourhood. About the only accolade it could be given was that nobody had ever escaped. Jesse wasn't likely to be the first.

'Lucy Ambrose to see Jesse Arens,' she said, tipping her dark, oversized sunglasses to the guard at the check-in. She walked through the X-ray machine and endured a pat-down by a very manly-looking woman. She wished they made hand-size versions of these things that you could just use to scan anyone. *How cool to actually be able to see through someone instead of having to guess.* Lucy was escorted to the visitors' boxes and she waited impatiently in the harsh white lighting until Jesse was brought out in cuffs. She watched him as he shuffled into his seat, bruised eye and sickly looking. 'Bail fail?'

'Nobody's opening their wallet for me,' Jesse said languidly. 'I know that.'

'You need a vacation,' she said, holding the visitors' phone about fifteen centimetres from her mouth so as to not catch germs, or poverty.

'So do you,' he said, realizing that Lucy looked just as battered as he did, if not worse. 'I like the raccoon eyes, but usually it's night-before makeup.'

'Even here, I have to be judged?'

Jesse smiled. Lucy smiled back.

'I need to tell you something.'

'How about starting with what the hell you're doing here?'

'That guy, Sebastian—'

'I know, I know,' she said, interrupting. 'You think he's a murderer. Well, I'm done with him. We all are.'

'No,' he cut her off firmly, looking from side to side warily. 'I think he's telling the truth. You know, somewhat.'

Lucy was shocked by his revelation. And suspicious.

'Why the sudden conversion?' Lucy asked, wondering if this wasn't some sort of reverse psychology ploy by Jesse to get back in her good graces.

'You asked me a few seconds ago, why I was here. It's because I wouldn't tell Dr Frey where the guy was. After I found you, I confronted him about the story he told me. He didn't like it. The cops were waiting.'

'You think he's lying about Sebastian?' A wave of nausea and guilt nearly overwhelmed her.

'I don't know, but something's not right.'

'You didn't tell them anything?' Lucy said, surprised he wouldn't sing like a diva in a West Village lounge to save his own skin.

'No.'

'What's your bail?' Lucy asked, reaching into her bag for her wallet. 'I'm getting you out of here.'

'Thanks, but don't bother. I'm on a seventy-two-hour hold.'

'Are you going to be OK?' It was the sincerest question she'd ever asked him.

'I'm not worried about me, Lucy.'

Jesse paused.

'What?'

'There are eyes on you.'

'Jesse, there are always eyes on me. That was our goal, right?'

'It's not a joke. They want Sebastian.'

'It's not my problem any more,' Lucy said. 'I just want to forget the whole thing.'

'But you can't?'

'I feel like I'm in limbo. Not really happy with who I was and not sure of who I am now. Something definitely changed in me, even if it was all just some kind of weird fantasy I got caught up in. Like the one my mom had me believe before she left. That she loved me for who I was. That nothing mattered but me. We all know how that shit played out. But, I don't know . . . This, he, was different. I felt connected to something bigger than myself. Something real. I can't explain it.'

'Well, fantasy or not, I don't think this is going away. Not until they get him, anyway.'

'Who's they? The cops?'

'Probably, but this whole thing is being driven by Dr Frey. He's afraid of Sebastian for some reason.'

'Stop with all the paranoia, Jesse.'

'I think you're being watched, Lucy.'

'You're scaring me.'

Jesse placed his hand on the glass to meet hers.

'Good.'

Agnes's Ecstasy

*A*gnes gave in.

In the middle of the night. Out in her backyard in the garden grotto by the koi pond. It happened. She felt as if she were leaving her body.

She opened her silk chartreuse robe, slipped it off, and lay bare on the rocks under the dogwood tree. Her auburn hair in a loose braid and wrapped around her head like a crown. One foot and one hand dangling in the water as gold, white, black, and orange fish nipped at her fingers and toes.

'Sebastian,' she whispered in a delicate, vulnerable voice. Calling him. Beckoning him.

She took a deep breath and got lost in the smell of his neck and hair. Spicy, warm – sandalwood, vanilla, frankincense, patchouli. He was not like any other. He knew love. He was love.

A flurry of cross-shaped dogwood blossoms opened up on the

bare tree above her as if it were springtime. Then they started floating down as if it were autumn – petals sprinkling over her naked body, adorning her hair.

'You are divine,' she heard him say.

She let out a sigh, closed her eyes, and let the petals float down on to her statuesque body. She glowed in the night, next to the black patent-leather-looking water.

Her lips waited for his, so much so that she could feel it in her whole body. She ached for him.

Trembling.

I won't hurt you.

She felt him. In every way.

Her spiritual lover.

She grabbed the back of his hair, which was her own.

Trying to get more of him. But the more she got, the more it wasn't enough.

Her scars, now dripping blood into the water, turned it red. The fish rose up and down into its warmth. Slowly.

She put pressure on her healed wrists to staunch the bleeding, but it flowed relentlessly. It was all out of her control.

She placed her lips on the wounds and began to softly move her tongue, stroking them. But, the sickly sweet smell of roses emulating from them was too much to swallow. It was so strong that she was sure it would wake up her mother inside the house.

Once she relaxed, it felt good.

She was euphoric.

It had happened.

'Sebastian.'

'I know your weaknesses. I understand your mysteries.'

Agnes believed.

'I am with you always.'

She looked down at the black water and saw his reflection. 'I recognize me in you.'

Agnes turned on her side, to face him.

'Each day I love you, I become more of myself.'

'That is what real love is.'

✦

23

The Birds and the Banshees

'Nature behaving badly,' Cecilia said, eyeing the piles of cicada shells covering the kerbs.

Ever since the storm, Brooklyn had been afflicted by plagues of insects and even rodents. Drugstore chains had sold out of insect repellent. Talking heads blamed it all on standing pools of water that allowed mosquitoes and other bugs to breed in greater numbers, flooded basements, cellars, and subway tunnels that drove subterranean dwellers like rats and mice aboveground. The threat of disease was very real and growing.

Everyone was talking, blogging, and tweeting about the unnatural cicada cycle, which was in full force and being aggressively exploited by some local businesses. SHUT THE

F*CK UP cicada T-shirts were made and sold and stir-fried cicada was being served as exotic cuisine in local restaurants. There were even cicada pops – carcasses, with their transparent, veiny wings and red eyes, frozen inside red lollies for the kids. It was all anyone could talk about after the tornado and the *We're Not in Brooklyn Anymore* campaign.

Brooklynites had pretty much separated into two camps. It either all made sense as a precursor to the end of days – all these unnatural occurrences – or it was beneath their concern. Cecilia was in the second camp for the time being. She'd had her fill of apocalyptic thought unless it had to do with her own day-to-day survival. The only thing on her mind right then was getting a gig. She was desperate to get up on a stage, any stage, and to play plugged into some sort of amp. She had so much inside to get out, and it was the only way she knew how to do that. Her therapy. She took off across the Williamsburg Bridge for Alphabet City in a single-minded quest for a dive-bar that would split the door charge with her.

The rumbling sound of cicada nearly shook the bridge as she crossed it, carrying her guitar. She might not have feared the clicking critters as a sign of the Armageddon, but for her it was disturbing on a much more personal level. As if Sebastian himself was shaking the truss work, reminding her of what she was trying so hard to forget. The storm. Him.

Once over the suspended span, she wandered through the Lower East Side up Ludlow Street toward the East Village before ducking into a small, dingy place on Avenue B. Somewhere she hadn't been in a while, where her fans wouldn't find her. They'd been texting and posting and wondering about her for days now, but she couldn't bear to respond, to face them. If they found her, then fine, but she wasn't going to make it easy.

Around there, club doors were frequently left open on to the street and you were just as likely to be playing in a place with power as not, which was more a function of the bar owners' bad personal finances than bad weather. She walked purposefully past the door guy and directly up to the stage and sat down on the lip of it. She slid her guitar case down next to her and opened it, revealing not just a beaten-up blonde wood Telecaster but some spare clothes and an awesome pair of shoes.

Cecilia kicked off the biker boots she'd walked in and replaced them with a pair of white suede platforms that zipped up the back with twenty-centimetre heels made of what looked like actual bone. Two tiny skulls peered out from each one, sculpted into the back of the heels. Her idea, Mrryah's art project. How she planned to stand on them was anyone's guess, including hers, but she felt compelled to wear them nonetheless for this one-off gig. She wore a slicked back 'do with spackles of white hair paint on each side, giving an illusion of a virgin Mohawk. She wore a vintage gold sequined backless minidress, and in her ears, a pair of large hoop earrings that she fashioned out of some old barbed-wire that she found on the roof. She gave the impression that she belonged there, so no one said anything, they just watched.

'This one's for you, Alphabet shitty,' she said into the mic, nodding to the house drummer on stage to get behind his kit.

She plugged in and let her guitar feed back for a while, and that's when it all started.

Cecilia strummed and sang softly at first. She was vulnerable. Her voice cracking in a beautiful mournful tone through the amplifier static.

The lights were flicked on.

She started sweating and could see her hands starting to bleed in the exact places where she was pierced by the iron maiden. It was coming on her.

The house drummer immediately joined her on stage.

She put a towel over her head and started stomping around to her own slow, dragging beat. Then she motioned to the drummer to kick in double time.

It was like she needed a soundtrack to coax out what was inside of her.

Feeling like she was on fire, she threw off the towel.

She could have sworn that she saw it burst into flames.

She started screaming as loud as she could. Screeching like an angry banshee or a feline in heat. It looked like an exorcism more than anything, and CeCe had more than a few demons to release.

The song was unrecognizable at first. A gritty, intense, punk

reading of something bluesy. Presented in Cecilia's style. Spare and violent.

This was a place where music mattered. And Cecilia was a girl to whom music mattered. A match made in heaven. It was her heart, her soul, and her reality.

And then the song revealed itself, or was revealed through her.

'Whipping Post.'

The tiny crowd of blasé music types gasped and a murmur built in the room. As live songs go, this was sacred.

Guest-listers from the bar started to pay attention.

She clawed and screeched, doubled over on the matchbook-size stage.

People, a mix between cool downtowners and hipster music geeks, immediately started pouring in from outside – either there was a murder in progress or one killer show. In this case it was both. Witnessing either would have been worth the money to them.

Cecilia scratched at her guitar and wailed:

> My friends tell me
> That I've been such a fool
> And I have to stand down and take it babe
> All for lovin' you

Cecilia and the room were at fever pitch. Whatever was happening inside of her was becoming unbearable to her, but

was apparently entertaining as well. The curse of the performer. Creating an *I was there* moment for the audience. And an I'm in hell moment for herself.

> I drown myself in sorrow
> As I look at what you've done
> Nothin' seems to change
> Bad times stay the same
> And I can't run

The club quickly filled to capacity, word of mouth spreading from dive to dive all over the neighbourhood. She was raw, oozing sensuality, vulnerability, defiance, and anger all at the same time. It was as if she were being channelled by greatness, being used as a vessel for something or someone else.

> Sometimes I feel
> Sometimes I feel
> Like I've been tied
> To the whipping post
> Tied to the whipping post
> Tied to the whipping post
> Oh Lord I feel like I'm dyin'

She screamed and began to roll around on the ground. The wounds from the chapel were still raw and unhealed. The more she rolled and scraped herself against the craggy floorboards, antagonized them, the more they swelled and broke open. She

felt something strike her back. Thinking it was a wayward guitar string, she checked her weapon, but all six strings were there. She looked up on the ceiling into the cracked mirror mounted on it and thought she saw a welt appear on her back.

Something was happening.

Cecilia looked out in pain, at the mosh pit, but she didn't see people – only pieces of them through her winces: hands, teeth, tattoos, elbows, hair, shoes.

She moaned in agony, getting verbal lashes from the crowd, typical of an otherworldly performance, and physical lashes from what seemed like thin air.

Lash after lash, whip after whip, she endured it in front of everyone. It was as if she was being beaten up by her own self. An invisible Inquisitor.

> Tied to the whipping post
> Tied to the whipping post
> Good Lord I feel like I'm dyin'

Singing those words was the last thing she remembered.

Cecilia woke up.

On the roof next to Bill.

'What happened?' she asked desperately. 'What is happening?'

'Things are different now,' he replied.

'I have to leave here,' she said.

'I know,' he began. 'What can I do for you?'

Cecilia gathered up some of her costumes that she had hanging to dry in an air duct vent and shoved them into her guitar case before disappearing down the stairs.

'You can write it all down.'

The Brooklyn Museum Gala, or the 'Da Ball' as insiders called it, was the social event of the year in the borough. Lucy never missed the opportunity to walk the red carpet, and this year was no exception. With Jesse in the House of D, Lucy went solo, which felt strange. They'd gone to the event together for the last few years – it guaranteed her coverage and him a ticket. It also guaranteed her someone to talk to. She was getting to be one of the best-known faces in town, but not the most popular.

She wasn't sure how her recent 'hiatus' would be perceived, but the key to being a successful *It Girl* was to never miss an important function. No. Matter. What. It was an obligation she had. To herself. Attending this event would be like getting back on the horse in the most public way. She still wasn't sure what she wanted going forward, so sticking to what she knew best seemed like the right thing to do.

The show must go on, she figured. And for Lucy it went on in an haute couture John Galliano black silk taffeta gown – off the shoulder with fitted corset and billowy bottom of intricate black taffeta swirls and train. Her face was flawless – pale and plain, even her lips were patted with concealer like the rest of

her face, all except for her eyes, which were covered from top to bottom with pink shadow, camouflaging the slight discolouration that remained from the wax burns in the chapel while, at the same time, creating the next high fashion trend. *Besides, she wouldn't be the first girl to walk the red carpet who looked like she'd just had a peel.*

Lucy's reasons for attending were more than selfish or self-promotional for a change, however. She'd offered herself to be auctioned off for charity at the gala dinner, an excellent way to meet influential people, she'd thought initially. But now, given the devastation from the storm, and everything else that had happened recently, she was genuinely excited about it.

The ball was known for its outlandish ways, and this year they outdid themselves, literally mixing things up. The red carpet followed the cocktail hour and dinner, an effort, the organizers explained via press release, to encourage attendees to mingle and most of all, stick around to bid at the charity auction rather than cut out after they'd taken a few pictures. The celebrities on the other hand, suspected that this was actually a great way for the gala committee to assure the press pictures of some tipsy boldface names tripping, falling, or nip-slipping their way down the carpet and into their limos.

Lucy couldn't have cared less. Whatever the motive, she figured it was much more interesting to spectators and newsworthy to the media to see celebrities' drunken antics after they'd gorged themselves on hors d'oeuvres and alcohol.

She noted the size of the crowd of professional fans, held at bay by rent-a-cops and velvet ropes, as she arrived, all waiting patiently to roar their indiscriminate approval at the party's conclusion, and knew it was going to be a successful night for her ego and her brand.

'You're late,' chastised a snippy, tuxedoed minder with a clipboard and walkie-talkie headset.

She was. Her sense of time was definitely not the same since the storm and without Jesse to wrangle her, she was lucky to have got there at all. Lucy went for the default excuse.

'My car was late.'

From the exasperated look on his face, it wasn't the first time he'd heard that one tonight.

'Rich-people problems,' he sniffed and pressed the talk button on his headset mic. 'I've got her.'

Lucy felt like one of those animals that occasionally escaped from the zoo and wreaked havoc. Rounded up.

Captured.

'What, no tranquilizer gun?'

'Dinner is almost over,' he said dismissively, taking her forcefully by the forearm. 'You're first up for the auction.'

As she was led around like an amateur dancer on a ballroom TV show toward the curtained back of the stage, Lucy noticed a line of heads dangling upside down under the lights above the hors d'oeuvre stations inside the dining area. They were all moulded in the likeness of the city's most rich and famous. As

the heat lamps above were switched on, the heads, made of actual cheese, started to melt slowly, drizzling on to the crackers of the patrons positioned expectantly below. The heated heads gave the appearance of a fire at Madame Tussauds.

Lucy noticed one of the heads was in her likeness.

She had been beheaded.

And set on fire.

Her features slowly disappearing under the lamps and dripping down in long strings into the hungry mouths.

She couldn't have been more honoured.

Lucy came to an abrupt stop and the minder released her at the foot of a small staircase. 'When they say your name, step up and out on to the stage.'

'Then what do I need to do?'

'Just stand there,' he said, resuming a crackly conversation on his radio with a colleague at some unknown location in the museum. 'You're good at that.'

A pack of obviously supercompetitive, well-married thirtysomethings, all members of the donor class, sneaked peeks at her over the rims of their half-empty champagne flutes, whispering. The knives were clearly out. Lucy became increasingly uncomfortable as she waited to be introduced. She felt their eyes on her, glaring savagely, picking her apart, appraising her outfit and calculating her worth. Covetous of her youth, her look, her ambition, her success. Lucy tried to hold her chin up high, but her head still hurt. She could

count the beats of her heart by the throbbing in her scalp.

'. . . *Brooklyn's own Lucky Lucy Ambrosssse.*'

She'd become so fixated on the pain, which instantly brought back thoughts of Sebastian, that she barely heard her name mentioned by the MC and the polite applause and catcalls that followed.

The minder came up behind her and gave her a shove. 'Go!'

Lucy burst through the curtain and practically galloped to the lip of the stage, hands on hips, ready to void the warranty. It was a confrontational pose, seductive, but if she knew anything, she knew how to sell herself. And on this night, she had literally offered herself up to the highest bidder. The crowd ate it up.

'All right, ladies and gentlemen, how much for a private dinner date at the River Café with this lovely young lady?'

Bids came in fast and furiously, one higher than the next, table by table, along with whoops and hollers, all decorum tossed to the wind. Well-to-do men, mainly, put down their utensils, wiped away the runny au jus from their chins, loosened their ties and shirt collars at the sight of her, and reached for their chequebooks. Husbands and boyfriends were watched closely by disapproving wives and green-eyed girlfriends. It was a primal scene as even the smell in the room changed subtly from a floral-laced scent thrown off by the table centrepieces to the raw musk of a hot, sweaty gym.

'The food pantries need filling, folks. We can't do it without you!'

She wondered what it must look like from the outside. All these people making offers for her time, her attention. It was all so transactional. Did they even know what charity they were supporting? She barely did, but like the bidders, she wanted to win, she wanted to be the most valuable, the most prized of the night. And besides, it wasn't up to her who paid the price.

'Make it rain, gentlemen!' she shouted brazenly. 'Give until it hurts.'

Lucy was caught up and she worked it. The higher the bid, the farther she retreated from the front of the stage, teasing them, coaxing them along with the MC to go bigger. It was demeaning and oddly empowering all at the same time. To have such control, such influence. To command such attention.

'Let's not have any short arms, deep-pockets people,' the MC barked. 'It's all for a good cause!'

With that challenge, a huge bid, double any other, came from the floor. The crowd was silenced as the MC called for a higher bid.

'Once.'

'Twice.'

'Done!'

'Miss Ambrose, please make your way to table six and meet the winning contributor.'

Lucy stepped down into the darkened dining room carefully, worried that the headache that was suddenly returning was affecting her vision. She stumbled past a few tables and arrived at her table, which was empty, except for a man seated at its head.

'Hello, Miss Ambrose.'

'Hello.'

'Wonderful event. And very magnanimous of you to put up with that. Even for charity.'

'Anything for a good cause,' she smiled. 'Congratulations, by the way.'

Lucy squinted for a name tag he didn't seem to be wearing.

'Dr Frey,' he said, standing and extending his hand formally for hers. 'Please sit down.'

Her hand went suddenly limp as she placed his name and withdrew her hand from his. She appeared ill to the doctor. Unsteady, she positioned her hand on the table to keep herself upright.

'Are you all right?' he asked.

'Yes. I'm fine.'

'So many were caught in the storm and got sick,' he said, looking at her closely. 'Headache. Red, puffy eyes. Bad flu. We're seeing a lot of that at the hospital.'

He was clearly probing her.

'I was inside.'

'Of course,' he said. 'That explains why we haven't seen

much of you in the news lately.'

'I wouldn't think a man with your responsibilities would even know who I am.'

'Quite the contrary. I know exactly who you are.'

She swallowed hard.

'Doesn't everyone?' he concluded with a smile.

Lucy's knees were starting to weaken, to buckle.

'I'm sorry, but I'm not feeling well after all. Perhaps I can have a rain check?'

'No worries,' Frey assured her, reaching into his pocket. 'Here is my card. Feel free to call and set up that dinner when you are feeling better.'

'Thank you.' Lucy turned to walk away, looking to see if he was following her, but he wasn't. He let her go. She bit her lip to keep from screaming.

'Oh, Miss Ambrose?'

Lucy froze. She had to acknowledge him. Others were watching. Listening.

'I'm surprised that you're not wearing your bracelet,' Frey said. 'For such a unique event, it would have been the perfect accessory.'

'Bracelet?' Lucy asked, knowing damn well what he meant.

'Oh, forgive me. I was referring to the white beaded one you had on in one of your photos online. Where did you get such a thing?'

'It was a gift.'

'Well, whoever gave it to you must know you well,' he said. 'It suits you.'

Lucy turned and flashed Frey a tense half-smile, keeping it together for just a few seconds longer. 'On behalf of the sponsors of the Brooklyn Museum, thank you for your generous contribution, Doctor.'

'You are worth every penny, Lucy,' Frey responded.

Lucy felt her head about to explode. She dropped his card to the floor and stepped on it, wiping her hand as she bolted for an exit, any exit, but found her path blocked by a table, a waiter, an admirer, a hater, at every turn in the busy room. Half-seated tables with papier-mâché Warhol head centrepieces vomiting roses sat surreally among litter and leftovers, lipsticked glasses and dirty plates holding the remains of roasted suckling pig and rabbit savagely devoured by savage beauties and their overfed dinner dates. It was like the storm fundraiser had turned into a fun house. She was overwhelmed.

'Please,' she begged, pushing her way through the crowd. 'I've got to get out of here.'

As Lucy made her move toward an open door, she was grabbed and pulled sideways, nearly out of her fifteen-centimetre heels.

'The red carpet is this way.'

The minder assigned to her was not taking no for an answer. She was pushed out of an exit and directly on to the walkway just as she'd been pushed up the stairs earlier.

Delivered.

Cameras flashed. Dozens of them.

'Lucy!'

The photographers screamed for her and so did the fans. All begging for acknowledgment like ardent lovers. It was loud and chaotic. Disorienting. Maddening. What was once such a pleasure seemed now a punishment. The flashbulbs kicked her migraine into overdrive and she began to claw at her brow in pain, dizzy and panicked.

'Help me!' she screamed.

In the black spaces between the strobing flashes, Lucy swore she could see Sebastian, breaking through the media throng, trying to get to her. Lucy called out to him to no avail.

'Sebastian!'

She ambled awkwardly down the never-ending carpet, all alone, on display, still scratching and still self-aware enough to realize that the photo editors just might get that humiliating picture they were looking for at her expense, when a frightening cry rang out.

'Oh, my God,' a blogger girl cried, pointing at Lucy's knees.

Sanguineous drops stained her legs as they formed a puddle of plasma on the carpet beneath her. At first, there was a collective gasp of embarrassment. It appeared to them that she had got her period, but when she removed her hands from her face and looked up, the true source was revealed to them.

Her tears were of blood.

The flashes went into a frenzy once again.

The whites of her eyes shone bright red in the bloodstream. She gazed up at the white tent above her and felt it fall further and further out of focus, until she could barely distinguish the massive canopy.

'My eyes,' she said, over and over.

She could see nothing until she closed them. And then all she could see was him.

An older woman, a waitress at the gala, had seen enough and ran toward the girl she'd watched bear the brunt of this full-frontal media assault. She helped Lucy behind the backdrop, out of view of the photographers, where the girl collapsed in her sympathetic arms. The event personnel began to crowd around, more concerned with their potential liability than with Lucy. A single look from the waitress was enough to disperse them.

'Should we call an ambulance?' the minder asked as he backed away.

'No,' the woman said authoritatively.

She pulled out a linen white lace hankie and placed it over Lucy's face, absorbing the blood and tears into the fabric. As she removed it, she noticed that a replica of the girl's face, outlined in her blood, had been transferred. The woman tucked the cloth in the front pocket of her smock carefully, respectfully, and proceeded to comfort her, wiping the matted hair away from her face.

'Oh, my head,' Lucy moaned. 'It's splitting.'

The woman gently took Lucy's hand and ran her fingers along her wrist in the exact place where the chaplet had been, and began making tiny crosses as she whispered prayers in Lucy's ear.

Lucy yawned.

Again and again.

'Good, let it out,' the woman said.

The pain seemed to escape through Lucy's open mouth.

She relaxed as the woman cradled her head in her arms.

'What was that?' Lucy asked, after a while.

'A *fatura*,' the woman said in Italian-accented English. 'The *malocchio*.'

'I don't understand.' Lucy said, wiping at her eyes and face.

'It's like a curse. The evil eye.'

'Oh, I don't believe in that stuff.'

'It doesn't matter whether you believe. The truth is what matters.'

'I don't know what's true anymore,' Lucy said, rising to her feet. 'Thank you for helping me.'

'No,' she said. 'I thank you.'

Lucy was flattered that she'd had such an impact on the woman. She never imagined her celebrity had trickled down so far, especially in her own neighbourhood, where she tended to be the least popular and most resented.

She hugged the woman tight, as she imagined she would

hug her mom if she ever saw her again. The waitress reached into another pocket of her smock and pulled out a gold charm in the shape of a horn of plenty and placed it in Lucy's hand.

'Who are you?' Lucy asked.

'Perpetua.' The old woman smiled. 'I live in the area. Near Precious Blood. I took him in after his escape, so they wouldn't find him when they looked in the church.'

'Sebastian?' Lucy asked, stunned.

They lived in different worlds. Until now.

'One has overlooked you. Three can save you. You understand me?'

'Yes,' Lucy replied. 'I think I do.'

'Then go back to him.'

24

Dis/Graced

'You must think I'm some kind of a psychotic, don't you?' Agnes blurted out as she gathered her things and headed for the door, her paranoia reaching new heights, feeling as if she were being watched, even inside the house.

'I only know what I see,' her mother responded casually, showing neither disgust nor sympathy as Agnes prepared to leave her again.

'Do I look crazy to you?' she asked, trying to prompt some kind of reaction.

'You look like,' Martha said frankly, looking her only daughter up and down, 'a girl with nothing to lose.'

'I'm praying for you,' Martha called out to her as she

walked out of the door.

'No, Mother,' Agnes began, putting on her lambswool poncho. 'I am the one praying for you.'

Agnes ran down her block and was stopped in her tracks at the sound of children playing and the sight of a little boy in the St. John's schoolyard. It was Jude.

She hurried to the towering silver cyclone fence surrounding the playground and grabbed hold of it for dear life, hoping to get some acknowledgement from him – a smile, a glance, anything – without much luck. He was standing with a middle-aged woman, a nun, before a handmade hanging figure. Agnes wanted to scream out to him, but checked herself and listened in on his lesson instead.

'The seven points on the piñata symbolize the seven deadly sins,' the sister explained, pointing a thin wooden rod at each. 'Greed. Lust. Pride. Despair. Wrath. Sloth. Envy.'

The nun raised a strip of cloth in front of the boy's face, folded it over, and began to tie it around his head. Once it was secure, she gently turned him in a circle a few times, explaining to him the deeper meaning to be found in this traditional game.

Agnes swallowed hard. The image of the blinded child disturbed her.

'The blindfolded person represents faith. Turning symbolizes the disorientation of temptation.'

She placed the stick in Jude's hand and instructed him to begin. Agnes was nervous for him. She'd played this game

countless times at birthday parties. It was hard and he was not 'typical', from what she'd seen.

'Striking the piñata recalls the battle against evil. Defeat it and the reward is revealed.'

Heavy shit for a kid, was all Agnes could think as she listened.

Jude held the rod in front of him and grabbed it with his other hand, steadying it. He tapped the piñata once, taking a measure of the distance between him and the suspended object. He drew the stick back up and over his head like a knight with a broadsword. Agnes could almost see how badly he wanted the sweets inside from the grimace on his face as he swung at the piñata. He smacked it top and bottom, side to side. Agnes was surprised at how on target he was, but there was no sign of damage.

Jude was obviously frustrated and getting upset the longer the game went on. The nun removed the stick from his hand and struck the piñata herself, also without result. She handed it back to him.

'Again,' she said, counselling both patience and perseverance.

The boy swung and turned the stick over to the teacher, who did likewise. Over and over.

Agnes marvelled that this was possibly the first combination of religious instruction and occupational therapy she'd ever seen. Other children began to turn their heads toward Jude, counting the strokes and licking their lips impatiently in anticipation of the sweets they hoped would eventually escape.

For her part, Agnes was beginning to feel bad for the piñata.

The nun's next swing was a productive one. She made a dent. But then Jude took his turn and cracked it wide open with a mighty whack. The sweets spilled and children came running.

'See, Jude,' the nun said, kneeling to help the children collect their sugary treasure. 'You can't always do it alone. Everyone has a part to play.'

Agnes smiled, not just at the boy and his achievement but also at the thought of Sebastian, Cecilia, and Lucy that came to her in that moment. There was more than a lesson in the game, Agnes felt, there was a message. A message for her.

To her surprise, Jude removed his blindfold and looked directly over at Agnes as if he'd known she was there all along. She beckoned him, and the boy, taking the opportunity while the nun was distracted, ran over to her, forgoing the sweets he'd earned.

'I told him,' Agnes said.

The boy kissed her through the chain link.

'There are snakes behind the rocks. You might not see them. But you know they're there,' Jude said in a whisper.

Just then the nun ran over and grabbed Jude's hand.

'You shouldn't run away like that,' the nun said sternly, looking him directly in his eyes.

'I think he wanted to tell me something,' Agnes offered, hoping to keep the boy out of trouble.

'I'm sorry, but that's impossible,' she said to Agnes. 'He's nonverbal. He doesn't talk.'

Cecilia awoke to piss-warm rain leaking through the street grate above and on to her in the filthy, white-tiled corner of the subway station she presently called home. She opened her eyes to confirm that it was indeed rain and not some pervert or bum getting his jollies by relieving himself on her. Or something worse.

She'd ducked into the subway for a nap the night before and had the eerie feeling she was being followed. The subway wasn't exactly the best place to hide, but it was the brightest place at that time of night, and that was a plus. Turns out she wasn't entirely wrong. There was a person, scrunched up in a foetal position, lying at her feet. Way too close for comfort.

'Hey,' Cecilia said, nudging the girl with her foot. 'Get up!'

The girl just moaned, turning over slowly and rising to her hands and knees.

Cecilia recognized her immediately, even though her long straggly hair was hanging down obscuring most of her face.

It was Catherine. The fangirl from Pittsburgh. What was left of her.

'Was it you following me?'

'No,' Catherine said quietly, lifting her head into the harsh light.

She was obviously badly battered and bruised. Her hair was

matted. Her clothes stained and weatherbeaten. This clearly wasn't her first night on the street. How long had it been since she'd seen her outside the club? CeCe pondered groggily. A week? Two? By the hollow look in Catherine's eyes, it might as well have been years.

'Who in the hell did this to you?' Cecilia asked, taking the girl's head in her hands.

'Does it matter?' Catherine responded through swollen lips, barely able to muster the strength to form words.

'Yes,' Cecilia said, already suspecting the answer. 'Tell me.'

'Ricky's band. They said I could sing a song in their set,' Catherine said. 'They said we were going to their rehearsal space in Williamsburg. That I could stay there with them.'

Cecilia didn't need to hear the rest. She knew.

'New York is not a place for someone like you.' Cecilia railed at the girl's naïveté. 'I told you. You need to go home.'

'I believed them,' Catherine responded sadly. 'I'm so ashamed.'

Cecilia stopped preaching at her, stopped trying to solve her problem. She'd been there too once. Made her share of mistakes. It was like looking in a mirror. She pulled a tissue from her pocket and wiped at the girl's eyes and face. 'We all put our trust in the wrong people sometimes.'

'What would you do? Would you really leave? Just give up on your dreams?'

Cecilia did not respond.

'That's what I thought,' the weary girl said through cracked

and scabbed lips. 'That's why you're great.'

Cecilia unpacked her guitar, plopped a few coins into a used coffee cup, and began to play.

'Still wanna be like me?'

'What happened?' Catherine asked.

'Reality. Sucks, but life is full of it.'

'Yes.'

'Yes, what?' Cecilia asked, putting down her guitar.

'Yes, I still wanna be like you.'

'Why? So you can sing for your supper, live on the streets, and drown in all the abuse?'

'I can't leave, just give up.'

Cecilia heard her words and thought of Agnes. She knew there was no way she could convince Catherine otherwise.

'Up to you, Catherine. You've paid your dues.'

'I don't even feel like I have a choice. It's like fate.'

Cecilia stared blankly ahead, thinking of Sebastian.

'I mean, I think our dreams choose us anyway, not the other way around,' Catherine continued. 'I'm supposed to stay, to do what I came to do. Whatever that is, you know?'

'I know.' Cecilia reached again for her guitar.

'Back to work,' Catherine said. 'Can I stay for a while?'

'Please do,' Cecilia answered, as she began to slowly strum a moody minor chord. 'At least I will be sure one person is listening.'

'One is all you need.'

'Goddamn right.'

Cecilia chanted a few words over the top of the chord changes that she played in the church.

'That's amazing,' Catherine said. 'Is it about a guy you know?'

'Yeah.'

'Have you ever sung it for him?'

A bit of the wide-eyed devotee returned to Catherine's face for just a moment, and CeCe smiled.

'Not yet.'

A train pulled loudly into the station, cutting off the conversation but not Cecilia's song. She continued to play and sing through the clanging racket, eyes closed, head hung low, as a few passengers ran for the closing doors and the last subway car pulled out. She shook her head and looked up at the emptiness and squalor all around and then up at Catherine.

'Does this look like a dream to you?' Cecilia asked, searching herself more than Catherine.

'No,' the girl admitted. 'It doesn't.'

'Well, what does it look like?'

'A calling,' Catherine responded.

'Decaf or regular, hon?' the waitress asked.

'Regular,' Lucy answered automatically out of habit.

She filled the white ceramic cup in front of Lucy, who was out of sorts from her experience at the museum. She found herself at a diner on Cadman Plaza in the wee hours. Alone.

As usual, she couldn't remember how she got there. Except this time vodka or Vicodin weren't the reason, it was a supernatural one.

She could feel herself being watched, but not by the regular gawkers and stalkers that followed her around.

'Need to wake up?' a nasal female voice asked, seemingly out of nowhere.

Lucy was startled. In the neighbourhood, she was usually left alone.

'The coffee?' the girl asked.

Lucy looked up. It was Sadie. She hadn't seen her since the ER that night.

'Sadie?' Lucy said, sheepishly standing up. 'Ah, how are you?'

There was a sadness in the girl's eyes and Lucy girded herself for the accusations she certainly had coming and the judgment she most certainly deserved. She prepared her defense quickly. *Jesse made me do it* was the first thing that came to mind. It was the truth but a very thin excuse for ratting out Sadie to him. She should have been able to keep her pregnancy and what she had done private. Lucy looked down at the girl's belly almost reflexively, but there was no sign of life that she could spy.

'I just want to thank you,' Sadie said.

'For what?'

'For helping me turn my life around.'

'Really?' Lucy said, genuinely shocked. 'How?'

'You exposed me.'

'I don't understand.'

'When the story ran with the picture you took, and the nasty looks from everyone started, the gossip, I realized what my life had become. Who my true friends really were. What was really important to me.'

It didn't sound much like a compliment to Lucy, more like a cleverly crafted diss, in fact. Something Sadie had been expert at.

'I still don't quite see . . .'

'I didn't have an abortion, Lucy. I had a miscarriage.'

Lucy bit her lower lip to keep it from shaking. Could she have been more wrong?

'I'm so sorry,' Lucy said, genuine concern and remorse welling up in her face.

She was sorry. Sorry for making the abortion joke, for taking the picture, and even more sorry for the tremendous loss that Sadie had to bear either way.

'It's OK,' Sadie said. 'I'm out of that world now. For good.'

'What about Tim?' Lucy asked. 'How's he taking it?'

'He's fine,' Sadie explained, forcing a smile through her tears. 'He is back with his girlfriend. He did tell his grandmother. She said that the baby would have been so beautiful, the angels wanted to keep it for themselves.'

'I'm sure she's right.' Lucy said, reaching for the girl's hand.

'I know she is.'

Lucy looked down at her cooling cup of coffee only to realize she'd lost her appetite.

'Just talking about it with you is making me feel so much better. I haven't told anyone yet outside our family. I don't care what everyone else thinks. Their minds are made up already anyway.'

'You know it's nothing to be ashamed of, right?' Lucy queried sympathetically. 'You didn't do anything wrong. It's not your fault.'

'Thank you.' Sadie sniffed. 'I'll try to remember that.'

Lucy cringed how easily she'd betrayed the girl in her hour of need, just as she had Sebastian. The tears began to come and she knew she had to make it right.

'I'm so sorry,' Lucy said again, hugging Sadie as tightly as she could.

'I forgive you.'

25

Last Call

Evening fell and one by one they arrived at the church. In the order in which they'd originally come.

Lucy.

Cecilia.

Agnes.

All out of breath, and filled with foreboding. Looking over their shoulders. They met only a little unexpectedly in the vestibule and smiled empathetically at one another. No hugs or air kisses. No words. None were necessary. Just sighs of relief and commiseration.

'You felt it too, right?' Lucy said to them.

They knew what she meant. It was a pull at the centre of

their being. A fire in the back of their heads and at the bottom of their hearts, burning hotter the longer they were away. A restlessness they'd each had even as children, and then more intensely as teenagers, that something bigger was in store for them. But more than anything, it was the desire to return to him. It was all the same compulsion.

'Yes,' Cecilia responded.

'Yes,' Agnes said.

Agnes explained to them about their namesakes. The legends of their saints and the influential roles they played. Their martyrdom.

'I told you, I'm not religious,' Lucy said.

'Virgin?' Cecilia said. 'That lets me out.'

'That's not the point. It was a different time,' Agnes rebuffed them. 'It's about realizing what's most important, what you are meant to be, meant to do. And what you are willing to sacrifice for it. They gave all they had for what they believed in. Gladly. A love, a duty, a calling beyond themselves.'

'Oh, yeah, and what is our calling?' CeCe asked.

'I don't know, but whatever it is, I believe it's something we can't do alone. Like opening the door to the chapel,' Agnes insisted. 'We've been thinking that he meant to bring the three of us here to him. I think what he really meant was to bring the three of us together.'

'We do know something else,' CeCe said. 'We know someone is trying to stop it.'

'But why?' Agnes asked.

'He can tell us.' Lucy yelled out for Sebastian without reply.

'Do you think he's still here?' Cecilia asked.

'He must be,' Lucy fretted. 'Maybe he's angry at us?'

'He's here,' Agnes said with certainty. 'In the ossuary.'

They stepped over the trail of warped plywood sheets, splintered beams, shattered glass, and the damp crumbled plaster that led down the side aisle, surveying the old church like a beloved landmark that was about to be imploded to make way for new construction. Through the sacristy door and into the vestry, which was still showing the effects of the rummaging they'd given it just a few days earlier. It didn't look like a single soul had been in there since.

The door to the stairwell was in their sight now, and Lucy held up.

'All our problems, all our questions started when we walked into this building.'

'They started way before that,' Cecilia said, shaking Lucy's grasp and reaching for the doorknob.

'Hey, Bill. How's it hanging, old man?'

The junkie squinted through his hungover eyes at the thin young man with the messy shag cut, strategically torn T, thick-linked wallet chain, and skinny jeans. Everything about him screamed asshole. In fact, Bill would have sworn it was a girl or a tranny at least, if not for the lowish voice.

'It's Ricky. Ricky Pyro,' he said, fidgeting. 'You've seen me play. I sampled your typewriter for one of my songs that time.'

Bill went blank, searching whatever brain cells might have dried out between then and his last drink. He still couldn't make the kid.

'C'mon. You know. *Ricky Rehab*. From Dr Frey's programme at the hospital,' the rocker said a little more quietly, leaning into Bill's ear.

'Oh, yeah, now I remember. Ricky.'

'That's right, Bill. Mind if I pull up some pavement?'

Ricky slid down on his bony butt, resting his forearms across his knees. The old man couldn't help but notice the paper bag the kid was holding. Ricky couldn't help noticing Bill notice it.

As expected, the bag was an icebreaker. Bill suddenly turned sociable.

'You're a friend of CeCe's, right?'

'Some nights,' Ricky said with a laugh, elbowing the old man like a frat buddy. 'Seen her around?'

'Not a lot lately, but she did come around last night,' Bill said, elbowing Ricky back less convincingly. 'She brings me my breakfast every so often.'

'She say where she'd been?'

'Oh, yeah. Even told me to write it all down.'

Bill pulled a few barely legible handwritten pages from his coat pocket and flashed them tantalizingly at Ricky.

'Sounds like a good story. Tell me about it.'

Bill was wary. He was an addict, not a sucker.

'Couldn't do that. She swore me to secrecy. A promise is a promise.'

Ricky tilted the bag back and forth. The familiar sound of a liquid rolling around inside a bottle was more than obvious to the old man.

'Yeah, but CeCe knows all about junkies and promises.'

Bill dropped his head slightly.

'All right then, Bill. I gotta go. Great seeing you again,' Ricky said.

Ricky started to get up from the ground when Bill grabbed his arm, the one with the bottle.

'What'cha got there, son?'

'Firewater,' the rocker said with a smile.

'Holy water, you mean,' the old man retorted with a small cackle.

'All depends on your point of view, I guess,' Ricky observed.

Bill's eyes glazed over and focused tightly on the bag, like a hungry cat in a restaurant back alley. The gentle sound of the whiskey sloshing to and fro as seductive to him as the lapping surf on a seaside resort. Ricky's tone turned exponentially more serious and demanding.

'Tell me about CeCe,' he said.

'I don't know,' Bill said nervously. 'It's real personal. I promised to keep it just between the two of us.'

'She'll never know, Bill.'

Ricky pulled the top of the bottle up through the bag and opened it, the aroma of alcohol wafting under Bill's nose like anesthesia. He could not resist any longer.

'OK, but don't be sore at me if it hurts your feelings. I'm just the messenger.'

'I won't. I swear.'

'She met some guy during the storm. I guess they hooked up and spent a few nights in that big old church they're converting. You know the one.'

'Yeah,' he said, his expression tightening, eyes narrowing. 'I know the one.'

Bill might have been old and gin-soaked, but the writer in him was good at reading faces.

'She said it was a spiritual thing. Never heard her talk like that before.'

'Me either.'

'I said you might get mad.'

Bill held his hand out expectantly.

Ricky stood up and looked down at the old man and held the bottle out just within Bill's reach. The old man grabbed it like manna from heaven.

'Thank you, son.'

'No need, old man. A promise is a promise.'

Ricky walked slowly down the block to one of the few corner pay phones left in Williamsburg, dropped a few

coins, and dialled a number.

'Dr Frey, please.'

'I'm sorry, he's unavailable right now. May I take a message?'

'This is Ricky Pyro, one of his rehab patients. Can you tell him that I have to cancel my appointment? I'm playing a special gig tonight. At Precious Blood Church in Cobble Hill. He's been asking about it. Tell him he shouldn't miss it.'

Cecilia, Lucy, and Agnes descended the cobblestone steps as they had before and stopped at the squat narrow door. It was ajar. Cecilia pushed it open and led the others in. It was dazzling. Every votive was lit and burning, throwing warm red light and thick shadows across the sacred fossils bedecking the chapel and a lone figure seated cross-legged, hands clasped, still, head bowed, swaying slightly, and facing the altar. He shimmered in the candlelight and shadow of the Sacred Heart fresco before him.

'Sebastian,' Cecilia whispered.

They were all nervous about approaching him. He seemed in a trance. Weak, breathing shallow and unsteady. Like a resistant captive in the midst of a hunger strike.

'Is he all right?' Agnes asked, wanting to run to him to find out.

Lucy shrugged, uncertain. 'He's alive. I think.'

Finally, he spoke.

'I have no idea what will happen, or in which places the pain

will come,' he mumbled, before opening his eyes to see them. They were cemented into a stare that left them to wonder whether he'd gone completely mad.

Agnes walked slowly toward him and fell to her knees.

'Sebastian, we're here.'

He smiled and brushed his hand against her cheek.

'Agnes.'

Lucy and Cecilia came and kneeled as well. He met each of their eyes with his.

'You came back,' he said.

'Of our own free will,' Lucy said.

'I think we are being watched. You've got to leave here,' Cecilia said.

'Why? There isn't anywhere to go.'

He was having trouble responding fully, almost seeming to hear and answer different questions than the ones they were asking.

They looked around in awe and trepidation, their memories of a few days earlier still raw and visible, bloodstains still on the floor. Their chaplets resting in the reliquary.

'What happened to us down here?' Lucy asked. 'We need to know.'

He did his best to explain and reassure them all at once. 'I would never hurt any of you.'

They wanted to be sceptical, to fight what they were feeling inside, but he was so beautiful, so genuine, so real, and now so

vulnerable, that it was almost impossible not to get lost in him.

'We want to understand,' Cecilia added. 'We want to believe you.'

Sebastian was heartened by their trust.

'I will tell you everything I know,' he said, gesturing then toward the bone-legged altar. It was surrounded by four pillar candles, one at each corner, and covered with the chasubles they modelled. A patchwork tablecloth of green, red, and white fabric with elaborately woven images of young men and women crowned with halos and clothed in glory. Atop it sat magnificent place settings, gold plates and long-stemmed silver cups glimmering. At the centre, the *Legenda Aurea* Agnes had flipped through on the lectern.

The girls joined him at the altar and sat on the antique short benches he'd arranged around it. They felt like royalty.

'What is this?' Cecilia asked.

Sebastian took a brass candle lighter that had been leaning against the altar and struck a match. He lit one candle and passed the rod around, asking each girl to do likewise.

It was a ritual, but unlike the ones they had experienced before. This was only for them.

When the last candle had been lit, Sebastian took the case holding the chaplets and placed it on the altar before them.

'We're getting them back?'

'Yes.'

'But Sebastian, they don't belong to you,' Agnes said.

'That's true.'

'Jesse said you stole them,' Lucy reminded him.

'I didn't steal them. I took them,' he admitted.

'I don't understand. You took them but you didn't steal them?' CeCe asked.

'I took them,' he explained. 'So I could return them to their rightful owners.'

'Us?' Lucy asked.

'These chaplets were made from holy relics, from the bones of St Lucy, St Cecilia, and St Agnes, as proof of their existence through the ages and held closely by generation after generation of men and women who worshipped them, were devoted to them, and prayed for their return when the world was most in need of them.'

'Now?' Lucy asked.

'Now,' Sebastian said. 'This legacy, these chaplets are your inheritance. I had to get them to you before Frey stopped me.'

'Why?'

'Because he knows who we are and will try to stop us however he can.'

'How can he do that?' Cecilia said. 'He has no control over us.'

'You said you thought you were being watched, followed. He is using you to find me. So he can get all of us.'

Sebastian turned suddenly grim.

'You aren't just being followed. You are being hunted.'

26

Altared

The corrections officer strolled down the cement-floored hallway of the Brooklyn House of Detention. Even to a seasoned veteran of the system, it was a scary place. But then, it was meant to be. In earlier days, it might be considered the kind of place where one might be sent to 'loosen the tongue', and it still had that effect. It was a snitch factory, especially for guys like Jesse, but he didn't break. He was proud of that.

'Arens!'

Jesse lifted himself from the hard cot slowly. The guard pressed the lock button on the side of his cell and the door slid open with an echoing clang. Jesse stepped out, cautiously, wary that this might be some sort of trick.

'You're free to go.'

'I'm sprung? Seriously? Did someone bail me out?'

His search for a Good Samaritan was unrewarded on a technicality, though he could hardly believe anyone he knew cared enough.

'You're not charged with anything. It's been seventy-two hours. You served your time.'

'So soon?' he asked snidely. 'I was never charged. Time for what?'

'For being a douche bag,' the officer said dismissively.

'Oh, well then, guilty,' Jesse said, holding his hands out for cuffs.

'Pick up your things at the desk and get the hell out of here.'

'Listen, I run a few nights at Sacrifice during the week. Maybe you might like to stop by with your boys. Let me know. I'll even comp you.'

'That's a bribe, prick.'

'You'd know.'

Jesse checked out of his accommodations and reached for his smartphone. He might have developed an instant reputation as a whiny bitch on the inside, but he made sure to play his rap sheet up for street cred on the way out. He threw on his shades, popped his jacket collar up, and put on his swagger as he hit the door. There was a photographer waiting to shoot him, as planned. Before he even got to the corner, the picture was posted, 'liked', and reblogged to every subscriber in the city.

The 'Free Jesse' slogan he posted across his main page in computer-animated caution tape was replaced by a 'Jesse's Free' headline and power-to-the-people fist icon. 'From felon to chillin' at warp tweet.' He was back.

He searched his competition as he usually did after a day or two offline, after holidays mostly, just to see what had gone on in his absence. He smiled at a folder of photos and an item about Lucy from Da Ball. He flipped through the JPEGS and captions casually, pissed off that she'd even gone without him. When he opened the last photo, his face went completely white and his jaw dropped. It was picture of Lucy and Dr Frey.

And then it hit him, all at once. Like a city bus.

'Oh God. How could I be so stupid?'

It wasn't just Sebastian Frey was after. He texted Lucy:

911. You are not safe.

He waved his arm in the air like a madman.

'Taxi!'

He jumped in the backseat of the first yellow cab that would have him and sped to the church.

'No,' Lucy said as she began sobbing uncontrollably. Agnes and Cecilia tried to pull away from Sebastian's grasp to comfort her, but he held them tight. 'I don't want this,' she protested hysterically, pulling at the chaplet.

'You do,' Sebastian said, a note of sympathy in his voice. 'You came back.'

'I like my life. These girls have nothing to lose!' Lucy screeched, pointing a finger at Agnes and Cecilia. 'I worked so hard to have everything I ever wanted.'

'Then you must be happy. Are you . . . happy?'

Sebastian waited.

A few sobs later, she gathered herself and looked up at the three of them, standing there, sacred hearts amid sculpted bones, bathed in the corona of candlelight.

'It's who you are. Who you have always been.'

Cecilia and Agnes reached out their hands, inviting her into their exclusive circle.

'You're not alone anymore,' Cecilia said. 'None of us are.'

She stepped up to the altar as if to the edge of a precipice and joined them. They stood like high divers about to take the plunge, anxiously awaiting the opportunity to jump. And then the tension eased. Hands clasped, they relaxed.

Sebastian, Lucy, Cecilia, and Agnes bowed their heads and felt themselves almost disappear into the smoke and fragrant heat, as if their flesh was melting away with the candle wax.

Revealed.

Stripped like the bleached bones that adorned the chapel.

At peace with themselves. At one with the chapel and with each other. A sort of music filled their ears, like the low hum of a generator or the soft chanting of a choir, which vibrated simultaneously through them and the ossuary, transforming it into a giant tuning fork. They channelled the powerful force, exchanging it with one another and with the room until everything was infused with their energy. It made the sudden intrusion of reality, the rumble of a passing subway train, even more startling.

Sebastian opened his eyes, raised his head, and stared at the stained-glass windows surrounding them. Scenes of pain. Scenes of sacrifice from the distant past fighting their way into the present.

'The faithful were not the only ones preparing for our coming,' Sebastian warned.

'Ciphers?' Cecilia asked.

'Ciphers are the leaders. They don't hide. They manipulate, they persuade, they seduce and pursue their agenda right under our noses.'

'Like Dr Frey?'

'Yes and many faceless others who do their dirty work but are just as dangerous. Vandals, some have called them. Destroyers of bodies and corrupters of souls. They are threatened by our very existence.'

'What is it that they are so afraid of?'

'Of the power inside you,' Sebastian explained. 'To be a wake-up call. To be living examples that things can be better.'

'Soul models,' Lucy said.

'Yes,' Sebastian said. 'People are lonely, hurting, empty. You will fill them.'

He reached for the book on the altar in front of him. He lifted the silk tassel marking a specific page. 'You asked me what this was all about. It is all about you.'

He walked over to the urn and brought it back to the altar as well, first removing a few hot coals and slipping them into the golden censer before him. He reached into the incense boat next to it and sprinkled a few resinous grains on to the coals and watched the smoke rise.

The air became heavy with the spicy aroma, the scent of cedar and rose. The candles burned brightly around them, almost singing their praise. Lucy, Cecilia, and Agnes felt an invisible pressure upon them, much as Sebastian had. The weight of the world.

Sebastian rose and stepped away from the table and toward the back of the altar where three linen wraps, secured with rope, enshrouded sculpted figures beneath them. One by one, he removed the ties and the coverings, revealing pristine life-size statues of beautiful young women, painted in the most gorgeous hues of blue, purple, red, green, gold, and silver. Wearing expressions both of joy and sorrow. All holding palm fronds. At the base of each statue a nameplate.

Saint Lucia.

Saint Cecilia.

Saint Agnes.

Their hearts jumped.

The girls were awestruck by what they saw. Symbols of faith and of purity worthy of worship. Saint Lucy, a wreath of roses and lighted candles around her head, holding a golden plate before her, her two beautiful blue eyes sitting atop it. Saint Cecilia, in flowing robes, with a violin and bow, a winged angel at her shoulder, eyes turned heavenward. Saint Agnes, long rivulets of curls flowing to her feet, surrounding her, a lamb tucked safely in her arm.

Sebastian returned to the altar and took his seat and held up the *Legenda* to his face, so that all they could see were his eyes.

'These are the long-forgotten legends of your namesakes, martyrs who gave their lives for something greater than themselves. Young girls. Teenagers, like us, who changed their worlds by their example and made the ultimate sacrifice. Human beings but divinely inspired. Subjects of art and architecture, poems and prayers. Their pictures enshrined everywhere. Their names literally on everyone's lips. They were superstars for nearly two thousand years before the word was ever invented. Eternal icons.'

'It is hard to believe,' Lucy whispered, speaking for them all.

Sebastian ripped the illuminated parchment pages from the old book and handed one to each. They were amazed. The sense of empowerment they felt was palpable. Something

in the stories, in his words, resonated with them to their very cores.

'You share their spirit. Their bravery. Their passion. Their purpose.' Sebastian proclaimed. 'Still yourselves. But something more.'

'You have sought attention. Adoration. Affection,' Sebastian went on. 'All aspects of love. Now you will find them. Not just for your own sake, but for the sake of all you touch.'

Sebastian removed his shirt. He looked deep into their eyes and reached in the reliquary box and removed Cecilia's chaplet. He detached the milagro, dropped it into the urn. 'Cecilia, the Messenger.'

He read out loud:

'Patron saint of musicians. A daughter of wealth and Roman privilege, but raised secretly among the faithful, she believed herself guarded by an angel. Betrayed by her jealous husband and turned over to the authorities as a heretic, she was to be beheaded but each of three attempts failed. She sang her faith for another three days even as she lay dying. Her body, exhumed centuries after her death, was found in an incorruptible state. In her determination, she found everlasting fame.'

Sebastian took the scalding hot milagro from the urn and pressed it on to his chest, branding her sword right over his heart. Despite the agony of his burning skin, he did not cry out

in pain. The girls winced as his skin sizzled.

'Your irresistible song will pierce the hearts and minds of others. It will fill their yearning souls, which have been left empty by doubt and false promises, with passion.'

He placed the chaplet back on to Cecilia's wrist.

Likewise he removed Agnes's chaplet, separating the flaming heart milagro.

And purifying it in the fire as he spoke: 'Agnes, the Lamb.'

He continued to read:

'Patron saint of virgins and victims. Sentenced to death for her beliefs, she was stripped and dragged through the streets of Rome and sent to a brothel to be abused and humiliated. The men who attacked her were struck blind. Her hair grew and covered her nakedness from head to toe. Tied to a stake to be burned, the flames parted so as not to harm her. Finally beheaded, her precious blood was soaked up from the ground by believers. Dishonoured by her adversaries but never defiled. In her refusal to compromise her faith or her body, an eternal testament to the power of love and innocence.'

He lifted the sacred heart from the fire and pressed it to his chest, internalizing the pain, and then placed it directly over the impression of Cecilia's sword, making it appear as if the blade was piercing the heart.

'Your compassionate heart and uncompromising virtue will

be an example to all who seek honesty and true love. You will bring comfort and understanding to the troubled, teaching them not only how to love another but to love themselves.'

Finally, he removed Lucy's chaplet and placed her double-eye milagro into the flames: 'Lucy, the Light.'

He read her passage:

'Patron saint of the blind, in body and soul. She gouged her eyes from their sockets to make herself less attractive to those who defile her, refusing to renounce her faith and remaining fearless in her suffering. She lost her sight and her life to her tormentors but never her vision. The way of light shining through the darkness of life.'

He took Lucy's milagro and positioned it strategically above the other two. His flesh was now completely raw there, but he did not hesitate. He lowered the charm down on to his skin and pressed it in so that the eyes were now serving as a guard for the sword.

'You are a beacon that will show the way out of darkness toward hope and a better life. An all-seeing leader whose unbreakable will and steadfast determination is the essence of faith.'

'The eyes keep watch over the sword that pierces the heart,' Lucy observed.

'There is no more need for books to tell your story and glass boxes to preserve your legacy. The waiting is over. You are here.'

Their milagros, the three of them, combined, burned into his body and into his soul, branding him and binding them together, for all eternity.

No longer merely legend, but living within him. In them.

A reliquary of the heart.

27

Divine Intervention

Jesse saw a familiar face at the corner. Dr Frey's.

'Take me around the block,' Jesse told the cabbie.

He jumped out, paid his fare, and walked around the back side of the church, unnoticed by Frey and the small ragtag group of arm-scratching, hollow-eyed guys encircling him. These were definitely not colleagues. Especially the big bald guy accompanying Frey. It was definitely Sicarius. What would Frey be doing taking him for a walk? Nothing good, Jesse was sure.

As for the others they were meeting, Jesse had never seen a psychiatrist sporting distressed leather and red high-top Chucks that he could remember. He did recall seeing a few rehab types wandering the corridors of Frey's loony bin, lining up for the daily dose of morphine. How hard would it be for the good doctor to roll them over to the dark side for a few extra hits? Not very.

'Crackheads,' he mumbled to himself.

In fact, he might have put it down to a drug deal or even a robbery if Frey didn't look so calm and in control. In command. The guys looked familiar to him. A local band, always looking for attention and always screwing up whenever they got it. It was almost like they just played music for the drugs. Took gigs to take the edge off the fact that they were waste products.

Frey sure gets around. No piece of shit was beneath his radar apparently, himself included, but then such a common touch was good for the hospital's rehab fundraising and the doctor's personal profile. He had pull with both the upscale Park Slope prescription pill poppers and cred with the street fiends who squatted along the polluted Greenpoint waterfront, leaving aside the fact that none of them were ever cured, which was never really the purpose anyway. Now Jesse understood why. Frey was an equal-opportunity enabler and not averse to a little outpatient treatment.

He watched Frey suddenly excuse himself to a café across the street, and the guys remained in a tight circle, nervously eyeing the boarded-up entrance to the church.

Jesse checked his phone. His palms were sweating and it

was getting harder to swipe his touch screen. Nothing from Lucy. He called and called. Again nothing. If she wasn't at home, the only other place she could be was in there. And reception was probably awful. He looked over at Frey in the café window, calmly sipping his espresso, and suddenly, his minions broke for the church steps, looking from side to side to see if they were being watched.

Jesse texted.

They're coming.

Jesse was out of options but desperate to help. He logged on to his site and updated his status. Time for a mob, he reckoned.

Can I get a witness?

He typed in the church address and hit send.

The candlelight was growing dimmer, bringing their moment together to a natural conclusion. But there were still questions to be answered.

'I know who you say we are, but I still don't get what it is we need to do,' Lucy said. 'Or why anyone would want to kill to stop us from just trying to be ourselves. Better people?'

'I don't think this was meant to be a self-help seminar, Lucy,' Cecilia interrupted. 'There has got to be a reason.'

Sebastian walked over to the reliquary and laid his hands on it reverently. He paused and then spoke with great deliberation.

'The day that I took the chaplets. It was revealed to me who they were destined for. And that I was to deliver them. At that time, my own fate was also revealed.'

'Like a prophecy?' Agnes said, naively. 'What did they tell you?'

'That I had to find you before they found me. Before they kill me.'

'Over my dead body!' Cecilia shouted.

'It doesn't matter what happens to me now. I'm ready to give my soul back. My only despair is leaving the three of you.'

Lucy was on the verge of tears. 'We will protect you, Sebastian.'

He put his hand to her lips.

'My mission is accomplished, but yours is just beginning.'

'Mission?'

'The answer to your question,' Sebastian said. 'Our reason to be here.'

'What do we need to do?'

'Two things. Call them miracles, if you like. The first, accepting who you are, is accomplished. The second you will have to find out for yourselves. Remember, they will not stop until your hearts do,' he continued. 'Until your blood is on their hands.'

Sebastian could see the resolve in their eyes.

By the first miracle, you are called Blessed. By the second—'

Agnes interrupted. 'Saint.'

Sebastian's eyes lit up at her understanding.

'You are the last of a line,' he explained. 'If one of you is defeated before performing your second miracle, then the scale will be tipped for ever in the direction of evil and the way will not be nor will it ever be prepared. It will either begin anew with you, or end with you.'

'Way for what?' Agnes said, boiling it down to its essence.

'For whom,' he said. 'It's a battle we've been losing for too long. It is a battle you must win.'

'Battle?'

'We are at war, and you are warriors. You are the fulfillment of almost two thousand years of devotion.'

'I don't know how to fight,' Agnes said nervously.

'You are all fighters. The weapons you need are inside you,' Sebastian promised. 'The gift you have received will strengthen your mind and body. Not just your soul. When you call on these tools, they will be there.'

'You said your mission was accomplished,' Agnes said. 'What was your second miracle?'

'You.'

The pride in his voice was tempered by the sadness in his eyes.

'You were different people when you left this room, than when you entered it,' he said. 'There is no changing it now.'

'So bring on the heavenly host, then!' She couldn't quite explain it, but Cecilia was itching for a fight. For her, passivity was not part of this process.

'You are the heavenly host, Cecilia,' Sebastian said ominously. 'There is no army of angels coming to save you.'

'Three girls and a guy from Brooklyn?'

'Why not,' he said simply.

His words hung in the air like a punishment. A death sentence.

'Save yourself,' Lucy whispered, recalling the first words of their meeting.

'Be yourself,' Cecilia summed up.

'Trust yourself,' Agnes said.

'You have to before you can save anyone else. Or love anyone else.'

'I believe you,' Lucy said.

'Don't believe me,' he said. 'Have faith.'

'What's the difference?' Agnes asked.

'A child believes. In magic. In fairies. In monsters. Faith is knowledge. Certainty. Without it, we fail.'

'But faith in what?'

'Start with yourself.'

'I believe in love,' Agnes said.

Sebastian reached for her hand.

'Love is just the faith you place in someone else.'

'Then I have faith in you,' Agnes said.

A loud noise from the church above suddenly intruded.

'They're here,' he said, preparing himself.

'I'm coming with you,' Cecilia demanded.

He took her by the shoulders gently, but firmly.

'No. You will be stronger together,' he insisted.

The rumble upstairs was getting louder and the enemy closer. He ran for the staircase.

'So, if we believe you, then we'll die?' Agnes shouted at him.

Sebastian stopped, his back facing them. He looked up to the ceiling, mustering all his strength for his answer.

'No, if you believe me, you'll never die.'

Monsignor Piazza took to his bedroom kneeler. He was agitated. Troubled. He removed his cassock and let it fall to his waist, exposing a scarred torso. He reached for the length of rope with knotted cords. *The discipline* had been preserved in the glass reliquary box in the chapel and was assumed to have belonged to one of the workers who died there, along with the rosaries, hair shirt, and other discouraged items of mortification used by the most faithful. It was the only thing he took. Father Piazza swung it over one shoulder and the next, again and again, in time, a click track to his suffering. He began to bleed. He began to pray.

The old man's lips moved silently, only occasionally speaking words out loud. Fragments of supplications he knew by heart. In this pain, he sought redemption and punishment for his sins. He literally beat himself up over his betrayal of the boy who was once in his care. With each stroke he did penance for his naïveté. With each tear in his back, he repented his arrogance.

He was the one who shut off the chapel, after all. He was the one who discouraged the cult that had developed around the 'subway saints', as the neighbourhood people called them. All in the name of modernity. He found himself on the slippery slope of secularity long before Sebastian ever came to him.

Raising his profile within the community, outside the church even, as a 'voice of reason', by certain public officials, for which he was rewarded with the trappings of status: board memberships, awards dinners, and weekend stays at seaside mansions. So that when Sebastian did come, with his unorthodox musings, wild eyes, sharp tongue, and spiritual fervor, he couldn't believe him, wouldn't recognize the truth staring him right in the face. Such people were crazy, not holy, he'd come to assume.

But now he knew. Now he did not celebrate. He suffered. He measured his legacy not in what he had gained, but in what he had lost, or given away at least. His church. His faith. And Sebastian.

In his urgent prayers he chastised himself and reminded himself of what he had gradually forgotten.

Bless all our life and the hour of our death.

The priest dropped the cord and clasped his hands tightly under his chin.

Amen.

'God forgive me,' he prayed, clenching his chest in pain.

'Sebastian,' he wept, striking his chest gently with his fist and bowing his head.

'Lucy.' He struck his chest again and bowed his head, continuing to do it after muttering each name.

'Cecilia.'

'Agnes.'

And with his last breath: 'Forgive me.'

28

The Girls Who Do It

Lucy, Cecilia, and Agnes heard footsteps descending rapidly down the staircase.

Their hearts raced.

'He's coming back,' Agnes said, relieved.

'No,' Cecilia said suspiciously. 'It's not him.'

CeCe looked down at her hands, her stigmata, and saw them starting to bleed. Her warning bell.

'What the hell do we do?' Lucy asked, staring at the other two in semi panic. The footsteps, which sounded more like an army, stopped for a minute outside the chapel door and the girls stood stiffly, expectantly, eyes locked on the door, until it was kicked open.

Cecilia recognized them as soon as she saw them.

'Look what Satan dragged in,' Cecilia said nonchalantly. 'Ricky.'

'You know him?' Lucy asked.

Ricky answered for her. 'She does. Intimately. Isn't that right, CeCe? Surprised to see me?'

'Not really. Playing basements is your thing, isn't it? How did you know I was here?'

'Your drinking buddy. It's amazing the covert intelligence you can gather for a pint of Jack. I should call the CIA.'

'Bill,' Cecilia gasped softly, a sick feeling settling in her stomach. Sebastian was right, she thought. It was those closest to you.

'Don't take it too hard. He probably doesn't even remember what he told me, poor drunken bastard. I would have found you anyway. We've been tailing you for a while.'

'Too much stalking, not enough rehearsing. I told you you'll never get anywhere that way, Ricky,' Cecilia said. 'Did you come to entertain me?'

'No. I came to kill you. And you. And you,' he said calmly, smiling through his nicotine-stained teeth and pointing to Lucy and Agnes. 'So did they, by the way.'

The guys behind him tightened up, ready for a fight.

'None of you is smart enough to plan this,' CeCe said. 'Who sent you?'

'A doctor friend I met in rehab,' Ricky said. 'Networking,

you know.'

Lucy and Agnes backed up, but there was nowhere else to go. They had their backs to the altar and the wall. Cecilia backed up as well, the heel of her shoe kicking into her guitar, which was leaning against the altar, making a terrible clang.

'New song?' Ricky said. 'A death knell, maybe?'

'A requiem,' Cecilia answered. 'For you.'

'Tough talk,' he said dismissively. 'Did I mention we're going to kill you?' Ricky said, feigning forgetfulness. 'But maybe a little fun first. What do you say, gents?'

The sound of shrill, compulsive, hormonal laughter, like a tribe of chimps, echoed through the tiny room.

'And who do we have here?' Ricky asked, approaching Agnes and stroking her hair. 'Fresh meat.'

'Leave her alone, Ricky!' Cecilia yelled.

'Awww, don't be jealous,' he said. 'There's plenty to go around.'

'Sebastian,' Agnes whispered, cringing in disgust, trying to make herself disappear.

'Don't bother calling for your boyfriend,' Ricky said, stepping up to the altar. 'He's busy dying upstairs by now.'

Ricky kicked the altar over and the book and stand and candles came crashing down in a racket. Bubbling trails of flaming wax flowed along the crevices of the wood and tiled flooring, seeking something to ignite.

He walked over to their statues and ran his hand lasciviously along their porcelain bodies, thrusting his tongue into each of their painted mouths.

'Cold as ice,' he said snidely. 'Not that different from kissing you, CeCe.'

'Did we kiss, Ricky?' Cecilia spat. 'I was sure that was a puddle of piss I was sucking in the other night.'

He picked up the statues off their pedestals and crashed them to the ground, one by one, huge shards of moulded plaster and painted ceramic exploded upward.

'Such a perfect place to die, wouldn't you say?' Ricky observed, smoke slowly rising up around him. 'A church and a crypt. One stop shopping.'

Ricky and his sadistic band eyed the girls threateningly, ravenously. However much they wanted to, Lucy, Agnes, and CeCe didn't flinch. There was no escape anyway. They stared their tormentors down. It was a stand-off.

'Time for a little ultraviolence, fellas.'

'Now that's original,' Cecilia said scornfully. 'A *Clockwork Orange* asshole. Still stuck in the Seventies. Just like your music.'

It was time. They all felt it.

'I always said I had a killer band, didn't I?'

'Save yourself,' Lucy said, just loud enough for the other girls to hear. They understood.

Cecilia started to count her enemies out loud. 'One. Two. Three. Four. Not a fair fight.'

'Life's not fair,' Ricky said bloodlessly, motioning to one of the guys, who stepped forward silently and headed for Agnes, grabbing a handful of her hair and sniffing like a pig, reaching for the button on the top of her blouse.

'Smells like teen spirit,' he hissed, his sickening breath puffing straight up her nostrils.

'Smells like shit,' Agnes said, spitting in his face.

In a split second, Cecilia reached behind her and grabbed the neck of her guitar and swung it full force into the head of the attacker.

He fell to the floor in a heap at her feet.

'I told you to leave her alone.'

She raised the solid-body electric and with a frightening screech slammed the gearhead right through the back of his head.

Lucy and Agnes were momentarily stunned but not afraid as they watched the life bubble out and around his head in a river on the floor. Ricky was impressed.

'Hunt you back,' she said with a smirk, resting her boot heel, like a proud forest ranger on a bear carcass, in his gaping wound.

'That's way inappropriate,' he scoffed, pulling a motorcycle chain out of his back pocket. 'Aren't you supposed to be saints or something?'

'Saints, maybe. Not angels,' Cecilia said, swinging her guitar overhead once more in a wide arc, keeping them all at bay and

slamming it into the bone legs of the altar behind her, shearing them off.

She tossed a length of broken bone to Lucy and to Agnes, who caught the clubs with the skill of athletes and stood at the ready, armed and dangerous. Full of a zeal and confidence that they could scarcely have imagined even a few minutes earlier.

'Don't be afraid,' she commanded.

'I'm not,' they said in unison.

Ricky and his crew bum-rushed the girls, swinging their chains ahead of them.

Lucy's attacker was on her before she could move. He swung wildly and connected, striking her in the jaw and knocking her back toward the urn and reliquary.

The vandal laughed and pulled a mobile phone out of his pocket.

'Smile,' he said, snapping her picture. 'That's bank when you're dead.'

Lucy gave him the finger with one hand, and tossed a hammer lying on the floor directly at him, hitting him in the chest.

'Bitch, this is your lucky day,' he railed. 'First I'm going to kill you, then I'm going to screw you.'

'Screw me?' she chided him. 'Alive or dead, I wouldn't feel it, loser.'

'We'll see about that.'

Lucy tried to call on whatever basic self-defence skills she

could muster in the moment but kept it simple. She extended her leg straight outward, her gold spiked designer heel first, and levelled it right into his balls.

'Flats are for quitters.' She smirked.

His face turned a bluish white, and his body began a slow-motion collapse to the floor.

'You should never think with your dick,' she huffed, helping him along with another kick, this time with the pointed toe, to his nose, shattering it, along with his cheekbone. She was about to bludgeon him with her bone club, when an awful cry came from the other side of the chapel. It was Agnes.

'Lucy!'

Agnes was bent over the kneeler. The vandal behind her had her by the throat and the hair, jerking her head back. Immobilized.

'What, no tramp stamp?' he said, noting her unmarked skin.

Agnes spasmed as he pulled a key from his chain and carved a cross into her back. Blood seeped up to the surface and Agnes was overcome with burning pain. She didn't cry out.

'That's better,' he said, admiring his cruelty.

Then suddenly, she felt a silky wave of comfort as her hair began to lengthen and grow down her back, to blot the wound and cover her nakedness.

'Agnes!' Lucy screamed, desperate to come to her aid.

Lucy suddenly felt a hand around her ankle and was unable to break free of the vandal's grip. Just behind her was the fourth

covered statue. She tore at the knot and loosened it, ripping the linen fabric from it, revealing the figure of a Roman soldier, in full armour, shot full of arrows. At the bottom it read SEBASTIAN.

'He's here,' she said. 'With us.'

Lucy pulled the sword from its scabbard and tossed it to Agnes, who was suffering in silence.

Agnes grabbed it in midair and raised the weapon as high as she could and drove it downward as hard as she could, right through the top of her attacker's foot. He was literally pinned, bleeding out quickly from his neck.

Agnes stood calmly and turned to face him.

'Sorry, I must have severed an artery,' she said calmly, watching the blood wash over her flats. She let her hair and dress fall to their natural length once again and bitch-slapped him, wiping his snot from her hand on his jacket. He was weakening and unable to defend himself.

'You like to pull hair,' she said seductively, slowly wrapping her locks around his neck and jerking him toward her. 'Me too.' She leaned in close to him. Face-to-face, close enough to kiss under less confrontational circumstances, and tightened her grip on the nest of hair now encircling his throat. He saw the fire in her eyes and she watched the life leave his slowly, like a sun setting into the horizon, degree by degree. She pulled and kept pulling. Until he was dead. She untangled him and let him drop.

The thug pulled Lucy down to the floor and covered her, his weight preventing her from moving. He tore at her blouse and made a juvenile effort to feel her up. 'They're real, despite what you might have heard.'

Lucy grabbed for his throat and dug in her nails, and he scraped at her eyes. Lucy pulled at his wrist until she could get a piece of his hand in her mouth. She bit down. He wailed in pain. She grabbed for the *Legenda* at her feet and pummelled the vandal on top of her with the heavy, leather-bound book. His forearm and ribs cracked easily under the force of her blows.

'Payback's a bitch. Even if it is a few thousand years late.'

Lucy brought the *Legenda Aurea* down on his face full force, killing him.

'Who says I'm not merciful.'

Ricky meanwhile had bum-rushed Cecilia, knocking her down hard. She was breathless and dazed momentarily and looked up at him, her vision fuzzy, knees and elbows scraped and bloody, as he removed his thick leather belt and folded it over, snapping it against his thigh. She'd seen him look like that before above her. With evil intent. Then, it was only her self-respect that was at stake. This time, it was her life. This time, she understood.

'Don't,' she said, still defiant, struggling to her hands and knees. 'You'll turn me on.'

Ricky smiled.

'You've been a very bad girl.'

He struck her. Whipping her back, her arms, and her legs savagely. Her skin flushed and welts appeared almost instantly. Tears of pain and humiliation rimmed her eyes.

'I have,' she confessed regretfully, taking the punishment almost to see how much she could stand.

With what strength she had, Cecilia crawled over to the votive stand and tried to scale it, lifting herself upright however which way she could. If she was going out now, she wanted it to be standing. She grabbed a votive cup in each hand and flung the boiling liquid at Ricky's face with all her might. He dropped the strap and fell to his knees, clutching at his face, screaming, but more in anger than pain. While he was blinded momentarily, she ran toward him and kneed him in the head, pushing him over on to his belly on top of the overturned wooden altar, stunned. But not dead.

'If you hit me, you'd better kill me,' Ricky growled, pulling gobs of wax from his face.

Ricky rushed her again, picked her up, and slammed her to the floor so hard she felt her lungs hit her rib cage. She gasped for air, lying motionless on her back. He stepped away and jumped up on the altar and kicked the glass reliquary, shattering it as he let out an ungodly harrowing wail, the veins in his neck near bursting as he swatted the remaining candles to the floor. 'You always wanted to be the centre of attention – the bride in the wedding and the body in the casket. Well, one of those is about to come true at least!'

Just like my dream, she thought.

'Saints alive!' he said in the midst of the rising smoke and fire, his raw face and gleaming white and bloodstained teeth causing him to appear as the wild beast he actually was, gloating over his prey, as she'd let him gloat over her many times before on lost and lonely nights. 'But not for long.'

Ricky jumped from the altar to the bone candelabra suspended from the chapel ceiling, hung from it, and began to swing back and forth, building momentum and staring down at Cecilia. A pendulum of unsalvageable human degradation twirling ominously above. 'I think it's time somebody knocked some sense into that thick skull of yours, CeCe.'

All she could bring into clear focus as she waited for the deathblow were the metal-studded soles of his hobnail boots. She waited for the nail heads to leave across her face the filthy imprint of the simple, mocking word they spelled out. DOUBT.

And then, as she stared up at him and waited, she thought she saw something else. The delicate pendalogues of the chandelier where Ricky was holding on, which were made from the bones of fingers and hands, appeared to slowly release him from their grasp. From her view below, it was as if they were holding Ricky up instead of him holding on. He began to count, oblivious to anything but her imminent demise.

'One,' he yelled. Cecilia noticed his grip loosen even more.

Century-old plaster from the ceiling broke free; fiery liquid dripped down and fell on top of her. She remained still, taking

the pain, all the while feeling a supernatural force was at work. Cecilia spied her fractured guitar neck on the floor beside her, gearhead aflame, and took it as a sign.

'Two.' He swung over her again, the whoosh of air from his motion feeding the flames that now nearly encircled her and kept Agnes and Lucy at bay.

She waited.

'Cecilia!' Agnes screamed.

'Thr—'

The candelabra canopy that affixed the chandelier to the ceiling gave way and came crashing down, along with the ornate bone chandelier. Cecilia quickly grabbed for her broken instrument and slid it under Ricky just as he landed, guitar neck pointed forcefully upward.

They lay face-to-face, centimetres apart, for what felt like hours but was just seconds, as they had many a night. She watched him turn white, gurgling for his breath and begging for his miserable life.

'How about showing a little mercy?' he gasped pathetically, his tone changing to suit the dire predicament he found himself in. 'Forgiveness.'

'Like you showed Catherine? Showed us?' CeCe countered. 'I don't do mercy or forgiveness, Ricky. I just work here. You will have to take that one up with the boss.'

As his breath became more laboured, she brought her lips even closer to his and whispered sweetly, 'I warned you never to fall for me, didn't I? Oh, that's right, too late.'

With all her might she tossed him off of her.

Agnes and Lucy grabbed the coverings from the saints' statues for protection and leaped through the wall of fire to CeCe and lifted her up. They brushed off the shards of glass and splinters protruding from their bruised and swollen skin and wiped the blood and ash away. Agnes lay her covering over the bones of the candelabra, which was now on the ground, as if she were respectfully burying it. Lucy veiled Cecilia with hers.

Four dead. Three injured. One missing.

'There will be others. You know that, right?' Cecilia said. 'They were just the opening act.'

The girls surveyed the carnage. A killing field of broken bones and broken glass, shattered bodies and splintered wood all around them. They'd turned the sacred chapel into a crime scene. More urgently, a fire hazard. Ricky's jacket exploded in flames and ignited the wooden altar, the fire seeming to lick the giant Sacred Heart fresco that was disappearing into the billowing smoke. Slowly incinerating the bodies and the evidence.

'Ashes to ashes, prick,' Lucy mused. 'Let's go.'

'Not yet,' Cecilia said.

She righted the kneelers, the only pieces of wood still not aflame and kneeled down to pray. Without exchanging any words, Lucy and Agnes joined her.

'We don't know what we are doing,' Cecilia said. 'But we will do our best.'

They prayed for guidance, they prayed for wisdom, they prayed for strength, they prayed for Sebastian, they prayed for one another, they prayed for themselves. Prayed like they never had before, because they never had. Most of all they gave thanks to the ones who'd come before, whose presence, strength, and bravery they felt inside the room and inside themselves now.

As she raised her head, Agnes was troubled. She was having an attack of conscience. 'Do you think that killing them makes us evil? Makes us like them?'

'I guess we'll find out someday,' Lucy said. 'But not today.'

'Time to go,' Cecilia pressed.

The fire was raging now, and the heat, smoke, and stench of burning flesh were stifling.

Agnes grabbed *Legenda Aurea*, flipped through it quickly, and tore out a single page. Lucy grabbed a length of bone from the ossuary, and plunged it into Ricky's burning body, turning it into a torch to light their way out. Cecilia bent down and picked up the hair shirt that had been thrown from the reliquary during the fight. She winced as she put it on her bloody back.

'Follow me,' Lucy said.

Agnes stopped as they reached the door and looked back.

'Are we the monsters now?' Agnes wondered. 'Did we ruin this place?'

'No!' Cecilia said, pulling her away. 'We restored it.'

29

Moths Have Come

Sirens began to blow before even the first few puffs of black smoke cleared the chimney. Jesse was instantly suspicious. He looked over in the café window and noticed Frey just hanging up from a call and collecting his things.

The smoke from the chapel fire began to escape through the old chimneys and vented out into the open air.

Jesse was panicking. If Lucy and the others were in there – and he was now sure they were – they wouldn't last long. Frey had played this perfectly. Creating a literal smoke screen behind which to operate.

His flash mob was late. The police were sure to be first on the scene, and Frey had them wired from the top down. A crowd, witnesses, was their only hope.

'Jesus,' he moaned. 'You can get five thousand kids to do the friggin' Macarena slathered in Hershey's syrup on Cadman Plaza but not a soul to witness a mass murder in progress.'

The doctor strolled casually across the street and up the church stairs.

'Arrogant prick.'

Jesse turned around and saw a few kids hanging around the corner. Could've been local rubberneckers now that a fire was going, but they seemed to have something else on their mind. Maybe there was hope.

Outside, he thought, would take care of itself. He was needed inside. He waited for a minute and followed Frey into the church.

Sebastian had been outmanoeuvered. The vandals had drawn him upstairs and sneaked down behind him while he searched the church, locking the sacristy door from behind. He kicked at the door over and over to no avail.

'God help them,' he prayed, tears and sweat mingling in sorrow and passion.

'Sebastian.' A menacing voice rang out from the back of the church, filling it like the tolling of a bell. It was not the voice of God.

Sebastian walked out into the church, facing the altar. His back to Frey.

'You know, priests used to say mass that way. With their backs to the people. Things change,' Frey said wistfully.

Sebastian preceded to the altar and climbed the stairs into the marble pulpit, facing out at the church and the doctor, who was not alone. From the elevated podium, he also saw another figure in the back. A head, nervously popping up from behind one of the back pews. It was Jesse. He didn't react, unsure if Frey knew the blogger had followed him in or not.

'You sure you want to come in here, Doctor?'

Frey sighed. 'We do what we must, you understand.'

'I do.'

'Another assistant to sacrifice?' Sebastian asked, gesturing toward the dead-eyed, uniformed psych-ward flunky Frey had brought with him.

'No,' Frey answered. 'A patient. Like you. I thought you should be properly introduced,' he explained snidely. 'You have a lot in common. Both sociopathic and violent. Murderous. Incurable. Though in his case it was young children, not teenage girls.'

Sebastian's jaw tightened. 'A death-penalty candidate.'

'Nearly. But as I explained to the court, he's not responsible for his actions.'

'We are all responsible for our actions, Doctor. And for the consequences.'

Dr Frey patted Sicarius on the shoulder, drawing a twisted smile from the defective delinquent. Frey's crunchy footfalls

echoed loudly as he and his assassin drew slowly closer.

'Still quite a mess in here. I have to make a note to speak to the developers about the status of my investment in the conversion.'

'Why are you so afraid of me?' Sebastian asked coolly. 'I understand the need for you, for what you believe, yet you see no place for me.'

'Not afraid. Concerned. As I am for all my patients.'

'Bullshit, you tried to erase my mind. My identity.'

'Erase you? Or treat you?'

'Same difference, Doctor.'

'You are sick, Sebastian. You think me evil, when all I've ever tried to do was help you, protect you from your own insanity. And when that proved impossible, to protect others from you.'

Sebastian fought the urge to strangle Frey right on the spot and kept his cool.

'Is that what you told the police? And Jesse?'

'I told them that you were a murderer and a kidnapper. A uniquely dangerous and delusional young man. The truth.'

'It all sounds so reasonable, Doctor – even to me.'

'It should. Those girls down there are in jeopardy because of you. Not me.'

'That's a lie.'

'You filled their heads with the same superstitious nonsense. We are long past the need for this,' Frey said adamantly, pointing to the altar. 'Or for those like you.'

'Why? Because now we have you?' Sebastian said derisively. 'You don't offer happiness. You don't offer fulfillment. You don't offer love. You prescribe it. Soulessness. In daily doses.'

'Whatever works,' he said blithely.

'What happens when the prescription runs out, Doctor?'

'You get a refill, Sebastian.'

'Here, I'm always full,' Sebastian said. 'I don't need a refill or an insurance card or a straitjacket.'

'No, just a small weekly donation.'

'No one charged me admission.'

'So romantic. I can see why the girls fall for it. Dangle a few bracelets, tell them you are destined to be together. Surely there are easier ways to get a date.'

'They came to me. They were led to me as I was to them.'

'There is nothing special about you, Sebastian. You are as deluded as a person who sees the face of Jesus in a bowl of cornflakes.'

'I know what I know,' Sebastian said firmly.

'You *know* nothing. You believe. You are spreading lies. Dangerous ones.'

'Nothing is more dangerous than truth, Doctor.'

'Science *is* truth. A rigorous process of study undertaken over years to arrive at answers to age-old questions. To separate fact from fiction. There are papers, reviewed and published, open to scrutiny.'

'All paid for by the like-minded, Doctor. Ever changing.

Evolving, as they say.

What I know can't be bought. It is eternal.'

'Why am I bothering? I had this argument recently with Father Piazza. You remember him?'

Frey could see that even the old priest's name was painful to Sebastian.

'Even self-styled men of God didn't believe you. Betrayed you. The world has turned, Sebastian.'

'Yes, it has turned. To shit.'

'And you and your little harem are here to give it a colonic? Is that right? Cleanse us all for the Second Coming? Please don't preach to me.'

'If you didn't believe it, Doctor, fear it, you wouldn't be here.'

'All hypotheticals, Sebastian. But keep telling yourself that.'

'Reality, Doctor. And soon everyone will know it.'

'No. The reality is that the police will be here shortly. Fire department too, from the looks of things. Your girlfriends will be dead. I will be a hostage. And you will be blamed. Or dead.'

'They can take care of themselves,' Sebastian responded. 'And so can I.'

'Such faith you have, Sebastian. But so rarely tested.'

Jesse poked his head up again and began to tremble, frightened out of his mind for Lucy and the girls, and for Sebastian. What was coming next was obvious to all of them.

'Sicarius,' Frey commanded.

Frey motioned to his lackey, who seemed to snap out of his stupor at the order, rushing forward down the centre aisle like a wild animal smelling blood. Sebastian jumped to the chancel floor from the pulpit to intercept him, defending the church sanctuary as if his life depended on it.

A last stand.

The massive collision carried them both over the altar and to the floor in a cloud of grit and dust. All of the assassin's weight was pressing down on Sebastian as they grappled and he struggled to free his arm before he was pinned, fatally. Sebastian elbowed Sicarius in the temple, stunning him, and pushed him off.

Jesse snapped picture after picture of the brutality as it unfolded.

Sicarius got to his feet first and grabbed one of the long, heavy pipes stacked next to the wall. He swung it down toward Sebastian like the handle of an executioner's axe, missing by centimetres. Sebastian tried to get to his feet, but Sicarius kicked him once in the stomach and then in the jaw, drawing blood from his nose and mouth. His breathing was laboured and he could taste his own blood.

From his position on the floor Sebastian spied an aspergillum, a holy water wand, and rolled toward it. As Sicarius raised the metal pipe to strike, Sebastian slammed the butt end of the hardwood and brass sprinkler into his leg and kneecapped the larger and slower man, shattering his patella.

As the killer buckled, Sebastian drove the wand into his solar plexus, winding Sicarius and incapacitating him. Sebastian wound up and struck for a third time, bringing the holy instrument down on Sicarius's bald head with all his might.

Sebastian stopped to wipe the blood away from his face and bent down, grabbing Sicarius by the collar of his jumpsuit and dragged him to the massive marble baptismal font in the chancel. He stared directly at the doctor, who was unmoved.

'They don't use these much any more,' Sebastian said, sitting Sicarius up and bending the back of his neck over the communion rail. 'Things change.'

Sebastian walked over to the holy water buckets the girls had placed around the altar to catch the leaks from the storm. He picked up three and carried them over to his broken adversary.

Through gritted teeth, Sebastian raised a bucket and poured the stale water into the man's mouth.

'Do you renounce Satan?' Sebastian asked, beginning the faux baptism ritual.

With his last bit of strength Sicarius spat the water out into Sebastian's face and tried to close his mouth.

Sebastian jammed the aspergillum into his mouth and down his throat, breaking teeth and forcing his mouth to remain agape.

'And all his works?'

Sebastian continued to question Sicarius according to the

ritual as he poured first one bucket, then a second, then a third, down his throat, until it was backing up out of his mouth, nose, and ears like an overfilled gas tank.

'And all his pomps?'

Sicarius's belly had swelled abnormally and his eyes rolled over. He was dead. Drowned. Sebastian pulled the wand out of his mouth and dropped it in one of the empty buckets with a loud clang.

The doctor spoke. 'Some might say such a thing is blasphemy. Unforgivable.'

'We do what we must,' Sebastian answered, echoing the doctor's own words. 'I'll take my chances.'

Exhausted, Sebastian recapped. He knew Jesse was there and he wanted it on the record for all time.

'You set me up and let me go. I find the girls. They lead you to me and them.'

'Simple, you have to admit, and flawless.'

'That's why they pay you the big bucks, Doctor. You have it all worked out. Totally rational, logical.'

'Thank you.'

'Except for one thing. What if I wasn't hiding? What if I was waiting? What if I wanted you to find me?'

'Why would you want to be found?'

'Maybe because I'm insane, Doctor. You said it yourself. Or, you can do the maths. I can decrease your kind by one, right here, right now.'

Sebastian and Frey were startled by a racket coming from outside as well as downstairs. Jesse's flash mob had arrived, hopped the fences, shimmied up the scaffolding, and begun banging on the boarded-up windows. From the chapel. Smoke began to escape through the doorjamb and out into the church soon after.

'I'm sure you would like to kill me, Sebastian, but I have done the maths, and judging from those slamming car doors outside, you are at quite a numerical disadvantage.'

Sebastian eyed the door and the thickening smoke with increasing trepidation when it unexpectedly flew open and Lucy, Agnes, and Cecilia burst out, bruised and bloodstained, from the smoke-filled sacristy, tongues of fire nipping at their heels. They ran immediately to Sebastian and encircled him in the tightest hug any of them had ever felt.

'You're alive!' he said, happier than they'd ever heard him. 'Thank God.'

Frey's expression was grim. Jesse, still ensconced in the balcony, was so relieved at the news he was brought nearly to tears.

'Agnes, dear. Lovely to see you again. Didn't we have a follow-up?'

'I'll have to reschedule.'

'He's a fanatic. You've just killed for him. How much further will you go?'

'Mind games,' Sebastian noted. 'Don't listen to him.'

'You're just enabling his fantasy and your own.'

Lucy spoke for all of them, holding tight to Sebastian.

'What happened down there was no dream. A nightmare, maybe. Not an illusion.'

'Miss Ambrose. I understand now why you haven't called. You've been busy.'

Frey was working them. Getting into their heads.

Suddenly, the windows were filled with police snipers. Sirens wailed, rifle barrels poked through empty spaces between the loosened boards in the lower and upper windows. The sound of static from police radios filled the air. Lights from news cameras booting up outside shone an otherworldly glow into the church. A third alarm sounded, alerting firemen in distant stations to head for the scene, creating even more chaos in the vicinity.

'I see him, but I can't get a fix on him!' an officer yelled. 'Too much smoke.'

'The hostages are too close!' yelled another.

A voice came hurtling from a megaphone.

'This is Captain Murphy. The building is surrounded. We don't want anyone to get hurt. Raise your arms in the air and walk forward.'

'We're not hostages!' Cecilia wailed to no avail, drowned out by the helicopter whirring overhead and the expectant mob surrounding them.

The fire chief ordered his men back until the police had

done their job, leaving the fire and the smoke to build. The crowd outside was growing.

Sebastian turned the altar behind them on its side and ushered the girls to kneel behind it like a shield. He stepped out in front. Vulnerable. A standing target.

'Step away from the girls,' Murphy ordered. 'This will be your last warning.'

Jesse was freaking. He was sure he'd be caught in the crossfire, that they all would.

'Don't shoot!' he stammered from the balcony, revealing himself. 'Don't shoot!'

Frey and the girls looked up at him in surprise.

'Call the police and tell them you are coming out,' Sebastian ordered Jesse. 'With the girls.'

'We're not leaving!' Cecilia screamed at him, holding him even tighter, more closely.

Jesse nodded nervously, but fumbled his phone as he dialled, dropping it to the aisle below.

'Shit,' he whined and raced for the staircase.

In that instant, the scene turned even more intense. Red and green lasers sliced through the acrid smoke, a spectacular light show unlike any they'd ever seen at any concert. Tiny glowing dots searching for targets.

'Get down!' Sebastian screamed to Jesse as he reached the nave.

Jesse hit the floor and crawled between pews, out of view.

Sebastian turned to them. Even in the haze, they could see the farewell in his eyes.

'It's time,' he said. 'I didn't know it would be this hard. But it is. Now that I know you. Now that I love you.'

'Sebastian, no!' Lucy cried. 'Don't do this.'

'We need you!' Cecilia screamed. 'Please.'

'Don't leave us!' Agnes wailed.

'I'll never leave you,' he said. 'If you believe nothing else, believe that.'

'Yes, you are leaving,' Frey said. 'In handcuffs or a body bag.'

'They aren't fooling around, Sebastian,' Lucy pleaded urgently. 'Just surrender. We will fight for you whatever happens. Don't let him win.'

Sebastian smiled sweetly. 'Don't you understand? He can't win, not now, it's up to the three of you.'

'The night isn't over, Sebastian!' Frey exclaimed.

'I told you there would be others, Doctor,' Sebastian said defiantly. 'The war goes on with or without me.'

'Collateral damage.'

Sebastian ripped his shirt off, revealing the brand, their brand on his heaving chest, spread his arms, and let out a loud yell.

'Brave,' Dr Frey acknowledged with a modicum of respect for his adversary. 'And foolish to the end.'

'It's not the end,' Sebastian corrected. 'It's the beginning.'

At that, Lucy, Agnes, and Cecilia jumped up and stepped in

front of Sebastian, forming a human wall in his defence. Frey smiled. Chaos was his friend and the odds of a happy accident, from his perspective, was still possible.

'Hold your fire!' Murphy shouted into the snipers' earpieces.

The tumult outside began to spill into the church with Jesse's flash mob banging on doors and whatever was left of windows. Sneaking smartphone pictures and video that prompted a frenzy of posting to social media sites by the thousands. The three girls, standing defiantly, risking their lives for love and mercy, were suddenly famous. 'Saints of Sackett Street' Jesse coined them.

'Shoot him!' some screamed in random bloodlust.

The scene, inside and out, was getting completely out of hand.

'Captain, we can't let this go any longer. The whole neighbourhood will go up in flames,' the fire chief insisted. 'You've got to end it.'

Sharpshooters had their itchy fingers poised on triggers, waiting for a clear shot. Any sudden moves and it was over. They all knew that.

'My heart is your heart,' Sebastian whispered to them, kissing each gently good-bye on the cheek. 'Remember what I said. Remember me.'

'Your choice,' Frey said, backing farther away from the altar and the smoke.

His words echoed powerfully. 'There was never a choice.'

Before they could restrain him, Sebastian broke through the girls' human shield and lunged for Dr Frey, who fell backward in his cowardly haste to retreat.

'I've got a shot,' a sniper said into his mouthpiece.

Murphy issued the command. 'Take it.'

A prolonged, guttural scream from the altar and gasps from the crowd outside filled the room. And then silence. Complete silence.

Five shots rang out and struck Sebastian. He stumbled to the tiled floor, mortally wounded.

Lucy, Agnes, and Cecilia rushed to him, surrounding him, comforting him and themselves, mourning him in the few seconds they had left together, brushing his hair from his eyes and covering his wounds with their hands, professing their undying love.

He was beautiful.

Serene.

If it weren't for the blood leaving him, he would have seemed an athlete resting from fatigue, catching his breath. A scent of clove and roses emanated from him. His gaze was distant, turned to heaven. With his last breaths he looked at them and recited from the prayer of the Sacred Heart:

> 'I will come back again
> and take you to Myself,
> so that where I am
> you also may be'

'We'll be waiting,' Agnes assured him through her sobs. 'Always.'

He smiled and took one last breath.

Frey looked on at the wretched spectacle unsatisfied, having achieved only a partial victory.

'*Ecce homo*,' Frey said to them mockingly. 'What do you see? A man. Just a man.'

'We'll see you again, Doctor,' Cecilia vowed through bitter tears.

'You will,' he concurred. 'One way or another.'

Frey dusted himself off and walked toward the exit. He spied Jesse's mobile phone on the floor and stepped on it. Crushing it and the evidence. He picked it up casually and placed it in his pocket, beneath notice in the confusion. He turned to see Jesse, still hiding in the pew.

'Coming with me?' the doctor asked him.

'No,' Jesse said.

Frey accepted Jesse's answer with an expression of derision and disgust and made his way out into the waiting throng of cops, EMTs, and reporters, quick to offer his story of the events that had just transpired for the record.

The police and firefighters crashed in, guns drawn and hand axes at the ready.

'It's over,' the police captain assured them. 'You're safe now.'

He was chilled by the girls' blank stares and quickly left this

business to his underlings.

Swelling hoses blasted rivers of water on to the burning embers fuming all around them. The runoff filled the holy water fonts, replenishing them, for the first time in years. One by one, the girls were helped up to their feet.

'We can't just leave him here,' Agnes moaned, wiping the blood and cold sweat from his face with her garment.

'We're not leaving him,' Lucy said, hugging her.

Lucy bent down and kissed his cheek and placed her hand on his.

'Rest easy,' she said. 'No one will forget what you did here today. I will make sure of it.'

Finally, Cecilia bent down. She reached for his hand and noticed that he was holding a black rosary. It was small, like a child's rosary, likely the one he received when he was an altar boy. The one he probably held on to in the psych ward all those years. He was gripping it so tight. She opened his hand and noticed that the crucifix was missing. Lost in the spray of gunshots. Cecilia took the rosary out of his hand and kissed it. She took out her earring and unfastened the charm that was dangling from it – miniature brass knuckles. She fastened it to the rosary where the crucifix was, put it around her neck and kissed it again. Then she kissed him.

As they were escorted down the centre aisle to the door, they stopped and looked back at Sebastian one last time.

And they saw it happen right in front of their eyes.

On his chest.

From each of the bullet holes.

One by one.

Arrows sprouted.

All doubt, all sorrow disappeared from them.

'Seeing is believing,' Lucy whispered.

'Saint Sebastian,' Cecilia said, awed by the vision.

Agnes ran back to him. And pulled Sebastian's *Legenda* page from her pocket that she had taken from the chapel and left it next to him.

'My sacred heart,' she said, kissing him for the last time. 'Pray for us.'

Agnes rejoined Lucy and Cecilia and headed toward the vestibule. Grief emptied from their hearts and they were filled with a sense of purpose. The black smoke inside was turning a grayish white. A decision had been made. The threat was over. But their fire inside was still burning.

They walked toward the church doors.

Jesse stood as they passed.

The unruly crowd was waiting outside. Restlessly. Whether to absolve or condemn them, what others would think of them, they didn't know. And didn't care. Perhaps for the first time in their lives.

Cecilia lifted her hoodie on to her head, sheltering her straight fringe and choppy bob.

Lucy veiled her head in a designer silk scarf, fixing it

loosely over her blonde locks.

Agnes placed the cowl of her lamb poncho over her long, auburn hair.

Heads covered, they joined hands and stood in the doorway.

Shouts and cheers rang out, cameras flashed, camcorders rolled, microphones were thrust toward them as they silently descended the church steps, humbly victorious. The lights from the cameras illuminated them, causing auras around them. The sea of law enforcement, media, and onlookers parted reverently before them as they were ushered into a waiting police cruiser.

A few reached out. Some to touch them. Others to rebuke them. Praised, cursed, and everything in between.

They marched forward, unlikely icons, their purpose clear, as Cecilia said to Agnes and Lucy flanking her:

'Thy will be done.'

The Word According to Sebastian

Seekers of Hope. Seekers of Faith. Seekers of Love.
Come to Me
And to These Three
Who Hold My Heart
And You Will See
All You Want and Wish to Do
Is Already There Inside of You
Fear Not
For I Am With You
Always
Even to The End.

ACKNOWLEDGMENTS

Thanks to my husband, Michael Pagnotta, for his undying love and support. This book would not have been possible without you.

Heartfelt thanks to the extraordinary team at Simon & Schuster: Jon Anderson, Justin Chanda – for believing, Anne Zafian, Zareen Jaffery, Julia Maguire, Elke Villa, Chrissy Noh, Lizzy Bromley, Lucille Rettino, Paul Crichton, Lydia Finn, Mary Marotta, Christina Pecorale, Jim Conlin, Mary Faria, and Teresa Brumm.

Special thanks to the people I have been blessed with in my life: Isabelle Rose Pagnotta, Beverly Hurley, Tracy Hurley Martin, Oscar Martin, Angela and Tony DiTerlizzi, Vince Clarke, Martha and Anthony Kolencik, Mary and Salvatore Pagnotta, Mary Nemchik, Clementina and Bill Morton, Thomas J. Hurley, Thomas A. Hurley, Denise DeCarlo, Heidi Holmes, Lauren Nemchik, Tamara Pajic Lang, Mary-Jo Pane, Abbey Watkins, Paul Sych, Adriana Beltrán, Natalie Shau, Andy McNicol, Laura Bonner, Alicia Gordon, Ellen Goldsmith-Vein, all at Aflaguara and William Morris Endeavor, and especially to my amazing publishers and readers around the world.

Look out
for the sequel to

The
BLESSED

COMING
IN 2013

If you've got a thirst for
fiction, join up now

bookswithbite.co.uk

Packed with sneak peeks, book trailers, exclusive
competitions and downloads, **bookswithbite.co.uk**
is the new place on the web to get your fix of
great fiction.

Sign up to the newsletter at
www.bookswithbite.co.uk
for the latest news on your favourite authors,
to receive exclusive extra content and the
opportunity to enter special
members-only competitions.